OPERATION EDGE

Also by Richard Joyce, featuring Johnny Vince

Operation Last Assault
Operation Blue Halo
Operation Poppy Pride

OPERATION
EDGE

Richard Joyce

OLIVER & LEWIS

British Library Cataloguing in Publication Data
A catalogue record for this book is available from the British Library

ISBN 978-0-9935750-3-7

Typeset by Amolibros, Milverton, Somerset
www.amolibros.com
This book production has been managed by Amolibros
Printed and bound by Lightning Source worldwide

ACKNOWLEDGEMENTS

Although there are references made to true military operations and people in this book, none of those in this story happened. However, I have tried to make the book as factually accurate as possible, and to show the courage and sacrifice involved.

First, I would like to thank those who have continued their support by purchasing my Johnny Vince novels, without whom I would not be able to continue to write and raise funds for military charities.

A massive thanks for the support of my loving wife, fans, and friends.

Like the last artwork book cover, I would again like to mention and praise the talented artist, Ant Holder. Jane Tatam, from Amolibros, thank you for enabling me to get this book published.

Lastly, please keep supporting all those who are suffering with PTSD, from all walks of life.

I dedicate this book to the brave soldiers who fought at the Somme.

ABOUT THE AUTHOR

Inspired in 2013 by his favourite author, Damien Lewis, Richard Joyce began to write his first of the Johnny Vince series. Right from the first book, *Operation Blue Halo*, he continues to finely blend historical facts and events, combined with raw emotion, suspense, and unexpected twists.

When not writing, researching, and editing in his 'man shed', Richard enjoys time with his wife and dog on beach walks; oh, and a sneaky beer. As well as raising funds for charitable affairs that are connected to his writing, he is now busy typing away for a new book, away from the Johnny Vince series.

EPILOGUE

I had never recovered from Operation Poppy Pride. The guilt, horrific scenes, leaving mates, losing the ones I had cared for, just to return to immense pressure of the death of my dad. I could not find my positive mindset.

That day of our argument when I had threatened him before leaving for Sumatra, he had gone to his local pub to console his mood. Visions of him staggering across the road in front of a lorry profoundly haunt me. It had been Ocker, with the help from Nico and Georges, that had tracked and rescued me from the tribe. I had blamed Ocker for the failure in his basic message to abort the mission.

Over the next few weeks recovering in hospital, Ocker's continuous questions and outrageous manner had got to me. I flicked the anger switch, not being able to get out of the red-zone, berating all the pent-up anger at him. Ocker returned to Australia, vowing he would never contact me or Will again.

Seven months on, the JD had become the amenity. Friends and family tried their best to keep me on the righteous, but their patronising comments riled me. The vivid nightmares and the increasing pressure from the voice haunted me. I suppressed in the shadows, negativity drowning me. The money I had saved from previous missions was depleting, along with my creditability. Fuck life, I would say, waking up with yet another hangover. The priority was to assure that I had enough alcohol to get me into a coma, helping me get through the night; I despised the voice.

On one occasion, when I had eventually decided to get my life in order, I drove to the cemetery where my dad was laid to rest. However, just encountering the church was too painful, and I sped by. That same freezing, windy day, I sat on the cliff, drained, staring vacantly out to sea. I went over memories of Operation Poppy Pride: desperate, sometimes pulling at my hair. Even with the new physical scars and Skedgewell's Omega watch, it was impossible to consider it had been real, fucking my mind.

That same cold night, the voice instructed I did genealogy on those that were involved in 1944. Knowing it was trying to crush me, I threw the Omega watch into the sea, laughing at the voice. I had won the first challenge in a long time. However, an argument followed. Against what it had advised not to do, I chucked my dad's Rolex. It was then I realised that is what the evil voice had wanted; I had failed.

Back in my lounge for the first time in three months, I threw the empty JD bottle at the wall. Like before, after the Afghan mission, life had become unbearable.

CHAPTER ONE

Securing a rope around a large boulder, then through a Petzl life-anchor, I checked all my gear. Clear from the outset, for once, I was at ease. Taking a stronghold on the cliff, I aimlessly peered around for the last time, then gently lowered myself over the edge, abseiling a few metres.

The sun was just rising, warming my numbness, lightening the dark place I had come from. The mesmerising sea crested the rocks, seagulls fluttered on the vortex of warm air currents. The strangest part was the *Déjà vu*: my nightmare after being knocked out by the German officer. So uncanny was this scene, I gazed out to sea to check if the perils of a storm smashed a boat, tossing it like a matchbox. I smirked at the idiocy of expecting to see my family holding on for dear life. However, this time I would have understood the nightmare of why my dad was not aboard that boat.

Getting a decent foothold, from inside my filthy jacket I retrieved the rest of the JD, half-guzzled before I had driven to here: Land's End. With the attendant's kiosk empty, I had parked at the furthest point away in the carpark and trudged along the beautiful coastline until I had found the precipice to the secluded rocks below. I had been to this spot before, hand in hand with Lena, the memory etched on the today's ominous journey.

I had not been rock climbing for quite a while, but then, these days nothing inspired me but the drink and solitude. Everything just irritated the fuck out of me. PTSD had been mentioned, but you cannot blame it on that if it's everyone else being complete twats. I just wished I did not attract idiots and they would leave me to get on with how I think I should live. No one had the right to tell me what to do. None of them had been through what I had since the 2013 Afghan mission.

Most days the guilt would suffocate me, knowing how selfish I had become, having the chance to live my life, unlike all my dead brothers.

After these thoughts, I would always despise my old squad because they were not living this nightmare. It was a vicious circle that I could only break by drinking. I had begun to enjoy the isolation of living away from home, my new adventure. There were no constant interruptions from my house phone and front door. With my stash of cash, and God forbid anyone who tried to mug me, I drunk when I wanted, letting the crappy takeaways soak it up. Yes, my family tried to intervene, but they could not help.

My stupid brother had dragged me back to his house after a fuelled night out, telling me in the morning he had found me in the gutter. His bullshit lectures wound me up, especially from standing there in his perfect life. After banging on for too long, a fight started, but I let him beat me, relinquishing his blame and guilt he had pinned on me for Dad's death.

As predicted, my mum joined the long list of annoying people giving me false sympathy. I knew she was hiding her hate, holding me accountable for everything. Constantly visiting and stopping me in the street was obliterating what self-esteem I had. One drizzly day, I was woken up on the beach by my mum and her friend. Telling my mum that "I wasn't fucking twelve anymore and to sort her own problems out", felt I had accomplished back control.

Feeling dejected that my saviour was only half-full, I spat out the screw cap, admiring the way it fell to the rocks and swell. I finished all but the last centimetre.

'Awwwww, shit,' I said.

A large burp belched; fumes rose into my watery eyes. I wiped the dribble from my heavy beard and then licked the back of my grubby hand. Tired from yet another restless night in my one-man squat, I stretched and yawned. A small recollection from yesterday filtered in, barred from another pub for abusive behaviour; I smirked. There were not many places left for me to have a good drink and let off steam. Not having returned to Karate since leaving hospital, setting alight my karate kit in my back garden, I had nowhere to vent my utter disgust for the society we lived in, and the MOD that had failed me. The more I seem to let people in on my trouble and secrets, the more I became branded.

I had let Simon and Trevor into my house. They rudely commented on its state and outrageously tried to tell me how I was behaving. How fucking dare they. What do they know? They even had the audacity to tell me to "grab a shower and a new set of clothes". It is what's in my mind that matters, not how I look. After an intense argument, exchanging keys back with Simon, that was the last time I had let either in. In fact, it was easier to ignore all the constant communications, feeling it right to walk on the other side of the street from anyone I knew. Sometimes I realised my actions were a result of what I had become, but the argument was lost when I thought of everyone's easy life.

It had been my choice to sleep rough. I could not be branded homeless as I had a home. In the three months of my new life, appearing homeless, many people did not acknowledge me or had kept their distance; just what I needed. My own personal space was away from the town's hustle. When a helicopter would fly over, I could huddle into my hide without them spotting me. I learnt what noises would spark off the flashbacks, quickly covering my ears and screwing my eyes shut. It had even worked, sometimes.

Visiting the psychologist from my hospital discharge had been a waste of time. I am sure whilst I was telling her about Operation Poppy Pride, she was doodling me in a straight-jacket. I had ignored her advice to leave the drink alone and, deciding I was going to sack her, I had turned up drunk to give her a deserved grilling. I was told to "seek further medical advice from a different professional". Oh, what grandeur words. Bitch.

Talking of drink, I wished I had brought another bottle, now looking back at the empty. What do I do with this one? I couldn't throw it into the sea, broken glass could wash up on the beach, causing serious injury to a child.

'Children,' I muttered, and scoffed.

Had I really put too much pressure on Lena to have children? I cannot recollect ever nagging her. Why didn't she tell me she could not have kids? Perhaps she could, finding it an excuse to run off with another bloke. All that love and war; what a waste.

'War? What's the point?'

I should have listened to my ex-wife, Ella, pleading me to leave the Special Forces. Images of Lee Brown and her making love behind my back knotted my gut.

'If you had not gone on Operation Blue Halo, then she would still be with you, Johnny,' I slurred, and sighed, rubbing my raw eyes, trying to rid the mission details. 'Ah, Operation Blue Halo,' I muttered. 'What a fuck-up.'

I hit the bottle on my helmet, wishing I could turn back time. But then, why should I have left the best unit in the world? I remembered being so proud at the time to have named the mission, especially knowing it had pissed off my CO, Dick Brown. From the point where we had extracted in the second Chinook, life had become one rollercoaster from hell.

I tried to think of the good times after leaving the SF, but the dreaded images filtered in of those left in my wake.

'Robert, Gary, Tony, and the crew,' I garbled, 'what a fucking waste.'

Without wanting them, other memories came back: Haleema's brown, silky hair tied in a bunch, mesmerising me. She elegantly turned around and gazed at me, her beautiful, wide eyes were a deep-brown. Haleema coyly smiled, just about showing her perfect teeth. Hearing her soothing voice, I was filled with a warm glow.

'Haleema,' I sadly murmured. 'The one angel who brought me back from near death.'

Opening my eyes, she had gone. I stared at my undone bootlace; how sloppy of me. Irritated, I leant forward to tie it...

BOOOM!

I shuddered. Haleema's naked, brown, slender body now lay in my arms. Wounds started to pour between the imbedded shards of glass and debris.

'Haleema, I'm so sorry I came back to rescue you,' I sobbed. 'If it wasn't for me, you'd be alive.' I spat out the bitterness.

But you saved Haleema and her mum from the evil Baha Udeen and his cronies, I thought. There was no comfort, I was spiralling down the self-pity route. It always happened after getting angry with myself, alcohol either numbing or angering the situation.

I held the bottle up to the sun, making weird patterns as if on fire. Why the fuck didn't I bring more alcohol? Jesus, I was at an all-time low. Perhaps it would it have been better to have died in the helicopter crash along with my mates.

'But what about Roy?' I said in defence. 'If it wasn't for you, Johnny, he would have been beheaded.' Good counterattack, Johnny, I thought, nodding my appreciation.

Feeling slightly better, I tried to envisage Roy at home with his loving family—blank. It was weird that only images of the good people I had lost now flashed before my eyes. I shook my head trying to rid more, but Kyle pictured, bleeding to death. Was it my fault that Kyle had died? Why wasn't Ocker and Will taking some of the blame?

I thought of the moment when I had phoned Will in the early hours of the morning, telling him that losing my dad was all his fault. The slanderous and threatening argument that had followed sealed his fate not to offer me another mission. OK, in the heat of the moment, I had mentioned that I would visit his shitty airport and wipe out all his SF staff, and personally throw Will out of his own junky plane without a parachute. Yet, he should not have told me I had lost my marbles. Anyway, his loss.

The leg cramps from my rooted feet took my negative thoughts away. I had to stay positive, I thought; but then, why? I knew why I was here. It's not all been doom and gloom, I had killed some evil people, I thought, trying to rid any guilt before the inevitable. At last, pictures of the slotted terrorist played out on my closed eyelids; I grinned with glee.

'That's it, Johnny, think of the bad shit you've slotted. All those terrorists, that drug lord and his henchman.'

Suddenly, the white lights and sound from an explosion startled open my eyes. I knew it was the repetitive image of Sameer's boat, but it still had shocked me. The pit of my stomach cartwheeled seeing his kind face and innocent smile. Slightly trembling, I searched the boulders below for the bottle, not realising I had dropped it. I smirked at the unreal importance of it compared to why I was here.

The better side of my mind, as it had been waiting to tell me, mentioned all those mad Somali pirates I had killed to save Ocker. Again, my morale was on the up, until I looked at the sand below: me and Ocker were fighting the hundreds of perusing enemies. Through the black and green seaweed swamp, something came to the surface. Focusing on a decaying hand protruding, my heart rate increased. Who the fuck is that? As the person locked eyes on me, I recognised it was Larry, decomposed. I sharply turned, quickly staring at the sun through my closed eyes, trying to rid the battle.

The roar of the sea was exchanged for the peace and quiet of the RAF field. Me and the lads were sunbathing after the killing house training; I blissfully smiled.

'Blondie, Spike, Churchill, and Benny, if the mission was real, I'm sorry,' I said.

Opening my tender eyes, I looked at the spray rising from the wash. Further questions came to the forefront, the same I had asked many times. Would they have died if I had not gone back in time? Did the rest of the lads make it out with the German boy driving? Why did my dad come back disguised as Tim? Was it to guide me through? When he used to say, "he hated the nickname Vinnie", and "son", how obvious it was now. I contemplated what I had just said, then slapped my cheek.

'What the actual fuck, Johnny?' I slurred. 'You know it was a dream. That's why each character was supposed to have represented someone from your life in the future.'

Nevertheless, there was the fact that I had come away with new scars and, frighteningly, Skedgewell's watch. How did all that happen with the lost tribe? Was my life planned from the day I was born? Fate, religion, the afterlife, what a bag of shite, I thought, rejecting the 'planned life' part. At least now I oversaw my own destiny, and on such a beautiful day. Empathy flooded me; the place went eerily quiet.

Unlocking the knife's blade, trembling, I placed it on the rope. Quickly, I lifted it, deciding to put it back on the purple pattern of the rope, unsure to why I hated the yellow colour. Taking a big sniff as the tears welled, I slowly dragged the blade, the nylon started to thread. I have not left a note, I thought, and stopped. Seagulls swooped and called nearby. Are they warning me or mocking me? Should I have left a suicide note? Where would have been the best place for them to find it? Perhaps killing myself would show I was not in control, when I was. But cutting the rope would prove it was not an accident. Would it have been better to have not properly secured the anchor bolt? To make it look like an accident.

I took the knife off. Did it fucking matter? I replaced the blade. But what about the poor RNLI crew that had to scrape me off the rocks? Would I float out to sea and never be found? Do I want to be found? Too many questions were confusing me.

'Why are you doing this?' I mumbled. Because no one can help you, I thought.

God, you're taking your fucking time.

'I wondered how long it would be before you raised your fucking ugly head.'

You know I like to come when you've had a few. Anyway, you weren't so abrupt when you pleaded for me when you were dying at the end of rope in Indonesia, were you.

'Yeah, but I survived anyway. I didn't need your help.'

You know that's a lie.

'I'm not having a conversation with you. Just fuck off.'

How rude. I tried to help you swing and grab that ledge.

'Rude?' I slurred. 'Since I've returned, you've done nothing but infuriate me about my dad's death and the loss of the lads on the last mission.'

I thought you told me, "it was a fucking dream".

'Yeah, it was. Now fuck off.'

You're being very disrespectful to your chums back in 1944. You've not even thought about the ones who have survived the mission under your shit leadership.

'What the fuck do you know?'

I know you're trying to hide the knife from me. And you know I've been right on so many occasions.

I brought the knife back up to show I didn't care it knew. 'Remember the first time you appeared? You were full of shit back then, like, "shoot the terrorist through my front door". You were wrong, it was my brother on the other side.'

Ah, but I wasn't wrong back then about your so called SBS mates using you to buy them a drink, planning get you into trouble. You wanker.

I gripped the knife. 'Your name calling is pathetic. And we've covered this ground so many times.'

I won't mention it was your wrong decision then.

'You were also wrong about the Chinook crash being all my fault. Your lies that the court were going to throw the book at me and throw me in prison. I was acquitted of any blame.' I folded the blade away, smug that for once I had not been beaten.

Yeah, you put that knife away, but like last time, I see you've gained jack shit, dude.

'What do you mean?'

You're on your own, you're a loser. You've lost your mates and your family have had enough of you. Again, you drink yourself into oblivion to hide your guilt. You've become a tramp.

'My choice. Now fuck off and leave me alone.'

No wonder your wife and Lena left you.

'You're starting to piss me off.'

Was it also your choice to leave Spike and Blondie to burn alive in that house?

'Fuck off,' I shouted, and smacked my forehead to rid the typical pain and the voice.

Hurry up and cut the fucking rope.

I opened the blade, the sky reflecting off it.

And how mistaken you were about Churchill hating Benny because he was black. I wonder what it's like to be burnt alive. Poor old Benny, if only you had listened to Churchill.

'Funny how you forget all the evil I've killed over the years.' I was breathing quicker.

You know you're just bullshitting yourself. Admit it, you wish the Germans had killed you or you had died in the Chinook crash.

'You're doing my fucking nut in.' I found the slight notch in the rope with the tip of the blade.

You can't even kill yourself without fucking-up.

'Shut the fuck up,' I yelled, and started to slide the blade across. 'If you had the bottle to stand in front of me, man to man, I would fucking kill you.'

You're lying. You know you've lost your fighting aggression.

'I fucking would,' I said, trying to convince myself.

Did you enjoy slapping your dad before you'd left, just to find some poachers? You should've realised your family meant more to you than the mission.

Breathing erratically the handle shook in my grip, nose drips ran down my beard.

Bet you wished you never laid hands on your dad and threatened him.

'Go away,' I sobbed.

I guess now you know why Ocker, Simon, and Trevor were playing your dad's favourite music whilst you were blissfully having fun with your new friends in 1944.

'And why there was none played for twenty-four hours because they attended his funeral. I'm not fucking stupid. And you mention Ocker playing my favourite songs, it was his fault I ended up taking that fucking mission. I'm glad he's gone back to Australia, the loud-mouth pikey.'

Are you sure about that, Johnny?

I scoffed, trying to hide that the voice was correct; I had become weak.

How could you miss his funeral? What a disgrace. You're feeble and pathetic.

'Arghhhhh,' I yelled.

Tensing up, I hit the side of my head, then pulled at the helmet, the blade catching my ear. Opening my eyes, all was silent. The blood trickled down my chapped cheek. I took a deep breath, then exhaled. At last, the voice had gone.

You know it was your fault he got drunk and strolled in front of that lorry.

Exasperated, but crushed, I placed the knife on the rope for the last time, not caring what colour it touched. The world around me darkened, the focus pinpointed on the blade's edge.

'Anything else to add?' I mumbled.

Cut the fucking rope.

'Goodbye pain.'

CHAPTER TWO

Shingle landed on my gloves. The world opened again. Instead of seeing Roy's legs dangling over the edge as I had dreamt, a snazzy florescent-yellow trainer cautiously took a hold on the lip. What was he doing? This was my spot. He wasn't in climbing gear, but creased jeans and a faded sweater. What was he looking at? Hadn't he seen me? More earth fell. I dusted myself down and shook the dirt from my helmet.

'Oi,' I yelled, 'you're covering me in shit.'

Appearing shocked, he said, 'Sorry, my friend. I... I... I never knew you were there.'

'Didn't you see my fucking rope?'

'All right, keep your frigging hat on,' he said.

He took the front of his shoes from the edge, more fragments fell. I glared hard at this middle-aged man. Placing his hands on his hips, he then curiously stared. I quickly took the blade off the rope, placing the knife to my side.

'Why are you cutting your rope?' he asked, then it dawned on him.

'Mind your fucking own. Now piss off and find another beauty spot.'

'This isn't a beauty spot with your ugly mug,' he said. 'Anyway, you don't own these cliffs.'

'I'll come up and own you in a minute.'

He purposely landed more dirt on me.

Feeding the rope back through the belay device, I heaved myself up, but stupidly dropped the knife.

'Bollocks,' I muttered.

'Are you clumsy, or just testing the theory of gravity?'

'I suggest you start running before I kill you,' I said, but it had sounded as lame as my real intentions.

'If I were immortal, I would work in an isolated shop and wait to see if anyone noticed that I hadn't aged.' He walked out of sight.

Ignoring his smart-arse answer, I made faster the ascent.

Once on top, I unhooked all my gear and threw it at the base of the rock. Lightheaded, I began to sway. The next thing I knew, I had face-planted the damp grass. Fortunately, I had not taken my helmet off due to the fiddly strap. A numbness glowed over me as my senses began to spin. My eyes closed on their own accord. The seagulls and wind became one tranquillity. In my dream, the ocean converted into a calm moving mass. The JD bottle that floated out to sea was hypnotic, swaying me back and forth with it.

Knowing it was coming, I opened my eyes and hauled myself to the edge. Peering at the aggressive wish-wash of blurry colours below, I spewed up. After the initial acid burning, I did again, and again. No breakfast, as I had not bothered, just rancid liquid.

'What a waste,' I mumbled.

Once the episode had finished, I wiped my chin and blew my nose. I turned over on my back. How long had I been out before I had spewed? I had not bought a new watch due to the relevance of losing my dad. The previous watches he had given me, I had misplaced. Also, every time I had looked at my divers' watch, it reminded me of the Rolex I had given to him. I checked the time on my phone: 08.52 hrs.

This time I easily undid the strap and threw the helmet aside. My head thumped. The seagulls started crazily flying around in circles, the odd one diving to my mess. Clouds started to patch over the blue sky. The recent January showers seeped into my clothes; I began to tremble. The voice was right when it had said: "You can't even kill yourself without fucking-up."

Sitting up quickly, regretting it as fast, there was an aroma of sick. I waited for my head to stop spinning before looking around for this middle-aged twat that had ruined my morning. Groggily standing, wondering where he had disappeared to, an urgency hit me. I carefully scrutinised over the edge, but he wasn't mashed on the rocks below or floating out with the tide. A faint whiff of cigarette wafted in on the chilli breeze. I spotted a haze coming from a dip in the ground on the next cliff contour.

'Time to vent,' I said.

Victorious, angry, smug, I stomped off in his direction, making sure I stayed away from the volatile edge. A joyful scene played in my mind of hitting him, but I knew I didn't have the balls.

I was not expecting to see him dangling his legs over a sandy edge that the weather had eroded. Still vexed with him, I jumped down a level.

With his back to me, he was staring into the chasm. A wash of spray bellowed up. A blue piece of folded paper fluttering under a medium sized rock stopped me going into a rant. He flicked away the cigarette. I looked back from its fall. He began to sob uncontrollably into his hands. I closed my mouth, my shoulders sunk. With a deep sniff and then a long breath, he then slapped his cheeks. I glared at what he stared at below him, then back at his precarious state. He placed his hands carefully by the side of him and inched forwards, possibly his last.

'You hear the voices, too?' I quietly said.

Shocked, he twisted, almost toppling over. Gripping to the rock covered in old man's beard moss, as we had called it as kids, he was slightly shaking.

'I thought you'd jumped,' he said.

'Who said I was going to? I came back to watch you do it. Is that a suicide note? How nice,' I said sarcastically.

I was slightly envious of that blue paper that he had snatched back, knocking the stone over the edge. Still holding onto the rock, he stuffed the letter in his jacket pocket.

'And going back to your first question, no, I don't hear voices. That's for proper mentally imbalanced freaks.' A wry smile followed.

'I'll leave you to your sane jump then,' I said. 'Make sure the bungee cord is tight around your ankles.'

I made my way back to my strewn gear, wondering if he would mess up like me. Whilst I collected my equipment and fastidiously put it away in order, a part of me wanted to go back and check on him; it was growing in strength. Once my small backpack was packed, I bent down and tied the annoying bootlace, eyes burning into my skull from the JD. It had started to drizzle, just to add to my crappy day. Blood dripped onto my wrist from the nick in my ear.

'Fancy a pint?' a voice said.

I turned around to see the failed jumper. 'Bit early for that.'

'Does an alcoholic ever stop?'

Did he mean me, or himself? 'What the fuck do you know?'

He frizzed his black and grey hair with his hand. 'I know I'm getting wet, but I don't know why you brought all that climbing shit with you. What was the point?'

Ignoring him, I placed the helmet on my head, the water ran down my face and neck. The rain became heavy as he began to stroll up the wet slope. I noticed *his* bootlace was not undone.

'Anyway, I'm off to the Whitehouse Inn,' he said. 'I want to see the bottom of a glass. You can see the bottom of the cliff. I'll see you there once I've had a few.'

As he was almost out of view, I looked back at the edge, and then the sea. Did he mean, "I'll see you there once I've had a few", as in, see me at the bottom of the cliff, or at the pub? I waited for the voice to answer—silence. Searching back for the jumper, he had gone. A massive wave of guilt crashed over me, followed by a back-surge of humiliation, pushing me to my knees. What the fuck am I doing? Angry that I had missed out on the opportunity of a free pint, knowing I had no money, I grabbed my backpack and hastily made my way up the slippery slope, trying not to fall.

The carpark had half-a-dozen cars in. Just as I reached the chalky stones, the rain now lashing, I spotted a black with red striped side VW Transporter leaving.

'Bollocks. Missed it,' I grumbled.

Peeling the penalty notice off the car, I quickly got in, chucking it on the passenger seat. I breathed a heavy sigh of relief, condensation forming, blocking out the view of the weird patterns that the rain made.

Cold, damp, I started the engine and waited for the air-con to clear the windows. Takeaway packaging and beer cans caught my eye in the foot-well. The back seat was no better. I tried to remember the last time I had been in my car for a night out of shenanigans, but couldn't. The parking attendant came into view. Catching his attention with a big wheel spin, I drove at full speed towards him. Startled as I neared, he backed up against a car. Within six metres, getting enjoyment out of his petrified expression, I hand-braked to a stop. I put the passenger window down and threw the fixed charge notice at him.

'Wanker,' I shouted.

'I'm going to report…'

Dropping the clutch, I span the shit over him, leaving him for dust.

After scraping a few verges and taking out a plastic bollard, I drove into a layby and killed the engine. I had only been driving for quarter of an hour, but my head was hurting. Still damp from the downpour, the glass quickly steamed up. Shoving the cliff episode to the back of my mind, I closed my eyes to sober-up.

★

Blondie walked into my thoughts trying to give me a bible, making me feel good. His blond hair caught the sunlight as he pushed his glasses up his thin nose, one lens still cracked. I pressed the bible back. His smile turned to a frown. Behind me strolled the other eleven lads all in the gear, ready to deploy. It was amazing to see them all jostle, smile, and laugh. I had missed these band of brothers. Planet waved at me, whilst Fish wound up his middle finger, Shrek giving him a dead-arm. Spike was telling Geordie that fingerless gloves were just hand vests. I laughed with Geordie, wanting all the fun back, desperate to join them, a new life. Looking at my clothes, I now did not have the vagrant persona, but was in full World War Two uniform. The old me was back.

I had heard it before I saw it: a damaged Halifax bomber. Where was that familiar era sound of the ambulance? The RAF crew were not on the balcony this time. I screamed at my mates who were walking aimlessly across the grassy runway, but my voice was muffled, as if blaring into a blocked tube. Blondie laughed. I turned to see his eyes were weird, his expression malice. From his shoes working upwards, he caught fire. With the flames becoming hotter, his eyes became pure-black, but at depths I did not want to look.

The Halifax crashing onto the grass took my transfixed stare. Careering out of control towards the lads, I yelled at them to move. It was no use. I sprinted, trying to wave my arms. They were too heavy. My feet sank into the soft grass, as if running on the spot. I began to work out the distance I had left compared to the bomber. Blondie's shrilling laugh was breathing down my neck, messing up my calculations. Within a few metres, sweating hard, I managed to hold my hand out to Rose. Just as we touched, the hulking mass of burning wreckage shot past, taking them all from me.

'Fuck,' I shouted.

The evil image and smell faded as I blinked hard. I stopped shaking my hot fingers. Water droplets ran down the front screen, as well as my forehead. I was soaked all over, again. My phone vibrated and, checking the screen in my trembling hands, it was a number I did not recognise. All my friends and family had been blocked.

'Hello?' I spoke. 'Hello?'

Someone was slightly breathing. Are they letting me know they were there? I waited—nothing.

'Bollocks to ya then,' I said, and ended the call.

Time check: 10.27 hrs. I had been asleep for about an hour. From the glove compartment I took a half-bottle of coke and gulped it down, distastefully flat, like my life. I contemplated what to do next. Where do I go now? I did not want to go home. I could not go back to the cliff, that part of me was over. I had to forget that life, taking this as the opportunity to change. However, an anxious part of me started questioning the reality, reminding me how I had got in this mess. Nerves mounting, I started the car and demisted the overwhelming fear.

'Just fucking drive away to another life, Johnny.'

With my vision clear, I thrust it into gear and left the layby. A long horn and a screech of tyres made me check my rear-view mirror. The angry driver behind vented his thoughts. Naturally, I gave him the middle finger.

It wasn't long before the vexed driver had caught me up, now flashing and swerving behind me. The bright stars suddenly lit up in the rolling black sky. Quickly, I fumbled to turn on the headlights to check the dusty track: the wadi was to the left. I knew it would be a bad mistake to take the approaching fork down into it. My Toyota screamed its nuts off. I fought to stay on the rutted road. Where was my SF training? Why wasn't it kicking in? In the rear-view mirror, the unmanned Dushka was flapping around. Where the fuck was Rabbit? I don't remember seeing or hearing him fall out.

Racing at speed, sweat pouring, I had to get my breathing and heart rate down. I couldn't, but at least I had made good ground from the pursuing Elkhaba. The rocks thundered under the chassis, dust making it hard to see how many were following. Fear was escalating. Why couldn't I control it? I had to make a greater distance so I could find the next slope, get out, and then grab the RPG situated in the back.

Going broadside around the next bend, the slope lay ahead. Skidding to a stop, slightly off the track with the front tyres entering the wadi's thick mud, I charged out and searched the rear for the RPG around the Dushka's stand.

'Fuck, where is it?' I yelled. 'Bingo.'

The chasing Toyota's engine screamed in the blackness, headlights bouncing into the eerie abyss. Trudging across the wadi's sticky floor, I turned to see the vehicle enter the slope. Without the time to take aim, the terrorist's car stopped. The door slammed. With my RPG raised, a loan figure walked in front of his Toyota's headlight beams. He then took a few steps towards me, but he stood still in the moonlight. My heart was pumping. I had the familiar dull pain to my forehead. I scanned his hands for weapons—empty. I looked through his Toyota's glass—empty. The cold desert air seeped into my sweaty clothes. What was he waiting for?

I regripped the RPG. Instead of this terrorist pulling an AK47 out from his white *dishdasha*, he began to shout abuse. My finger caressed the trigger. I tried to translate his Arabic, but it was no good. The Elkhaba leader's aggression blazed through his eyes under the black turban and *shemagh*. My lips had become dry through heavy breathing, so I licked them. He walked backwards with more gesticulating and Arabic spewing. Once his vehicle started to leave, I released my iron grip off the RPG.

The dust cloud made his rear lights invisible. Even though I was fortunate that this fighter had no comrades with him, and for some reason no weapon, I knew it would not be long before he was back, fully loaded.

'Excuse me, is everything all right?'

Daylight made me squint. I spun to see a man dressed in a suit walking across the wadi, sand being replaced with tarmac. Behind him was a building with people staring through a large window. The sign above read: The Whitehouse Inn. Checking to my left and right, I was standing in a grassy field, mud on my boots. Confused, I noticed the baseball bat in my hands. I lowered it after seeing his manager badge. He stayed back in the carpark. I tried not to show him I was trembling.

'Do you want me to call the police?' he said.

'No, it's fine.'

'Would you mind moving your car as you're causing an obstruction.'

I looked at the open boot on my mud splattered Audi, the rain washing it away. I had left the engine running. Steam rose from the underside and brake-discs.

'Sure,' I said, still dazed.

'Thank you.'

As he walked back towards the restaurant, someone shielded by the crowd at the main window was filming me on their phone.

Back in the safety of my car, I hastily drove down the hill into the second carpark area. Fearful of the Elkhaba returning, I headed towards the exit. I stopped, having spotted the black with red striped side VW Transporter parked. My stomach gargled as the smell of food sifted through my open window. Reversed into a space, the thought of brunch had been overwhelming. Do I wait for this bloke I had met on the cliff to leave? Sod it, he did not bother me. But what about the humiliation? What would the crowd be thinking if he had said he knew me at Land's End? However, if the onlookers had seen the Elkhaba leader chase me, then they would understand. I was not going to feel ashamed for the carpark altercation.

Walking up the stairs, I banged as much wadi mud off as possible. Before I fully opened the main door, I put my ear to the gap, expecting lots of laughter, but the ambience was normal. I took a deep breath, then entered. Warm air encapsulated my damp clothes. Behind me I had left a trail of mud on the blue and white flecked carpet. I thought of the hideous flooring at Aden International Airport. I smirked, but images of me being grabbed by the airport staff filtered in.

'Table for one, sir?'

I shook the thoughts. 'Err… yeah… sure,' I said.

Rubbing my neck after reliving the pain from being seized, the young waitress was still staring at me, covering her nose with the palm of her delicate hand.

'I'm sorry about the terrorist problem,' I said.

'Please, follow me.'

Perhaps everyone just excepted it these days, I thought.

I purposely ignored her cute arse and her breasts that pushed through her blouse. I knew who she reminded me of, but now wasn't the time to think about the Afghan doctor. My libido had been the lowest, no, extinct. It was not like me. I passed a lot of business-like people, some appearing suspicious of me. Some of the adults told their kids not to stare. Too damn right, I thought. How many children these days knew what it was like to get mucky? I fought hard not to stick my middle finger up at them.

Ahead were a pair of fire-exit doors. The chef, standing in an open-plan view kitchen, prepared some steak with a large, sharp knife. Other dangerous knives were placed in a rack around the tiled wall. From the corner of my eye, I checked to see if he had clocked me; he had. Was the chef getting ready to attack? The manager now watched me. Had he called the police? I didn't trust him; I had to watch my back. A gold combination-locked black briefcase was next to a suited gentleman. I ignored his eye contact. With the humid temperature and growing pressure, without drawing any attention to myself I sat down at the table the waitress had showed. My mind told me that there might be a pistol in the briefcase, and to observe covertly. The person on the table behind had a paper covering their face. The headline read: 'Staggering Number of European Jihadists'. Who was behind it? Who wrote that headline?

'Can I get you a drink?' she asked.

I shook the thoughts and looked up at the waitress. She kept her false smile. I picked up the menu, slightly covering my face.

'Sir?'

'Yes, a pint of lager, please,' I softly said.

'What type, sir?'

'Erm…?' I couldn't remember the brand I liked. Hands sweating, I gripped the menu. Had someone turned the heating on?

She impatiently tutted.

'What have you got?' I blurted.

'We have Fosters, Carls…'

'Yeah, that one,' I interrupted.

'Carlsberg or Fosters?'

Knowing my irritability levels were rising, I swallowed hard. I had to remain the grey man. I drew my eyes back from the suspicious on-lookers, then looked at her with a deadpan expression.

'Carlsberg, or Fosters?' she harshly repeated.

'Fosters.'

'Thank you, sir,' she said flippantly.

Taking the menu by the corner in her index finger and thumb, as if it had been dropped in shit, I covertly spotted cars entering the grounds. I relaxed, having not seen a Toyota with a group of young fighting males seeking revenge. My sixth sense told me that the bloke behind was studying me. Was this person behind the paper one of the European Jihadists? The hairs on my neck raised. Maybe when my beer arrives, I should knock it over to see if he drops his paper, a distraction. I slid the table knife up my sleeve. No, that would cause more of a scene if he was not a threat. I secretly shook the weapon out. But why the feeling of dread running through me? My hand covered the knife. Perhaps I should go to the toilet and on the way check the person from the side. I stood up and took off my sodden jacket, food particles and dirt falling. The waitress, at arm's length, placed down a pint of lager, her nose twitching.

'There you go, sir.'

I gulped it down, catching the drips with my other hand.

'Have you chosen your food, sir?'

'For God's sake, stop calling me bloody sir,' I blurted.

I tried to hide the belching beer gases, also concealing my stupidity from those who had turned around. The man to my right pulled his briefcase into his legs. What *was* in there? The chef stopped working and said something to the manager. What?

'He's had a tough morning,' the man behind said. 'Give him a few minutes, please.'

I turned sharply, ready to attack my growing fear, but it was the jumper. He folded his paper. In front of him was a tumbler with the remains of ice.

The manager had taken a few strides over, so I sat down.

'Well?' the waitress asked.

'I'll have a full English and a round of toast,' I said, 'but I've got no money.'

'Erm?' she said. 'I will need to check if the manager lets homeless…'

'Don't worry yourself, pretty lady,' the jumper interrupted, 'I will pay for his.'

'Pot of tea or a coffee?' the waitress asked me.

Was she taking the fucking piss? Tea? Coffee? After the morning from hell? 'I'll have whatever he's drinking,' I said abruptly.

'I'll have a full English as well,' the jumper said. 'Fancy joining me?' he asked me.

I pondered why he had not eaten yet, but I decided to join him.

CHAPTER THREE

To start with, the kitchen staff and the children had been too noisy, but gradually I began to relax and enjoy the Gin and ample food. I couldn't remember the last time I'd had a breakfast. From time to time, I would glance up, catching the jumper studying me, but straightaway he had lowered his eyes. It must have looked odd to others that we had both not said a word. Is this why the diners were looking at me strangely? The mysterious man with the briefcase had left. Now I wasn't bothered about what was in that case. In fact, the more I drunk, the more the life around appeased. I wasn't even concerned about where the exits were.

Finishing the bacon, I then gulped down the second large Gin. It was then I noticed new food stains on my dirty shirt. The waitress came over and started to collect our plates, so I ordered two Jack Daniels. The jumper nodded his appreciation. I was itching to break the awkwardness, but I did not know where to start the conversation.

'So...' the jumper said.

We held eye contact; I folded my unused napkin.

'Yeah... so,' I said—silence.

We spoke at the same time, then both offered for the other to go first, but none of us spoke. It was comical in the awkwardness. He gestured around my mouth and chin.

'You not going to use that napkin?' he said.

'No.'

'Perhaps a toothbrush?' The jumper licked his teeth.

I picked the food out of my teeth and then ate it from my dirty nails.

'Strange way to hold a baseball bat,' he said. 'Light anti-tank weapon?' He scoffed.

I narrowed my eyes at him. 'RPG, actually,' I retorted.

'Oh.'

The waitress plonked down the two drinks, the ice clunking braking the quietness. I caught another glimpse of her tits popping out of her blouse. This time it stirred something. It must be the Gin, I thought.

'What's your name?' he asked.

'Johnny.'

'Second name?'

'Are you MI5, surname division?' I asked.

He frowned at me, his crows-feet showing his age. 'I'm Chris, Chris Breedon. Monkfish to my mates.' He pushed back his black and grey bushy eyebrows.

'That's some nickname,' I said. 'Military mates give you that?'

'Yes, but I'm ex-military now. You look like you've been in a few scraps. You a bouncer or a thug, Johnny?' He smiled.

'Bit of this, bit of that.'

'You also stink. You a tramp or a sewage worker?' he asked.

'One for the road?'

Monkfish looked at his watch.

'Got to be somewhere?' I asked.

'No. Not even sure why I looked at it. And yes, why not. Make it a double, you're paying. Oh, I forgot, you're a homeless guy that drives a nice expensive car.'

'How did you know that?' I retorted.

A waiter came across, keeping his distance, also pulling a small expression. I took a sniff of my armpits but couldn't smell anything. He nervously rung his hands.

'I'm sorry, sir, no offence, but you really need a shower and a change of clothes,' he said.

'Punch him in the face, Johnny, and then say, no offence taken,' Monkfish said—I sniggered. 'Only jesting,' Monkfish said to the waiter.

The shocked waiter half-smiled, then nervously finished taking the order of drinks.

A group of three lively lads strolled in. They were giving the waitress quite a bit of saucy banter. I bet she now wished she had carried on serving me and Monkfish. Turning back to Monkfish, he had a weird grin. I narrowed my eyes, trying to work out what he had in store.

'Fancy a free meal and drinks, Johnny?'

'It was going to be free for me anyway.'

'You were being serious then? You have no money?'

I nodded.

Monkfish tutted. 'OK, *none* of us pay for what we've had.'

'Sounds like a plan,' I said curiously.

'Follow my lead when the time comes.'

'What lead?'

Monkfish did not reply, but surreptitiously watched the burly group of lads sit, still acting the fools. All three of them looked trouble, especially the biggest bloke, having a neck like a bucket and a physic to match any World's Strongest Man competitor. On the back of his neck was an English flag over a bulldog. Monkfish inconspicuously slid a basket of rolls towards him before secretly taking two. Without drawing notice, he placed the basket under the table and winked at me. Was that my lead? What was I supposed to do? I searched him for answers, prompting another que.

With no warning, Monkfish viciously lobbed a roll at one of the three. Quickly, I looked back at the menu. Monkfish started making random conversation, and then took another drink.

'Who fucking threw that?' the victim shouted.

The place fell quiet, even the smells seemed to evaporate. I turned to them and, trying not to nervously laugh, I gave my best innocent look. After some deathly glares off all three, the blokes sat back down, grumbling between them like a band of gorillas.

'Want to bet I can hit the big fucker on his neck tattoo?' Monkfish whispered.

'Bet you a round of drinks you can't.'

'That means when you get paid, right?'

'I've enough money to last me the rest of my life,' I snapped.

'Not much then, as you were on the cliff.'

My eyes bored into him.

'Joke, Johnny.'

Monkfish waited till the ambiance had returned, and the meat-heads had started to pay more attention to the menu and bollocks they were talking. With ferocity, Monkfish threw the small hard-baked roll, right on the money. The skinhead brute stood up and ripped his chair from behind him. For some reason, his eyes burned into mine. Uncomfortably, I started to redden. Monkfish sharply pointed at the two young men who sat slightly right of us. The seething gorillas were going off their tree. The tattooed brute picked up his chair and lobbed it at the two stunned blokes. Astonishingly, they both launched at the thugs. And that was it: a fight erupted. In the confusion, other people started to join in, whilst a few tried to break it up. I nervously laughed at it. As the manager and chef came running, Monkfish told me to join in. Just as I stood up, not really having the bottle, Monkfish bashed opened the fire-exit doors and was soon sprinting across the carpark. Sneakily, I followed.

Brakes blazing before every country lane corner and blind brow, I speedily followed his Transporter Sportline. Even with the amount of alcohol we had consumed, we still managed to keep the rally going. It felt like I was escaping my recent past, now a chance for a new life; I did not want to lose.

Catching him on the straight at a hundred and twenty miles per hour as we came down to the Newquay roundabout, I heavily braked and followed him left. Suddenly, he hit the anchors hard and handbraked it into the garage. I didn't have time to handbrake, nearly overshooting the entrance. Pulling alongside, his brakes glowing and engine steaming, he lowered his window and started to laugh. I joined in the amusement.

'Did you see that shot with the roll?' he said. 'You owe me a round of drinks.'

'What about the two poor lads on that table, though? They got a pasting.'

'Ah, don't worry about them. Being spontaneous is just a nicer way to say no impulse control.'

I pondered what he had just said.

'You have to admit, that's the kick you needed. Better than the alcohol. We should hang around together more often, and I don't mean at Land's End.'

I was still thinking of the two lads. A small part of me felt like a bully, something I despised, but I had to admit that it had been a fantastic thrill. I had not had a rush like it for a while, and with the car chase, both had fuelled my adrenalin.

In my rear-view mirror an ambulance and police car drove past at high speed. Lifting back up, I stared at Monkfish. He shrugged his shoulders, then looked sorrowful.

'It's pretty messed up that we live in a world where everyone that works so much needs stimulants all the time… only jesting,' he said. 'Nice to be young again, hey?'

'See ya around.'

'Somewhere less dramatic? Here, take this. We should go for a drink.'

Turning over the white card, it had his business details: Diving Instructor.

'Yeah?' he persisted.

'Perhaps.'

Back in the prison-like confinement of my depressive house, the steam rose from the kettle. At the same time as staring aimlessly at it, I relived the restaurant fracas and high-speed, adrenalin surging chase home, missing the rush. The kettle button popped, which was a good thing as images of the knife on the climbing rope came to bear. I opened the fridge to the sour milk and a green chicken. I had not been home for three months before I had collected my car-keys and gear this morning. Wading through the rubbish and clothes on the floor, I tipped the collection of the bad nights in off the chair, and then slumped down. I could not remember how the TV had become smashed, but I had a good idea.

I did not go much on the black coffee, but without a drop of alcohol left, it would mean I would have to venture to the shops, a big adventure of its own kind. Perhaps if I go today, people will leave me alone and stop offering me money. On the next bitter sip, I looked at my collection of signed military books through the glass-lined oak cabinet: some were missing. When would I learn that they were important to me and to stop blaming them for my destructive path? Throwing some across the room had seemed good at the time, but now I resented it. All this excitement and exercise had taken its toll, so I shut my eyes.

Opening them to my phone ringing, I answered—silence. Immediately ending the call, I checked the phone history, being the previous number. How long had I been asleep? My mug had dropped to the floor, being soaked up by the rubbish. Pungent odours wafted in amongst the living room disorder. Annoyingly, the phone rang again.

'Hello?' I said abruptly.

A faint breathing rasped.

'Car-phone warehouse? PPI? Bloke from Nairobi wanting to help me sort my Windows virus?' I waited... 'No? Well fuck off then.'

I was about to block the number when there was a loud banging at the door. Expecting it to be the police, I crawled my way through the mess and slowly lifted one of the closed blind slats: the postman. I still checked the road both ways.

Slightly ajar, just enough for me to get through, the postman peered around the door. Baffled, he handed me a parcel and letters, asking me to sign his electronic gadget. I scribbled any old shit, pushed it back, and slammed the door, bolting it after. Walking back into the lounge, I threw the bills one by one, and then chucked a postcard as I sat down, leaving me with the parcel. What had I ordered off Amazon? Tearing at the packaging, I chuckled remembering the trouble I had got into for winning a cement mixer off eBay, one evening when drunk. I had received a warning from eBay for threatening to use the mixer to bury the seller. But he had kept chasing payment.

Inside my new parcel was a book: Canadian Rockies. National Geographical Destination Map.

'What the fuck?' I said, then scoffed.

Bang, bang, bang!

'Johnny, I fucking know you're in there.'

Bang, bang, bang!

'I saw you answer the fucking door.'

It was Trevor, my ex-*sensei*. I had sunk into my chair.

'If you don't open it, I'll fucking kick it in,' Trevor yelled.

You won't, I thought, I have added three security bolts. Why was he so angry? He was normally calm and reserved, using his fists to do the talking, not swearing. Not knowing why I had pissed him off, and why again I was on my stomach crawling through the mess as the blinds were shut, I made way to the hallway whilst the raging continued. I stopped worrying when the front of the postcard had caught my eye: Emperor Falls. Canadian Rockies.

A new sound took my attention away. Were those weapons being loaded outside? I turned my head to the window: a tank.

'One last chance to open the door before we blow it off its hinges,' Oliver shouted.

With the added pressure from my brother, I stuffed the folded postcard in my jeans pocket and scurried to the back door. The noises and abuse stopped. I knew they were making their way around to the rear. Quickly, I fumbled for the keys and unlocked the door, including all the dead-bolts I had fitted. Heart thumping, I dashed to the end of the garden. A hand came over the gate, tattoos giving it away as Trevor. Fuck. Cunningly, I silently opened the shed and slid in. Through a tiny gap I listened to the grunts as someone climbed the gate. Why did they want to kill me? As the first form went by, I pulled the door closed. With my eyes shut, visions of gunmen walked by. I checked the gap, relieved to see Trevor and Oliver go by. But then, who was the first person earlier? Crooking my neck around, pushing the gap open as much as I dared, Simon walked through the rear door that I had left open. Bollocks, they have infiltrated my base. I picked up my rifle and sprung out of my OP, but I went jelly-legged as I thought of taking on the intruders. Instead, I ran out of the open rear gate.

Sprinting up the hill past the war monument, I occasionally checked behind me. At the top was the French farmhouse. I knew the Germans were loitering. In the eerie-black night, out of breath with my back against it, I touched the nobbled wall. Making sure my Enfield was loaded, I peeked around the corner. The impenetrable, scary forest stared back; mutts barked. Were explosives strapped to these Alsatians? Where was my squad? Are they waiting inside the farmhouse? I tried the front door, but it was locked. Hold on, the squad? I hit the side of my head. The Special Raiding Squad I was assigned to was over. What is going on?

'It's locked, man. Do you want to go inside?'

The contrast daylight hurt my eyes. I was stood in front of the Huer's Hut. I let go of the cold railing-gate and turned to see a big guy with keys in his hand. He took off his cap.

'Yes? No?'

'Are you the town's keeper?' I bantered.

'No, I'm the key holder. Jon G...'

'I know who you are, Goodman; everyone does. You've been here so long, you're part of the scenery. I reckon you're on every postcard and photo.'

He grinned. 'I guess you're the man causing a bit of mischief lately in town.'

'No,' I said, and then looked at what Jon was nodding at. 'Just coming up here to do a bit of weeding.'

'Fitting one of the descriptions of some perpetrators involved in a restaurant scuffle this morning, I would take your hoe and attend some weeds at the lifeboat lookout hut.'

'Amazing how a food-fight can get out of control. Thanks, Jono.'

'No worries. Just listen to your bro occasionally. Get the original Johnny Vince back on track. See ya.'

This man was a fantastic representative for the town's people, always with his finger on the pulse. I wondered why he was trying to help me. Had he mentioned me going to the lifeboat lookout because he knew my hideout was close by?

Half-way up the road, I turned around. 'Jono, have you ever heard of an old guy in town called Weaves?'

'Sure. Did you not read about his funeral last year on June the sixth? Or was you on your own mission?'

A chill ran through me. 'Yeah, D-day,' I said, and left Jono standing there looking confused.

Heading towards the peninsular, I thought back on what Jono had said about Weaves. That was one of the sticky points to the trip back to 1944 being a weird dream. If it was just a figment of my imagination whilst in a coma, how did Weaves know back in the Australian Bar about the death of my squad in Afghanistan? Perhaps he had read it in the newspaper and knew it was me. Why ask why I was in uniform that night in the pub? Was he crazy? Am I crazy? Maybe the tribe had stolen my mind and planted the watch on me before Ocker, Nico, and Georges had found me.

A little while later, making sure I was not being followed by my assassin friends and brother, I found the little hollowed-out cave that sat on the overhang of the last rocks. Me and Oliver used to fish from it as kids. Now it was my new home. After throwing out the layers of damp cardboard, I got comfortable on my sleeping bag. Around me were a collection of empty JD bottles with candles in. I had kept the rest of the area clean of waste, the only bit of pride remaining.

I was still wondering how Skedgewell's watch came into the hands of the tribe, when I noticed the carved inscription on the wall: 'Johnny & Ella. Together for ever'. Even though I had read it every day whilst living here, my head sunk into my hands. I tried to control the emotion, but the images of me and Ella entertaining the lads at a barbecue at our house in Poole, and on regular nights out on the town, became too overwhelming. Our love life was damn good before that fateful mission, even as far back as the day we had met. If only I could go back to those days.

A large cold spray of water awoke me from my sleep. No nightmare, I thought. It was an amazing feeling to have slept so sound, slightly marred that I was stiff as a surfboard. The waves had become more torrent and the sun had moved out of sight. I suddenly remembered the postcard and I delved into my back pocket. After studying the beautiful Emperor Falls, I flipped it over to see who was having a better time than me in life, which could have been anyone I knew. However, it was blank. Why would someone send me a blank postcard all the way from Canada? The postmark was true enough. Perhaps they did not have a pen—stupid thought.

Thinking back on the Amazon parcel, I tried to remember if I had been drunk chatting to someone about meeting them, and that's why I ordered the map—blank. But where would I have ordered it from? I had not been home for months. I needed to check my Amazon account to see when and what time I had ordered it. However, I could not go back to my house in case Trevor and his entourage were waiting to ambush me.

'Hold on, Johnny,' I mumbled. 'Why would there be a tank outside your house?' I sighed. 'I doubt Trevor was even hammering the door down, let alone threatening me.' I need some help, I thought.

Studying the business card, I decided to phone the mobile number.

'Monkfish. This is Johnny. I need to get a few things off my chest. Seeing you've been through the same shit and ended up on the same cliff, I wondered if we could meet up for a chat and coffee, but no alcohol,' I said, leaving him a voicemail.

Before leaving the nostalgic cave, I took one last look at the fishing paraphernalia entangled in the rocks, but shied away from the inscription. Time check: 16.26 hrs. With one last large inhale and exhale, I backed away from the sea and started to walk home in the sunset. I knew that would be the last time I would visit that cave, that home, that life.

No one seemed bothered me carrying a hoe down the street in the dusk; however, I was unnerved to see all the lights on at the front of my house. It could be mum cleaning. I knew she wanted to talk to me about losing my dad. Past arguments hummed through my mind: the nasty shit I had said, or caused others to retaliate, and that is what I could remember. Worse came: a police car pulled up. One officer knocked on my door, Oliver let him in.

Buzz! Buzz!

In the shadows of a closed surf-shop's doorway, I opened the text:

'Love to go for a coffee and chat. I'm not working tonight. Where and when?'

Just as well you're not teaching someone to drive with that recent fuelled breath, I thought, and then sent a reply:

'Don't want to be in Newquay tonight. Need a clean break. How about Padstow? Harbour Inn at 8.30. I'll grab a taxi as my car hasn't enough fuel.'

I had lied, but looking at my Audi outside my house, it was in view of the lounge window and, frustratingly, the blind had been pulled up. A few regular surfers walked past and nodded. I did the same courtesy.

The reply came in: '20.30 hours don't you mean. Slacking, Johnny. Sure, my friend, meet you there. Don't forget you owe me a drink for lobbing the roll dead on target.'

'I'm on the wagon.' I quickly replied.

'OK, me too. I will pick you up at 20.30 hours from the garage where we parked earlier.'

CHAPTER FOUR

There were only so many places in three hours that I could have hid; also, not letting my mind take over. I did not want to return to the cave, my house; the memories hurt. At least the voice had not returned. Not taking the plunge on the cliff had given me the chance to sort my troubles out; it had been a sign.

My phone read it was dead on 20.30 hrs. Where was Monkfish? I was sitting just on the garage forecourt's peripheral lights, not to be seen, but not to look suspicious. A traffic-cop had already been past, twice. I was beginning to get agitated, entwining my fingers together.

'Come on, Monkfish,' I said.

Beep!

The VW headlights rose as the low-profile tyres bounced up the drop-kerb. Music blaring inside, he leant over and opened the door, aftershave wafting. I spotted his gold chain with a gold ring attached.

'Turn that shit off,' I said.

'Shit? This is eighties and nineties classic house music, my friend.'

As soon as I climbed into the black and red leather Recaro seat, I hit a few dials on the radio. The music eventually stopped. Monkfish ejected the CD.

'You're fucking late,' I said.

'Bloody hell, only three...' He stopped. 'Sorry,' he continued. 'Anyway, why do you still look like a tramp? You could have at least had a shower and shave, let alone a change of clothes. No chance of pulling a woman for sex tonight.'

'I'm not interested...'

'Why do we shout "fuck" when having sex?' he interrupted. 'It's like yelling "football" when playing football.'

Monkfish seemed to have a gag for everything, and almost cringingly set himself up to say the same old jokes.

'Are you ever normal?' I asked.

'I could act normal, but it would be acting, and wouldn't be normal.'

I thought on his words. Perhaps he was just smart, like his clothes. He looked like he was going out on the razzle with his trendy jeans, leather shoes, no socks, and a flowery shirt.

'You smell like the perfume counter at Debenhams,' I said.

'If we're into the smell test, you're like an out-of-date fish cake.'

'Maybe your new nickname should be "Face", as in the A-team.'

'Why?'

'Black van with red stripe, and a tart who thinks he is clever with the ladies. Oh, and listens to eighties shit music. Drive on then, Face.'

'Hmmmm, sucker,' he said in a terrible Mr T impersonation.

Whilst I admired the funky interior in the rear, he turned the radio on. Coldplay blared out. Threatened, I punched the radio. Monkfish tried to get it to work but swerved to miss a car on this narrow lane.

'Wanker,' he said. 'Sorry, my friend, I meant that driver.'

I doubted he did.

'It wasn't loud or eighties music,' he challenged.

'I can't listen to certain music as it brings back too many bad thoughts.'

'Bloody hell, you're in a bad way. Mentally complex.'

'Do you know what, take me the fuck home,' I snapped. 'I'm not enjoying this.'

'Sorry, Johnny, that was insensitive of me. I wish I could uninstall thoughts from my brain sometimes. Let's just go for a quick coffee and bite to eat. No more banter, hey?'

On the remaining journey, we did not speak. I had a lot going around my head. Did he? Did he wonder why I was quickly over the cliff episode? I had thought that about him, a miraculous change.

As he was reversing into a space in the Padstow Harbour carpark, a thought came to mind.

'Thought your business card said you were a driving instructor,' I said.

'Ha, very funny, but my parking is brilliant. So, are we back on the banter?'

'I meant; how do you teach people to drive in this?'

'I have another car. This is my shag wagon.' He grabbed his groin.

Monkfish held the Harbour Inn door open for me, but I stopped and stared inside. Taking a step back outside, I took a deep breath, then exhaled.

'Listen, my friend, you don't have to do this,' he said. 'I can take you home.'

'No, I've got this.'

'I know it depends on what part of the world you come from, but do you fancy getting stoned?'

'I'd rather get *stoned*, than do drugs.'

'Religious folk care more about how the Earth was made more than Earth itself.'

'I'm not religious,' I retorted. 'Now shut the fuck up and let's get inside.'

Re-opening the door, a few people checked us out: well, more than likely just me. Just as well the place was almost empty, as I had thought of the *Lady and The Tramp*. I made a quick move for an alcove table next to the fire-exit and stuck my dried muddied boots under the table. Inconspicuously as possible, I searched where Monkfish was. He was having a laugh with a group of lads at the bar. Please do not bring them over, I thought. Whilst waiting, I tried not to tune into the music.

Monkfish placed a coffee in front of me and sat opposite, annoyingly supping a pint of beer. I frowned, purposely not looking at the beautiful golden bubbles that rose.

'Thought you were on the wagon,' I said.

'Sorry, I forgot. I'll drink it at the bar.'

'Bollocks. Sit down. I have a strong will power.'

'You must have.'

'What's that supposed to mean?'

He didn't reply.

I sipped my strong coffee, not tasting like his refreshing lager, as I had imagined.

'Look, I don't want to beat around the bush, but you did ask me here so you can get stuff off your chest,' he said. 'I guess that's why you were up on... you know... the...'

'On the edge, metaphorically speaking,' I interrupted.

He lugubriously nodded and took a larger gulp. I took a longer sip of my coffee, my nerves jingled. Was the caffeine having an adverse effect already?

'I owe you a drink for that lost bet. Be back in a tick,' I said, but stopped. 'I've not been home for my wallet.'

'That explains you smelling like you do.'

On the way to the bar, I became agitated that all my friends and family had descended on my property as if they owned it. I would have had a shower and change if they had not been there. One of the lads at the bar stepped backwards into me, turned, and frowned.

'You lost homeless old man? Looking for the gay bar? I mean, touching me up like that,' he said—his mates laughed.

I went to tell him his cock could fit in a matchbox, or that's what your girlfriend said when I had got off her, but the words wouldn't come out.

'Well?' he said.

'Sorry, dude.'

I moved further down the bar, ignoring their continuous jokes about me. The barman came over, but the gobby shite told the barman that he was first. When the barman looked at me, I nodded in agreeance; smugness rose on all three of the lads. Whilst I waited as they deliberately prolonged what to order, I nodded at Monkfish who looked on with interest. A bar lady came out and asked if she could help. She frowned at the comments from the lads, the barman also telling them to pipe down. I went to give my Jeremy Clarkson's smug face at the lads, but decided it was best to not to.

After I had ordered a lemonade and pint of lager, an image of agent Ronaldo Gomez flashed in my mind, who looked like Jeremy Clarkson. I had given Gomez the nickname. I knew what was next, and rightly so, my thoughts turned to the other bent Yanks: Red and Tommy. The Heckler beams flicked around my mind as we entered the pitch-black building. I gripped what was in front of me.

'That's five pounds sixty-five, please,' the lady said.

'Make that a double Jack Daniels as well,' I huffed.

She muttered I was rude and went to the end optical.

'Fuck off,' I mumbled.

'There you go. That's eleven pounds fifty.'

'I need some ice, *please*.'

After chucking some ice in, she held her hand out. I placed a twenty note on the bar and told her to keep the change. On the way back with the drinks, the gobby lad stepped in my way. What was his problem? Quickly, I side-stepped him and found another route, much to their enjoyment.

'Problem?' Monkfish asked, taking his pint.

'Yeah, I needed a drink.' I took a meaningful sip. 'So, why were you about to jump?'

Monkfish spat his lager back. 'Are you always this straight to the point?'

'No, I'm normally very tactful. Just thought I would start the chat before you get wasted.'

'Any change?' he said.

'From you getting wasted, I doubt it.'

'No, any change from my note?'

'No, I left a tip.'

Monkfish scowled. 'Hadn't you better save your money to pay your carpark fine?'

'More to the point, why the hell do you buy a parking ticket? A cry for help?'

'Ouch. That was low,' he retorted. 'Anyway, I thought it was you that wanted to get some shit off your chest.'

'Right, stop the chit-chat and get down to the practical details. Shortest version will do.'

Monkfish stayed opened mouthed whilst I sipped on my drink, then said, 'After being kicked out the Regiment, I...'

'You were in the SF?'

'Yep. I know it doesn't look like I was.'

'If everyone looked like they were in it, they would be easy targets.'

'Good point,' he said. 'I was discharged from the British Army. It hit me hard. We moved to Cornwall and then to Odiham. I had to as my wife was in the RAF.'

'I hope we very soon get to the bit why you ended up wanting to get off the world, but first, I need a top-up,' I said, and held my hand out for more money.

He sighed.

At the bar I ignored the twats' pathetic banter from a table nearby, all trying to look big in front of the girls that had joined them. I took my round and headed back. Monkfish took his pint and change.

'Thought you said you were on the wagon,' Monkfish said.

'Carry on the story.'

'After we moved to Odiham, my wife's job took over her life. I became a drunk and did some stupid stuff. But then, I've made all my worst mistakes stone cold sober, and after some considerable thought.' He laughed—I frowned. 'My son joined the army and went on a few tours. He was killed in Afghanistan a few years back. Last year my wife left me. June gone; my dad died of a heart-attack.' Monkfish turned away and wiped his face.

'Fuck,' I said sombrely.

'Don't worry about the marriage, ninety per cent of it is shouting through walls. I deserved to be dumped: alcoholic, gambler, drugs, wanker. I only say gambler because nobody thinks you are if you win a lot.'

'Did you have no friends to help? No support groups?' I asked, but I knew the answer.

'Looking for a tiny strand of hay in a massive pile of needles would have been easier. Apart from one brother that I don't get on with, and the ex-army mates that have forgotten me, that's it for me. I've tried to come off the drink, but it tends to help me get through the twenty-four hours.'

'Who was the letter to?' I asked.

Monkfish narrowed his eyes at me.

'Sorry, I shouldn't have asked,' I muttered.

'No, it's OK, it just hurts. The letter was to whoever found my body.'

There was an awkward moment as we both stared into our glass. I twirled my ice with my finger. The bloke at the fruit machine won the jackpot, delighted, and his mates joined around him.

'Some people get all the luck,' Monkfish said.

'Why were you discharged from the Regiment; well, the British Army?'

'I'm a bit embarrassed to say, but as we have become good friends, I got caught smuggling a weapon. Not sure who grassed me up.'

'Have you been living the same life as me?' I blurted.

Monkfish looked uncomfortable. 'What do you mean?'

'I'll tell you after another drink.'

'You're costing me a fortune.'

Whilst ordering at the bar, one of the gobby lad's cronies stood next to me. I stared hard at him. He turned and observed me, trying to look unbothered. After ten seconds of us locked in a gaze, I slightly lifted the corner of my lip and squinted at him, a bit like Clint Eastwood. His nerves were buckling, and he turned back to the bar. The JD was fuelling my strength and reducing my tolerance.

I took out my phone and decided to phone Mike, unsure to why I would have such thoughts about Monkfish. I held two fingers up at Monkfish, mouthing two minutes.

'Mike?'

'I fucking told you never to contact me again, you motherfucker.'

'I know, Mike, and I'm really sorry,' I said, not really knowing what I had done to enrage him; just join the list, I thought.

'Sorry? You fucking threatened to expose me for sending the Sig back to Joe. You utter wanker.'

'There's nothing I can say, Mike. I was in a bad place. I don't even remember the phone call.'

'So, you don't even know if you fucking grassed me up.'

'Just one favour, that's all I ask. You know I wouldn't dob you in.'

'No.'

'I need you to check out an ex-serving brother, Chris Breedon. Says he was discharged for handling an illicit weapon. His son...'

'Is this a fucking wind-up? "Handling an illicit weapon".'

I hit the side of my head. 'No... no, I didn't mean anything by that.'

'Where's the old Johnny Vince gone? Stop running from it and face it like Johnny.' He ended the call.

In a growing bad mood, I threw a tenner at the bar girl and stomped off back to our table.

'Who was that?' Monkfish asked.

'No one.'

'Bloody hell, I would hate to think it was someone you had known who could piss you off that much.' He smirked—I didn't.

'You really want to know how I ended up on that cliff?' I asked.

'Is it going to bore me to death?' he said, and grinned.

'Right, in short. I was also in the Regiment and lost some of my best mates on a mission. My wife left me; my life fell apart. I quit the army and tried to rebuild myself. After another dumb idea to visit Afghan to pay my respects to the fallen, and for closure, it went tits-up. Knowing I missed the buzz of action, and because life had become mundane, not fitting in to civi-street, I took on PMC to Yemen. That was a fuck-up. Me and Ocker...'

'Ocker?' he interrupted.

'You know him?'

'Err... no. Just a weird name.'

'Tommy White?'

'Nope.'

'Oh, it's just you sat back slightly as if you knew him,' I insinuated.

'What happened to you in Yemen?'

'Barely got out with our skin on our backs,' I continued. 'Anyway, are you open-minded?'

'I'm not sure if I'm open-minded and non-judgmental, or just don't give a fuck about people.'

'I need you to be serious and broad shouldered,' I said. 'I took on another private military contract, but it was meant to be "easy", as Ocker had said.'

'Did you go with Ocker? I mean, after all that shit in Yemen.'

'No. Ocker was then working for the PMC boss. He sent me to Sumatra to track the poachers' traps and main camp, but the mission ended up me being the hunted. This is gonna sound fucked-up...'

'No more fucked-up than T-rex moved around like kangaroos,' he butted in.

'I'm being fucking serious, Chris.'

'Sorry.'

I rubbed my wrist where I had worn Skedgewell's watch. 'I was transported back to a mission a few days before D-day.'

Monkfish spat his beer, appearing to choke, but exaggerated. 'D-day? What the fuck?'

I slammed my fist on the table. 'Are you fucking mocking me?'

'Err... no... just a bit hard to comprehend. Please, go on.'

'On my return to this world, I found out I'd lost my dad. The alcohol numbs the pain. With terribly similar troubles to you, I didn't want to see the sun come around again.'

Whilst downing my JD, Monkfish stayed silent, possibly going over in his mind what I had said. We had now both run out of drink.

'Why were you wearing a safety helmet if you were going to cut your rope?' he said.

'I was hoping there was a glimmer of hope that I couldn't do it.'

'Lucky I was there to save your life then.'

'But you were going to do the...'

'Fancy another?' he interrupted.

'No. I'm pretty pissed-up. Take me home. I need to sort my life out.'

Monkfish's eyes followed someone across the room. 'Sure. I'll just grab a wee.'

I twisted to see who had caught his attention. 'Stay away from that dickhead lad.'

'You want to come to the toilet with me in case he tries it on in there. Don't worry, I was trained in how to do a runner.' Monkfish chuckled.

I was not sure if it was the JD or the stress of telling him my past, but I had an uncomfortable feeling something bad was going to kick off. Surely trouble would stop following me around, but then, did I give a shit anymore? I shook my head. No, I did give a shit, I wanted the old me back.

CHAPTER FIVE

Outside, waiting for Monkfish, a few loved-up couples walked through the beautiful town. I pondered about my non-existent love life and the two women I had let down. At least Doctor Kay was just a one-night stand. What a fun night with no ties; she was amazing. If only I had married a doctor, I thought, but then I felt guilty for Haleema.

Monkfish came out in a hurry. 'Let's go. I've had enough of their bullshit in there.'

'Just ignore the twa...'

'Oh look, there's the other faggot,' the gobby lad interrupted—again, his friends laughed.

I waited for the anger to run through my veins or a show of defiance with a cool remark, but nothing happened. I decided to stomp off to the carpark. It was not long before Monkfish caught me up.

'As we never got to eat in the pub, fancy fish and chips?' he asked.

'I'm fucking starving.'

'That's a good sign, my friend.'

'I could eat a pasty through a wicker chair.'

'Hey, I do the jokes,' he said. 'Let's give Rick Stein's a miss.'

'But Steins is only there.'

'Chip Ahoy is around the corner.' He pulled my arm to go in the opposite direction.

At the top of the cobbled road, a silhouette came walking towards us: the gobby lad, on his own. With a mouthful of chips, he muttered something as he went by. Monkfish stopped me.

'You going to let that go?' he said.

'What did he say?'

'He called you a "chicken shit". If only he knew what you've been through. Maybe you should catch him up and tell him.'

Something snapped.

Before I knew it, I was uncontrollably striding after him. 'Oi, fuck-face,' I yelled.

As he turned, I ripped the chips from his hand and lobbed them at his chest. Monkfish stood next to me, the lad looking like a lost puppy.

'Listen, man, I don't want any trouble.'

'Fucking shame, as you've woken the dead,' I fumed.

'Yeah, giving it all the large in the pub,' Monkfish added. 'Where's your mates now?'

'I'm sorry. It was only banter.'

'Banter fucking works when two or more enjoy it. Next time watch your fucking mouth,' I said, and started walking back to the chip shop.

'God, you've lost your Elite bollocks. He deserved a thumping,' Monkfish said.

I span around and went back up to the lad who was rearranging his chip paper. I fired a light jab to his chin, but he went down like a sack of spuds. Suddenly, he started to uncontrollably shake, eyes rolling.

'Fuck me, Johnny,' Monkfish shrieked. 'How hard did you hit him?'

'I hardly touched him.'

Monkfish bent down and tried to stop him fitting. The lad stopped, not moving at all. A group came around the corner: his friends. Monkfish began to check the lad's airway.

'You've killed him,' Monkfish said.

One of the girls started to scream. I wanted to tell her to shut the fuck up as the whole town would hear. Breathing heavy, I glanced at them. They looked back with such hatred, sadness, mixed with anxiety. I took a step back as Monkfish repeatedly pushed down on the lad's chest. The girls started to cry. Monkfish told one of the friends to take over, and he then grabbed my arm, taking me back a few metres.

'Take these and fuck off,' he whispered. 'I will phone you.'

Once Monkfish had slapped his keys in my trembling hand, he then barged the other lad out of the way who was continuing the CPR. I was rooted to the ground. Without warning, the street was exchanged for the factory in Yemen. Blood was spurting from Kyle's neck. Ocker was hunched over him. I went to shout to stem the carotid artery and to check his chest from the shotgun round, but the words never came. My world started to spin as I took in more oxygen.

Run. Fucking run.

I can't leave a man down, I thought.

Too late. He's dead. You're going to end up in the slammer.

Panicking, I ran through the girls towards the carpark, pulling over my hoodie. The less people who identified me, the better.

Out of breath, I spewed up as I reached the VW. Fumbling with the key-fob, I opened the door, jumped in, and started the engine. The crash at the back told me I had hit the barrier to stop you going over into the sea. Heart racing, I crunched into gear and span away. With blurred vision, I came out the carpark, catching another car or a bollard. Thrashing the nuts out of it to get away, something was niggling me: do not draw attention to yourself.

Leaving the town and incident in the rear-view mirror, I began to slow my speed. Trembling took over. Driving on the main costal road to Newquay, a police car lit up in my headlights, before going by. Immediately, I checked my mirrors, and then punched the steering wheel.

'Fuck, fuck, fuck,' I yelled.

On the longest straight, headlights shone behind. Had the police turned around? There were no blue lights. As the beams went into a hidden dip in the road, I killed mine. Underbraking, I quickly turned right down a narrow road. On black-light, I carried on going to the end. The behind car went by on the main road. At the bottom of the lane was the Bedruthan Rocks carpark. I pulled up on the handbrake, letting the van roll gently into the knee-height fence. Once the engine was killed, I turned the interior light off. Where was my phone? Stupidly, I was sat on it, so I took it out of my pocket, the postcard dropping onto the seat. I had not cracked the screen, neither had Monkfish made contact.

A breeze whipped up as I got out. Silently, I closed the door and waited for my eyes to adjust to the dark; weird shapes moved in the bluster. I waited ten minutes, alone with my thoughts; I had dreaded it.

Blindly following the coastal path, the crash of the sea alerted me to the cliff's precarious edge. Sitting on a wet grass mound, I knew this had become all too familiar. The silence was deafening. I thought back on Mike's words, "Stop running from it and face it like Johnny."

It's no good running. They will catch you.

'Sorry, I can't hear you. I'm an obnoxious twat,' I said, and falsely laughed.

You need a drink.

'La la la la la,' I rambled, putting my fingers in my ears.

That's so pathetic. Drive back to town, find an off-licence, and get a stiff drink. You can always come back here, close to the edge.

'De de de, la la la.'

Is that a song by Coldplay or Frank Sinatra? Go put the radio on in the van.

'I'm back on track now. Coming off that cliff was the turning point. Leave me alone.'

Never. Unless you jump.

I hated the voice, there was no point arguing. I shuffled on my arse towards the edge.

You can't outrun your life.

Three metres…

Keep going. You know you've killed that young lad…

Two metres…

Even Monkfish was shocked at your bullying ways…

One metre…

Go meet your lost friends and dad.

Acid in my throat, I dangled my legs over the precipice of life. The soft sand spread between my grip; the edge moved slightly.

No use thinking of who you can turn to, you have no one left.

Through watery eyes, I looked at the white waves crashing, breath held.

Buzz… buzz… buzz…

Bam! Realization hit me. I scrambled back and held onto the mound behind, shaking all over.

Buzz… buzz… buzz…

Still trying to catch my breath, I searched for my phone. 'Hello?'

'Johnny, it's me.'

'Monkfish. Where the fuck are you? Did you save him?'

'I tried, my friend, but he's dead.'

'What? How? I hardly hit him.'

'Bleed on the brain. I reckon as he hit the kerb. I left when I heard the sirens.'

I felt nauseous, so I laid back on the grass and held my forehead, sand fell onto my face. 'Where are you?'

'I got a taxi home. Where're you?'

'That was a dumb fuck idea, now the police will know where you live.'

'Oh fuck, I never thought of that. I'll say I don't know you, we just met in the pub. Listen, there was loads of police swarming towards Padstow when I'd left.'

'Can you meet me?' I asked.

'Sure. Where are… hold on, I've got an incoming call. It's the wife. I'll phone you back in a few minutes.'

The sounds of the sea came crashing back, along with the wind. That is the last time the voice tricks me, or I venture near any cliff. Quickly, I got to my feet and backed up further from the edge. Damp, cold, I ran to the van with my phone in hand, ready to answer. Around the toilet-block's edge, I made sure there were no police sniffing about. I mentally cursed about how the van stuck out like a diamond in a baboon's arse; Ocker came to mind, one of his sayings. That was it: I had to get out of the UK. Perhaps Ocker would forgive me and put me up, but I doubted it. I racked my mind who abroad I could rely on—no one. Did it matter? If I carried on the right positive mindset, maybe the old me would return. If I could find my previous self, I could be planted anywhere in the world and survive, I thought. The challenge was set.

Inside the warmth of the VW, I stared at the phone. Time seemed to speed up. Was the net closing in on me? I searched the glove compartment for just the possibility there was a bottle of Gin to numb the nerves. After pulling out notes of paper, I reached the bottom, but I was out of luck.

As soon as it rang, I answered it, 'Monkfish?'

It was the silent caller, just the breathing.

'Fuck off,' I barked, and pressed end.

A few seconds later it rang again. This time, unlike before, I checked the number.

'Monkfish?'

'Sorry, my friend, the missus was really upset as her best friend's husband, Roy, has been missing for months. She does tend to get overwhelmed by the littlest things. She has mentioned this bloke before. He's in the same sinking boat…'

'I'm down at Bedruthan Steps,' I interrupted, not interested in small talk. 'Do you know it?'

'Yes. Look, to be honest, Johnny…' He paused. 'Look…' He went quiet again. 'I don't…'

'You don't want to get any further involved,' I said it for him.

'I want to re-build my life. Meeting you on the cliff saved me from jumping. Keep the van for a bit. I haven't any driving lessons booked in this fortnight, so I can use my car to go and make sure the ex-wife is OK. As much as she hates me, she really needs my support as she lives alone in France.'

'Where the fuck am I going to hide a big black van with a distinct red-stripe?'

'I'm sorry, Johnny. Any more pressure and…'

I hung up on him and threw my phone behind me. My world seemed to close in.

Aware that nobody at the scene had known me, and even Monkfish did not know where I lived, I drove back onto the main costal road towards home. Around the corner on Pentire Road, I parked the van, making sure no one was around. I picked up my phone before dashing across the road into the grassy area overlooking the sea. Trying to stay out of the lamppost's beams, I took as many back-routes as possible. At the back of my property the gate had not been locked. After getting annoyed with whoever had left it open, I then scoffed at the little importance.

Simon's house next door had the lights on. I found my hidden spare key and literally tip-toed in through the back door. I opened the cupboard under the stairs, the creaking irritating. The house maintenance job-list would now never be finished, I thought, as I quietly felt for a torch. Even worse, the familiar stairs creaking now gave the impression I would wake the street.

In my bedroom, I slowly drew the curtains. With the Maglite between my teeth, I quietly lifted the bedside table across. In the chilling dark behind me, I felt a presence; my hackles rose. I swung the Maglite around. For some reason I was looking down the same end of the AK47 that I had taped the torch to in Operation Blue Halo. A bullet riddled body lay in the corner of the room, his red mist on the wall behind. Eyes on stalks, I held my breath. Suddenly, the dead terrorist's eyes opened, my heart came into my mouth. Blood flowing from his wounds, he started to get up. The light beam flickered as I squeezed the trigger. I was plunged into complete darkness. Slamming back against the bedroom wall, I had nowhere to run. I shut my eyes.

What the fuck was I thinking, I thought, and opened my eyes.

'Arghhh,' I yelled.

Two inches from my face was the dead person's face, his putrid, cold breath was rapid. I squinted as he put his finger in the bullet hole in his forehead. Pushing myself further on the wall, I turned away sharply. Daring to look back, he had gone. I slumped to the floor in a jabbering mess. I'd had nightmares frequently, but this new one had been the worst.

The torch beam was facing my feet on the floor and, picking it up, I shone the shaking light in the corner, just to double-check. I sat back, reliving the same moment when I had checked the prison corridors searching for Rabbit. Time for a fucking large drink, I thought.

'No,' I hushed. 'You need to pull yourself together, Johnny. No more alcohol.'

Like taking smelling salts, those recently said words, "get back on track", rushed me into pulling the carpet back and lifting the adapted floorboard. Torch back in my teeth, I undid the combination lock on the metal box. It had been a while since I had opened it. I took a deep breath. The feelings had not changed since I last put my earned cash and passport in there. I exhaled as the memories came flooding back. In the beam, the passport photo reflected, not just younger, but more confident, fearless, no troubles; I sighed. How much money do I need? Will had paid me handsomely for the last mission, even though I had not completed the task. I did not want it, but he had insisted. Perhaps it was guilt on his part. I wish I had not said those terrible things to him.

I counted out five thousand in fifty-notes, dribble dripping off the Maglite onto the remaining items in the box. Quickly, I dropped the rest of the cash and wiped the photo. I stared at the picture of Planet, Fish, Shrek, and Ella at a barbecue before the inconceivable events that have taken hold since. Part of the photo was already ruined. A thought of me tipping a drop of JD on it and throwing the frame across the room sprung to mind. Even though I knew I shouldn't, I started looking at the rest of the photos, hoping to reminisce. Days with the SBS lads, Ella, and Lena. There were many of us on exercise to look through. I stopped when I got to my favourite one of me as a kid on Newquay beach with mum, dad, and Oliver. Sniffing back the tears, I vowed to make it up with them and visit dad's grave once the dust had settled.

Feeling positive for the first time in a long time, I came to the last photo which was face down. Curious, I picked it out and turned it over: me and Rabbit at a piss-up six months before the Chinook crash. It was funny to think back then that in this group photo we disliked each other, but now the bond was inseparable. I hope he had coped with his demons.

Bam!

Like a smash in the head, a wave of guilt and terror had hit me. I tussled with my phone and rapidly searched for Monkfish's number. Surely not, I thought, too coincidental.

'Come on, come on,' I said as it rang.

'Johnny.'

'Monkfish. You mentioned your RAF wife's best friend. What's her name?'

'Err… Christine. Why?'

'Oh fuck,' I said.

'What's happened? Johnny? Johnny, are you there?'

I shook the thoughts from my mind. 'Christine Franklin, right?'

'Yes. You know her?'

'I know both her and Roy.'

'Oh shit, my friend, I'm sorry for putting my foot in it.'

'No, Monkfish, I'm so glad you did.'

'What are you going to do?'

'I'm going to visit her. Don't mind if I borrow your van, do you?'

He paused. 'OK, but please take care of it.'

I winced at the damage I had caused. 'Sure. I owe you, Chris.'

'No you don't. Well, actually, I was thinking I need to spice up my life. I hate being a driving instructor. What's the chances of giving me Will's details so I can take a private *mercenary* contract?'

'That's military, not mercenary.' I scoffed. 'I've blocked his number, but I will text you some details when I find them. I know I've got them written down in code somewhere.'

'Thanks, my…'

I looked at my phone, the battery had died.

Over the next hour, I had quietly but quickly showered, shaved, changed, cut my nails, charged my phone, and packed a large over-night holdall. I could not believe the difference as I stood naked in the mirror. Where my grotty beard used to be was now sore with spots. My cheeks above were different in colour and texture. The bingeing and no exercise were plainly evident, along with scars of previous conflicts, including my recent self-harming. Those could be easily fixed or hidden, but as I stared deep into my eyes, it was my mind that I had to mend. No matter how many fails along the way, I had to bounce back.

I had left no traces of the secure box hiding place. I had a good guess the police would soon be kicking in the door. The worry of Roy whizzed around my mind. I was fucking angry for nearly ending my life as he needed my help. I had not been in contact for a few months or so. Was this why I had just had a flashback about the dead terrorist guard who had beat him to an inch of his life? I realised it must have been fated to have started looking at the pictures, perhaps even meeting Monkfish on the edge of life. I had never been a believer in God, the afterlife, spiritual mumbo-jumbo, but some of that had changed since meeting Blondie in the water tank.

There was no way I was going to find Will's details in this mess,

Monkfish would have to wait. Before I shut and locked the rear door, I meaningfully looked back. Was this the new turning point in my crumbling life, something to focus hard on?

CHAPTER SIX

Pulling into the Exeter service station after a thought-provoking two-hour drive, my phone rang. Quickly, I swung into any old space. An unknown number showed so I answered it.

'Are you wanting something, Mr Heavy Breather?' Then it dawned on me. 'Rabbit? Is that you? You can talk, dude. I under...'

They ended the call.

I stored the mobile number under the name Roy. Just that small thought it was him boosted my morale ten-fold, as if my past problems were being washed away.

With my baseball cap on to keep back my long, un-styled hair, I ordered a Double Whopper and black coffee. I did not want to draw attention to myself, but at the same time, not be recognised by any security cameras. I stunk of cigarette smoke from Monkfish's van, hating it. I was itching to phone Christine at home but did not have the bollocks to tell her I was on the way.

It was the best burger I'd had in ages, most probably because I was sober for a change. The next admission that I had worked out was when I was drunk, I heard the voice, but when I wasn't, I couldn't live with the nightmare thoughts and my changing self. I had to break the cycle. It was going to be a massive challenge, but I was up for it. Knowing Roy needed help took my mind off all the other shit.

I stopped the van on the corner of Mildmay Court, then killed the lights. Without anyone to talk to on the two-hour journey, my mind had gone into overdrive. This new me, or was it trying to find the old me, was proving tough. Time check: 05.55 hrs. I yawned; the coffee had worn off. I was not a hundred per cent on the house number, and in the strange crack of dawn lighting I could not see the numbers. Then I spotted Roy's new car he had bragged about ages ago: BMW i3. Even with the mist clearing, it was far too early to wake Christine and the kids, especially with the shock of seeing me. After setting the phone alarm for eight, I pulled down my cap and curled into a ball to sleep.

★

It was great to be back under the sun with Roy, even though I knew we were evading all the crazed religious factions in Afghanistan. I'd had the dream so many times, but this time it did not bother me to see him all beat up. The banter and trying to escape from the crazy shrieking man-lookalike woman for stealing her food was becoming funnier. Even though it played out that Roy was shot in the neck as we tried to escape in the Nissan, I knew he had survived. Unexpectedly, this time I sat up in the hospital instead of the Chinook. This was not an ordinary hospital; I had been here before: Camp Bastion. The room was cooler than I remembered. Strangely, I was dressed in black trousers and shirt, realising after that it was what we had deployed into in Operation Poppy Pride.

I put my black shoes on and went to the square wire-meshed window situated in the door. Rows of beds with human forms lay under crisp-white blankets. Why was I at the morgue?In the stillness, the door mechanism clicked as I opened it. Without warning, a cacophony of jumbled sounds hit me. I shut the door. Listening to my memory, I deciphered the mass: explosions, gun-fire, planes, screams, and music.

'Face it,' Mike said.

I vigorously opened the door—silence. Something drew me to the first sheet covered table. Walking over, a hand fell out; I flinched. The hand only had a finger and a thumb. I thought Shrek had made it in Operation Poppy Pride. Stepping slightly back, the next sheet covered someone with a big stature; so, Planet had died. Dizzy and nauseous, I walked backwards until my back hit the cold door I had entered. It was locked. Viewing through the window, I was shocked to see an unrecognisable burnt face staring at me. Smoke poured from what was left of his mouth and nose. Only the German emblem on the officer's melted cap remained intact. I staggered back and, breathing erratically, I became aware there was no other exit.

For some reason, a voice told me to count the others, but I knew who they were. Small items were now laying on the chest of each person. After seeing a bible and a Fairburn fighting knife, I skipped to the last one that did not have anything. This solitary sheet was black. I counted them again, it was number thirteen. Why would Weaves be under it? He had not been on the mission. A faint beeping started and, walking towards the table, the sound kept in rhythm with my steps, but my heartbeat was going faster. Gripping the sheet at the head end, I then whipped it back.

'Arghhhhhh,' I hollered.

Controlling my breathing, I leant forward and grabbed the phone off the dash, turning off the alarm. My sweat became very cold, the same temperature of the van. The image of my dad mashed up had stained my mind; I swallowed hard. Laughter diverted my thoughts: a group of school kids all having fun. I missed those days. Instantly, I recognised some of them to be Roy's children, all grown up. I waited till they were around the corner.

Taking my baseball cap off, I went to open my door, but a car rushed past. The black Merc with blacked out windows parked next to the BMW. The suave bloke that got out was dressed in an expensive suit and black shoes. He had clocked me, only subtle, but enough to recognise I had been compromised. From the car boot he took a large black holdall and then went to the front door. With his own key he let himself in. Who the shit was this guy? Was he muscling in now that Roy was troubled? Time to fucking ask.

Once I had bumped the back of his Merc with the VW, I wiped the sweat off my face and neck. Marching up the drive, banging on the door, the van's door chime played out.

'Johnny,' Christine said, but then she slapped me around the face.

'I deserve that,' I said.

Hugging me, holding on, she began to sob. 'He's gone... he's gone.'

I should have embraced her back, but my arms stayed awkwardly by my side. She let go of me. There was an uncomfortable pause as I stared into her teary eyes. She appeared older than I remembered.

Eventually, I was invited in. The first thing I noticed was the expensive black shoes under the radiator in the hallway: size ten. Through the next door, I scanned the area: the dining room table was a littered with breakfast paraphernalia. A cup of half-drunk tea was next to the sofa. I went over and touched it: warm.

'Do you want a coffee or tea?' she asked.

'I'll make you a fresh one.'

'No, that's fine, Johnny. You're my guest.'

I did not listen and burst into the kitchen; he wasn't there. 'Not what I expected to find,' I insinuated.

'I'm sorry for the mess, I've not got on top of it.'

'Not what I meant,' I said.

Whilst I waited on the sofa, having cleared a space, I tuned in above the frantic tidying-up in the kitchen. A tiny creek from upstairs alerted me.

'Youngest off school?' I said.

'No, she's at my sisters. Bless her.'

I took the cup from her and said, 'Thought I heard someone. Are you alone?'

'No,' a voice said.

I twisted to the pensive, tall, dark-haired bloke stood in the doorway to upstairs, the light reflecting in his light-blue eyes. I plonked down my tea, spilling it, and quickly stood. I fucking loathed him, even more that he was handsome.

'Who the fuck are you?' I blurted.

'Johnny, this is...'

'Steve,' he interrupted Christine, pulling his shirt cuffs down past the end of his jacket.

I took my eyes off the silver cufflinks. 'Steve who?'

'No. Steve.'

'Steve Steve? That's fucking a cock name. Right, Steve Steve, why the fuck are you here?'

He smirked, then sharply breathed out through his nose.

'Too fucking good looking to answer?' I raged. 'I could arrange that you do reply, and you would become an ugly fuck after.'

He smiled again, adjusted his tie, and looked over my shoulder.

Even though I wanted to smash his smooth chisel jaw, I knew I was lying deep-down, hoping Steve would not accept the contest.

'Johnny, this is...'

'Steve, her friend,' he again interrupted Christine.

'You wanna go on *Britain's Got Talent* with your ventriloquist act, Steve Steve.' I faced Christine. 'Friend? Are you fucking sure? Not trying to fill Roy's shoes already.'

She burst into tears and sank into the chair.

'Tut tut,' Steve said.

'I never heard Rabbit speak about a Steve. You sure you fucking know him?'

'You're right, I don't know a Rabbit, only a Roy, who I've known for years,' he said calmly.

'Well, you wouldn't have called him that if you were in my circle of friends.'

'Your circle of friends?' he mimicked.

'What do you fucking mean by…'

'Johnny. Stop,' Christine shrieked.

'Now why don't you fuck off and leave me and Christine to talk.'

'Because you would upset her, even more, Johnny. Now, hadn't you better shut your van door.'

After slamming the door and kicking the tyre, I went back inside the house. In the obstinate mood, I waited till Steve had made Christine another drink. In that time, it struck me how haggard and distressed she was. Had I been a total twat to insinuate that Steve was some sort of lover? Who was Steve? Why his vagueness?

It transpired over the next hour that Roy had been mentally suffering for the last ten months; guilt consumed me. I had tried to put up a fight to why I had not been in better contact, but it had been rejected, probably because I had purposely never mentioned my personal troubles.

When it came to the part of Roy going missing, Steve took over Christine's emotional story; she couldn't find the words. Three months ago, Roy had decided to walk to work instead of taking the car. He never made it. A full-scale search had been done, but the press and police lost interest once a letter had been received saying he had left Christine and the kids. The postmark was from Cornwall. Christine had blustered that "this wasn't like Roy".

The payments on the fancy BMW had not been kept up on time, adding to warning letters. Debt, worry, and guilt was suffocating this family. I had offered her financial cash to tie her over, but it had not gone down well. However, I had still left the Jiffy envelope containing some cash on the coffee table.

With my anxiety growing, I went outside for some much-needed fresh air. Steve had decided to follow, but I doubted for a change of atmosphere. I smiled when he looked disgruntled at the back of his Merc where the VW had pushed into it. Expecting some sort of aggressive reprisal, I kept my distance.

'Get in. We need to talk in private,' he said.

'I'm not getting in your pile of shit. Jump in the A-team van, mad Murdock.'

I was enjoying taking the piss out of Steve as I walked around to the driver's side, it calmed the nerves. However, he seemed to have a cool, untouchable air about him, something that sparked a little nostalgia in me. Opening the door, he picked up all the paper and pens off the passenger seat. It was then I noticed it: a blue folded letter. I quickly snatched it from him.

'Something of importance?' Steve said. 'Anything to do with the whereabouts of your friend Roy?'

'No. It's a poignant speech written by another friend. Anyway, even if it were, why the fuck would I share it with you? And shouldn't it be, *our* friend Roy.'

'Because...' He paused and picked up the postcard. 'When did you get this?'

I went to snatch it, but in lightning reaction he grabbed my wrist, staring at me with his piercing eyes. He then released his grip and handed the card to me. Steve got in and calmly shut the door.

'You touch me again and I'll bust your face,' I said.

'Yes, I've heard. So, you've been sending postcards out.'

'What the fuck do you mean?'

'Christine received the same postcard.' He studied me for a reaction.

'That's not what I meant.' I waited for him to reply about his "Yes, I've heard", but he remained tight lipped. 'Oh, yeah, stupid me, I went all the way to Canada and sent myself and Christine a fucking postcard. You twat.'

'Well, Johnny, you have been missing for a few months,' he said, imperturbable.

He really was battering my bollocks. 'You really are getting under my... How did you know that?'

'Did you receive a map from Amazon?'

I scrutinised him with narrowing eyes, unnerved he had so much info on me. Perhaps Steve had sent the cards and map. Was this why he was muscling in? Had Steve sorted Roy? A cold chill went through me as I thought he could be the abductor. I moved closer to the door, trying not to make it obvious.

'Well?' he said.

'You know I received a map.'

'Where is it?'

'On the junk pile at home.'

'Did you open it?'

'No. I was getting away from a tank parked outside my house,' I said seriously.

'For someone who was trained, you're an ignoramus.'

'If you get a lie-detector, you will see I did hear a tank,' I said haughtily.

'I *meant*, you're an ignoramus for not checking your map.'

Steve reached inside his suit jacket and pulled out a map, the exact one I had received. Unfolding it, he slapped it on my knee. I studied the map: a small red pen-dot was marked next to the name Valemount Hotel. Next, Steve placed the identical postcard next to mine. With his perfectly kept hands, he pointed to some tiny writing under the postmark: RF. Really, Roy's initials? Was Steve asking me to believe this is where Roy was? Why the discrete code? If this was true, why send it to me and Christine? Why would he go all the way to The Rockies and then make contact in such a stupid way? Why send a letter from Cornwall saying he had left? Maybe Roy's mind was more fucked than mine. Not only was my brain misted, but now the windows were.

I went to tell Steve that *he* was the ignoramus, but he rudely put his finger over his lips; I closed my mouth.

'We have received intel that he checked in at Heathrow on a non-return flight to Calgary International Airport a couple of months back,' he said.

'Intel? And you use the word "we". Who is we?'

'Christine and me. Have you been to Calgary recently?'

'You say, "Christine and me". Are you sure you haven't misplaced some intel where Roy really is? Perhaps slipped your mind that you buried him under the patio.' I scoffed.

He didn't answer.

There was no way Roy would fly to Canada and leave his family. Steve must be behind it. The mysterious phone calls sprung to mind. Shrewdly, I took out my mobile and phoned Roy's new number, self-righteously smiling and nodding at Steve being the silent caller. Bollocks, I thought, as someone else but Steve had answered it.

'Rabbit. Listen, dude, it's me Vinnie,' I said. 'We go back quite a way and we've been through some serious shit together in Afghan. Where are you?' I waited… 'At least let me know this is you or you're in Canada, as this prick next to me thinks. I'm sorry…'

The person cut me short by ending the call.

'Do you really think Roy wants to be reminded of his troubles in Afghanistan?'

'It's personal. Got it, fucktard?' I threw the postcard and map at him.

He didn't flinch, but curiously stared, as if getting the measure of me.

'I can't believe Rabbit never mentioned his complete dickhead friend called Steve.'

'Roy told me a lot about you, the off-record stuff. Been a lot of *rogue* trouble since Operation Blue Halo.'

Was I the only one getting really worked up? I thought about smacking him, but the new nervous part of me kicked in, becoming all too familiar.

Buzz... buzz!

Steve leant over to see who had texted, but I held it to my chest. He grinned, showing his perfect teeth. Leaning back, I opened the text. It was from Roy, but all that was written was: 'Yes'. A part of me felt great I had made contact. Steve had gotten out his phone and was looking at his screen. He showed me the same text to what was on my phone.

'Roy's new contact details. Thanks, but why keep it a secret?' he asked.

'How the fuck have you got into my phone?'

'Time to book a flight. If you want to travel to help locate Roy, then you need to get your passport. Oh, and get your haircut, Hillbilly.'

'I've already got it with me,' I retorted, and deleted the text, quickly regretting it.

Steve got out and fastened his suit jacket. 'Really? Where were you heading to, and why?'

'And you just by chance had your passport before working out he was in Canada, or is it you live local, and I mean local.' I nodded at Roy's house.

Steve looked up at the house windows and then reached into his back pocket. 'From Cornwall,' he said, and respectfully closed the door.

Did he ever get pissed off? I was stressed that he was trying to pin some blame on me.

I looked at the envelope that he had given me: Christine's typed labelled details on the front, the postmark from Newquay. The date was sent a few months back. Surely, he doesn't think I sent this. Fuck. Had I sent this in one of my off days? Had he insinuated to Christine I might be involved? There was nothing familiar about Steve, except something unique. I could not quite put my finger on it.

Itching to read the contents, I took the letter out. Feeling that I might have written something bad, I had an urge to have a large JD to caress my worry. It read:

Christine,
Apologies are not enough anymore to all of you. I have tried to come off the drink, but it tends to help me get through the twenty-four hours.

This is the last time you hear from me as I am starting a new life, alone. Don't search in the last place you would look because that is where you would find me.

    Love,

       Roy.

I read it again; in fact, several times, trying to pick it apart. My hands trembled. All those years of marriage, his wonderful kids, his amazing ability to fly a Chinook into any war zone, and it comes down to a few lines. But then, I had written nothing in my plight.

Searching the empty void where Steve had sat, I questioned everything about him, trying to remember if Roy had ever mentioned a Steve. A tiny niggling fact said that I had seen him before, maybe many years back. Whatever I couldn't get to grips with, one resolute fact was that there was no way I would be travelling all the way to Canada with him, let alone believe his nonsense story of Roy being there.

CHAPTER SEVEN

After my request, Monkfish's van was put in Christine's garage. Steve had disappeared for forty-eight hours, leaving me to deal with the enormous awkward guilt of facing Christine and the kids; I did not get much sleep on the sofa. On a secret mission, I had searched for some alcohol to help, but there was none. Perhaps it had been removed because of Roy. I am so glad Christine was there to help me stay sober, to help me become the new me.

The journey to Heathrow with Steve had been one thing, but sitting on a plane for just over nine hours to Calgary International Airport was going to be unbearable. As we began the numbing four and a half thousand-mile flight, I thought back on the events that had taken place before…

Steve was overly attached to his holdall. He had even fitted a pathetic small padlock on the zip. What did he have in it? Did he think I would rifle through it? I was travelling light, the same gear almost as when I had travelled to Yemen to find Larry Schultz; that thought was quickly buried. I'd had my haircut for the first time in a year, and had tried to have another shave, but the previous cuts made it sore. Steve had purchased me a tube of shaving balm. Wanker.

Steve had changed into a new black suit, white shirt, but no tie. The jokes about him going to a funeral, as Spike had said before we had left for D-day, did not fare any better. Expressionless was an art for Steve, not helping with his dazzling-blue eyes.

It was only minuscule, but I had noticed, even checking my paranoia radar after. Steve had nodded to one of the security staff at the passport control. A new member of staff had taken over the x-ray machine whilst Steve went through the detector. There had been no chat or eye contact as Steve took his holdall off the conveyer-belt. Was Steve in the security sector? I had asked him loads of questions since we had met, but he never answered any of them.

I had sat away from him in the waiting area. From time to time, he would just stare at me or type something in his phone. He would come back from the bar and hand me a spring water. I would send him back for a slice of lemon, just to irritate him, but he did with pleasure.

Well into the boring flight, I ordered a large JD off the sexy stewardess.

'Please do not serve him alcohol, he's in recovery and has to drive once we land,' Steve said.

I was furious, but even my best plea to her saying it was banter, was wasted. That was it: I could have thrown him off the plane. Part of what he had said was true, but surely one drink would not hurt? Was it a guess that I had become an alcoholic? Admitting that was a revelation. I knew it was a good thing, and I hated him even more.

Whilst I relieved the water that I had drunk, I noticed I had been shaking a lot since not having any alcohol for a few days. An idea came to mind: I would order Steve loads of soft drinks and when he visited the toilet, I would bust open his black bag stored in the overhead locker. Yes, he had guessed right, I would rifle through his holdall. However, possibly intuitively on his part, two hours on, he had said no to each drink order. Yet, I spent many visits to the toilet. Wanker.

The stewardesses were around him like bees around honeypot, or like flies around a big turd, as I had whispered to him. The craving for some of the attention increased the more the flight went on. Jealousy wasn't me, but I had always got on with the airline ladies. It was like being the only stripper at a nun's convention, but at least my eye for the ladies was returning.

Like on previous trips, the first thing I checked out was the airport décor. I loved the number of Canadian flags on show and how modern it felt. Jesus, was I becoming a Laurence Llewelyn-Bowen on airport décor? The people milling about at nine in the morning all seemed very friendly, compared to some of the hostile places I had landed at. Worryingly, those who came to greet others were all wearing full winter clothing. I had only invested in a puffer-jacket.

Steve knew where he was going. The wind howled through me as we walked out of the skywalk. It was fucking freezing. He either had layers of thermals on or was superhuman. I shivered doing up my padded coat over my Animal lightweight jacket. It was so cold that an image came to mind of training with the SBS in winter. Although my mind had been conditioned to the cold, I hated it, not just the freezing climate, but why suddenly was I thinking back on those days. Apart from the recent photos in the locked box, I had to banish such thoughts due to the frightening flashbacks. Did he have a car and driver waiting? I hoped so, with the heaters on. However, who would be driving? Maybe a chauffeur driven Bentley or an Aston Martin, I thought; that would suit Steve.

Casually walking up to a box-standard family four by four, Steve got down on one knee and quickly undid the padlock. He pointed what seemed to be a three-inch cylinder black object, like a smaller version of an Amazon Echo. Once the silver Pajero doors unlocked, Steve opened the passenger door for me and then hurried to the driver's door. The key flicked out of the cylinder object and Steve slid it in the ignition. After a few seconds, a tiny green light illuminated, and he started the engine. What kind of key-fob was that? Steve stared at me as if waiting for the question, but I adjusted the seat back. There was no way I was letting him have the pleasure of telling me to mind my own business, that is if he would have answered.

Out of the airport, a slight settling of snow lay on the roadside. Instantly, I switched on the hot air. Steve placed his bag on the back seat; my eyes followed.

'Hire car?' I asked.

'You could say that. You don't like the cold.'

'Rhetorical question, Steve Steve?'

Steve pulled out his phone and began texting.

'You know that's illegal,' I said, then cringed.

'Rhetorical question, Johnny?'

'Fuck me. You're so cool, no, deadpan, no, boring. Are the heaters not thawing your humour out?'

Steve placed his phone on the dash in front of the speed dials, as a satnav. 'I've heard about your wit.'

'Roy and I didn't get on to start with, but we worked it out. We had to, the pressures we were under were immense. You know he saved my life.'

'Modest of you, Johnny, knowing it was the other way around. It's a shame you were the only two to come out of that dreadful conflict.'

'I lost some big guys.'

'Especially your best mate, Robert.'

Relaxing slightly, thinking Steve had understood, I pictured my best mate Planet. It was nice not to feel the dread, the pain. A faint heart never fucked a pig, I thought. I had not said that in… well, too long.

We had only been travelling for another ten minutes, but I was becoming too warm, so I took off my furry hat, then stretched my legs.

'Large stature Robert had,' Steve said, from nowhere.

'Six feet ten of solid reliance,' I boasted.

'No, he was six feet seven.'

'No he wasn't, he was six feet ten,' I snapped.

'Through your rose-tinted glasses, maybe, but he wasn't as big as your obsession.'

I was stunned at his mocking. 'I'll give you a smack in the mouth in a second.'

Steve pulled up onto the snowy verge, got out, and closed his door. Calmly, he walked around to my door and opened it.

'Let's be having your best shot,' he summoned.

Steve took a step back; the three inches of snow covered his shiny black shoes. He eyes appeared more striking than ever, piercing my soul. I went cold, not just for the minus-three chill. At best, I tried to keep his glare.

'I'll fucking sort you if I get out,' I wavered.

I reached down for the seatbelt, but hesitated undoing it. Looking back, Steve nodded and closed the door. Was that a test? Was he satisfying what he already thought I had become? I turned the heating down and took off my coat as a hot flush had come over me.

For the next hour and a half, we had never said a word. The scenes of mountains capped with snow and ice, vast open spaces, had been idyllic, simplifying my mood. The snow had now become heavier.

Just before a sign that read 'Banff National Park', Steve veered off right down a smaller road. The trees dropped snow onto the screen—beautiful. After about five minutes of slipping and sliding at speed through the densest part of the forest, of which I was impressed with his driving skills, a bright light reflected in the distance. The phone said, 'You have reached your destination.' It was like entering a new world. Not only did the sun seem magnificent, but the bright crystal-blue-green lake mirrored its beauty. The only dark thing was my thoughts on what Steve was up to.

To the left of a basic carpark, a timber pontoon with boats had iced over. Only the middle of the lake was not frozen, out of the wake of the mountain's shadow. Steve backed the Mitsubishi a couple of metres from the edge, not the only edge looming. Something did not feel right. It had been a long time since my sixth sense had rattled me, probably because of the mess I had been in. As much of the new admittance relevance, new signs took my mind into a mistrust overload: no hire car details, lady's sunglasses in the door pocket, open packet of chewing gum in the centre console, and the whiff of nicotine. This was not a hire car. Why had I only just clocked this info? The door was locked as I went to open it. Why? When did he do that? My heart began to race.

'I need a piss,' I blurted.

'Your dick will freeze out there.'

'Open the fucking door or I'm going to do it right now.'

'Sure. Didn't even realise it was locked.'

The door lock clicked; I was out like a caged animal. Behind the Pajero, I slowed my breathing, telling myself to get out of the fear-zone. The sound of another vehicle approaching alerted me. Escape wise, there was not much option but to grab my warmer weather gear and make a run for the woods. Would I remember my arctic training? Weapon, I suddenly thought. Quickly, I opened the rear door. A pram and kiddie's boots lay on top. I peered around the side as Steve was now out, with his holdall.

'Come on, Johnny. You'll freeze to death,' Steve said, and gently jogged over to the approaching silver Merc off-road jeep.

Still looking at the new driver, I fumbled around under the hardboard floor panel until I found what I was looking for: a wheel brace. Keeping the situation in sight, I went back to my foot-well and picked up my coat, hat, and bag, slipping the brace inside, the zip left open. Walking cautiously over, putting my hat and coat on whilst holding the strap in my mouth, a muscular, broad bloke stepped out the Merc. Steve could hardly get his arms around him as they patted each other on the back. It was then the new guy clocked me; his eyes narrowed. The bloke released Steve, then slightly pushed back his black beanie-hat. I stared at his old, rugged face, trying not to count the scars. Everyone's warm breath raced into the freeze.

'This is Johnny Vince,' Steve said.

The solid bloke's eyes lit up as he stared at Steve. What was he thinking? My hand slid to the top of the bag's opening. I contemplated where to add the next scar, but a part of me doubted I could hit him. Eyes locked, he strutted towards me, then continued walking around the back of me as if looking at a new car.

'This is him?' he said incredulity, with a slight Irish accent. 'Not what I expected.'

'You mean, not what you remembered. We've met before somewhere,' I probed.

'You reckon?'

The voice rattled around my head, on the tip of my tongue. He held out his huge, thick-skinned hand; tattooed on the top.

'What's your name?' I asked.

He smiled.

'Both in the car now,' Steve said. 'We need to find Roy.'

For a second, we both squeezed harder, before I released first, my cold hand throbbing. He strode around to the passenger door; I opened the rear.

'And, Johnny,' he said, 'this Merc has a wheel-brace, so you can ditch that. Call sign, fucking outrageous.' His deep laugh seemed to echo across the lake.

I was glad to be in the warmth, in the rear where I could keep an eye on them both. I had kept the brace. Without warning, Steve stuck it in reverse and looked over his shoulder. The smash made me look behind: the Mitsubishi skidded onto the ice. The Mitsubishi's rear suddenly crashed down, and it wasn't long before just the top of the roof was exposed. Steve headed back towards the track.

'Call sign, fucking awesome,' the new bloke said.

'Paddy, isn't it?' I said.

He turned, again his menacing eyes penetrated me. 'Too fucking obvious a guess. I'll let you into a bit of intel: my name is Ant.' His grin showed a silver tooth.

My mind raced at all the names and voices I had heard, trying to put it to the face. 'Bit old to be playing games.'

'Nothing better than mind-fuck games, oh, except combat. I love to be the one standing over a corpse not giving a fuck.'

'Do you even know Roy Franklin? I mean, why the fuck are you here?' I asked.

'Always good to have an extra hand to watch your back,' Steve answered.

'Let me just remind you two tiny-brained morons, we're just going to find Roy. It's not some fucking mission. That's even if you've ever put a fucking pair of boots on the ground.'

'Wake me when we get there, unless I'm dreaming with a boner,' Ant said, and put his rear seat back, almost touching my knees.

Deliberately, I kneed the back of his chair. He chuckled to himself and then pulled his beanie-hat over his eyes. Pissed off, I placed the bag at my feet and took off my coat and hat as the car temperature inside was warming.

Over the next three hours, even with the stunning scenery, I could not get these two out of my mind. I reckoned Ant was mid-fifties, whereas Steve was late-twenties, early-thirties. Not only did I not believe their names, but the whole thing did not make sense. One growing in speed concern I did have was that they thought I had something to do with Roy's disappearance. I was not in control of this journey to find Roy; my stomach was in knots. I tried to kid myself food would help. I didn't know whether to tell them to stop for something to eat and drink. I needed to grow some balls. Here goes, act assertive, I thought.

'I'm fucking ravenous back here. This journey is frigging worse than being stuck on a boat with Ocker.'

Ant stretched and yawned before leaning across at Steve's phone. 'Fucking brutal dream, mate,' he said to Steve.

Bollocks. You think you're so hard, Ant, I thought.

Expressionless, Steve pulled into layby that had a large mound of snow where the road had been cleared. Ant did up his jacket and got out. I tried to look cool as he went to the rear and opened the doors, the chill running down my neck. After he shut them, he got back in; I relaxed. He tossed me and Steve a bottle of Coke, and then pulled out a box from his bag, handing it to me. Inside were scrumptious bite-sized donuts. I popped one in my mouth.

'Timbits, mate,' Ant said. 'Better than licking a lizard's nuts in the jungle or squeezing the juice from goat's droppings in the desert.'

'I've noticed that you two always prying for me to react to my past,' I said.

'On a mission, life is always on a tightrope. You need to understand the balance of what fear is, and what is the job.'

My mind wondered back to previous tours.

'Rob, Gary, and Tony's bodies were never found,' Ant said. 'Funny that.'

I started to choke.

Steve gave Ant a little shake of the head.

Regaining my composure, I stared evilly at Ant, then Steve. 'What the fuck is this all about?'

'It's OK, Johnny, Ant is just teasing you. I filled him in on that dreadful mission in Afghanistan.'

'Yeah? Fucking say it again, Ant, and I'll fucking squash you like one.'

Steve sighed and pulled back onto the road.

Ant grinned again; the remnants of a donut stuck between his teeth.

'Your bollocks must be retracting taking me on. You must be more careful who you go on missions with.'

'I doubt you've even made an army ant.' I sniggered. 'You don't have the right to take the piss out of my mates. If only you had met my ferocious mate who fought by my side. Shrek was fucking aggressive, possibly a lunatic, when the time was right. A true friend. He'd tear you both apart.'

'Gary Harding?' Steve asked.

'You two couldn't have even stood in his shadow.' I was getting too emotional.

'I think he saw you as the lunatic, sorry, the complex mate,' Ant said, and laughed.

'I'm fucking getting sick of you disrespecting...'

'Oh dear, Johnny is going to piss his nappy,' Ant interrupted.

'Don't go over the top, Ant,' Steve ordered.

Ant went to say something, but Steve stared hard at him.

The satnav's lovely voice broke the ice with a direction change.

'Call sign, fucking disgraceful,' Ant said.

Back on route, I mulled over what was said. Although embarrassed, I had to admit I was glad Ant had not taken my threat further. In the past, I would have taken on whoever had said nasty shit about my mates, whether my friends were dead or alive. I needed the old Johnny back. Perhaps I could find some alcohol at the next petrol station, flare up my mood. How did Steve know so much about Robert and Gary? Roy would not have known that much, would he? Would Roy even have had brought such details up in conversation? It was obvious that Steve and Ant had been chatting about my past, but why discuss it all now? Why were they trying to upset me? Then it dawned on me, something Steve had said: "Rogue". Was that meant to be me? And what about, "You must be more careful who you go on missions with"? Was Ant referring to me, to himself, or Steve? Either way, except I'd guessed they were both ex-military, I had nothing else on them. I was not facing this head-on like the Johnny of old. I needed my control back to get out of this world of shit.

'Johnny, grab your shit.'

Startled, I opened my eyes to see Ant leaning over the back of his seat, smirking. We were parked outside a hotel. The snow had been cleared in the carpark, except what was falling. The rear doors opened. Steve impassively looked at me as he moved stuff around. Ant looked at his watch.

'Enjoy your little nap... oh... of two hours,' he said.

'You can tell the time, Ant? Shit me,' I said.

'Four o'clock, mate.'

'Don't you mean sixteen hundred hours. Yeah, I'm onto you, Mr Walter Mitty who needs to think he's on a mission as some hard-man.'

'Time to bag some baddies.'

'You're a twat,' I said.

'Pass me your jacket and hat, Johnny,' Steve said.

'Why?'

'Because you won't need it.'

I curiously handed them to Steve, and he shoved them in the boot. Returned to his seat, between them they studied an A3 piece of paper. Ant was going over details of what he had recently observed. When had Ant done a recce? Why not just knock-on Roy's room? I leant inquisitively forward.

'What's that?' I asked.

'That, Johnny,' Ant said, thumbing at the hotel over his shoulder.

'All clear?' Steve asked.

'Crystal,' Ant replied.

It clicked: Valemount Hotel. 'Right, let's go in and surprise Roy,' I said, not believing he could be here.

Steve was looking at me in his mirror as he put a tie on. 'Probably best you stay here, Johnny.'

'Why?'

'Do you remember how to lead? Be a team player?' Steve asked.

I contemplated his questions.

'Thought so. You need to find your bollocks,' Ant said.

I went to reply but was stopped by him swigging out of a bottle of Canadian Club Whiskey, imagining it going down my throat. I licked my lips.

'You can't stop me coming in,' I said. 'I know Roy better than any of you.'

'Pull up your school socks on that last remark?' Ant said, his annoying laughter booming.

Ant nicely held out the whiskey bottle to me. My fingers touched it, but Steve seized it again in a quick reaction. He thrust Ant's hand away, with a stern look. Ant scoffed, nodding, as if I had failed a test. Steve placed what looked like a small radio on the dash, pressed a couple of buttons, and then placed it in his holdall.

'Is that the music for the welcoming party?' I jested.

Ant sighed. 'We don't want your ugly mug on the CCTV, it will ruin our looks. Music. You bellsmack.'

'Slight change of plan,' Steve said. 'Johnny, you push Ant in the wheelchair. I'll chat to the receptionist.'

'What the fuck?' I said.

'When the enemy play your plan, then it's Horlicks and an early night. Now shut your hole and follow me and Steve.'

CHAPTER EIGHT

Nerves were getting the better of me as I pushed Ant in a wheelchair across the gritted tarmac. I suppose the anxiousness was due to seeing Roy as messed up as I had been, hoping it would not bring back any of my demons. Not knowing what the plan was, or even why there had to be such a strategy, Ant had his cap on and was hunched over with a tartan blanket across him. It was a tight squeeze in the wheelchair. Steve hastily, but in control, walked slightly ahead. Infuriatingly, flashes of all missions I had carried out went through my mind. Not now, I thought. Trying to take my mind off them, I studied the wooden ornate shutters on the side of the windows and the big 'China House' sign. A CCTV camera was above the door. Did Steve's gadget really scramble the security?

Finding it hard to get a grip on the lightly snow-laden car-park, I made a quip about Ant being a fat bastard. He told me I was pushing my luck. Gripping the white railings as I took a breather, I began to shiver. Steve came within a foot of me.

'If you're going to have a bilious attack, then I suggest you go sit in the car,' he said.

'Call sign, wanker,' Ant muttered.

'I'm fine, only tired from the journey, and a bit nervous for meeting Roy.'

'You've done the extreme before,' Steve said, and tapped my shoulder.

Deliberately, I gave Ant a bumpy ride as Steve opened the door; also, catching Ant's knee on the frame. His low growling made me smile.

A 'Wet Floor' sign stood on the slate floor. For a laugh I ran the wheelchair straight into it. The clatter appeared to echo through the oak pillars in the dining area. Ant shook his bowed head, but I missed Steve's reaction as he had faced back towards a sign: 'For room rental please see bar attendant'. I looked at the empty bar and lounge. Where were all the guests? It was strange to have no staff. Perhaps we could help ourselves to the drink, I jovially thought.

I followed Steve into the lounge area and smashed Ant into the bar, pissing him off. Three pine barstools sat at a laminated wood-effect bar. I shook the thoughts of the weird saloon shack in Indonesia. Surely no strange shit was going to happen today. Memories flooded in of me saying and thinking this sort of thing before, and then trouble followed me. I mentally cursed.

'You OK?' Steve quietly asked.

'Yeah, why?'

'Stop muttering to yourself. Focus,' he whispered.

I hadn't realised I was.

The pub smells were enticing. It was not long before I was admiring the rows of optics. My mouth dried up looking at the JD bottle, hoping Roy hasn't been affected by occasional drinks; I really could do with a party.

'Service,' Steve said.

Five seconds later, a young man poked his head around the side door, straightening his tie.

'*Bonjour. Comment puis-je aider?*' he said.

A warming thought of Fish crudely speaking French to the Germans made me snigger.

Steve was not impressed with me. '*Bonjour. Nous en sommes venus à visiter…*'

'Can you not speak in French, guys, but English,' I blurted.

Steve's eyes narrowed at me for interrupting him.

'Yes, of course, sir,' the bartender said.

'We are here to surprise our good friend who is staying here, Roy Franklin. Please can you give us his room number,' Steve graciously said.

'I am sorry, sir, but I am not permitted to give out guest details.'

'We've travelled along way, and grandad here is dying, literally, to meet him,' I said.

'Fuck off,' Ant barely said.

'Again, sir, I am not permitted to give you any details. I could phone his room.'

'That's exceedingly kind of you, but that would give the surprise away,' Steve said. 'Surely on this occasion you could just give the room number. No one would ever know.'

'Not exactly busy are you,' I said. 'Plus, grandad here is gonna shit himself soon as he needs a toilet.'

Ant growled.

'Again, sir, I am not permitted to give you any details. There is a toilet situated at…'

Ant exploded from his chair; a holdall fell on the floor. Shockingly, he pointed a pistol at the young lad's head.

'For fuck's sake, you jobsworth, grow some bollocks,' Ant said. 'I'm going count to five, and if you don't give me the fucking room number, I'm going make two neat holes in your fucking forehead. The back of your head isn't going to be so fucking pretty.'

The colour drained from the barman's face. Just for a second, I wondered if he had thought it was a joke, but then he looked as if he was going to vomit. The lad searched me for answers, but I was unsure if Ant meant it. I half-grinned—pathetic.

'One…'

'I would do as he says,' Steve said.

'Two…'

'Yeah, grandad here gets damn grouchy when he fills himself,' I said, and waved my hand in front of my nose. I sneered—nobody else did.

'Four…'

The lad frantically pressed the touchscreen at the bar, but it didn't work. Confused to why, he then pulled out a diary and frantically read down the pages. '*Chambre douze.*'

'And which way is that?' Steve asked.

'*À travers cette porte, monter les escaliers, première porte à droite.*'

'Fucking English,' I prompted.

Steve reacted first by quickly grabbing the barman, and then Tasered his neck. Holding the stunned lad tight, Steve flipped the pen-like Taser around and stuck the other end in the barman. The lad went limp, Steve dragged him over the bar.

'Door to the left, up the stairs, first door on the right. Room twelve,' Steve calmly said.

'Johnny, do you speak any language? You cretin,' Ant scowled.

Ant helped Steve put the lad in the wheelchair. OK, I had to admit, this was as weird as the lookalike cowboy saloon in Sumatra.

'Dispose of him, Johnny, then meet us at the bottom of the stairs, and rapid about it. Can you fucking manage that?' Ant said.

Perplexed to what was going on, I took hold of the handles as Steve and Ant went through the door signed to the hotel rooms. The place fell eerily silent. Even though insane for just finding Roy, I did understand a part of me had retuned: the buzz.

Once I had sorted the lad in the wheelchair, I raced through the door. I sharply stopped, surprised to see Ant aiming at me down a sub-machinegun weapon; a type I had not seen before. Steve was standing half-way up the stairs. Ant tapped his watch.

'Where the fuck have you been?' Ant hushed.

'Why the fuck have you got that? What make is it?' I asked.

'Time to search and destroy. Get with the fucking mission.'

'Johnny,' Steve whispered, 'time to switch on.'

Steve threw me the Taser pen gadget. I looked at my weapon, before glancing at the empty holdall stuffed under the stairs, envious I only had a biro-pen, almost.

'Anyone who comes out of their room, show them they need to fucking mind their own business. Got it?' Ant said.

Steve coolly undid his suit jacket and pulled out a pistol. With it by his side, he walked to the top of the stairs, us close behind him. Ant sighted the door that we had entered, whilst I studied Steve's pistol: a black Walther PPK. Steve checked the door gap. The oppressive feelings came; I knew they would. The stairwell's lighting darkened, almost to a pitch-black, but weirdly, I could perfectly see the green laser beams that searched. Through the next door were the blue and red room, the one holding the Somali pirates. I shouted to abort the mission knowing Kyle was going to die in shotgun blasts through the side wall, but no one was answering my calls on the headset. A hand touched my shoulder; Ocker was ready. Kyle appeared very enthusiastic to get stuck in.

'Remember the fucking Elite unit you were in; fearless, fearsome,' Ant hushed in my ear.

The lifelike situation changed: I was back. The demons did now not bother me, I was pumped with adrenalin and aggression. It did not matter that I only had a Taser, use my fucking bare hands if I had to. Brain power will be supremacy with any weapon; it's me, or them.

'On me,' I whispered.

Both looked at me and smiled.

Steve quietly opened the door and started walking towards the first door on the left. Ant got down on one knee covering the length of the corridor. I had my foot at the closed door we had entered. All was silent. Ant retrieved a black rubber cup from his leg pocket and gave it to Steve, who then handed it to me. It was a strange contraption. Steve frowned at me, making a gesture to watch him, now having an identical object. He aligned the cup's centre tube over the door's spy-glass, pressing the cup edges around. Looking through a hole in the cup, he waited a few seconds, before nodding at the door directly opposite. Once I had done what he had, I looked through.

'Fucking ace,' I muttered—someone tutted.

My eye looked excitedly around at the main room in a thermal image. At the bottom of the image was a continuous moving digital line, presuming a sound wave. I twisted to Steve and hand signalled no contacts. Surprisingly, Steve did the same action. I wasn't sure if I was disappointed because that there were no contacts, or that Roy wasn't in there. Perhaps he was in the bathroom.

I reluctantly passed Steve the thermal-view gadget, he swapped it with another device from Ant. Steve handed me the credit card object that had an electronic device on top. I shrugged my shoulders, embarrassed. Steve came up close to my ear.

'Switch it to lock, place it in all the other doors, and wait for the green light before taking it out,' he whispered, and nodded to make sure I understood, but patronisingly.

Letting the insult go, I started to do as instructed. The clicking of the magnetic card slotting in and out appeared very loud; I cringed. After the doors were done, I handed it back to Steve. I was still grinning at the 'boy's toys'. However, that was soon wiped as he motioned me to stand by the main stairwell door.

Steve placed the device in door number twelve. As soon as the green light illuminated, he slightly turned the door handle. Staying aside from the door, he placed his polished leather shoe at the base of the door. As if well-rehearsed, Ant then flicked on a red beam and sped in, followed sharply by Steve. I, however, felt like a chastised kid. Within seconds the lights flickered on. A large hand came around the door frame, beckoning me in.

Ant locked the door behind me with the card and followed me into the main room. I was pissed off not to see Roy. Was this some sort of sick joke using this amount of force? Ant was peering through the net-curtains.

'Well, that was as lame as watching John Major having a wank,' Ant said.

'You don't want to get that old heart ticking, grandad,' I bantered.

'You can shut that shit up. I wouldn't have gotten Kyle Slater killed.'

'Where's that come from, you sick fuck?' I raged. 'Did your mum and dad leave you on a doorstep when you were born? No one wanted you. Is that why you pretend you're in the army?'

'Fuck off,' Ant retorted.

'Or was it you didn't fit in at school or borstal?'

'Why the fuck did you join up?' he countered. 'Family troubles? Bit of a *special* kid, were you? And look at you now, for fuck's sake.' Ant did a fat man walking impersonation, then rubbed his eyes as if crying.

'Bollocks. I didn't enlist for the stereotype reasons. My upbringing was brilliant, I was good at school and had no life troubles. And what's "special kid" supposed to mean?'

Ant sat in an armchair trying to look cool, but I reckoned I was getting to him. My hands slyly gripped the dressing unit I had sat down on.

'Then why did you join?' he asked. 'Wanted to be a real man? Your tiny cock is no revelation, according to Ella.'

'Very funny, but predictable. I wanted to be like those in my dad's signed book collection; simple.'

'You sad motherfucker. Oh, yes, your dad. Didn't you recently inherit those books from him?'

'Like you inherited that gaping hole in your arse from yours,' I frothed.

I moved quickly towards him, infuriated. Steve quickly stood between us. Ant lowered his main weapon and put his arms behind his head. Steve eyes stared into mine, before glaring at Ant. There was an awkward silence.

'Good to see the fire hasn't quite gone out,' Ant said.

'We need to find some clues to where Roy is,' Steve said, unruffled. 'Johnny, keep watch on the carpark below.'

'Bollocks, Steve Steve,' I said.

Taking myself off to the bathroom, I locked the door. Shit, that was a close ruck, I thought.

I let go the comments from Ant that I was crying, and I got the feeling Steve was giving him a little chat about his conduct.

Once the trembling had almost subsided, the nausea of the situation hit me. I started to question what the fuck was going on. I thought back to when Steve had said, "You've done the extreme before." Had he meant the cold, or referred to the SBS? Who were these guys? Why were such gadgets and weapons required? Who were they expecting to meet? Had Roy lost the plot and had an arsenal at his means? How did they have so much info on me? It was seriously grating on me how they used it against me. Perhaps they were really going to kill Roy and blame me. But why?

I had seen Steve before somewhere, but this was over-shadowed by the more familiarisation of Ant. I thought on, then smacked myself on the side of the head; I was supposed to be finding a desperate mate. I should not be putting those fuckwits and me at the hub of attention. I felt sick. Images played out of me on the cliff with the knife on the rope, but my mind put Roy in my place. I hated the thought that could have been the end of the line for me, scoffing at the metaphor. Primarily, I had to find Roy.

Knock, knock, knock.

'All right in there, Johnny?' Ant said patronisingly.

'Sure,' I lied. The acid was still in my throat, I tried to swallow it.

'Have you worked out why you joined the Elite, yet?'

Staring at a bar of soap with an arrow sign carved in it, my mind backtracked to the beginning of training for selection. How epic to have had the chance for selection. The revulsion increased of what I had left, to what I had become. Lifting the toilet-seat, fingers down my throat, I tried to disguise the sound of the coke and donuts that spewed up, the pressure with it. Clearing my eyes and throat, I noticed a small plastic bag at back of the seat hinges. Strange, I thought, wiping my mouth on back of my hand.

'No sign of him staying here,' Steve said disappointedly.

I put the lid down, made myself more respectful, and went to press the cistern button, but immediately stopped when I had relooked at the arrow facing the toilet.

'Forward thinker,' I mumbled.

Once I had retrieved the bag, I opened it and removed the piece of paper. It read: 'Cabin. 2 klicks east of Swiftcurrent Falls.' I grinned. Roy was a forward thinker, always planning, but why leave this clue? What was his game? Was it a call for help? Did he really know I would come all this way and find it? I was now sure that Steve and Ant had nothing to do with his disappearance. I thought about turning my phone on and contacting Roy. Would Steve see the text? Would his gadget in the car stop the signal? Is that why the electronic reception register never worked?

After washing the sweat from my face, I took the time to brush my teeth. Spraying some freshener, I flushed the toilet, hopefully with the old me away; I did feel different. Back in the room, both looked a little pissed off.

'You remember why we're here,' Steve said.

'Well, it appears this isn't a normal find a missing friend,' I replied, nodding at Ant's weapon. 'So, I thought I would take the opportunity to now appear better.'

'Forgot your basic training, Johnny? No soap or deodorant,' Ant gloated.

'I don't think he meant that, Ant,' Steve said.

'Too intellectual for Grandad,' I said—for once, Steve chuckled.

'Call sign, fuck off,' Ant said.

'Sitrep: Ant owned,' I smugly said. 'Oh, by the way, this is the clue you two twats have been searching for.' I handed Steve the tissue paper.

Ant looked on.

Steve made a note on his phone and then handed it to Ant.

'I would've found this, it's only that you got there first,' Ant said.

I mimicked his voice, 'Pull up your school socks on that last remark.'

Ant brashly let me know it was a rubbish Irish accent.

'We need an Ops name,' I said.

'No we don't.'

'Sure we do,' Steve chipped in, 'but for now make yourself as inconspicuous as you can on the way out.'

I arrogantly grinned at Ant as he cautiously followed Steve out.

At the bottom of the stairs, Ant put all the gear in the holdall and then held his hand out. Assuming he wanted to take back the Taser, instead I gave him the middle finger.

'Operation Fuckwit,' Ant whispered.

'Really? That's no way to speak about Steve Steve.'

'Stop your stupid games, you two, and stay switched on,' Steve ordered.

Steve led us through the reception, but he suddenly stopped. I had parked the wheelchair at a lounge table and put Ant's cap and blanket on the lad. In front of the hunched lad, I had placed a bottle of vodka and filled a glass half-way.

'What the fuck is that all about?' Ant whispered.

'I had to make it look real,' I said.

'You were supposed to dispose of him,' Steve said.

'Literally?'

'Do it,' Ant said.

Both left me standing there. I walked across to the wheelchair and took the bottle of Vodka, hiding it under my Animal jacket.

Back in the cold, Ant chucked me the bag, ordering me to put it in the back. By Ant's tone and Steve's glare, they were unimpressed. I realised I needed to stop larking around, grow up, and take the situation seriously, perhaps my life.

In the jeep's rear, gear of all different shapes and sizes littered the floor, my bag and wheel-brace pathetic in contrast. Just as I began to un-zip Ant's to get a better look at his weapon, the bottle of vodka slipped from my jacket. Luckily for me, it hit the boot liner. With the shock subsiding, temptation embedded my mind. Quickly, I crouched, unscrewed the cap, and swigged. The amazing feeling made the gulps continue. As soon as I stopped, my throat and chest burned, something I had not felt for a long while: three and a bit days.

Ant shouted something. Like a troublesome, guilty teenager, I replaced the lid and tried to cover the fumes I had belched. Contraband hidden, I skulked around and snuck in. Both were checking a route on a folded map, adding the details in Steve's phone's satnav. Concentrating hard, I slid the bottle under Ant's seat.

A white BMW entered the carpark. Steve did not look up but started the engine. As this vehicle pulled up to the main doors, we gently crept through the carpark and back onto the main road. I sensed something was wrong but was unsure. Steve and Ant were not even checking their mirrors. As soon as we got around the first bend, Steve floored it. Ant took out his 9-mm semi-Browning pistol and held it on his lap.

CHAPTER NINE

The atmosphere in the car changed, something serious was going down. For once in a long time, I felt in control of my emotions, and a tiny part of me wanted some action.

'We've been pinged,' Steve said, composed.

I checked behind. The first car to come around was a silver Chrysler, but not gaining. Ant had managed to get his bulking frame next to me, barging me as he lent over the rear, possibly deliberately. Leaning back again, he had his main weapon. My eyes must have been wide as he made a comment about being caught in the headlights. I went to reply that I wanted one of those weapons and not this stupid quill, but our four-by-four jeep slid around a sweeping bend, G-force making us grip the seats. There was nothing behind us except the odd car that zipped in the opposite direction. My shoulders relaxed, at last, but the excitement stayed.

We were still driving at high speed. Oncoming cars flashed at us, some sounding their horns.

'Contact,' Ant said.

Sharply, I looked behind, but it was difficult to see through the spray. I waited for the rear wiper to sweep again. In the far distance was the white X5.

'Get the mines ready, Ant,' Steve said.

'Call sign, fucking ace.'

Ant lent over the rear again. At the same time as to curious to what Ant was speedily retrieving, I studied his compact weapon. Above the main silenced barrel was another fitted mini-tube barrel, which I guessed to be some sort of grenade launcher. I had seen the optical sight and red-dot configuration earlier but wondered why the stock appeared to have a battery pack fitted. Before I could get to see the transparent mag's markings, Ant retuned. He pulled both pins and the tops sprung up.

'Get ready to fucking lay these, carefully,' he enthusiastically said.

He handed me the two square objects. The inch-and-half thick heavy plates were about ten inches by ten inches. The top looked like tarmac, with at least fifty holes in. I went to press on the top, but Ant screamed at me to stop. I looked at him, dumbfounded.

'Hold on tight,' Steve ordered.

Ant held against the driver's seat, whilst I carefully placed the plates between me and the back of the rear seat. I gripped fast. Suddenly, around the next corner, Steve slammed the anchors on, the ABS trying to stop us skidding. Screeching and swerving ceased, I released my grasp.

'Lay them in the road, now. Get it fucking right,' Ant ordered. 'Don't squeeze the fuckers.' He grinned.

I took my supporting hand off the seat and leant behind for the handle, shoulder-barging the door open. A waft of fumes hit me. Ant was aiming out of the rear window, whilst Steve just looked ahead. Carefully, but quickly, I sprung out holding each plate upright on my forearm. All I could think about was the BMW coming around the sweeping bend and squashing me between them and the Merc. My fast breathing made cold patterns. As if I had loads of time, or was it in slow motion, I worked out the trajectory of the approaching vehicle and combined it with our tyre marks on the wet road, disappearing fast. After laying them, I sprinted back to the revving car, catching sight of Ant's silver tooth as he was grinning.

I had hardly got my other foot in as the powerful engine roared. The spray from the road stopped as I slammed the door. Looking back out the window, two explosions ripped. The X5 lost control into the woodland on the other side of the carriageway, barely missing an oncoming lorry.

'You twat,' Ant shouted. 'The driver missed the lorry.'

I continued to stare.

He friendly punched me on my arm. 'Johnny? Johnny?'

As soon as he slapped the back of my head, I turned and grabbed him around the throat, pushing him into the door. Gripping tighter, he squeezed my arm and tried to pull it away but couldn't. Ant then looped his hands under and over, breaking my grasp. He pulled his fist back to hit me but stopped. Instinctively, I had my fist back, the other ready to block. It felt good.

'Remember your fucking control,' he said gruffly.

'Remember not to fucking slap me again.'

'Good, lad,' he said, and then climbed awkwardly back into the passenger seat.

'Nice placement, Johnny,' Steve said.

Pride flooded as I began to shake from the comedown. I held my hands together. 'Were they stingers?'

'Traditional stingers would allow the enemy to follow, even if you had managed to hit one tyre,' Ant said. 'These, when pushed, electronically fired armour-piercing rounds. Angry little fuckers, a bit like you, Johnny. Operation Spikey Fucker.' He laughed.

I couldn't be bothered to answer him. 'Steve, who were they?'

Steve just glanced in his mirror.

'Why all this cloak and dagger stuff?' I added.

Steve placed his pistol inside his jacket.

'I'm on this mission whether you like it not,' I tried.

'You're starting to realise then,' Ant answered.

'I mean, why bring me?'

'All in good time, Johnny. For now, both of you get some sleep,' Steve said.

'Well done, Johnny,' Ant said—that felt good.

I leant back, placing my feet under the chair, the bottle clunking against the metal seat runners. Upfront never noticed. Ant put his beanie-hat on and, rolling it down over his eyes, made himself comfortable. It wasn't long before his deep breathing like snore was grating on me. How the fuck could he sleep after that encounter? I couldn't relax, no matter what position I had tried. Images of the vodka bottle were at the forefront of my mind. At least it would make me sleep, I thought. Without making it obvious, I took the empty coke bottle from the door-card holder. Subtly retrieving the vodka bottle, I started to covertly decant, trying damn hard not to spill a drop. With the label peeled, it appeared to be a bottle of water. The vodka bottle stood between my feet.

Taking the ruse further, I even nodded at Steve who checked his mirror. I licked my lips and then began to sip, resisting the urge to gulp, even though it tasted great. Finishing each drink, I had made no expression of its strength. It wasn't long before I needed a refill, so I went through the whole process again. However, I was becoming sloppy, spilling some on my trousers. Bollocks. After another refill, I didn't care about the drips, the world was becoming nice, addictive.

'Can't sleep, Johnny?' Steve asked.

Ant made a snoring sound like a demented pig.

I went to answer, but my lips and mouth didn't keep up with my brain. Instead, I nodded and shut my eyes. Peeking, when he was not looking I downed the rest of the bottle. The fumes burnt my chest, a familiar effect.

Once the Vodka bottle was empty, I carefully let it tip over, covertly pushing it under the seat. I managed to stay as coherent as possible as I finished the last drops from the coke bottle. The sounds and movement became one. Even the thoughts of the hotel and chase became mellow. I was now invincible.

Who are you trusting?

No one, I thought. Who the fuck invited you on this mission?

You're slurring.

Whoopy-fucking-do.

You know these two are out to kill you don't you.

Retircl… ratoric… stupid question. And you don't bother me anymore.

★

Rabbit and I were giving it large banter in Afghanistan, no nightmare this time. I was laughing at the runny shit I had left after having a poor diet and strong goat's meat. Who knows what else I caught after that goat herder had hugged me? Rabbit was wiping my diarrhoea off his boot. His expression when I told him it was an Afghan mountain bear that had shat, was hilarious. Did I ever tell Rabbit there was no such bear, or had he worked it out by now?

The scene changed: I was sat next to him on his sofa at his house and he was on his i-Pad searching for Afghan bears. We discussed that lucky chance meeting at the RAF fete when Roy caught me and my brother having a fight with some RAF lads in the marque. I remembered the look on his face when I turned up at his RAF base before the C-17 flight to Akatori. He had even called me Mr. Castleton.

More thoughts entered: we were on the run from the crazy knife-wielding woman, which lead onto when he said I had been eating our food loot like a crazed pig. I chuckled even more. Such good times, I thought, but then the happy memories started to fade. Instead, I was left with the vision of Roy struggling in life. Guilt washed over me. Roy had his head in his hands. I tried to comfort him, but the words would not come out. Surely, we could share our problems, lifting the burden.

My head was banging as I prised open my eyes. The car was empty. I had missed the chance to tell Roy, I thought, then realised it had been a dream. That was it: once we were home, I would book and pay for us to go on a month's holiday, somewhere warm and tranquil. Over few beers I would tell him everything, and most importantly, listen to his problems. We could both encourage each other to find professional help.

I began to shiver. How long had I been here? An unnerving silence surrounded the chill. Shame flooded me as I realised that I had let myself down with the vodka. Sobering up, I focused on the ground and surrounding trees that were covered in a beautiful snow blanket. The sun was setting, a weird orange glow filled the sky, silhouetting the tall pine trees. Behind me was a log-cabin. A slight glow came from a single window. Warmth, I thought. My mood quickly darkened as to why I had been left in the car. What were they up to? I quickly checked the jeep's rear area, all the bags were missing, including my gear. The car began to spin a little as I sat back. Had they found Roy at last? Were they celebrating without me?

Now that Steve was out of view, I dug my numb hands into my pocket and retrieved my phone. Turning it on was difficult. Under my jacket, I lowered the screen brightness, but was too late for the sound of an incoming text alert. Thumb on the volume, I checked to see if anyone was coming over from the cabin. The text was from Mike: 'Careful who you trust. You need to see the world through Johnny Vince. Don't contact me again. By strength and guile.' I read it again, my breath misting up the screen. Suddenly, my door opened.

'Awake then,' Steve said.

'Very perceptive of you. Where's my jacket and hat?'

'You must have left it at the hotel.'

'No, I...'

'How's the head, you idiot,' he interrupted. 'When are you going to learn?'

Had they both known all along? Why did they let me drink it? I studied his military arctic clothing and webbing, looking toasty. I slid my phone into my cold pocket.

'No answer,' he said.

'Why the fuck have you left me in the car? I'm fucking freezing.'

'Go inside and get warm off the Agar. Do not forget your phone can be tracked by the right surveillance. You should have remembered that basic lesson.'

'Is Roy in there?'

'No. I'm off to scout the area. You're on the right path back to the old Johnny.'

With a holdall in his hand, Steve headed off into the wilderness, leaving the only tracks in the snow.

Eager to get inside, I had not accounted for how much vodka had passed my lips. The refuge was only about ten metres away, but it was proving problematic. I was glad that Steve wasn't with me. How belittling that they had both known, both letting me make a fool of myself. I thought about the mention of the phone surveillance. Was that a hint that he had seen the message from Mike? Or was it he was reminding me of what we had been taught in the SF? Perhaps both. More images and questions flooded my head: the jumbled mass of the hotel, weapons, being chased, the distrust; all getting the better of me. I leant over and spewed up the rancid liquid. Wiping my eyes, I then concentrated on the steam at my cold feet. Again, I was sick. This repetitive mess had to stop.

'There has been too much fucking thinking on this mission, and not enough action,' I muttered.

Feeling slightly better, but as hungry as I could eat a horse and chase the jockey, I got myself more respectable.

'I'm pissed off with all the bullshit,' I said. 'Time for some fucking answers.'

Ant was sat with his back to me in an old rocking chair. The wall lantern cast his shadow on the varnished timber boards. The ice clunked as he took a drink. I crept forwards; a sinister smile crept as well. It was like sneaking up to prank a woman who had a ravaged hangover and PMT. I pulled out the Taser pen and turned it on, all the time looking at the back of Ant. The rest of the room's sights and smells disappeared, even my boozy and sick breath.

Four metres…

I gripped the Taser…

Three metres…

I almost stopped my breathing…

Two metres…

I lifted the pen like a dagger…

One metre…

I slightly glanced at movement to my right, catching the same mirror image as Ant's wide-eyed stare. Fuck, compromised. Time seemed to stop. In desperation, I lunged at his neck, but he swivelled, the pen making a static sound as it hit his cheek. Momentum sent him back, but I tried to keep the contact. He yelled, hitting it aside. The aggression switch was flicked. Immediately, I punched him hard in the face, but it seemed to have little effect. I thrust the Taser back into the side of his head, a waft of singed hair hit my nostrils. Ant's eyes went mad. Gritting his teeth, he seized my arm, ripping it away. Now up close, I head-butted him. For a second, I was dazed.

I spun the pen around to inject him, but he double-punched me on the chest. Almost flying, I landed on my back and slid on the floor. Ant discarded the chair out the way as if made of paper. Fuck. Wearing just a tight Lycra vest, and boxer-shorts, he was solidly ripped with muscle. My first kick he caught, but I swiped his other leg below his knee. Buckling, he let go. Rapidly, I scrambled back until I could go no more, but Ant came in blazing. The sound of his fists hitting me was strange, like an out of body experience. Bam! I had managed to get a boot to his bollocks. Ant slightly staggered back holding his groin.

Shuffling to the left, I clambered to my feet. His expression said it all, and again he attacked. My skills took over as I blocked as many punches as possible, but I was breathing like an astronaut on the G-test. An elbow strike startled me. Where did that come from? Angered, I struck a powerful palm strike to his solar plexus, sending him stumbling back a few steps. It had been just enough for me to front kick him further away, crashing him over the oblong coffee table. Earthquake over, he roared with defiance and contempt as he came at me. His straight punch got past my block—too strong. The crunching meant he had busted my nose, the coppery taste confirmed it.

He knew I was affected, and he threw me across the open-plan-kitchen into the cupboard doors. Pain rippled through my head. All became shadowed as his great bulking frame stood over me. Ant's excavator like hands grabbed my shirt and skin and pulled me up close, whiskey apparent on his breath. Blooded, he grinned and then pulled his fist back. A little flashback appeared. I urgently felt for it and then hit him with the bottle, shocking him. Ant searched what was in my hand. I whacked him again in the face. He released me onto the shards of glass as he held his blooded injury.

Fearing he was getting even more vexed, I scrambled across to the lounge area and picked up the thick wooden table leg. He had not fully turned when I walloped him as hard on the back. The air was sucked out of him, spurring me on to hit him harder. This time he fell to his knees. Suddenly, Ant returned with an almighty swing; thank fuck it missed. Swearing and lashing out, he was possessed. When would this fucker go down? I thumped him again as his arms wrapped around me. After what seemed an eternity of grappling and strikes, he lay face down on the rug. My breathing was erratic, pain flooded every part of me. I did not feel triumphant, just barely alive.

First, I tied his trunk-like wrists together behind his back with the blind's cord. Next, I heaved him over and sat him against the Ikea-styled sofa. Feeling a bit shite, as it was not meant to be that brutal, I padded tissue on his bleeding wounds. I then began to sort mine out, having plenty. Apart from falling over drunk, the injuries were the most I had received in a long time since returning from any mission. Whilst I cleaned myself up, I decided to think of an operational name, but was interrupted by Ant's cursing and writhing as he came to. I gingerly hauled myself up on the worktop and smiled at him, pretending I was OK. It infuriated him.

Once he had calmed, there was silence, but then he began to laugh. Weirdly, he just stopped and eyed me. Blood dribbled from his head wound.

'You're in a lot if shit now,' he said.

'No more than normal. All I wanted were some answers.'

'You can't even see what we're trying to do to you, can you.'

'Keep pushing my buttons to wind me up.'

'Why, Johnny?'

I shrugged.

'And what about me and Steve letting you in on the action,' he said.

'Steve Steve? Just another wannabe.'

'Bollocks. And you know it. You didn't have to attack me for answers.' He tried to loosen the cord, but to no avail. 'Untie me and we can chat,' he said nicely.

'Oh yeah, like our last little chat.' I showed him my wounds.

He smiled. 'Call sign, fucking good ruck.'

I slipped down and pulled out Ant's pistol from my waistband, deliberately marvelling it. Upping the tension, I checked the mag, surprised to see armour piercing rounds. I loosely pointed at him.

'Question one: who do you work for?' I asked.

'You can't interrogate me to talk. Don't you remember me?'

The familiarity returned as he asked me some further questions in a different commanding voice. Then Ant started to shout orders and questions in a richer Irish accent—it clicked.

'You were the twat in the RTI training. The one shouting abuse and muscling me, putting me in horrid stress positions and sitting in on the interview in your balaclava.'

'I should have let my Rottweiler chew you a bit more.' Ant laughed.

I now recognised the laugh, the fucker who was always on my case. 'So, without the balaclava, this is how fucking ugly you are. Why did you always wear that? Fetish? Bit of extra bum-fun?'

'Because I knew one day, I might meet up with little pricks like you. Although, I thought it would be you dead first and not some of the other fine lads that passed selection.'

That one cut. I cocked the pistol.

'I'll only answer questions I want to,' he said. 'My name is Anthony Holder.'

'Who do you work for?' I asked.

'Steve.'

'Why?'

'All that SAS undercover expertise, I had to keep my skills alive. For about five years now.'

'What's his surname?'

'Don't know,' he answered lamely.

'Who does Steve work for?'

'Don't know.'

'Why are you both here?' I asked.

'I'm here to assist in finding Roy. Now that you know, untie me.'

'Bollocks, that's only the part truth. Why would you both bring such weaponry just to find a simple friend in a desperate state?'

'Anthony Holder is my name.'

'Who were the enemy chasing us?'

Ant looked over my shoulder and grinned.

I knew this was trouble.

CHAPTER TEN

Steve methodically took off his special winter jacket, trousers, and boots. Underneath he was wearing a tanned suede-jacket, black trousers, shirt, but no tie. He was focused as he slipped on his black shoes.

'Not a good look, Steve Steve.'

'Some say trouble follows you, Johnny, but I say you make it your own,' he said. 'This is how you repay Ant, is it?'

I didn't know what that last sentence meant, but did it matter, I knew the storm was coming. Steve took off his cufflinks.

'Lost your tie?' I mimicked.

'You OK, Ant?'

I turned to hear the shit Ant had to say but saw Steve in the broken mirror, quickly coming up behind me. Half-facing the threat, Steve thrust me backwards into the wall, grabbing me around the throat. My other hand was shoved up by the side of my head.

Bang! Bang!

My ears were ringing. Steve smashed my hand twice against the wall, and then with ferocity, slung it across my chest. I dropped the Browning. As I pulled my arm back, Steve grappled both hands around my throat and pushed. I hit him hard in the face, but it didn't release his pressure. Thinking quick, I dropped my hands and sharply lifted them up amid his elbows, forcing them out, breaking his grip. In an instant, he held onto my jacket. Lifting me, he forced me back into the wall. Grunting, I kicked him hard in the knee, then struck him on his inner thigh with my knee, but he didn't relent.

Desperation hit me as he clenched my throat again. Placing both hands behind the back of his head, I pulled him in. As he resisted, I used this a leverage and butted him on the forehead and immediately again on the bridge of the nose. Both battered, the blood converged. He mumbled as I smacked him in the temple. His eyes glared through a calm but possessed face. He threw me aside the room and I clattered over the worktop, pulling the cutlery draw onto me as I crumpled on the floor. Fuck me, he was more powerful that Ant. I stretched out a powerful kick to his shin as he attacked, and then twisted another to his outer thigh. That surely must have hurt, I thought, as Steve stumbled back without showing pain.

Rising quickly to my feet, I tried not to slide what was underfoot. I grabbed a knife, but Steve seized me from behind at elbow height and squeezed a bear hug. I should not have turned my back. Fighting for air, I back butted him in the face. However, he lifted me till I was on tiptoes and then tossed me behind. I still had hold of the kitchen knife as I scrambled to my feet. I thrust the knife, but from nowhere he blocked the tip with a chopping board. Instantaneously, he sharply kicked me on the hip and then ripped away the board and embedded knife. My following fast punches and elbow strikes he blocked with the same ferocity, far superior in Martial Arts.

In an aggressive attempt to gain back control, I rugby tackled him over the sofa. On top, I punched him in the gut, ribs, and face, but he showed no agony in the brutal assault. I had forgotten Ant was in the room, until I had heard him screaming for Steve to show me no mercy. Steve's fingers clutched my face and ripped at my skin; I yelled. Eyes watering, he lifted me over the top of him with his knee, crash landing on the mess caused by the fight with Ant. I was to my feet at the same speed as him, but instead of attacking Steve, I moved away, throwing anything at him that came to hand. Ornaments and objects smashed into him as he came forward, but Steve managed to block some of them. He kept coming, and I had run out of things to throw.

Panic started to set in as the sweat, or was it blood, blurred my vision. Blinking hard, I blocked his barrage of strikes, but he speedily dropped on one hand and leg swiped me. Laying on the floor, winded, I seized a large piece of mirror, swinging it into his thigh. I followed a toe-punt to his groin. For the first time, Steve appeared a little stunned as he staggered back. Spurred on, even with my immobilised leg, I raced to a stand. I hit him in the face; one, two, three, and then trailed with a crunching elbow strike. Somehow, he seized my arms, pirouetted me, and launched me through an open door to another room.

Steve stood in the doorway, blood dripped from his nose and wound, but no sweat, unlike my soaked body. I chucked more objects to disoriented him, to give me a split-second to reevaluate. Managing to stand as he swatted the items away, I retreated to the back of the room, spotting a broom. He must have read the situation as he made a move, but I had picked up the broom and tried to swipe him. Knowing he would block it, I switched course and jabbed it into his throat, pushing him away. Steve snapped the broom in half with a strike, plummeting me onto him. In desperation, I struck lower body blows, pushing him back into the main room. I was breathing heavy.

Both upright, fists in guard, we began to trade blows. I was knackered. Intuition took over: never give up; however, I had become weaker. Images of Baha's cronies overpowering me flashed before my eyes. I did not want to lose. Clutching onto him like an out of steam boxer, I found the glass imbedded in his leg and twisted it. He didn't scream, but that pause, that tiny release, gave me enough strength to shove him away. Groggily running for the exit, my shoulders were twisted around, but my punches seemed as if I was carrying an anvil. The slow thumps managed to make contact, but he wasn't really defending them. Was he conserving energy? Suddenly, his forehead came in, the pain splashed through my skull as the psychedelic shapes turned the lights off.

First into the blurred vision was a light with a person leaning over it. My face ached. I went to touch it, but my arms had been restrained by my sides, tied to a chair in only my boxer-shorts. Sore, and now seriously pissed off, I crooked my neck to the left and right.

'Are you going to be a good lad?' Ant asked.

Looming out of the shadows, Ant was wearing the same artic military gear that Steve had on earlier, except his pouches were full of grenades and ammo. His head wound had been stitched. The room was a mess. Ironically, the chair I was on was the last bit of furniture to survive. I began to tremble, blaming it on having no heating.

'You must be hungry,' Ant said.

Through a gap in the blinds, it was pitch-black outside. More strewn items caught my attention. Blood splattered the floor. Steve was leaning over a mini-laptop on the kitchen side.

'Did you not hear what I said?' Ant asked.

My body was red and was aching all over. Even so, I tried to move my wrists and ankles from the restraints. The frustration, combined with the humiliation, was eating me.

'If you're calm, I'll untie you and give you some painkillers,' Ant said.

'Go fuck yourself,' I said, hoarse.

'Some fight. I did warn…'

'Like I said, fuck off, Ant. I've still got plenty in me to see…'

'Johnny, listen in,' Steve interrupted.

'You can go fuck yourself as well,' I blurted.

Steve sighed and then continued looking at the screen, without a care in the world.

'How's the leg?' I asked him.

'We need to sort a few things,' he answered.

'You had the chance to sort me, so why didn't you finish me?' I croaked.

'We've got a few questions, as I'm sure you have. Right?' he said. 'Ant, untie him.'

Ant nodded and then slipped around the back. The rope was cut to my ankles first, and then my arms. They fell forward. I didn't want to show the pain. Ant stood in front of me and slid his knife away, slowly, making sure I got the message. Impulsive thoughts told me to grab the weapon and take them on, but I overruled.

'Yeah, I have a few questions, but before you answer all of them, I need a brew and some scoff. Can you manage that with your busted body, Ant. Shocking, hey?'

Ant rubbed his neck and cheek where I had zapped him. 'Fucking outrageous.'

'Well go on then,' I demanded. 'Or do you need to ask Steve Steve,' I said patronisingly.

Ant half-grinned and went back to the kitchen, moodily kicking the stuff around his feet.

Steve grabbed a large, cubed leather poof and sat about a metre away; glass crunched under it. He studied me. I felt slightly unnerved but could not help but smile at his lumps and abrasions. I managed to pacify my revenge to launch at him. I started laughing with them. I had not laughed for ages, it was painful.

'Fuck knows what the other guy must be like,' I said.

'You are a feisty fighter,' Steve said.

'Fighter? Girl more like,' Ant chipped in.

'Says the over-sized, hormonal woman,' I retorted.

'I see from your scars you've lost a few fights,' Ant said.

'Just trophies,' I said, and hid the self-harming.

'I find it incredible you returned to Afghanistan on your own after the first disaster, let alone for a female doctor, but what exactly happened in Yemen?'

My mouth could have dropped open. 'That was straight to the point, Steve Steve.'

Taking a cup of coffee from Ant, I didn't retaliate that I had actually wanted tea. I took a sip through my inflamed lips. Steve gently took a sip of his.

'I know you headed to Hordio,' Steve boasted, out of the blue.

How did he know? Why did he want me to fill the blanks? What the fuck has it got to do with finding Roy? Shit, Roy. Had the trail gone? Guilt followed. Ant waved his hand in front of my face.

'Johnny? Operation Vacant,' he said.

I swatted his hand away, which he didn't like—good. 'I'll do a deal with you, Steve Steve,' I said. 'I'll let you in on the missing gaps, including my recent time in Indonesia, if you tell me why you are here. Deal?'

'OK.'

Ant put the sofa back on its feet. I sat down on it first, spreading out, overdoing the comfortable feeling and that there was no room. Ant begrudgingly handed me a bowl; my fingers still swollen.

'What the fuck is this?'

'Tined peaches, Johnny. Thought you may find it easier to swallow.'

'Cheers,' I said sarcastically.

Over more drinks and tinned fruit, I had shared parts of Operation Blue Halo. I was surprised there had been no questions, but Steve had stated details that I had purposely had not mentioned. When it came to the short version of Operation Last Assault, Steve had asked quite a few questions, but nothing specific, more so what happened to key people. I had answered all with the truth. It didn't shock them how I had dealt with Abishua and his henchman. I had changed the names of Simon and Trevor; also, not replying to any personal probing about my family. Ant had kept quiet the whole time, not even any stupid or insulting comments.

When I started to tell them about Operation Poppy Pride, Steve started to get into his white and black winter-ops clothing—rude. Had he heard enough? Once I got to the bit where I was dangling off the cliff, I stopped, having been in this situation telling this part before, many times. I had never believed it properly, let alone anyone else. It was still a mind-fuck. Again, I pondered on how to continue, but was urged to get on with it. I told them the whole story, right up to when I awoke in the hospital back in my time, leaving out the private part about my dad.

The sound of me eating oat biscuits seemed loud, exaggerating the awkwardness.

'How did you end up at Roy's house?' Ant asked.

'I've not been right for a while, lost my positive mindset. You know, not normal.'

No one replied whilst I stared hard at the floor, my eyes welling. There was no encouragement to continue, but no sympathy either. I slowly released my pent-up breath.

'I've been sleeping rough for a few months,' I said.

'Where?' Steve asked.

'Somewhere I could let my troubles float away with the wash, and let the stars keep my hopes alive.'

Ant pulled an astonished expression. 'Sorry to hear that, mate.'

'I wanted to get away from people. I found it easier to drink the days and nights away to rid the darkness that was inside me.'

Their concentration was palatable, and Ant moved forward on the chair.

'I've become a drunk, a tramp, as Monkfish had said.'

'Monkfish?' Ant cried. 'Chris Breedon?'

'Yes. I met him on the cliff's edge when it was the end for me. I was about to cut the rope when he interrupted me. He was up there for the same reasons. You remember him, then? He passed...'

'We know him,' Steve interrupted, and looked at Ant.

I tried to evaluate the stare.

'That doesn't explain how you ended up at Roy's,' Ant said impatiently.

'Me and Monkfish met for a drink after; well, we obviously didn't jump,' I said.

'Why was he on the cliff? I mean, I know why, but how did he end up in that position?' Steve asked.

'Because he had been through the same shit as me, losing his loved ones and not adapting to civi life. Something you would know nothing about.'

Both scoffed.

I didn't like the smirks on their faces. Steve started to put his webbing and other kit on. Aching still, I retrieved the blue letter from my trousers that lay crumpled on the floor. I thrust it at Steve.

'It's true. Look. Read it,' I demanded.

'Was this what you snatched from me in the van?' he asked.

'Yes. At the time it was none of your business.'

Steve read it, then handed it to Ant, who moved it in and out until he could focus. He stared at me, folded it, and gave it back.

'You've not read it. Why?' Steve asked.

How did he know? I rubbed the letter anxiously, pondering how to answer.

'I don't think anything else will shock us about you, Johnny. You've been through too much shit. You've let the black dogs in,' Ant said.

'Black…' I stopped, knowing what he had meant.

'Take your time to answer, mate,' Ant said, and leant forward and meaningfully patted my knee.

I tried not to clam up, holding back the tears. 'I only found the letter in Monkfish's van after I got into a bit of trouble in Padstow.'

'So, what's the big deal?' Ant asked.

'I ended up gently punching a guy in the face for being a twat.'

'Gently?' they said simultaneously.

Steve stroked swollen his nose, whilst Ant held the back of his head.

'Honestly,' I exclaimed. 'The next thing, this young lad went down like a sack of shit and started fitting. Monkfish tried to help with CPR. He then pulled me aside to say I should leave. Later, Monkfish told me the lad was dead.'

'What from?' Ant cross examined.

'I assume from hitting his head on the road. I wasn't going to hang around to find out. Cowardly, I know, but I couldn't deal with it in the state I was. I was about to leave the country when Monkfish let it slip about his ex-wife knowing Christine, and that Roy had gone missing. Or something like that, it was all a daze.' I looked down at the crumpled letter, annoyed I could ruin something so personal.

'One last question: do you know why Monkfish was thrown out the Regiment?' Steve asked.

'Are you asking me do I know because you know?'

'It's a simple question, Johnny?' Ant chipped in.

I sighed. 'Like me, he had smuggled an illegal firearm and was found out. However, I got away with it.'

'Thanks for your honesty,' Steve said.

I took in a deep breath and exhaled. Something had been lifted. I held out my cut and bruised hand to Ant; we gently shook.

'I'm sorry for the way it turned out between us, Ant,' I said.

'Mate, how can you be ordinary after serving in the sex before suntan?'

I half-smiled as I had not heard that SBS saying for many years, even though there were a few variations.

'Sure, your mind currently is like emptying a cutlery draw onto a trampoline, but who the fuck can criticise you after the shit you've been through. Just keep the black dogs in their kennel. The MO that gave you some *tablets* should have done more to keep up your counselling. You had the wrong CO, mate.' He winked at me. 'At least you're dealing with your problems head on now.'

'And Johnny's alive to hear that,' Steve added.

It was like I was back in a team, at last. I thought of my CO, Dick Brown, for setting me up for the fall of the helicopter crash—nasty traitor.

'And, Johnny, stop thinking about the past negative,' Ant said. 'Would you want to return to that bad shit?'

I nodded my head in recognition.

'How about, Operation End of The Line?' Ant blurted.

'What's that got to do with this mission?' I asked.

'A metaphor, like when you were going to cut the line, your rope.'

I frowned, showing my displeasure.

'You've stopped handling your emotions, Johnny,' Steve said.

'Well, except the unrestricted violence,' Ant said, and showed me the table leg.

'Lucky it wasn't the table,' I bantered. 'So, Steve Steve, what's your background?'

'I'm going to be short as we've a job to finish to find Roy. Outside what I belong to, you are the first two I have ever told.'

'He's going to have to kill us after, Johnny,' Ant said—the timing wasn't funny.

'Both my parents died when I was young,' Steve begun. 'I became a bad boy going through different foster parents, schools, and hostels. Still the outlaw teenager, I was approached in a detention unit by a kind man in a suit, offering me a new beginning. To wipe the slate clean, to forget my past. I was left to think about it over a weekend. After another big fight where I got a pasting from a group of men, I decided to agree. I had to; I was barely sixteen.'

Steve delved into a bag and chucked me some thermal trousers and vest, instructing me wear them. About time, I was still cold. Hopefully, I was getting the rest of the full kit like theirs, I thought. Steve picked two pills from a ready pack and swallowed them. Ant handed me two tablets from a small bottle. I mistrustfully stared at him.

'You don't want his 'stay awake' tablets, believe me,' Ant said, and held open his eyes and crazily twitched. 'These are large painkillers.' Ant swallowed one.

'Why do I get two?'

'Because you've had two beatings,' he replied, and chuckled.

'Funny, not.' Trusting him, I swallow hard and then faced Steve who looked wide awake. 'Who was the bloke in the suit that visited you in prison? Did he shop at the same shit shops as you?' I laughed—only Ant joined in.

'This man saved me from spiralling out of control,' Steve said. 'He introduced me to the organisation I'm still with now. After six years of specialised training, and I mean seven days a week, and a few medical operations, I was ready to work for them.'

'Who is "them"?' I asked.

Steve snorted. 'They are the eyes and ears of every British special-ops. We are a select surreptitious Elite who have been trained beyond any calibre. We lurk in the background, or use specialist equipment, watching, listening, making notes, making important decisions.'

'Hold on. Are you telling me that on black-ops, you lot are there? That would take a hell of a lot of secret manpower and gadgetry.'

Steve smugly nodded. 'We also watch certain individuals after, infiltrating their families and friends.'

'I don't get it. Why?'

'In case some of you go rogue, off the rails, blabbing to the highest bidder, the next criminal mastermind, etcetera. I've seen many serving and ex-serving wind up like you.'

Uneasy, I thought about the next question. 'Are you above MI5, an assassin?'

'I've been in that moment your life flashes before your eyes, and you try to think of loved ones. The freeze point, that blank instant, where a muzzle is put to your head, but I'm the one standing over the rogue.'

I let it sink in what he had just said, provoking the same situation I had been in, but at the end of a barrel. 'Do you think it's me who killed Planet, Shrek, and Fish?'

'No.'

'What about Kyle and Sameer?'

'No.'

I tried not show my relief. 'Was I justified to kill all the evil that came my way?'

'Perhaps.'

'Aren't I just the same as you?'

'No.'

'Not after all his medical experiments,' Ant said, but then realised he opened his big gob.

I looked at Ant for more info.

'Parts of my brain and nervous system has been modified,' Steve admitted. 'I hardly feel pain, and the fear receptacles have been tampered with.'

I was astonished but knew there was more. 'Fear keeps you alert.'

'I hardly sleep,' Steve said. 'I don't stop when I am exhausted, I stop when the job is done.'

'And there was I thinking you were the one who was behind Roy's abduction,' I mocked. 'Am I the rogue?'

'I think you would know,' Steve replied.

'Why didn't you kill the kid in the jungle?' Ant asked.

That's odd to bring that up, I thought.

'I would have,' Ant butted in. 'Just another target with a weapon. I don't give a fuck.'

'I reckon you would have gotten along fine with Planet, Shrek, and Fish,' I said. 'Like two dingo balls in the same sack, mate,' I said in an Australian accent, like Ocker.

'Why are you saying that in a Pakistani's voice?' Ant said seriously. 'Dingos are Australian.'

'Piss off.'

'Fish was a bit of a dead head,' Steve blurted.

'Fuck you. Most intelligent bloke I know,' I retorted.

'Thick as a turd after five pints of Guinness,' Ant uttered.

For a second, I was going to explode into rant about disrespecting the third mate, but realised their test was to see if I would have lost control. They had been doing this from day one. Why? Then it became obvious: this was to get me back to my former-self and to keep the black dogs chained up.

'He was cleverer silent, than the diarrhoea you two speak,' I said, relaxed.

Both smiled.

This could go on all night, I thought, and Steve looked itching to move on. 'One more question you've skirted around: who were the enemy at the hotel?' I asked.

Beep... beep... beep!

A small alarm had sounded on the laptop. Steve rapidly got up and checked the screen.

'Get dressed. We've got company,' he calmly said.

'Who? Where's my kit?' I asked.

Ant slapped my old clothes on my lap and then made his pistol and main weapon ready.

'Where's my gear?' I asked.

Steve systematically placed a plastic fuel-can on the vintage Aga oven's already hot plate.

'Where's my jacket and hat at least?' I pleaded.

'Perhaps you need to be reminded of your Elite skill,' Ant said.

Steve put on a white full-face mask and pulled over his hood. The corner lamp's light was killed.

'Stand by,' Ant whispered.

CHAPTER ELEVEN

Even though with only jeans, a t-shirt, sweater, and a jacket to wear, I didn't even have time to tie my Cat-boot laces properly. The silent pressure from Ant and Steve, and the thought of being cooked alive, was growing. At the back door, Steve mumbled under his mask. Ant turned and told me to cover my eyes. He was wearing an identical mask. I stared Ant's one-way lenses. Frustrated, he nodded at me to do as he said, then pulled down a black outer lens. Grabbing me by the scruff, he felt the door liner, then blindly touched the back of Steve. Could he not see? What the fuck was the point of that?

In the moonlight, Steve rapidly opened one of his chest pouches and loaded the grenade into his weapon. He waited, searching the forest, and I guessed, tunning in. Had his hearing been modified? What a stupid thought. Why were we waiting so long? The thought of the melting fuel-can almost made me take off on my own path. I hoped Steve and Ant had remembered. I was just about to speak up when Steve tapped Ant's hand. Ant warned me to shut my eyes. I heard the pop, a small fizz sound echoed, then an extraordinary bright light flashed—intense. Even with my eyes shut I had to shield away.

Suddenly, I was on the move, trying to keep a grip on the snow laden floor. Another pop came from the front, followed by the penetrating blinding source. I still couldn't face the light. We stopped, then a metal on metal clicked, followed by a small beep. Ant's fingers dug in, dragging me along again at speed. One further forceful light grenade was fired.

I really needed to open my eyes as I was now being hauled down a bank. Twigs and branches smacked me in the face, igniting the recent injuries. Was the fucker getting his own back for the wheelchair knocks?

BOOOM!

Debris gusted over the top of me, and I almost tumbled over the back of Ant; he cursed me. A wave of heat wafted above, then my feet began splashing through water, leaving the crackling popping behind. The pace was forceful. Twice I had stumbled, nearly twisting my ankle, swearing Ant to slow-up.

Without warning, as if lost in no man's land, the grip on my shoulder had released. I touched what was in front of me—nothing. I had to open my eyes. Peeking, there stood Ant and Steve. Both had lifted their black visors. Even with their masks on I could tell they were amused. It was like watching Star Wars clone troopers tilt their heads. I was ankle deep in very cold water. Ant gave me the wanker sign.

'How fucking long ago could I have opened my eyes?' I ranted.

'Did you not hear me shout at you could back at the car?' Ant said faintly.

'Bollocks did you. And what was that explosion?'

'Deny everything into the enemy's hands,' Ant said.

'And what's with the Halo gaming mask? I bet you sit playing your Xbox with it on.'

'What the fuck's Halo? We're too old to...'

BOOOM!

My neck sunk into my shoulders; both their masks reflected the huge fireball. I swung around to see the orange and yellow glow, followed by flames licking into the black night. The fierce light beyond the crest lit up the whole area, like an alien's craft had landed. Bits of the wreckage clunked into the trees.

'Hope you didn't leave your vodka in the car,' Ant jested. 'Oh, no, you drank it, you drunk.'

It was something I wanted to forget, and my discomfort must have shown. I had no counter reply.

'Let's move,' Steve ordered.

I was having big trouble breathing through my nose, so I held one side at a time and blew the shit out—painful. The mess landed in the stream below. It was then I realised how cold and numb my feet were. I went to give Steve and Ant grief about the lack of suitable clothing for me, but lifting my head from where I was running, they had made at least ten metres up stream.

'Wankers,' I muttered.

Leaving the burning smells and carnage behind, I tripped and stumbled to try catch them. Pissed off, I jumped out and ran along the foot-high level bank. Steve half-turned, then continued facing forward. Ant stopped and put his hands on his hips, body language showing he was not impressed. As I reached him, the distant sound of mutts barked. Ant pointed behind. Fearing the worst, as I had not had good previous with mutt chases, I looked at my tracks in the snow. Fuck. Ant didn't have to point at the water for me to get in, he must have known I felt a careless dickhead. I told him it was all right for him in his designer babygrow and boots, but the joke must have fallen flat as he put his finger on his mask to tell me to shut the fuck up.

I know I have not been karate training and keeping fit, and on any other mission since Poppy Pride, but keeping up at their medium jogging pace through the foot-high water was impossible. I had begun to fall back, too far. If we were in the open desert at night, like Roy and I were, I could get lost. Trudging along, I thought of that escape and evasion in Afghanistan. It kept me and my morale going, the mind overcoming the body's request to stop. Digging deeper, the tiredness and pain went. I had not felt like this for many moons. I thought on about Roy. Whatever was going on with him, I hoped he was thinking back on our miracle escapes, remembering more than once he had saved my life.

Stupidly, I had not realised the icy water was now above my knee until I was almost at a standstill, bogged down with weight and exhaustion. Fortunately, Ant had stopped on the bank. I took hold of his glove and he heaved me out.

'Where the fuck is Steve?' I asked.

Ant pointed to my left.

I followed his hand signal to a large boulder below a rock face, but couldn't see anything, even after opening my eyes wide and then squinting. Ant pulled down his hood and took off his mask, shutting his eyes, then blinking furiously. His head was steaming into the brisk night. I placed the warm mask against my face and stared where I thought Steve was. Incredibly, it was like looking through yellow day-driving glasses. Even better, they had a retina display that followed the eye, with a hub at the bottom.

'Your standard torchlight, car headlights, and bright light doesn't interfere, but the latest "eclipse grenade" can be viewed through the shield,' Ant bragged.

Steve was stood on the boulder's edge sighting his weapon in the direction we had run. A thin white beam pierced out of his weapon. The bottom of the mask's hub stated 'friendly'. I started to look around, like the first time you look through any night enhancement. This was way beyond anything I have seen. Ant pressed a button on the side.

The view went to thermal image, but Steve's suit and weapon did not register—I wanted a mask.

'Commander Steve Steve,' I said.

He looked down at me.

'Ant said I could keep this,' I lied.

He shook his head.

After a little childish struggle, Ant eventually got the mask and he wiped the residue where I had been rasping. For ten seconds or so I could see jack shit. Unbeknown to me, Steve had returned. Frostily, Steve took Ant away. By their body language, Ant was getting a roasting. I smiled. Once they had finished, both started to plant spiked white objects in the snow.

'Trip flares?' I asked.

'Coupled with an electronic countermeasure,' Ant said.

Steve pressed on a handheld gadget similar to a GPS. It appeared not to work as the screen was black, but they continued to talk about the direction. Steve set off. In the excitement of the new gadgets, I had not realised my sweat had turned me even colder. Shivering uncontrollably, I gritted my teeth and followed, my steps more of a plod compared to their quick tab. I suddenly realised they had been testing my skills from the time I had met them. Therefore, they had kept back my clothes.

The stream opened into other tributaries. We had followed a main torrent upstream for about a klick, crossing large boulders at times. As we now tabbed across a plateau of cervices, my boot came off. Whilst my freezing hands tied the frozen bootlaces, I knew they were looking on; embarrassment was the only warming thing.

Again, it was not long before I needed a rest, but I didn't want to admit it, which was dangerous. My fitness and resilience were also being tested. I had kept up fairly good, but they had slowed down to make allowances. In the end, I yelled at them I needed a break, and then sat on a large rock. First to sit next to me was Ant. Steve kept watch. I could not feel my feet whilst I blew into my numb hands. Ant took his glove off, dangling from a cord from his coat.

'Your mum tie string through your coat so you didn't lose them,' I said, and laughed through chattering.

Ant held my hands; unbelievably hot. 'Lovely, heated suit this,' he said. 'How's your Marks and Spencer thermals?'

'Heated? How? From what?' I arched back and stared at Steve.

He put his thumb up.

'Wankers,' I mumbled.

'I bet you wish you were back in the warm Indonesian jungle with Shere Khan,' Ant said.

'Shere Khan? Oh fuck off,' I said, realising the tiger joke.

'Here you go, mate,' Ant said.

Extraordinarily, Ant handed me a heated ration pack, a sublime feeling in my numb hands. When did he cook that? I ripped the top off and squeezed the mushy contents into my mouth, not knowing what flavour, but sweet, heavenly.

'Mind the pubes in that,' Ant said.

'What the fuck?' I said.

'That wasn't warmed by electrodes and a battery pack. Got that from my sweaty bollocks, mate.'

I grimaced.

'How about, Operation Cliff Hanger?' Ant blurted.

'Will you shut the fuck up with mission names, unless they have something to do with finding Roy,' I blasted. 'I'd rather work alone.'

Ant tapped his ear. 'Sorry, mate, did you just say, you wear cologne?'

'Let's move,' Steve mumbled under his mask.

Standing up and stretching, was testing. Northwest was a silhouette of large mountain looming into the star-filled night. Except for the water running, the tranquillity was stunning. I had navigated by the stars on many occasions. Feeling my good past was returning, Ant took his time to marvel the same views, taking a big sniff of fresh air.

'Do you ever think about what the world was like before humans?' Ant asked. 'Probably nice.'

'My mate, Spike, once said, "We don't even know what dinosaurs sounded like. They could have spoken fluent Italian for all we know."'

Ant laughed. 'You've got some fucking weird mates.'

'Yep, and you're on the top of the list.'

'That's Whitehorn mountain. Oh, that's if you get lost, because your top mate on the list leaves you behind,' he said facetiously.

'Where are we heading?' I asked, bringing the conversation back to seriousness.

'An emergency retreat-shack half a klick west of Emperor Falls. Apparently used by bear hunters.'

'How did…'

'Steve found a GPS co-ordination left on a pad,' Ant interrupted.

'Steve knows a lot of stuff,' I said, and pondered… 'Were you there in Operation Blue Halo, Steve Steve?'

'Yes. Now we need to get moving, if you have stopped both being such idiots, that is.'

'How did you get extracted?'

Steve had started to climb up the next boulder but stopped and looked back at me. 'By Chinook, an hour later after you guys were extracted,' he replied.

'But there were no more Chinooks, as one was out of…' I had realised. 'Fuck me,' I fumed. 'That's why we were told there was only one Chinook. Cunts.'

Ant looked at the ground.

I climbed up to Steve's level. 'Did you fly over the crash site, Steve?'

'Let's move,' he said.

I went to grab his shoulder as he had turned to head out, but Ant grabbed my arm and shook his head.

As we crossed different terrains, rocky pastures, forests, and frozen water, I had navigated by the stars that we were heading east. Of course, I could not get what Steve had said out of my mind. I was seriously pissed and wanted more answers. I had warmed up considerably. Was it the food, or was it I was enraged?

The snow in places was above my boots, making it difficult moving, but seeing Steve ahead, I wanted to get closer. Ant suddenly held his fist up at the base off a snow-covered rocky hill. Water flowed close by. I went down on one knee whilst Ant swept the area. Steve, weapon in his shoulder, carried onto the base of the rocks. I hated not having the same weapons, or any, in fact. Was this another test?

In what appeared an eternity in the cold, deathly silence, I noticed the snow melting around Ant's white snow boots. Surely not? My mind started to go into a rant, but then Steve returned. He took off his mask, immediately rubbing his eyes.

'Found a lie up position till the morning. It's…'

'I hope it has fucking central heating, Steve Steve,' I butted in. 'Oh, you two don't fucking need it, do you.'

'Being an elongated cave set a far way back in the face, we'll get a fire going. Let's move,' Steve said.

'Great. And you two telly-tubbies can get the fucking wood,' I ranted.

Ant tapped me on the back. 'Pull up your pre-school socks on that last remark?'

'I fucking can't, they're frozen in my boots,' I retorted.

As we entered the cave, Steve passed me a torch, then flipped his mask. I shone beam forwards; shadows dauntingly moved in the chasm as my hand shook. Walking in further, my teeth chattered.

'Did you follow me when I returned to Afghan to have closure on my lost mates?' I asked.

Steve sighed, his breath catching in the beam. 'You were being tracked, but not by me. Other operatives were already in the area.'

'You mean your lot watched me struggle, nearly losing my life, right from the parachute insertion?'

'No. We lost track of you. We only picked up messages that were intercepted after the car explosion at the hospital.'

'You know who sent the messages don't you.'

'One of David Charles' ex-members who was in the shadows watching the hospital.'

'So why didn't your guys come and rescue me from nearly getting my head cut off?'

'A lot of other trouble was going on at the time out there, and you were a hard person to keep track of. Plus, David's friends sorted it. You must have been nuts to be alone in the middle of Kabul, and just to find a woman.'

'If you had the manpower in Afghanistan, why the fuck didn't you rescue us at the Chinook crash?'

'I had no orders to.'

At the end of the cave, Steve and Ant took off their packs, whilst I stuck my hands under my armpits. A stale odour wafted as they kicked at the sandy floor. What was it? Like shit mixed with the smell of a zebra pen. For a moment, it took my thoughts off Steve, but my frustration soon returned. Ant put on a lamp-light.

'Did you track me across to Yemen to find Larry Schultz?' I asked.

Steve stayed silent.

'I'm fucking asking you a question.'

'Let it go, Johnny,' Ant said, 'remember when it's right to flick...'

'I'm not fucking speaking to you, so keep your busted face out of my business.'

Steve sighed. 'I wasn't assigned to that mission, but I had interest in other rogues who had been on the radar for quite a while. However, I heard about you again once you touched down in Washington.'

I was speechless.

'Now, if we don't get a fire going, you will die of hypothermia. Remember?' Steve walked by.

I stood in his way. 'What about Indonesia?'

'Once you had left Minangkabau International Airport, it was impossible to monitor you.'

'That's bollocks.'

Steve pushed me back, the torch beam bouncing around. 'Out of my way.'

'You and your agency had watched me in the shadows, but when I'd hit the lowest point and ended up nearly cutting the rope, you do absolutely fuck all,' I said, too emotional.

'I had no ord…'

I hit him square in the face.

There was a big scuffle with a mass of punches and kicks. I wasn't even sure if it was Ant or Steve I was connecting with, and vice-versa. Eventually, it was Ant who pinned me to the ground, also making sure he kept Steve off me. Ant leant into my face.

'You've got to stop kicking off at us,' he yelled. 'When was the last time you had any part of the brotherhood?'

I relaxed my grip, thinking.

'When was the last time you felt this energised, positive, a part of something, rather than pissing it up every day? When was the last time you stopped fucking up your life and feeling sorry for yourself? Hey?' Ant shook me.

I reapplied my grip on his jacket.

'We've been through more blood, sweat, and emotions together in the last twenty-four-hours than most that have worked together for years. Now fucking sort your shit out whilst me and Steve collect some firewood.'

I took my hands from his jacket.

Getting to his feet, he bonded my hand with his and pulled me up. 'All sufferings have rewards, mate. It's never over, just remember that.'

It had not taken them long to get a fire started, and for the wetness of the logs and branches to evaporate. Chilblains gripped my naked feet as I curled my toes back and forth in front of the fire. My hands stung with the new warmth. Steam rose from my wet socks and boots. We sat around eating and drinking rations, reminding me of previous SBS exercises; also, when me and Roy had lit a fire in the Afghan cave. This exposure to my previous life to bring me back from desperation was working. Ant had given me some painkillers. I wasn't sure if it was these making me feel relaxed, or the glow of the fire.

'Steve, you managed to trick Christine into believing you were Roy's best chum, how?' I asked.

'You're not going to kick off, are you?' Ant said. 'Hey, Operation Kick Off.'

'No,' I said. 'I feel I've vented enough. And thanks for the little chat by the way.'

Ant nodded his appreciation.

Steve stopped sorting his kit and said, 'I just turned up pretending to see an old mate. I had enough intel on Roy to fool Christine that I had worked with him. It just unfolded from there.'

'Why did you turn up? Has Roy gone rogue?'

'No.'

'I won't let you kill him.'

'I understand.'

'You sent me the map and postcard, didn't you?' I asked.

'No.'

His one-word answers normally grated on me, but this time I couldn't be bothered. I yawned and rested on my side, watching the glow. Yet, more thoughts niggled me.

'Why are you tracking Roy?' I asked. 'Has it got something to do with the enemy that are after you?'

'All will become clear in the morning,' Ant answered. 'We promise we'll tell you. Operation Edge is on, and it's going to be fucking exhilarating.'

'Operation Edge?' I mumbled, my eyes closing. Fucking exhilarating, I thought, be careful what you wish for. Again, my recollections turned to Roy.

★

My dream played the memories again, but different from before. Everyone was in good spirits. I was having a beer with my dad in Newquay. He was so proud of me. It was a fantastic feeling. Ella, now single, came to the pub the same day. We cried, laughed, and flirted. No one discussed my past problems. Why would they? They were over. I had a new drive in life. We chatted about the animal paradise and wonders of the Indonesian jungle. I told them about each character I had met but left out the deaths. After more beer and stories, my dad asked if I had seen the majestic tiger. The music stopped; the lights dimmed. A deep roar echoed around the pub; gun-shots quickly followed.

Shocking me into opening my eyes, the fire had reduced to glowing embers. How long had I been asleep?

Bang, bang, bang!

Sitting bolt upright, I first noticed Ant and Steve were missing. Had the enemy found us? The same roar from my dream reverberated down the cave. My heart came into my throat.

CHAPTER TWELVE

A bulking mass blocked the moonlight shining into the cave. A deep, husky breath resounded off the walls. Gradually, inconspicuously, I scraped backwards till I found the cave wall, squeezing myself tight into a crevice. Again, the grizzly roared. It suddenly charged, paws thudding, the vibrations coming through my body. I held my breath, but it skidded to a stop a metre from the fire, sending dust over me. Through the smoke from the embers, the bear grabbed the kit from the floor and violently shook it in its teeth, growling, snarling. What fell out, its huge claws ripped at, then it violently chewed. The embers abruptly caught ablaze with one of the torn backpacks. The emitting light shimmered off the cinnamon-brown fur. This made the bear angrier, making its rage known with a bellowing growl. The colossus stood up on it hind legs, before punching to the ground. The shockwave rippled through its powerful brawny forelegs to the muscular hump on its shoulders.

Whilst I was breathing in short bursts, the bear's snorting became lame. It took a few wobbled steps backwards, crashing to the floor. The odour I had smelt earlier became stronger. A loud belly growl reverberated, but I could not see what this probable fifty-stone beast was doing due to the smoking and fizzing fire. I waited.

The fumes were becoming unbearable, along with trying to disguise my choking. I nervously reached out and placed a wet sandy sock across my mouth and nose. I dared to scrape out of my hide, inch by inch. Cautiously standing, I searched for some sort of weapon, but my eyes were still watering. I had to get the mass of burning pack off the flames.

Everything that was not on the fire was wrecked, including the transparent mags. Thank fuck the two remaining grenades were not on the fire. I didn't want to risk waking the beast, but I had to clear the haze so I could see my way past. Putting my hand inside the only available boot, I slowly pushed the smouldering, gooey mess off the flames. The embers lit up the ceiling. Coughing in my throat, I slowly covered the burnt mess in earth. A weird sound came from the bear, the beast I still could not see properly. Heart fluttering, I scarpered back into my original hide.

Once the fire had died down to embers and the smoke had cleared, I raised my eyeline to see the dished-faced bear staring at me. A cold chill ran through my bones. Locked in perpetual fright, I noticed a dark liquid forming under its neck and snout. Apart from the odd crackle, peace cloaked the cave. Was that blood? Was it dead? Why? How?

From the glow, I looked down at my trembling hands, clenching them after. Gradually, I pulled myself out and half-stood. Barefooted, I crept around the fire. Fuck. I held in the agony as I rapidly scraped the burning ember off my sole. The cool sand quenched the pain. Eyes wider, I checked the path that I needed to take towards the bear. At the back of my mind, I had visions of it springing to life; the roar played out. It was fucking huge. Shredded white material clung to its evil claws. I stopped and listened for the slightest breathing—nothing. The embers glowed in its eyes, tiny in comparison to the rest of the bulking beast. Painfully slow, I edged past, but out of the shadow I became interested in the liquid oozing into the dirt. Bending down, heart beating like a steam train, I leant out and touched it. Up close to my face, the warm blood felt good on my cold hands. Stupidly, I got onto my knees and put my ear to its mouth—lifeless.

Overwhelmed, but then furious that this bear could have ripped me apart, I stood up and kicked it. The adrenaline and relief trembled through me. I cursed it for good measure, but then a part of me realised the sadness to see this magnificent creature dead. I touched its fur, a surreal moment. Oddly, I wanted to see the size of its teeth. Up close I lifted the huge top lip. Its large teeth were covered in blood and small remnants, like it had eaten a steak. Fuck. What the hell was I doing? Steve and Ant, I thought.

I leapfrogged the eight-feet body and ran out of the cave, only to be confronted with like that of a horror scene from the *Texas Chainsaw Massacre*. Adrenalin blocked out the churned snow and blood mix. I continued across the rutted ground. Suddenly, I stopped at the forest edge. Freezing to the spot, I opened my eyes as large as possible, even looking at the moon, as if asking for some help on what I could not see properly. Instantly searching my pocket, I pulled out a mini-torch that Ant had given me in jest: "the only thing I could properly use".

The beam carefully waved across the fur. Around its dead body were bits of clothing mixed with blood and gore. From under its forearm, a pink hand protruded, almost as if grabbing the air. In a panic, almost dropping the torch, I sprinted to the bear and heaved back on its neck, but only managed to move the shoulder six inches. However, gruesomely, it had exposed the mashed face of Ant. Again, I grappled, heaved, and with a new amount of strength not seen for a long time, I managed to pull Ant out.

I knelt on the bear to keep my feet out of the snow. Because of the severe lacerations to Ant's neck and face, I could not find a pulse. Ant's left hand had fingers missing. His right hand still held his pistol. Waiting desperately for a pulse from his wrist, I was captivated by Ant's ripped clothing and the amount of blood and flesh that protruded across his torso. I swallowed hard. A small cough brought me back from the horror.

'Ant,' I said.

I quickly put my ear to his mouth. Ant coughed up a load of blood, it ran down my neck. Fuck, I need a serious medi-kit, I thought, frantically trying to stop the bleeding from numerous wounds. Thoughts of Kyle flashed into my mind. I realised I really needed Ocker here. What a total twat I had been to him. Ant began to splutter and mumble, his eyes shot open. Blood ran from his mouth. I gripped his right hand that held the pistol.

'Stay with me, brother. I'll get you fixed up,' I said.

'Where's... where's the fight?' he barely mumbled.

'There's no fight left, Ant. You've finished the fucker.'

I looked at the bear, knowing he had killed it, whereas I had cowered in the cave. I had to change. Suddenly, I realised it was wrong what I had thought, it was OK to be scared. It's how you deal with it, use it, that mattered.

Ant grimaced in pain, then released his scowl. 'It's never over,' he managed, and took in sharp breath. 'Go... go...'

'Come on, big man, let's get you inside for a few plasters,' I said.

Ant was taking short breaths. 'Back... to your... roots... Johnny.'

Ant half-grinned and tried to pull his wrist away from my grasp. I didn't catch what he said, so I placed my ear close to his mouth. He plonked the weapon on the back of my head.

'Take... this. Massive... pleasure serving... with you... brother.' Ant stopped breathing.

I remained silent, still, waiting, wanting.

An overwhelming wave of guilt flushed through me. The arguments and the recent fight played out in front of my tightly squeezed eyes. Realisation that Ant and Steve were trying to get me back to the old positive me was impossible to stomach. Shit. I opened my eyes. Steve.

Quickly, I picked up the Browning. With the torch by its side, I searched down the sight. In the beam, about ten metres away, a large patch of churned snow and blood remained. Standing at the edge of the battle, one blooded, ploughed trail headed back to the cave. The other, gorier, disappeared into the forest.

An object poked out from under the snow. Clearing the trampled ground, I found Steve's main weapon, but it had been damaged beyond use. Even so, I slung the sling over my shoulder and headed into the forest, alert to any movement. My shivering breath rose into the clear, freezing night; the snow crumpled under my icy feet. Something thrusted out as my light shone into a heap of foliage: Steve's pistol. Locked on, I slightly increased pressure on my trigger, ready to react with more aggression.

'Tell me that's you,' Steve's whispered.

'If it weren't, you would be dead,' I said—insensitive. 'Not sure why you're hiding, not only does the trailed lead here, but it's the only bush without any snow on it.' That remark wasn't any better.

After clearing away the branches, I was shocked to see Steve covered in blood. For once he looked unrelaxed, flustered. Had he seen my stunned expression? Steve dropped his hand and then his head, taking a deep breath before exhaling. As I checked his body, he had also been attacked. Cradling his arm against his stomach, I observed that part of his glove and hand was missing. Not making a fuss, I took off my soaked shirt and wrapped the wound. It reminded me of the situation of finding the imposter Tariq, aka Baha Udeen, the Elkhaba leader in Afghanistan. The main differences were, I had no medical kit, no vehicle, and it was below zero.

There was a bit of resilience from Steve about me helping him back to the cave, but I told him to dispense with the cool James Bond bollocks. He let me take charge. I tried to keep the view of Ant from him, but I guessed he had seen. Even as we entered the cave, Steve had his pistol out in front, holding back slightly as the bear came into view in the beam. With his odd little pants of breath, I made him comfortable at the back the cave. It was only now I got to grips with how cold I was, not being able to stop shivering, realising I could not feel my hands and feet.

The cave looked like a teenager's bedroom after a massive tantrum. The objects that could burn, I shoved on the embers. Through the rest of the kit, I managed to salvage some water and ration packs. Without any complaint, I cable-tied Steve's left wrist to stop the blood loss. The melted rucksack had nothing of use, nor was my other burnt boot. Perhaps the two grenades would come in use, especially if I could find Ant's main weapon.

As the fire came to life, we however, did not. I knew what I had to do. Outside was silent, only the nightmare was left. It appeared colder than before, my red-raw, chilblained feet trudging through the snow. Feeling stiff from shivering, I started undoing Ant's torn suit, trying not to stare at the frosty lashes on his open eyes. As I removed his artic boots, I could hear him telling me in his Irish accent that I was a pikey. Ant was now booming with laughter as I took down the rest of his suit, adding many crude names at me. Then, once he was stripped, he went quiet. Dashing back to the cave, I spotted the rucksack under the bear, but I was too numb to stop.

Putting on the blooded clothes, one of the gloves was not on the wire. My joke about Ant's mum tying string through his coat so he did not lose them came back to haunt me. Steve watched me, half-smiling.

'Looks like Johnny's returning,' Steve croaked. 'Adapt and overcome.'

Not being able to answer as my jaw was clenched because of how cold I was, I held my feet one by one in quick concession in front of the fire, hiding the pain that convulsed. Once life had returned, I slid on Ant's boots. Looking down, it appeared I had been through a shredder. However, feeling better, perhaps proud that I was in Ant's gear, I headed back outside.

The jacket's hood had been ripped off, the cold starting my headache again. The size of this grizzly was smaller than the other encountered in the cave, but still a deadly beast. I dug the snow by its gut and hauled out the backpack, still warm and covered in hair and blood. Knowing there was Ant's main weapon under the bear, I foraged further, but could not get under enough. I cursed, but then it felt like I was blaming Ant. Heaving the huge animal was useless, using up energy.

Over the snow-lined fur that moved in the breeze, I peered at Ant. Again, I swallowed the shit hard to the bottom of my churning stomach. He was a mess of bites and claw marks.

'Get a fucking grip, Johnny,' I muttered.

Exhaling, I stood and started to collect snow, placing it over his body.

With my hand that had no glove, I placed it inside my jacket to thaw. The hot swelling pain after was pathetic in comparison to what lay in front of me. Looking around for an object to place on the mound, something fluttering caught my eye in the beam: the blue suicide letter. After cursing for losing such an item, I unhooked it from the bark at the base of the tree.

I returned to Ant, determined to read it; unsure why. However, shockingly, it was blank. Again, I turned it over and over, as if I were mistaken. "You've not read it". Now I knew what Steve had meant. Had I picked up the wrong letter? No, I could not have as it was the only one. Surely it wouldn't have been blank? More importantly, I had nothing to say over Ant's grave, but then it came to me.

'Anthony Holder, my brother, you've not died in vain. I will return to the real Johnny Vince, I promise you. As a mark of respect, this mission to find Roy will be called Operation Edge, even though I knew it was a piss-take of yours for me being on the cliff. Time to fucking ammo up.'

I unzipped his backpack and sifted through until I found it: his black beanie-hat. I imagined Ant pulling it down over his face. I backed up to the cave, still staring at the mound.

'Sorry, Ant, I would place this on you, but I'm too fucking cold.'

The trees gently shook as a wind blew through them. Small ice particles formed on his face. I had closure.

Inside the cave, I instantly felt the heat on my face. Steve looked a little stunned to see I had Ant's hat on. For a moment, had he thought Ant had returned? The tears in his eyes reflected the fire. Inside the backpack, annoyingly, there was no trauma-pack. I handed Steve two painkillers, but he swatted them back. I tried to take his pistol from him and exchange it with the remaining water bottle. He gripped the weapon, studying me. Instead, I held the water to his bloated, blue lips, the blood and water dripping onto his jacket.

'I've buried him,' I said sadly.

'Once I had met the father-like man who visited me in the detention centre, he continued to visit me for a few months in my new home.'

Why had he admitted that? It was like he was waiting for me to ask something, but I wasn't sure where he was going with this. Was he becoming delirious? I checked his pulse again, then gave him some water.

'I never saw him again,' he said. 'He had other underprivileged boys to recruit. Ant took over the fatherly role. It's a shame you never saved any of that vodka.'

'I'm sorry. I mean, sorry for your loss, not the vodka.'

'You would be, you understand,' he said.

I thought of my deceased dad whilst he studied his injured hand.

'You're different from the rest,' he said.

'You mean complex.' I smirked.

'You have all the qualities required to be in the Elite, it's just you have become clouded by confusion and depression. You have the scars to prove it.'

I thought about his words. Did he mean mental scars, or the inflicted battle scars? 'No confusion or PTSD anymore. Thanks, Steve, for helping.'

'The PTSD will never go, you know that, right?'

I nodded.

Steve appeared pleased I had acknowledged it at last. 'Can you get some more wood, Johnny.'

'Sure.'

Outside, the wind occasionally whipped up, sending up swirls of snow and ice crystals. Whilst collecting as much scattered branches, using Ant's rucksack to store, I thought about Steve's mood. I knew he said he could not feel pain and fear, but he looked like the last man standing. I had recognised that lowest point. A worrying thought crossed my mind due to him losing his hand: was this the end of his career? Had losing Ant, the dad-like figure in his life, tipped him over the edge. I pictured him with his weapon, then I ran back to the cave.

Steve was gazing at his pistol which he held close to his face. His bright-blue eyes seemed duller. Was he contemplating it? I purposely emptied the wood onto his feet. He cursed, which was unlike him. I then placed a few logs on the fire.

'Sorry, Steve Steve.'

'Got anymore cable-ties?' he slurred.

'Why?'

Steve tried to tear open the rip in his trouser leg, but holding his weapon made it difficult. 'Need to stem the flow,' he said softly.

'What?'

In the warming light from the fire, I held open the material gash. Fuck. Rapidly, I pulled Steve's boots off, blood dripped from the inside. Once I slid down his trousers, he was covered in puncture marks. The top of his right leg was slashed. His recent bandage on the wound I had caused with the glass had rolled down; guilt followed. He was still losing blood. I went to tell him he should have fucking told me, but I didn't.

I doubted he could have felt the injury. Perhaps he had checked when I was gathering wood.

With his knife, I cut Ant's beanie-hat into the right-size pieces and stuffed it into the wounds. The largest gash, I retrieved my Animal jacket, cut it up, and then tied it tight around the makeshift bandage. Lastly, I bound up his hand, loosening off the cable-tie. Next, I unzipped his main jacket. He still had his expensive shirt on, now turned red. On further investigation, he had many puncture and claw marks.

'Not good is it,' he said.

'You're alive,' I bluntly replied.

'Can you imagine what Ant would have said if he saw you cutting up his infamous beanie-hat come balaclava?'

I smirked. 'I can hear him now.'

After I had finished dressing him the best I could, there was a long pause as we both gazed at the fire. He took the water bottle from me, breaking my stare.

'I need to know exactly where Roy is,' I said.

'Where's my GPS watch?'

'Probably in the that great big fucker's stomach.'

'I had already slit the bear open before firing three rounds in him.'

'Met your match at last,' I bantered.

'No, the hairy cunt did.' He laughed, dribbling the water.

I joined in the chorus.

Once we had stopped, just the wind howling through the trees filtered in. The embers and haze lifted to the ceiling. The ambience had changed, the pressure was building of the obvious situation.

'You know I can't go on,' he said, releasing it.

'I'll find Roy and bring him back here. We'll both help you back to the lodge.' I frowned; having forgotten we had destroyed it.

'That's not what I meant. I can't live like...'

'Don't you fucking go all...'

'Shut up and listen,' he interrupted. 'One klick south, following the base of these cliffs, is where Emperor Falls is situated. Half a klick west is the emergency shack. You know how to navigate.'

'And I can navigate back to pick you up.'

'You would both be better off leaving me here and escape and evade as quick as you can.'

'Bollocks to your plan. Who am I up against?' I asked.

Steve smirked. 'You are going to have to use all your old skills, Johnny.

Even though you had retrieved my main weapon, it's the latest Canadian smart-weapon. It will only work to my retainer and prints.'

I went to lighten the mood about cutting off his fingers and prising an eye, but that would have gone too far. 'Give me your pistol.'

'No, it's personal. Anyway, you will have to think smarter on this last part of the mission, especially without Ant and me.'

I knew I would be causing trouble if I tried to grab it, even though I had an inkling to why he wanted to keep it.

'You might have no fear, I've excepted mine,' I said. 'I want to turn it into aggression. Tell me who the fucking enemy are.'

'OK, you have the right...' Steve stopped.

'Well?'

'Shhh,' he demanded.

'I need...'

'Shhh,' he hissed. He arched his neck forward, his expression concentrating hard towards the cave's entrance. 'Listen.'

I couldn't hear anything, wondering if he was going mad, or he really had superhuman hearing. Maybe I was going deaf after the years of battle, but all I could register was the breeze. Then, voices sifted in on the same wind. We locked stare.

'Go, Johnny. Find Roy.'

I gathered up everything, including the wood, and left it by his side. He made ready his pistol.

'Are they the same who have been tailing us from the start?' I asked.

'It's not Mother Theresa. You need to leave, right now.'

'Who then?' I cautiously headed towards the entrance.

He didn't reply.

I glared back my frustration.

'Targets,' he replied.

'It's no time for games.'

'Anyone who uses the phrase, "my friend", isn't.'

I went to question what he meant, but the voices were growing louder. Instead, I made ready the torch and Ant's pistol. I dreaded leaving Steve behind.

CHAPTER THIRTEEN

The increasing wind blustered the ice crystals that lay on the ground and trees, fortunately hampering the sight of the cave. However, I could not tell what direction the voices had come from. Touching the mountain's side, I stared at Ant's disappearing grave, along with the carnage, a distant chilling memory. Then I heard them, but with the trees swaying, they echoed from all around. I could not let them find me or Steve.

With my arm across my face, the other gloveless hand felt the side of the cold, uneven cliff face. Large dumps of snow fell from way above. I hoped there weren't rocks in those. What a fucking time to have a storm. What else could go wrong? Shut up, Johnny, I thought.

The moving woodland to my right played tricks on my senses. However, I just pushed on. Hopefully, the tracking enemy were having trouble navigating. From time to time, I am sure mutts had barked, along with their owners shouting. I was not going to let the negative get to me. I was spurred on that I had once been part of the most feared unit in the world. Nothing was going to stop me finding my mate Roy.

My left hand had become so cold that I had to let go of the precipice, placing it in my pocket. The freezing wind and snow drifts had become worse. I was numb, probably due to the suit not working correctly, but nothing as bad as just in my civi clothes. I wished the storm would stop, but then I thought of being able to be seen. Could the enemy mutts get my scent in this weather?

To take my mind off this, I thought of meeting Roy, killing anyone that got in my way. At the back of my mind, I had a niggling worry that Steve was going to end his days. I had to rescue him. What had he meant by, "Anyone who uses the phrase, my friend, isn't"?

'Monkfish,' I chattered.

He had used the saying on numerous occasions, but surely, he had nothing to do with Roy's disappearance. Mike had said, "Be careful who you trust." Did he mean Monkfish? No, that is absurd, because I was up on the cliff when he had stumbled across me. But why the empty suicide note? It was me who found him at the restaurant. Pure coincidence? And what about Monkfish lending me his van to help me escape from the lad I had killed? Confused even more, I pushed on, even though the only bearing I had was the mountain's jagged rocks.

Eventually, the storm relented, along with my questions. Like in other desperate situations, I counted my steps to get some sort of idea how far I had travelled. The snot had frozen to my freezing skin, and my hair was solid. Yet, I was now glad of the visibility of the stars.

Stopping on one knee for a breather, I took my numb hand from my pocket. It was then I found I was clutching the mask. I smirked, knowing that would have helped me through the storm, keeping me from getting severely chapped. Typical Ant, I thought jokingly. Trying on the mask, it did not work. I checked further, pressing the side buttons, but noticed it had cracks in. The thought the bear's weight cast a gloomy shadow.

The moon and stars were stunning as I worked out the next direction. The tranquillity that enveloped was like the storm had never happened. A part of me thought that some strange power had helped me escape, the other told me not to be so fucking stupid. Suddenly, I noticed a red-dot on the cliff rock ahead, moving slightly towards me. Without hesitation, I had sprung into a sprint. The rocks to my side exploded over me. Fighting the shards in my face and the deep snow, I bounded forwards, heart racing, Browning in hand. This insulated suit was making it hard to run at speed, or was it I was out of condition? However, fear kept me going. Further ricochets hit the wall, and I am sure I spotted the snow puff in front of my feet. Perhaps the person using the weapon was a shit shot—I hoped.

A small ditch lay ahead. Out of breath I jumped into it. The ice below cracked, almost taking my feet as I continued to squat-run in the direction it led. At least the metre-high bank covered me from the following red-dot. My mind instructed me to take the fight to them, but I had no idea how many were pursuing; also, unsure how many rounds were left in Ant's pistol. Three shots had been fired in my sleep, and more when I had woken. I thought of camouflaging in the snow with a surprise attack, or even a dog-leg ambush. Then, I heard the dreaded mutts.

From deep, I found the energy to increase my pace. The tree next to me exploded, sending the debris into my face. I had been in this situation before, and survived, I thought, boosting my morale. The ditch turned slightly left so I carried on sprinting. Quickly skidding to a halt, I turned down onto one knee and raised my pistol. Facing the hunters, I controlled my heavy breathing. As soon as the first mutt appeared, I fired two shots; the first having missed. It crumpled to the floor with a yelp, but teeth showing, it scrambled up. Aiming hard, I fired off another two shots. Just as it slid on the ice, another mutt jumped over it. With its killing intent, the gap was closing. I held my breath. Within four metres, I relaxed and breathed out, then fired off three shots. The mutt's blooded body slid into me.

A red beam and shadow were next around the corner. I laid prone. Whether the enemy had not seen me, or was distracted by the dead mutts, he had stopped. Aligning my sight, I fired off two shots. His red beam caught the tall trees. The target was at least down, but he was scrabbling back. He fired his weapon in my direction, but he had no idea where I was. Even so, the familiar sound whizzed close. Someone else reached around and dragged him back around the bend. I cursed as my next two rounds missed the new assailant: instead, hitting the first bloke.

I was up and running in a split-second, breathing heavily through a clenched grin. Suddenly, I had to put the brakes on. The iced ditch abruptly disappeared over a drop into a black world of uncertainty. Sat on my arse, I pulled in my legs from the edge and rapidly turned over, facing the way I had escaped, scanning my arcs. This was nuts, as they could come down on either side bank. Scrambling up the heavy snow laden side, I headed left.

Trying to stay quiet through the forest, but at the same time trying to achieve as much ground as possible, I continued around the cliff's edge. After about five minutes I took refuge behind a tree, tuning into the situation. Once the blood had stopped pumping around my head, I heard water crashing nearby. This had to be the Emperor Falls. The thought of being close to Roy boosted my determination. This time I did not feel sick; in fact, I had a buzz from what had just happened. If only Ant and Steve were here to have witnessed.

Over the twenty-metre edge was a rocky plateau. Facing out, to my furthest left and set up a lot higher, was a stunning waterfall lit up by the moon. Behind me were snow covered tall trees. It didn't feel right to go back into the woods. Something was drawing me to continue along the edge down to the level below. Was it my sixth sense returning at last? Had the words "Operation Edge" from Ant been a sign? What the fuck was I thinking? I had to stop this physic bollocks; I didn't believe in that kind of mumbo-superstition shit. However, Blondie in the sealed water tank came to mind, again. This time I really did miss his divine intervention.

With one eye scouring for any potential threats, I checked my pistol: two rounds. Fuck. At the first chance, I would grab an enemy's weapon. Failing that, use my knife or invent something. Any fucker who gets in my way will lose, like the PTSD voice had. There was no way that was ever coming back. I did not feel humiliated anymore knowing it was me all along, but victorious, boosting my optimistic attitude.

The odd creaking and thumping echoed from the forest behind me. I contemplated staying till dawn just in case the chasing party had night-vision goggles. Perhaps with one man down they had fled. If I had known I had killed him there and then, would I have heard the robotic gaming voice?

'Mutts neutralised,' I said in a gaming voice—it was silly, but it made me smile.

Daylight would put us on an even keel for spotting each other, but then what about Steve? Would he survive the night? It wasn't his failing suit that worried me, nor the weather, but his injuries did. Have the enemy found him, or worse, another grizzly? I thought about him mentioning that he could not carry on. Did he mean his career?

'Career,' I mocked.

I shook my head at the stupid choice of word. Could he kill himself? He had no fear. It was a horrible thought. I flicked on the positive switch, something I had powered off for nearly a year. Closing my eyes, I imagined finding Roy sitting there smoking and drinking beer. I sneered at the thought that he was missing making more babies.

Opening my eyes, I realised I had drifted off, knowing I could have been found. I slapped my cheeks, not to wake me, but to smack a bit of sense into me. Peering hard in the surrounding area, I searched for any sign that Roy might be out there—too dark. How long till first light? I checked for my phone—gone.

'Fuck.'

Not happy with my OP, I carefully moved down the sloped edge, but stopped when I spotted a small ledge below. I contemplated if it was a too risky to climb down. One slip and it was game over. Yet, if I took on the danger and did not fall, the position would conceal me. It would also shorten the unforeseen journey till the cliff was low enough for me to climb down safely onto the plateau. From this little hide below, I could observe the area till dawn, and then try to take a direct route to the land below. It's not as if I hadn't been in the same situation before; however, in Indonesia at least I had rope. Go for it and die? Go for it and survive? It was a calculated risk.

'Who dares wins,' I muttered.

Steadily, I turned onto my belly and held on to the small tree. I lowered my legs over the edge. Clasping my fingers together around the trunk, I shuffled down further, imagining the last drop to the ledge. Suddenly, I heard voices. I froze. They were English. Now that I was out of the snow, would my camouflage look odd against the black rocks? I pushed my face into it. Snow from the ledge fell onto my head and neck. Fear escalating, my ears pricked up following the sound from my right. Being casually loud, I took it they had given up looking for me; it's all I had to keep me positive. I tried to heave myself up on my elbows, but the crumbling edge fell. The voices stopped. Bollocks. Could I let go of one hand and grab my pistol out of my pocket? If I fell, at least I could land on the ledge.

Whoever was out there, they had started chatting again. They were close...

Ten metres...

Pull yourself up and slot them...

Nine metres...

What if there are more than two?

Eight metres...

Fuck. Was the tree sliding down? I stared up at the disintegrating soil, showing the roots...

Six metres...

I released my grip.

As soon as my feet hit the slab, I leaned forward to stop going backwards, digging my fingers into the rock face, a stinging to my left index-finger. The jutting rock appeared to sway as I held on for dear life. Frozen like a statue, I controlled my breathing, tuning in to the above, squashing negative thoughts of a red-dot on my head. My feet had only fallen about three metres onto this tiny ledge. I was sure the surface area was larger from when I was above. Slowly, I released my poor grip, slightly relaxing. Turning my head to my left, I scraped my numb cheek on the rock. I had to see why my left hand was irritating me: blood ran down my pale hand. I had ripped part of my nail off.

'Wanker,' I mumbled. 'Why did Ant have to lose a glove?' It was dark, but it made me smile.

Cautiously, I shuffled around till I was facing out. Operation Edge; how fitting. Without warning, something Monkfish had said bared to mind: "What's the chances of giving me Will's details so I can take a private *mercenary* contract?" I had never mentioned Will's name. How did he know Will? Why did he want his details? One thing was for sure: I had a lot of questions for the fucker when I got home. For now, I had to bury it all and continue to find Roy.

Getting down onto my arse had not been easy. I was curled up with one hand around my knees, the other inside my pocket. I pushed my face into my body, deducing the time to be in the early hours of the morning. My breath thawed my face. I closed my eyes.

Abruptly, I opened them, unsure how long I had been asleep. I had not had any dreams that I could remember. Chilled through to the core, I wondered if Steve's suit battery had failed like this one. Hopefully, the embers were still glowing, adding what logs were left.

Lifting my face off my knees, my neck cracked. I rotated it, then slapped my cheeks again. I ruffled my sweat-frozen hair, adding to the headache. The moon was disappearing out of sight. A faint smell wafted in, possible burning wood. Like an animal, I stuck my nose out to get a better fix on it. My gut rumbled as soon as I had smelt food cooking. It mentally tasted like stew. On the edge of my vision, I am sure I could see a faint light. Blinking and refocusing positively identified the glow. That had to be the shack. The major problem was Roy was also alerting any nasty people that may still be out there. I had to move quick.

The drop below was worrying me as I laid flat against the rock's side. I inched my way down. A boulder came away. Before I knew it, I was crashing down. The jagged rocks penetrated the suit. I tried to keep the grunts and groans to a minimum. My legs buckled. Instinctively, I covered my head as I hit the ground, all happening very quick. I let the shingle and stones stop, as well as the rippling pain, before looking around. After feeling for any potential bones sticking out, I turned over on my back and looked up at the stars, wanting a bit of camaraderie from some of the old squad. I began to chuckle.

'What a fuck-up,' I said.

Exhausted, I placed my hands behind my head, needing a rest, a big sleep. I knew this was not the time, but with all the emotions and physical stuff I was not used to, I wanted to take timeout. It was a strange situation: to lie back as if on holiday taking in the scenery, but at the same time, knowing there were killers hunting me. Nevertheless, even though it felt amazing, I had a mission to complete.

'I hope you appreciate this, Roy,' I said quietly. 'Chinook pilot? Bloody glorified bus driver.'

What was left of the moonlight silhouetted the cold, barren landscape. The only sound, apart from the blood going around my frosty head, was of crashing water. I looked at the little ledge I had fallen from, the height daunting. For reassurance, I pulled out Ant's Browning. Time to move out, I thought.

Whether it was due to the thought of at last finding Roy, or the tantalising smell of food, I made quick ground across the spacious rock level, jumping at speed over the channels carved in the stone by years of water erosion. Also, in the back of my mind was the thought of the weapon with the red-dot scope, knowing there were at least two still at large. Within fifty yards of the target, I scaled a large boulder and went prone. Concealing my heavy breathing and the moisture it exposed, I told myself I would get into shape when I returned home. I tuned in to the environment and scanned the area. My sixth sense told me Roy was in the log cabin. Under my jacket, I made sure the torch was working.

There were scattered trees in the inky-black behind the cabin. The light inside was still glowing, possibly a lantern or a fire. I knew I was outnumbered and had no weapon match, but I was so committed. I had not come all this way, lost friends, and been beaten for nothing. God forbid any fucker who tried to stop me now. I made sure my knife, along with the pistol, were ready.

After checking the whole area was sterile, I silently ran the short distance to the shack's frosted timbered side. A small amount of smoke filtered out the rusty metal chimney pipe. Logs, not food. In the shadows, I pulled out my torch and held it next to my pistol, thumb poised on its rear button-switch. First, I made my way around to the rear, carefully placing my feet. Three water buts and a shed full of cut wood were at the rear, wind howling through the gaps.

With no rear door, I carried on around the side, sticking close, making no sound. The building was about the size of a double garage. Crouched at the front, I studied the door: timber with a large, rusty ring handle. A small amount of light seeped from under. The window above my head was covered in a thick algae-like substance, but just enough to see light inside. Perhaps it wasn't so dark in there after all. Ignoring the sound of the distant water cascading, I slightly closed my eyes and listened for the slightest sound from inside—nothing.

I pondered my next move. Do I gain entry by power and force? Shall I go stealthily? I smirked at thinking of laying a breaching charge and throwing a few thunder flashes for good measure, and, the best bit, the look on Roy's face. Noticing a corner of the glass was missing, I eased my eye up to it and peered in. A warm waft of air flowed out. Instantly, I ducked, my heart almost missing a beat. In that split-second of the low light, I had spotted a figure sitting in a chair facing the door. Concerningly, a red laser protruded from his main weapon in his lap. Fuck. Had the enemy spotted me advancing and now lie in waiting? Was it the same bloke who tried to slot me earlier? Fuck. Had he killed Roy? My anger intensified. Wait, I told myself, where was the other crony?

To be certain, I lifted very slowly, centimetre by centimetre, squashing the negative that I was going to get a face full of lead. Breath held, one hand gripping the pistol, the other on the slippery, thin frame, I peered in. I was right, the weapon's beam was aiming at the door. The person who sat there was in black puffer-jacket and trousers. Spookily, he was wearing an old-styled SAS balaclava, but his head was bowed. The stupid twat had fallen asleep. I carefully let go of my breath. There were no other rooms. An iron Furness glowed at the rear. Next to this was two wooden bunks, both had been slept in. In the lantern's gloom, on the rustic wood table were two used plates and tin mugs. In the centre was a pot with a lid on, a small amount of steam filtered out. None of this made sense.

Apprehensive, I lowered and looked to each side, then behind me. In the far distance the torrent waterfall could not be seen, but other shapes teased me. Even with the foreboding odds against me, weirdly, I was looking forward to this. The fearsome Elite had returned. By strength and guile, I thought.

'Fucking ammo up,' I silently muttered.

I cautiously reached out and placed a hand on the handle and, millimetre at a time, turned it until it came off the latch. Out of the way of the door, I placed the torch to the side of the pistol, half-stood up, then took a breath. The fright did not bother me, I was not going to die today.

Crash!

As soon as I booted the door, my thumb clicked on the light, I was in.

Bang! Bang!

The assailant tipped backwards on his chair in his own red mist. Darting behind the open door, I searched the rest of the room. Alone, I shut the door, but there was no bolt. Dashing to the dead man's body, I heard the old voice, '*Threat neutralised.*' It lifted me ten-fold. I picked up the Heckler and switched off the sight. At speed, I extinguished the lamp. Sharply back at the window, I tapped out a pane with the butt and switched off the torch. Even with the thick walls, I knew those shots would have been heard for some way. I waited, watching.

Five minutes or so later, I began to tremble a fantastic feeling. With no sign of advancing trouble, I automatically took out the mag to check the rounds: unbelievably, it was empty, including the chamber. What the fuck? In slow-motion my mind played out the entry, the bloke with the Heckler had woken. In that millisecond, I saw his wide eyes, the fear. With no main weapon, I had to either find another, or flee.

Knife out, backing up to the fallen chair, I turned to look at the body. Not noticing before, strangely the dead man's ankles were bound to the chair. Compelled, I kicked his hand aside and lowered onto my knee. In the pool of blood, I grabbed the balaclava and ripped it off.

'Noooo,' I bawled.

My world spun as I tried to get a hold of my breathing. In a panic and fury, I hit the chest of this dead man, then shouted again in disbelief. Emotions flooded me. Transfixed, I couldn't keep it in, and I started to sob and shake. What the fuck had I done? It didn't make sense. A sound behind me alerted me. I grabbed my weapon and swiftly turned. Through watershed vison, the stock smashed my head.

CHAPTER FOURTEEN

Ant and Steve helped me to my feet. Wearily, I held onto the table, the other hand on my head wound. They found it highly amusing as I held back the flap of skin on my forehead. Staggering slightly forward, I searched on the floor for my weapon.

'Hey, fuck-face, this is my Browning,' Ant said.

I looked at Ant as he slapped in a new mag. He then pointed the pistol at my chest. I wiped the blood from my eyes and looked at Steve for reassurance. Steve glared at me, hard, nodding, giving me the impression that I was a dumb-fuck for believing I wasn't the rogue. He cocked his Waltham.

'What's going on, Steve?' I asked.

'Do you really think I would tell you who I work for and why we're here?' he said. 'It's time to turn off Johnny Vince, the rogue, forever.'

I sat back on the edge of the table and folded my arms, then stared at Roy's body at my feet. 'So, it was you that abducted Roy. I fucking knew it. But why kill him?'

Both laughed. 'Call sign, you killed him,' Ant said.

'You two fuckers made me,' I blamed.

'Good-bye, Johnny,' Steve said.

I shut my eyes as he squeezed the trigger.

I opened my eyes, stopping the nightmare. Face to face with a pair of eyes, I wriggled backwards on my side, frantically gasping. The horrendous sight of Roy's gun-shot wound to his forehead brought my gut acid into my mouth. I vomited it out. Looking back, he was still staring at me; this was not a dream, but a real nightmare. For some reason, like me, he was stripped to his underwear, if it could get any more degrading. With my hands tied behind my back and ankles bound, I heaved myself up in the sitting position, spitting the remaining sick. The chair that Roy had been tied to was missing. I could not stop the lump in my throat producing flows of tears. Even with the warming sunlight creeping up the dirty panes, I could not control my dark thoughts. There were no words of comfort, just brutal dejection. Further down Roy's body, he lay in blood from the second double-tap entry and exit. A deathly silence and guilt enveloped me. Shock took over any explanation. I did not give a shit about my throbbing forehead wound.

Every time I opened my mouth to speak, the words wouldn't voice; apologies were entirely pointless. Images of Christine and the kids played out, adding numbing justice to the sickening blame. I still wanted this to be a dream, but I knew I had come all this way and killed the very person I was here to save. With my bare toes, I pushed his eyelids closed. I sunk my head back against the log wall, demoralised. I shut my eyes, hoping I would not wake. Perhaps in an hour or two, I would be frozen to death.

Strangely, an odour of nicotine filled my nostrils, but I shrugged it off.

It's never over.

'Oh fuck off, voice,' I mumbled.

A faint heart never fucked a pig.

Realising the voices weren't that of the PTSD, but of Ant and Planet, I opened my eyes. They weren't in the room. My heart sunk, realising the voices had been my figment. Roy still laid there.

'Sorry, Planet, not this time me old mate,' I muttered, my breath making cold patterns.

The one person who I really needed to talk to would have been my dad. He had such a level-head. I wondered if my mum and brother would forgive me, the trouble I had caused. How could I explain this, let alone live with it? I knew I was going into a negative spiral, but the sadness was mixed with nostalgia. Feeling pathetically sorry for myself in front of my dead mate made it worse. I started wishing I had made that jump at Land's End. I smashed the back of my head against the wall.

'Roy... Roy... I'm...' I couldn't finish; I was finished.

'Who's that?' a voice croaked.

Startled, I peered into the shadows. 'Who's there?'

Face down on the bottom bunk was a body, just in pants, the same as me. The person was hooded, looking at where my voice had come from. Why weren't they answering? I searched for the nearest object I could use as a weapon, but then, we were both tied up.

All sufferings have rewards, mate.

Did he just say that? But it sounded like Ant. Now wasn't the time for mind-fuck games, I thought.

The person tried to shake off the cloth hood. I found myself doing head movements, urging it to come off and reveal who it was. Yet, deep-down, I kind of knew, but it was too confusing.

'Who's there?' he said, frightened.

'Johnny Vince. I've got a weapon pointing at you.'

The person feistily scuffled into a sitting up position and used the bunk above to remove the hood.

'Monkfish,' I yelled. Maddened, I tried to shimmy to my feet. 'The last place you want to be is here. I'm fucking gonna kill you with my bare hands.'

'Johnny, it wasn't supposed to be like this,' Monkfish pleaded.

'You fucking tricked me.'

I managed to get to my feet by using the rough wall. Pain swept through me, along with adrenalin. Stable, still shouting obscenities at him, I methodically hopped along on both feet, but still could not get my hands free. As I neared him, I lurched forward and deliberately smashed my forehead on the side of his face.

'Arhhh. Stop, Johnny. Let me explain,' he begged.

Again, I head-butted him, cursing him.

Monkfish must have brought his knees up, as the pain in my bollocks sharpened. Now angrier than ever, I tried to bite his face. Yes, I had lost control, but it seemed the right level; I was not in a combat-zone.

Eventually, he managed to push me off and I fell back on to the wood-planked floor. Something else clanged to the floor close by. Gasping in air, I studied the timber on the roof as the sun crept in further. We were both breathing heavily. Laying on my hands, my finger injury stung like crazy. A cold breeze blew under the door, and with no fire going, I began to shiver. The top of my head was touching Roy's head. I wasn't sure if I should move mine away or not.

'Johnny. Listen my…'

'Save your fucking breath, Chris. You best make your escape before I loosen these ropes.'

'You need…'

Not listening, I lifted my feet to check how I was doing, noticing the recent burn blister on my sole had burst.

'Has it not crossed your mind that I am bound, beat up, the same as you?' he said.

I arched my head to see the sunlight shining on his bloated and cut face; dust danced in the rays. The recent beatings looked bluer than his cold body. My own torso had begun to take on a numb shade. I plonked my head back on the boards, the anger dissipating.

'Then why the fuck are you here?' I asked.

'I'm not sure how much time we have, but…'

'Do you know what, I don't give a flying fuck anymore. I've just killed my mate. What will be, will be.'

'No, listen, you've been set up,' Monkfish said.

He moved forwards to the edge of the bunk, groaning in pain as he did. Turning away from Roy's soul, I tried to sit up again. Eventually, I leant back on the wall.

'And you had nothing to do with this,' I said facetiously.

'It wasn't supposed to go this far. I had no idea it would end like this. I promise.'

Bollocks, I thought. 'There was no suicide note. Right?'

'No, it was blank. I'm sorry.' Monkfish lowered his head. 'How did you know?'

'It doesn't fucking matter. And all that about your wife leaving you, your son dying on tour and your dad dying of heart-attack, that was a load of bollocks as well. Right?'

Monkfish lifted his head, appearing a little fuelled. 'My wife did leave me,' he said, trying to make amends. 'But she…'

'You scumbag traitor,' I blasted. 'I don't want to listen to your shit anymore.'

'I'm sorry I took advantage of your lowest point.'

'Bollocks. How much of anything you've said is truthful.'

Monkfish rigorously was trying to release his hands behind his back. At the same time, he pulled his legs back and forth. Did he have another motive? Seeing he was trying to break free, I had to release myself first in case he decided to attack me. It seemed to have become a race to free first.

'I was in the Regiment, but I wasn't thrown out because of handling a weapon,' he said. 'I had intel on you, and I tried to make me more believable. You know, in the same boat as you.'

'You will never be like me,' I said.

'I'm fatherless.'

That enraged me further. 'You had a father?' I countered. 'I doubt that, you bastard.'

'I'm telling the truth.'

'OK, you want to start getting stuff of your chest. The kid I killed in Padstow, all rigged?'

His guilty silence followed.

I sighed a massive relief, but still felt the need to beat him. 'I've been fucking going out of my mind with guilt and worry. You crazy sick fuck.' I gritted my teeth as my bounds burned into my wrists.

'Everyone has a crazy friend. I've just never met anyone who is crazy.'

'Oh my days, you still try to mock every situation. I hope I get free before you. I'm gonna make sure you don't joke again.'

'Look, Johnny, I can't say I'm sorry enough, but if you need to end my already messed up life, then so be it. In all honesty, I'm just so glad you didn't jump off the cliff. If anything, I saved your life.'

'Yeah? And I've gone from bad to worse.'

'You're not the only fucker out there with problems and mental issues. God. You can be a selfish twat. I'm in debt up to my eyeballs. I've lost all my dignity and loved ones. If I could turn back the clock and not have tricked you, I would.'

At last, the rope around my writs were loosening. I stopped what I was doing for a rest, and to gain some composure.

'It's true,' he said.

'Who the fuck paid you?'

Monkfish must have slipped his restraints as he now had his arms around the front. Instead of fully standing up, he cried in pain as he hit the deck. Slowly, he dragged himself towards me. I scuttled away, trying even harder to break the wrist ties, but the lantern's broken glass stopped me. Monkfish raised his face from behind me. He had been savagely beaten. Even though his eyes were teary, he managed to smile through swollen lips. A tooth was missing.

'I'm not making it out of here, mate. They've busted my ankles good and proper,' he said, and began loosening my rope—I wasn't expecting that.

'Are you sure you want to be releasing me, freeing my inner demon on you?' I scowled.

'My son did die on tour and my life did fall apart when I was thrown out of the army,' he admitted. 'I grew up fatherless, so who knows if my dad is alive. I have an empty heart with my wife gone. They stole my necklace and wedding ring. I'm struggling to make ends meet. That's the truth. Yes, I make stupid jokes and sayings, but it hides the pain.'

'Is that the truth?'

'On what's left of my life,' Monkfish said.

'Who are you working for?'

'Johnny, you need to get the fuck away from here. I'll take my punishment.' Monkfish sighed a relief as he had released me.

Blood flowed back into my hands. I rolled over and grabbed Monkfish around his already bloodied throat. 'You sent the letter to Christine didn't you.' I didn't let him reply; I knew.

Monkfish seized my wrists as I squeezed.

'Yeah. Fucking rhetorical,' I fumed. 'A few clues gave it away: the postmark, Cornwall. And the written part in it, 'I've tried to come off the drink, but it tends to help me get through the twenty-four hours.' You've said that yourself.' I gripped harder, boiling inside. 'And the quip, 'don't search in the last place you would look because that is where you would find me.' It's so fucking you. So fucking obvious now.'

'Obvious now because you're sober,' Monkfish gasped.

Releasing one hand, I punched him hard in the face. 'Roy's dead because of you. Ant and Steve are dead because of you.' I hit him again; this felt good.

Monkfish's head came back, snorting blood. 'Who?'

Fist in chamber, I stopped, realising I had gone beyond what was necessary. He was not going to fight back. I released my grip around his throat, shoving him away in disgust.

'As if you don't know who Ant and Steve are. And if you really don't know, they were bloody warriors,' I said.

Bending forward, I undid the ties around my ankles and groggily stood to, leaning against the wall for support. I threw the rope at him in revulsion, then limped over to the broken window. My near-naked body was a mess of cuts, bruises, and blood, along with old scars. I had fought with the best, and worst.

'I don't know how far up the chain this fucked-up deceit goes, but you best disappear from here, mate,' he said.

'How the fuck? I've no fucking clothes, no transport, no weapons, no food and water, and no fucking communications.'

'About half a mile west through the forest is another shelter, a vehicle, and weapons. Its quicker this way than follow the track to it. From here you can get yourself sorted, and then head out on the only road that leads back to the main highway. Wrap up in this bedding and go.'

Monkfish was draining in colour as he gently rubbed his bruised shins. I hated this bloke more than anyone, but a part of me knew at one point we had served in the same brotherhood. Perhaps he had been through the same shit as me. However, the loathing part knew he had tricked me into finding, and perhaps killing, my mate. Who was behind setting me up, and why? I had to find this other emergency shelter. If I did and made it back to the highway, where would I head? I had no phone, passport, or money.

'You'll work it out,' Monkfish said, as if reading my mind. 'You can't take me. I will hamper your escape, then we both die.'

Guilt took over my anger towards him.

With outside being clear, I hobbled back over to Monkfish. Standing over him in the new light, he really was in a bad way. The cold would kill him before his injuries, that is if whoever brutally beat him didn't return.

'I'm fucked, mate,' Monkfish said.

'If I leave you here, they could beat you further. I could protect you.'

'With what? Take anything you can and piss off.'

I knelt, and instinctively as a former medic, I started looking at his wounds. 'I could come back with Steve if he's still alive.'

'Steve who?'

'I'll go and get him first.'

However, even if Steve had survived the enemy, cold, or not bled to death, with both mine and Steve's injuries, we were not up to carrying Monkfish to the shelter. I doubted I could make it back to the cave and then back here in just a few blankets, let alone climb the rock-face. I was not being negative, just realistic. When I reached this new shelter, I could drive the car back to here, I positively thought. But what about Steve?

'Johnny... Johnny, did you hear me?' Monkfish interrupted my plans.

'What?'

'I'm fucked here, and in the world out there. I've nothing left, materialistically and credibility. Ironic, I had the chance on the cliff. Go now, Johnny.' He took my hand and bonded it, slightly squeezing. 'Forgive me, mate.'

'Who the fuck paid you? Who set me up?'

'If I tell you, do you promise to finish this scum once you leave me here?'

'You have my word,' I said. 'Just tell me who is behind this.'

'It was...

Psst... psst... psst!

Still holding Monkfish's jerking hand, his body writhed, then his head dropped back. The door burst open. Behind the silenced Heckler stood a form hunkered into it. Daylight behind made it hard to see the face, but the killer had something recognisable about him. Cordite hazed in the sun's rays. He took a few steps in, treading on the window glass. Why hasn't he slotted me? I let go of Monkfish's lifeless hand and turned to his blooded body. A mix of emotions surged through me. Worse, I had not had the chance to tell Monkfish that I had forgiven him. Switching my sadness to anger, I faced the loan enemy, having to cover the brightness around the figure.

'Johnny fucking Vince. We meet again.'

Implausible, almost horrified at who I was looking at, my jaw must have hit the floor.

CHAPTER FIFTEEN

'Andy fucking Ludkin,' I gasped.

'How the fucking tables have turned. I've waited a long time for this moment, ever since you deserted me on Hordio with the Somali pirates.'

'Oh yeah, Operation Last Assault,' I said lamely. 'I see you've grown a beard to match your last pathetic goatee since I first met you, Ludkin. Or should I call you Union J.'

'I see you're still in the same fucked-up position when I'd first met you.'

'I thought you'd been boiled along with some vegetables,' I sneered. 'Still obnoxious.'

'It's only just returning actually. I've not been myself for a while,' I gloated.

'I know how the trained mind works. Behind this false facade, you want to attack me because you're scared shitless.'

'I can't believe you've spent all this time worrying about me. I've not given you a second thought.'

'Well, now you are.'

Ludkin took his eye from the sight, back-stepped and closed the door. He then rapidly put his hand back on his weapon, whilst I thought of my next move to survive.

'Looks like you've had quite a party here,' he said.

'Yep. Who the fuck invited you? This is a "pants only club".' It was dark, but it's all I had in the way of spirit. I spat in front of his feet. 'You're not even worth that.'

Ludkin tightened the stock in his shoulder.

'You were a shit shot back at the mountain,' I said.

'I was meant to miss you. Get on the bed.'

'Blimey. You *must* have enjoyed all those Somali pirates bumming you.'

Ludkin fired a shot at my feet—I flinched. 'The next one is between the fucking eyes. Fucking do it.'

Trying not to clamber disrespectfully over Chris and Roy, I covertly checked Chris for a pulse. I shuddered when Ludkin fired two further rounds into Chris. Another two rounds were fired into Roy.

'Roy's already fucking dead,' I shouted.

'Like my squad are when you left us for dead on that island.'

'Along with your morals and honour.'

His face had dropped. 'Don't you want to know how I survived?'

I sat on the lower bunk, the warmth from it touched my bare legs. 'Not really,' I replied, equanimous. 'But I bet you want to know what happened to me after your little holiday on Hordio beach.'

Ludkin was glowing with anger. He pulled out the remaining chair and, slowly dragging it across Roy, infuriating me, he sat down to the right of the window.

'Sure,' he said.

'Your mate, Bushy, sorry, Red Six, sorry, real name George Spaatz, was slotted with his own sniper-rifle. Good old Ocker.'

Andy's lip curled. 'What happened to Ocker?'

I thought back to the pub when Monkfish had taken notice of Ocker's name. I now knew that Ludkin had instructed him to find out about Ocker.

'Well?'

I shook the thoughts. 'He died.'

'Damn shame.'

'Remember Jeremy, AKA Marshal Brad Hilton, real name Agent Ronaldo Gomez? He was rescued from the group that you left him for dead with.'

'Think I've heard enough,' he said.

'I'm sure you want to know that Gomez was working for the USSS.'

Ludkin quickly stood. 'You can shut the fuck up, now,' he snapped.

'Oh, and remember Night Stalker, real name Leon? Well, he was also working with the USSS main man, David Mclachlan.'

Andy's finger caressed the trigger, aiming at my forehead. 'You're lying.'

'Whoa,' I said, holding my hands up. 'Hold on, I'm nearly there. Tommy, sorry, Marshal Jones, probably ended up as fish bait. That's after he made some dodgy porn with an old man and young girls.'

'Say goodbye, Johnny.'

'My final words before you slot me, please.'

No shot fired.

'Remember Enu Kofana? Your boat charge hand. He helped me and Ocker escape. We shared your money from the safe.' I smiled.

'You don't know when enough is enough, do you. Your fucking death wish is here.'

'Are you not interested in what happened to Larry and the formula, L16BY?' I quickly added.

Ludkin blinked and slightly lifted off his sight. He then lowered his weapon, scrutinising me.

I relaxed.

'I thought Abishua had it,' he probed.

I did a silly buzzer sound and said, 'Wrong. And for your information, Abishua and Ramario are dead, probably injecting some shit in hell as we speak.'

'Unlike Kyle, who was too wet behind the ears.'

I tried not to tense, not letting him know that he had got to me.

'Oh, and poor old Sameer. Mincemeat for the sharks,' he added.

Obviously, I was not good at hiding my disgust, as that remark had also provoked, and he knew it. I pulled the blanket around my cold shoulders. Chris' hood fell to the floor.

'Look, we can go around in circles with this jabbing banter,' I said. 'Now, you can either slot me, or I could tell you where the unencrypted formula is, along with Larry.'

'In exchange for what?'

'My life.'

'Is that it?' he said sarcastically.

'No.'

'There's a surprise.' He lit up a cigarette. 'Nice of Chris to leave these fags for me. What else then?'

Every part of me detested this piece of shit, but I had to stay calmly in control of the situation. 'You help me take Roy's and Chris' bodies home to their family.'

'Deal. Now, where's Larry and the formula?' Ludkin sat down, blowing out the smoke.

I snorted through my nose, slightly shaking my head, letting him know I knew he would not honour the deal.

'No deal?' he asked.

'Now that we're friends, first tell me how I ended up in this shit with you,' I said.

'Be my pleasure, buddy. After leaving me on the island with hundreds of Somali pirates, I managed to escape. You must have forgotten who I had served with. Eventually, I made it across...'

I exaggerated a yawn and looked at my wrist.

Ludkin flicked his fag at me in disgust. 'He says you're a bastard.'

'Oh really. Who is "he"?'

Ludkin looked uncomfortable, then quickly glanced at the door, before back to me. 'Anyway, on that arduous journey back to safety, I thought nothing but revenge. It took me a while to track you down, but I couldn't just turn up and blow my cover. You're too smart for that. Chris Breedon, who I knew a few years back...'

'Were you dealing drugs with him?' I said jokingly. 'Did he get found out by the Special Forces, like you had with drugs?'

Ludkin looked shocked at the revelation, then slammed his boot on the floor. 'Are you fucking going to let me finish? For fuck's sake.'

I now understood the truth to why Chris had been chucked out the Army, and how they knew each other. 'Be my guest, but the short version, please.'

'What's the rush? Looking forward to dying?'

'No, my ears are starting to bleed because you're so fucking boring, and I want to take you to Larry.'

Ludkin shook his head in disbelief.

Really though, I was scared, trying to spot an opportunity to attack him.

'We found out that Chris was struggling with money, so we offered a big cash incentive. After a little digging around, I found out about one of your mates; well, one that was still alive: Roy Franklin. Chris befriended him with the intel we had on Roy and managed to lure him to Cornwall. It was easy as Roy had gone a bit loopy-loo. Once there, Chris persuaded Roy to join him in Canada. Once here, we looked after the *bait*. We knew you would come looking, boy.'

'You forgot to tell Chris that he was expendable.'

'I think Chris enjoyed the mission. I'm amazed he thought of all these plans to get you both here. The map, postcard, and even the silent calls from us; genius. However, live by the sword, die by my weapon.' He chuckled to himself.

'You've said "we" and "us" a few times,' I quizzed.

'You'd be amazed how many people want to meet up with you.'

My distaste levels were sky-high, but I had to remain calm. 'You fucking idiot,' I blurted. 'You really think Larry is alive. My shit has more brains than you. He's at the bottom of a swamp on the island you'd left. And the formula, that's in the hands of David Mclachlan, insurance that Abishua's estate was eradicated.' My heart was beating fast.

Ludkin stood up and kicked the chair, then the table. I lifted my hands up as he came over to hit me with the Heckler. Suddenly, he stopped, a sinister smile lighting up his angered face. I feared it worse than the fight I wanted. He took a few paces back.

'You know what, Johnny,' he said calmly, 'I think you wouldn't mind me killing you now, especially after losing so many mates in the past, including today. But I wonder if there's someone you would hate more to end your sorry, pathetic life.'

I didn't want it to, but my mind started searching for names. 'I can't think of anyone,' I said unconvincingly.

'Oh, I'm sure there is. Think harder, Johnny.'

I squinted at him, trying to picture who he was on about.

'Be careful what you wish for,' he said.

'All I'm wishing for is you lower that weapon and fight me man to man.'

'You're too lethal.'

Ludkin backed up to the door and, with his other hand, he opened the door and backed out, still watching me. My mind raced for answers, and a way of escaping. What could I use as a weapon? If he went out any further, would I have the time to rush him? We had reached the pinnacle of my survival or dying. Different voices were talking in my mind, mainly encouragement to take the fight, to keep going. Shall I test him to see if he had the balls to kill me? Stupid thought.

Ludkin turned to his right and signalled at someone. I stood up, dropping the blanket, and picked up a piece of glass. I was in control of the situation. Ludkin turned around. I made evil eye-contact with him. He re-gripped his Heckler, tightening it into his shoulder. I took another two steps forward, brandishing the glass. I wasn't sure what I was doing, but it felt I needed to. Ludkin looked concerned. A shadow appeared at his feet; he smiled.

'Welcome home, Vince.'

The glass dagger dropped, along with my jaw.

Dick Brown barged past Andy, stomping towards me. I bent down to pick up the weapon but felt the thud to my chest. Sprawling back, winded, I scrambled to my feet. Instinctively, I went into my karate stance. Dick swung around a piece of wood from behind him and hit the palm of his hand. I realised it was a Hickory handle, possibly from an axe; at least the head was missing. Ludkin had lowered his weapon and was beaming. I had lots of quips that I wanted to tease my old CO, but decided to shut up, for once.

Working out his move just after he coiled back for a swing at me, I stepped in close and fired a punch to the back of his large tricep, his muscular bicep hitting him in the face. I followed up with a damaging left blow to his left kidney, then a swooping open-palm strike to his bollocks. Somehow, the Hickory still contacted the top of my scull; the characteristic sound rang. Slightly dazed, I took two quick steps back and front kicked him on the inside of his thigh. Switching my other leg forward, I raised my open hands in front.

Dick had kept in shape, looking like a rhino in a kid's t-shirt, and snorting mad like one. A warm tickle flowed down behind my ear. Instead of coming at me again, Dick moved to his left and viciously side kicked the table-leg. Everything on top trashed to the floor. As he picked up the leg, I thought he was going to give it to me, as if to even it up—stupid. Grinning, he chucked it back at Andy.

Ludkin placed his Heckler deliberately slowly on the ground and intentionally marvelled the new weapon. Dick made some comment about not only breaking ankles, but I had missed the rest as I had glanced down at Andy's main weapon. That was my saviour, his mistake. Before Ludkin had the chance to square up with Dick, I launched my attack. Body blows and kicks sent Dick to the floor. I followed in, listening to his grunts. Just as I stood tall, the table-leg swung in. My not quite fast enough block didn't push it all the way past. The stinging, tingling sensation spread rapidly from my shoulder to the tips of my fingers; the whole arm paralysed.

Annoyed that Roy and Chris were being trampled, I swung a fast strike to Andy's temple, stunning him. Then I side kicked him to the top of his knee. Dick got up, red in the face. I put my right hand up for defence; my left just flopped by my side. Dick yelled and, lowering his stance, ran at me. Even though it's not in rugby rules, I kicked him to the top of his head. However, his overbearing size continued. I fell, the back of my head hitting the bunk. I lashed out, fist after fist. The sound was exciting. I knew I was winning. Suddenly, my world went black.

★

Back at HQ, Dick was speaking to us as we prepared for Operation Blue Halo. I wondered how much he hated that I was going instead of his son Lee, let alone me leading the mission that I had named. As Dick left, he gave me a weird grin. This time I knew there was going to be trouble. Planet, Fish, and Shrek all congratulated me after the briefing. As we got our shit together, the other SAS lads came in, rowdy, excited. We were on top of the world.

As the fantastic feeling evaporated, I forced my eyes open. My head thumped like a numeric drill. Once the strange shapes came into focus, the reality I had been knocked out came to bare. Sick and tired of being out-cold on numerous occasions, I cursed. Laughter came from the corner of the room. Groggily, but not to show I was beaten yet, I sat up. Strangely, my hands and feet were not bound. Weirder, Andy's Heckler was next to me. After seeing my pistol laid next to that, I slowly lifted my stare. Dick and Ludkin stood leaning against the wall. Dick held up a pump-action shotgun. Was this a duel? Andy walked across to me and, at arm's length, held out a bottle of water.

Thirsty?' Ludkin asked.

In training, we had been taught to accept food and water. I sipped the water through my swollen, dry blooded lips, then cleared my throat. Even though it did not taste fresh, I needed the boost, so I drank some more. After, I tried not to smile at their injuries.

'Pick up the Heckler?' Dick ordered. 'One false move and I'll spread your insides across the wall.'

Looking down, I marvelled the weapon in my hand. Thoughts raced in my mind: why would they give me this? They know I would kill them in a blink of an eye. I noticed only Monkfish was on the floor, having been moved slightly. I placed the weapon back down, cynical of their plan.

'Where's Roy?' I asked.

'On the top bunk,' Dick said—I cringed. 'This is how it's been worked out: when they find you, you will either be frozen to death.'

Ludkin opened the door and then elbowed out the remaining window glass.

'Or, with the remaining round in the chamber, you'll shoot yourself,' Dick finished.

'What makes you think I wouldn't escape and find you?' I asked.

'In just your shorts? Hashtag: minus five,' Dick said.

'Surprised you know what a hashtag is. Hashtag: old Dick-head,' I retorted.

'It was nice to bump into Andy after all these years,' he said. 'Fancy him and Lee knowing each other from days gone by.'

'Lee?' I scoffed.

'Even better to hear, Andy wanted to kill you. How could I resist after all the shit you dumped me in?'

'Jesus fuck. Are you still pissed off that your pathetic son never got to lead Blue Halo?'

'He lasted longer than you did in the Reg.'

'Sorry, I forgot the Rupert, Richard Reddin, dismissed you from the Elite, not long after I quit. What a jolly good chap he was,' I said.

'You should have named it Operation Johnny Vince's Fuck-up,' Dick said.

'Operation Kill my Mates,' Ludkin added.

They both laughed.

Whilst they found this highly amusing, strangely, my anger did not rise; instead, I felt passive. 'How's Lee these days? Ever get his penis enlarged?' My laugh was odd, as if it came from somewhere else.

'He's left the Elite and now has a lovely high-paid security job, and a beautiful family; unlike you. It's a damn shame Ella didn't stay with Lee.'

'Yeah, shame,' I slurred.

'If you hadn't of interfered, Ella wouldn't have been raped.' Dick grinned.

'What?' I mumbled. My rapidly dropping energy levels did not allow me to pick up the Heckler to slot the motherfucker.

'Oh, didn't you know?' Dick asked facetiously.

'You, like Ella, really ought to be careful accepting drinks from strangers, especially me,' Ludkin said.

Fuck you, I thought, dribble seeping.

'Right from day one, you have played emphatically into our hands,' Ludkin continued.

'It was strange to see Chris' phone video of you in the restaurant carpark. I'm not sure what was going on, but I knew one day our paths would cross,' Dick added.

'You both should never have had the privilege of wearing the badge,' I said lamely.

'You see, when you wake tonight dressed in just your shorts, you will have either gone stiff...'

'And I doubt he means your useless non-baby making manhood,' Ludkin interrupted Dick.

'Or, you will have survived. However, with no means of heat to survive, and blankets and transport to get you the thirty-five kilometres to the log cabin...'

'The one you blew up along with your car, you stupid twat,' Ludkin butted in, again.

'I've managed… to kill most who have… chased us, including your… fucking dods,' I said softly.

'I think you meant dogs,' Dick said. 'Yes, you have single handily stopped all the hired hands, but you've missed the two most important. Your downfall.'

'Threat neutra…' I couldn't finish.

'Now, that's why I have kindly left you one in the chamber,' Dick finished.

'And with the thoughts wildly going around your head.' Ludkin put his fingers to his temple. 'Bang.'

Not being able to keep myself up, I slumped onto the bed, nose touching the Heckler. It was so near, but so far. Just one shot, that's all I needed, I thought.

'Once someone finds you frozen in years to come…'

'Or perhaps with your brains blown,' Ludkin continued the double-act.

'They will surmise you killed Roy with your pistol, and Chris with your Heckler, as your prints are now on it,' Dick said. 'With statements from your friends and family, they will say you killed yourself because of your PTSD. That's if you have the bollocks to even put the weapon to your head.'

I blinked away the water and focused on the doorway. Someone was walking in the far distance. I took in a sharp breath and held it, rehearsing the words in my mind.

'Has it not crossed your tiny pea-brains how I've managed to stay one step ahead of you dickheads on this mission to find Roy?' I slurred, then gasped oxygen.

'What do you mean?' Ludkin quizzed.

I had to stay awake, I thought. 'Wasn't… single… handed,' I mumbled, closing my eyes, but didn't want to miss out. 'You're… the… rogues.'

Bang… bang!

The gunshots were muffled; the thuds made me happy. I dozed off.

CHAPTER SIXTEEN

The slaps around one side of face and the constant shaking annoyed me, but intoxicated, I could not stop it. At least the pain from my injuries has subsided. Steve's shouting was like that of yelling through a pillow. I could only imagine him with his wounds, dragging me up and half-placing me over his shoulder, a surreal out of body moment. My words as he heaved me outside made no sense, even though I knew what I was trying to say.

The sun dazzled my already blurry vision. The world was a whiteout. Weirdly, I could not feel the cold on my near-naked body, unlike my throat and lungs. Close against the white floor, I tried to guess why Steve had laid me down. Next, something was placed over my head. Steve rapidly cleared the way for me to breathe. Was that snow? Why the fuck was Steve trying to freeze my brain? Again, he abused me. I wanted to tell him to stop, or at least slap him back. Without warning, he dumped my head back on the ground. All went silent. I listened in, totally mummified. My breath began to freeze my lungs. Was I shivering?

After what seemed a lifetime of nothing, I was on the move again, but this time dragged. The blurry bright sky and surroundings bounced off my face. Counting steps was easy; well, not my feet that were all over the place, but Steve's trudges. At last, my yelling and swearing sounded more like it should, but so did the cursing back from Steve. I knew I was smiling.

A door opened, but before I could work it all out, I was bundled into something. Further yanking got me in a sitting position. Different shapes teased my mind. My head leant forward against something transparent. Steve was talking next to me; what, I don't know. Suddenly, a huge light flashed, followed by a muffled explosion. I shut my eyes; the image still bright. Further clunking and purring sounded. Being rocked around, I began to relax and enjoy the peace. This was a nice place.

Warm, cosy, I tried to turn on my side to give Ella a hug and, perhaps, a bit more. I was as randy as virgin teenager at an LA beach party.

'Glad you have returned to your sanity. Well, almost.'

I took my hand off Steve and sat bolt upright, head spinning. Wiping the dribble from my chin, I then touched the aching head lump.

'You OK?'

'Where are we?' I croaked. 'What happened?'

'On the way…'

'Why am I in my pants,' I interrupted.

'It wasn't down to Ella.' Steve laughed.

Rushing to take my seatbelt off, I was reminded of the injuries before and after the encounter with Dick and Andy, but I continued to check the rear seats. He wasn't in the rear boot area either.

'Where's Roy's body?' I asked.

'I'm afraid we couldn't bring him, but he got a good cremation.'

'Is that supposed to be fucking funny? Happy to stop the fucking car *this* time.'

Steve slowed up, glanced at my stern look in his rear-view mirror, and then gained speed. 'I had to hide all the carnage. I have been on many assignments, Johnny, but never have I had so much trouble and mess to deal with. Is this your normal life?'

'You know my past, Steve.'

Gingerly, I climbed back into the Honda's front seat and searched the glovebox. For the first time I noticed how pale Steve was in his blood-soaked winter suit. He threw me something: the hire car agreement. Reading the front, it was Dick's name.

'So, that's it, we just left Roy and Chris,' I said.

'I had to leave behind my comrade Ant.'

'Don't be so anal,' I barked. 'You can say friend or mate, for God's sake.'

'Oh, and now it's Chris, is it. A bit more respectful than Monkfish.'

'What happened back there?'

'It was easy to follow your trail with the dead dogs and one enemy. I'm surprised the rest didn't follow your tracks.'

'That's because they wanted me to get to the shack,' I said. 'Dick and Andy had deceived Monkfish into getting Roy to Canada, and…' I paused. 'You knew, didn't you.'

'Rhetorical?' he asked.

I waited for him to answer my question.

'I wasn't aware of Monkfish being involved until you had said, but both Dick and Andy have been on the list for some time.'

'Why the fuck didn't you tell me?'

'Work that out, Johnny.'

I wanted to yank up the handbrake and beat his not so good-looking face, but I was remembering wanting and doing are two different things. The non-talking as I looked at the scenery was getting to me.

'And Will, is he on the list?' I asked.

'Will? No, he's just runs a simplistic airport in Cyprus.' Steve winked at me. 'Oh, and thanks for saving me would be pleasant.'

'Ditto.' I folded my arms in a huff. 'I need some painkillers. And some clothes.'

Steve clumsily drove with his knees, almost skidding off the track. Pulling his hand from his side pocket, he handed me a packet. It was stained red, but I was desperate to stop the pains. With no water, I swallowed four. Steve looked on. I stared back, wondering what the fuck we both looked like: me in just my pants and battered body, and him in a blooded, ripped, camouflaged artic suit, with half a hand. I hope we do not get stopped by the police.

'So, that's it then?' I asked.

'Yes, that's the last of the sleeping tablets.'

'That's not what I meant.'

'Oh, the mission.'

'Sarcasm as well? Jesus. I meant for finding rogues.'

'Dick and Andy? Err, yeah,' he said stupidly and sarcastically.

'How come now you're coming out of you shell?'

Steve smirked. 'Must have listened to you and Ant for too long.'

'Perhaps.' I thought of Ant. 'Hold on. Sleeping tablets? Why the fuck did you give me those instead of painkillers?'

'I had no painkillers. Now get some sleep. It won't be long before this mission is over.' Steve clumsily changed down a gear as we came back onto the main road, and then floored it.

Not only did I try to fight off the thought of punching him in the face, but also the grogginess that enveloped me. Not in control again, my thoughts turned worrying. Where were we heading to? Has he drugged me on purpose? What did "won't be long before this mission is over" mean? I thought it was over. As much as I battled to keep awake, the nice feelings of sleep overtook…

★

Clearer images of Steve killing Dick and Ludkin and the explosion at the shack played out in my dream. I relived the scenes where I first met Monkfish, right up till the last phone call. His deception was now obvious. Even though I held him in contempt for getting me to the shack, especially that I was vulnerable, he had not squeezed the trigger on Roy. I believed Monkfish had not known the severity of what he was getting himself involved in, not just by his admissions and beatings, but he had paid the ultimate price. What a fuck-up Operation Edge had been, except the death of Andy and Dick. How would I tell Christine about Roy? Do I lie about the mission? The scene played where I told her and the kids that I had shot him. It was horrific. I tried to wake up but wasn't ready to. In the docks, the judge read the damning statements from everyone involved, including Steve's untruthful events. Even the lad at the hotel lied. As I was led away in hand-cuffs with two-life sentences, I looked up at my inconsolable mum, my angry brother, and standing on the end, a sorrowful Ella.

'Ella,' I yelled, as cold water had been splashed on my face.

Wiping the liquid from my eyes, I stared at Steve. I was confused at first to why he was holding a bottle of water, and then to why he was wearing a suit. His injuries had been seen to. I looked around at the disused, snow-covered factory on a vast-open wasteland. Tyre tracks and footprints circled the area.

'Am I dreaming again?' I muttered.

'No. This is reality,' Steve said, non-friendly.

'Why didn't you give me that water when you gave me the tablets?'

'You didn't ask,' he coldly said.

There was no concealment he had slid his weapon onto his lap. The air thickened with an uneasy prediction to why we were here.

'Back to James Bond,' I said.

He didn't reply.

I searched the derelict factory and grounds. 'How come you're all changed? Who helped you?'

'You need to stop blaming yourself for the loss of such friends who decided to enter the world you work. It was their choice.'

I wasn't excepting that. 'And the images and dreams?'

'Ignore them.'

'Pull my fucking socks up?' I snapped, thinking of Ant.

'OK. Get drunk. Disrespect yourself and lose everything you have worked so hard for. Abuse those that care about you: your friends, your brother, and parents. Perhaps jump off a cliff.'

I was gobsmacked. 'My dad is dead.'

'I know,' he snapped, then punched the steering wheel with his good hand.

Confused to the reaction, I said, 'Did you know him?'

Steve was breathing hard, his crystal eyes filled.

'Are you OK, Steve?'

'There must be another way to end all your suffering and self-pity.' Steve looked at his weapon.

'I could snatch the pistol and shove it up your arse,' I retorted.

He half-smiled. 'What were you like before that helicopter disaster?'

'I was the best, positive in everything. It didn't matter what challenges were laid out; I mentally set out to complete them. If I failed, I would get up again, and again. Not only was I a brilliant leader, but I also respected my followers. Without them…' I stopped; it had dawned on me.

Steve nodded at me.

'I wish I could turn back the clock, revisit…'

'You can't physically return to your past. Going back to 1944 was a figment of your imagination, the positive role you subconsciously want. Return to what you know best, Johnny. Or you could kill yourself.'

'Can you stop fucking saying that. I'm not ready to die.'

'Are you sure about that?'

'My family and friends need me back,' I muttered.

Steve took his stare off me and checked his watch, then he looked at the disused factory.

'I need to go back to my roots, as someone had said recently. Find the real me, where I was most fulfilled,' I said.

'Stop judging your personality, complex as you say. You are who you are. Perhaps you should ask your mum how she saw you as a child.'

Where did that come from? It had no bearing on what we were chatting about. 'Leave my family out of this,' I barked.

'You bring a unique set of survival skills, aggression, leadership, the thinking soldier, and caring levels to the table, Johnny. That's all I am saying.'

'I know, but why should I ask my mum?'

Steve checked his rear-view mirror, then readied his weapon.

My body was suspended in time; my eyes side glanced at the door handle. Was Steve giving me the chance to go? How far would I get? In shorts and no weapon, not far. Would he shoot me in the back? He had it on his lap, the end pointing at my side. Were his reactions quicker than mine? I was still tired and beat up.

'Decisions,' he mumbled.

I went to reply, but stopped when a black BMW saloon roared past, skidding to a halt about twenty metres away. Not being able to see through the blacked-out windows, I twisted sharply to Steve, who appeared sorrowful. My heart started to race when two men in sleek suits got out, armed with machineguns with silencers. I narrowed my eyes at Steve.

'Is this it?' I asked. 'Do I not get to change?'

'I have a choice to make.'

The two guys slowly walked over. The quiet ticking clock now sounding like Big Ben. I tried to keep my composure. Thoughts whizzed around my mind.

'Are you thinking of grabbing my weapon and using me as a bargaining deal?' Steve asked.

'No. Fucking slot you, and then take on the other two morons.'

Steve handed over his pistol, then from inside his jacket, a passport. 'You will have special clearance at the check-in.'

'I'm free to go then?'

'I don't want you on my radar again.' Steve quickly got out; the two-armed suits stopped.

'So, I was on your list,' I muttered.

'Your change is behind you,' he said, and gently shut the door.

Holding the pistol ready whilst scrutinising Steve talking to the other men, I discreetly started to shift over to the driver's side. The discussion between them seemed to go on for ages, before eventually, they led him to the waiting BMW. As soon as the door was closed, the saloon sped off.

I must have sat still for a minute checking the rear-view mirror, before realising the cold silence. Was that it? It was like nothing had ever happened. The snow started to fall. An empty feeling engulfed me. I started the engine, noticing the passport on the floor. Opening it up, I stared at my photo, unsure to why. That was the old me I so wanted back.

What's stopping you?

I looked around for the different voice but was alone. Was that Monkfish's voice in my mind? Had he said this to me before? Even with Roy dead, the fact was that Monkfish had saved me from cutting the rope. I had forgiven him.

Flicking through the passport, looking at the stamps of all the places that I had managed to return from, two loose photos were on the last page. The first was of me when I was young. I held it up and studied it, not ever seeing it before, wondering who had taken it. It was me in army uniform as I passed SAS selection, pleasing to see. I turned the other over. Surprisingly, it was my dad in a suit standing next to a lad. The boy was not me or my brother. Because I wanted more answers from this small photo, I held it closer. In the background was some sort of prison, like a detention centre. Dauntingly, the lad looked like a younger version of Steve. I went cold.

Checking the rear boot area of the Honda CRV from outside was not the best idea. I thought the freezing temperatures might take my mind off the images and feelings of my dad and Steve, but the thoughts kept processing. My bollocks had retracted quicker than the land speed record. Surely my dad could not have been that man who visited him in prison.

On top of a blue gym-type bag was a neatly folded suit. Under this were shoes and a tie. I smirked thinking of what Steve had said, "Your change is behind you". And there was me thinking he was being meaningful about my life. Inside the holdall was my phone, but the screen was cracked. I marvelled the cylinder object, the type that Steve had used on the random car at the airport. At the bottom was a ticket for a flight at 14.30 hrs, and a hundred and fifty in British cash. And that was it. It was a shame he had never left the thermal gadget. Tosser, I thought, and smirked.

Once dressed, feeling weird in such fine clobber, I strolled around to the driver's side, wiping the snow off my new shoes. Again, I sneered at how everything fitted perfectly. Not thinking about the importance of it before, I placed Steve's personal Waltham in my inside suit jacket. Something else was in there. I pulled out a torn piece of black cloth, leaving my fingers slightly tinged with red. An image sprang to mind: Ant pulling down his beanie-hat.

'Fucking hell, Johnny,' I said, 'you're turning into *Mr Ben*.'

Not having a clue where I was in Canada, I set the satnav to the airport, pleased to see it was only twenty miles south.

After leaving the airport's multistorey, I stood on the walkover gantry, taking a long look back. Next to me was a bin, so I put the special car key and black material in it. I pondered on the pistol as my hand touched it, deciding I did not want any further hassle of handling illegal weapons; done that, wore the t-shirt. After ripping out the phone's sim and breaking both, I chucked them in as well. New start, I thought.

With a new spring in my step, I found the main check-in desk. At best, I ignored the confused looks of a well-dressed man with a face that had seen better days. I made all sorts of stories why I had no luggage but a gym bag, and where I had been. I knew the following questions were security ones. My charm had returned, along with the libido, as the stunning staff acted all coy, blushing to my flirting; or that's how it felt to me.

At the passport clearance, an older gentleman gave me a quick raised eyebrow, but waved me through. I wondered if I would have passed through with the weapon, as Steve had said. Perhaps he knew I would dump it, a test. I felt super-special, like that of an agent, but walking to the waiting area, I knew this wasn't me. However, I was going to milk it whilst on the flight with the ladies.

During the long flight, even though the stewardesses were trying their best to make me feel good, I chose not to have anything alcoholic. Resting my body and mind was better. I knew where I was going and what I had to do to get there. Back on track, I was not going to derail. The black dogs had been put down.

Touching British soil felt everything good had returned. Again, I glided through the airport with ease and made a detour for the shops. Once I purchased what I needed to, spending all the money, I went to the toilets and changed into jeans, a sweater, and trainers. OK, I was now looking like a branded celeb, but the suit had started to chaff. Hopefully, leaving the expensive tailored suit and gym bag, someone would have it. Perhaps the cleaner I passed as I left.

Strolling across the main hall, I had no money or a phone. Shit. It was going so well.

'I thought you'd retired,' someone said behind me.

I turned to see a blast from the past, then put my hand out to shake his. 'Still working the security beat. And you still got that fucking sissy tattoo,' I bantered.

'I could fucking shoot you just for touching me.' He beamed; his mate got the gist of what was going on.

'You mean that pea-shooter is loaded? Fuck me,' I said.

'We've intel that there's a wanker lurking through the airport.'

'Dressed like a model's chihuahua,' his colleague chipped in.

I exaggerated the look around me, before stepping back aghast when

I faced them both. 'I think that's two wankers that should be on your radar. I would sack the head of intel.'

They both chuckled.

'I'm Dave.'

'Johnny,' I replied, and then looked his mate.

'Dave,' he replied.

'Yeah, right,' I said.

'What brings you through this time? Not had another visit to the US president?' Dave-1 asked.

'Bollocks to politics,' I said. 'I need a favour though.'

'If you're after high heels and handbag to go with your attire, you can fucking buy it yourself,' Dave-2 said.

'I've lost my wallet and can't get home.'

'Have you reported it?' Dave-1 asked sarcastically.

I pulled a dumb face at him.

'I could arrange a lift home for you,' Dave-2 said.

'Fuck me. Dave and Dave, the comical duo. If I gave you any indication of where I live, I would be expecting a large knock at the door.'

They both nodded.

'Can I borrow some cash to get a train back to...' I paused as they looked too intrigued, 'to wherever it is I need to go?'

'I take it "borrow" means that of the Elite: to borrow what isn't yours and never return it,' Dave-1 said.

I smiled. 'You remember then.'

Dave-1 looked inconspicuously around before delving under his protection vest. He opened his wallet and quickly pushed a bundle in my hand.

'You're lost, sir?' he said loudly. 'Take this London underground map, this should sort you home.'

I leaned over and whispered, 'Your acting skills are a bag of shite.'

'Don't come to my airport again,' he bellowed.

After he had made a spectacle, he harshly turned me around and shoved me away. People stopped and stared. I didn't want to turn back to see Dave and Dave smugly smiling.

CHAPTER SEVENTEEN

I had been home for three days. In that time, I had managed to clean my house from top to bottom. Most of it I had binned, cleansing my past. I had even had pleasure having my car fully valeted. Even with the blinds and windows open, and many trips to the charity shop and local tip, no one had come around. Could I blame them. However, I was at least expecting Simon from next door to have popped in to see what the noise was about. Having cleared out my ex-military gear, except one uniform and a pair of boots, I had packed it away into two Bergans, along with a little money. After having heaved these two packs around town, I had found some old homeless chums and gave them the haul, taking a while for them to sink in who I was.

Like my problems in Poole had been, I was in disbelief I could have got my new house and life into such disarray again. These new changes were the first steps of my new plan, something I had thought hard about on the flight home.

Before I knocked on the door, I took a deep breath. Exhaling, I banged and stepped back. The familiar form through the front door's glazing appeared. I wrung my hands nervously. My mum, startled at first, burst into tears and then hugged me. This time I did not get that recent awkward feeling and embraced back. We stood on the doorstep for ages, before she put me at arm's length and sighed a big relief. Mum studied the cuts and bruises on my face. I told her the wounds have healed. She knew what I had meant.

It wasn't long before she was in the kitchen making tea, and more than likely getting a few snacks ready. The characteristic smells and sights harmonised me. Photos on the wall and furniture showed us all from an early age, up to recently. I looked differently at them, searching to see if I could see any problems that I might have had back then. Seeing Dad was amazing but upsetting. There was one photo taking centre position on the fireplace, a copy of mine that was in the locked chest under my floorboards. My heart ached. I was surprised to see Mum had one of us four and Ella at our wedding day. I thought she had thrown it away after Ella and I had separated. Perhaps Mum was still proud of this day, five of us together.

Emotional again, I took another relaxing exhale. I loved this house as a kid; I had come home. To enrich this beautiful nostalgia, Mum carried in a tray of doorstep sandwiches, cakes, tea, and a bottled beer. Hiding the sentiment away, I started to make small talk, but it came out all a load of squeaky, rambling nonsense. Mum smiled and told me to first have some food and a drink. I declined the beer, much to her enjoyment. Maybe the alcohol was a test.

Once I had relaxed, I briefly went over the mess I had got into because of the PTSD. Just admitting this was energising, lifting. I told her that I had gone away to Canada to get my mind straight, met some old friends, and I am now back in pole position. Most importantly, I would not be returning to those dark days. Fit to burst, her joy was palatable. Nothing was mentioned again, and the day-to-day chat flowed.

Whilst Mum made another brew, I leant back and put my hands behind my head. There was a knock at the door. Mum, almost running, shouted she would answer it. I heard Oliver talking. Mum must have messaged him. I sat up defensively. Oliver stood in the doorway, silent. Mum made some excuse about the tea getting cold and then disappeared. Oliver just stared. I stood to, expecting a punch to the face or a kick to the balls, but he started to well-up. I told him I was sorry.

After a long-lost brotherly embrace and some back slapping, he went into a rage about letting down him, Mum, and Dad. I soaked up more abuse, deserving every bit of it. Once he had got everything off his chest, he stormed into the kitchen, a beer opening shortly after—my beer. I smiled.

When they came out, the mood was passive. I recapped where I had been, the shorter version of why. I never told them I was up on the cliff. There was no need to bring them any further pain. Oliver told me what he had been up to. He was a bit surprised at my non-reaction that he had a boyfriend. I shrugged it off, saying I had already guessed. I think a bigger weight had been lifted off his shoulders, and perhaps Mum's. I looked at Dad's picture again, wondering if he had known. Did it matter? Oliver kept his answers short to my questions about Trevor and Simon; it was up to me to chat to them. Apparently, Lena had found a new flat in Newquay. I tried to make out I wasn't interested.

I knew it would come, and when it did, it hurt as much. Mum, with yet more snack delights, carried in Dad's wake photos, including the church service sheet. It was the hardest emotion to deal with. Mum said dad would have gone to the pub that day whether we had argued or not. Oliver agreed. It was a regular thing that he had a few pints and then staggered home.

After looking through the photos, I told them I wanted to go and see him. Stupidly, Oliver's boyfriend was sat in the car. For some reason he looked nervous when he saw me approaching. For a split-second, I thought about a prank, going into a rage about not a suitable bloke for my brother, but decided this wasn't the right time. After the greetings, making no fuss about it, Orion relaxed. He drove us to the funeral. Part of me wanted the closure, part of me was shitting it.

Trembling, I held my mum as we walked together. Orion did the decency thing and stayed at the gates. Once at the grave, I read the inscription. Oliver patted me on the back, then they left. I sat down on the damp grass. The birds were singing, the sun shining. I said my peace with him. For once in my life, I believed that beyond death someone could hear me. It was strange. One of the biggest burdens had been lifted. I must have sat there for an hour, telling him about Operation Poppy Pride, thinking, staring.

On the way home there was a silence. We must have all been thinking of dad.

'So, Orion, are you named after one of those eighties car that all the sisters drove?' I asked.

There was stunned quietness, before Orion said, 'I'm too young to know. But these days, it's the Audi the *sisters* love, especially white ones.'

I laughed. 'If it's not the car your parents named you after, it must be the mythical hunter.'

'Yep, big strapping huntsman me, biceps to prove it,' he said, taking the piss out of himself being skinnier than Oliver—I liked this guy.

Driving back into Newquay, we all agreed to my request of going to Dad's local. It was shock tactics on my behalf, but I needed to submerge myself in the deep end to get over it, and quick. The bar staff looked awkwardly at me as I walked in. Was it I had been barred recently? The manager came up to me, but instead of telling me to get out, he heartily apologised for letting my dad get so drunk. Our shoulders relaxed at the same time, or that's how it felt.

I cornered Oliver on the way back down from the toilets and asked him if he knew a bloke called Steve. He did, but only at school, an older troublesome kid who had been expelled. Oliver could not remember his second name though; how weird. The photograph I produced stoked a reaction, but Oliver frowned at me asking what this was all about. In the end, I just said I found the photo years ago and thought it was me, leaving it at that. Before we headed back to the now rowdy table, as other friends had joined, I held onto Oliver's arm.

'What was I like as a kid?' I asked.

Oliver probed me with a look. 'Do you have fantastic memories?'

'Yes,' I said.

Oliver patted my shoulder and walked away.

Even though they were drunk at the end of the evening, myself not touching a drop, I told them I was sorry for all the pain I had caused, and this was the end to it.

The very next day, I decided to drive all the way to Christine's house. Like the pervious journey, my thoughts and nerves started to get the better of me. I couldn't stomach any food. I must have prepared a speech, and then corrected it many times; also, fighting temptations to turn back.

Parking where I had last time, it was strange not to see Steve's Merc, and depressive not to see the BMW. At the door Christine appeared different, lighter; perhaps happier. After the hugs, participating myself this time, we entered. I still looked for any inclination that Steve was here.

Sitting with my brew in the now tidy lounge, I did not know where to start.

'It's fine, Johnny. You tried your best,' she said.

Had it been that it obvious that I had been looking uncomfortably around? I blew onto my tea. Come on, Johnny, grow a pair, I thought.

'Johnny?'

'I have something to tell you,' I murmured.

'You don't have to apologise. Steve contacted me and told me all about your endeavours to find Roy, and that you couldn't bring yourself to show me his last letter to me. Perhaps one day they will find his body at the bottom of the lake.'

I was speechless.

Christine came over and gave me a massive hug to console me. 'It's tough for us all, but now he may rest in peace. Without you, he wouldn't have made it back from Afghan, and would have been brutally murdered at the hands of terrorists, paraded on the media. At least this way he got to die with dignity, remembering his family and friends, as he wrote in the letter.'

I cleared my throat, the pain. 'Can I see the letter? I'll understand if you don't want to show me.'

'It was meant for you as well.' Christine went to the sideboard, then returned, leaving me alone with it.

I looked at the photo of Roy on the unit, before looking down at the writing:

> To my loving wife and family,
>
> Although this last letter may seem sadly desperate, it's not. Right now, all I can think about are the happy times with you and the children. I want to stay in this place, so I won't be returning. No more unhappy times for my loving family and children. I know my time has come to look over you from a different world, so I sit in this shack and write this letter knowing Johnny will try to free me from my troubles.
>
> I hope he survives the battle and passes this letter, my love, and devotion on to you. Without such a solid friend as you, Johnny, I wouldn't have enjoyed so much.
>
> You know from here on Christine, my darling, you, and the kids will all be looked after, and I want you all to live your lives.
>
> Thank you for such lovely children. Looking down on you all now, happy again.
>
> Love forever,
> Roy (Dad)

I read it again, the authenticity of it was incredible. The writing was in pencil on blue paper. The red stains had been washed. Had Steve found this on Roy? Roy must have known his time was up in the hands of those evil bastards. Had Monkfish given him the paper and pencil? Many emotions flooded me, but instead of putting them to the back of my mind, like normal, I let them out in the way of anger and tears. Christine stood over me and cared.

As I was about to leave, she handed back the envelope containing the cash. I made sure she knew I would not, could not, take it. I told her to pay off the debts, but Christine explained that Steve had transferred an exceptionally large amount of money, as a loan, until Roy's life insurance paid out, when his body had been found. I knew Steve wouldn't be asking for the money back and would now disappear forever. Christine eventually agreed to take the money, but for the children. Also, according to Christine, Steve had taken my VW van back to Cornwall. I went along with the lie, knowing that Steve, with the organization he belonged to, sorted out Monkfish's stuff. After telling her that I had a new phone and had lost Steve's mobile contact, she gave his number to me.

Sunday morning, whilst trying to get back to fitness, I jogged past Trevor and Simon going into the local café for a sneaky breakfast: a big fry-up, no doubt. Because I knew the owner well, I snuck in the back door. Once they had ordered the biggest breakfast with side orders to match, as expected, I got Robin to take out two plates with just an inch-square slice of bread with a sprig of parsley on top. Next to this, half a raw mushroom; both hated mushrooms. I stood out the back and listened. Robin told them that the new chef had said they were two fat fuckers that needed to go on a diet. Their angry reaction was hilarious. Simon shouted for the chef to come to the table. I quickly grabbed a blue hairnet and placed it over my face, then wrapped a towel around my head. Large kitchen knife in hand, I rushed out into the main eating area, shouting off the little Arabic that I could remember. Trevor was up first into a Karate stance, followed by Simon lifting a chair. I told them they were fat fuckers; it dawned on them.

Once the other diners had realised it was a prank, we sat down. The jovial mood was soon swapped for awkwardness. I started to make my apologies but was interrupted saying they understood. I insisted they let me finish. It was good to get it off my chest. The breakfast appeared, and nothing was said whilst we ate. However, as we reordered more tea and coffee, the banter came in subtle, which then twisted into full blown. Some of it was harsh; probably having lots of meaning. I had to endure it. Before we left, I asked Trever if I could come for some intense training.

'No, you're a fat fucker,' he said—I think he meant it.

Over the next eight weeks, whether it had a bearing on the next person I wanted to visit, I hit karate training, the gym, and a strict diet like a man possessed. It nearly killed me—irony. I had ordered a second-hand Karate Gi off eBay, but no cement mixer this time. I had managed to get Mike to answer his phone after non-stop plaguing. The conversation had started out to be an aggressive explosion on his part. I had no armour on, I just took the defeat. Eventually, once he had calmed, I said my apologies and explanation. We had not parted as best mates, but there was a mutual respect.

Tracking Will down had been like looking for Shergar in a dodgy Irish burger factory. After many days of leaving messages, he returned the call. I knew he would be frosty, no, guns blazing, and he had not disappointed. The threats to kill me had gone over my head, remaining passive. We eventually half-made up, promising to send him the most expensive rum I could buy—I did.

On one beautiful Newquay evening, I sat in my living room with a fresh milk and a chicken sandwich after a good work out at the gym. I had ended the call numerous times before it had been answered, not knowing how to start the conversation with Ocker. We had been through as much as me and Roy had in Afghanistan. Both had saved me from certain death. What kind of fucked-up place had I been in to ruin what we had? This time I was pumped-up to make the call. It rang for ages—no change there then.

'G'day?'

'Don't hang up, Tommy. I just want to profusely apologise,' I pleaded.

'Profound pommy twats aren't on my agenda today, so profusely fuck off,' Ocker replied in a terrible posh English accent. He ended the call.

I had to phone another five times, before he answered. 'Tommy, I just need to apologise for my idiotic blame for the death of my dad. I was in a bad...'

'Yep,' he interrupted. 'Ya turned into a fucking bitzer alright.'

I smiled. 'I thought I was a green-eyed mullet?'

'That's a brown-eyed mullet, ya stupid pommy dropkick,' he said, more caring.

'What have you been up to?'

'Ya small talk is about as good as ya tiny pig-dick, mate.' Ocker laughed.

'Listen, Tommy, I'm sorry I blamed you for me missing my dad's funeral, and...'

'And for his death, don't forget that,' he butted in.

'Yes, and that, and all the other things I've said.'

'The list goes on, mate. Longer than an Abo's burger fuzz.'

The image entered my mind, I cringed. 'So, we're all square then?' I waited, hoping.

'OK, grouse, but you pull that croc shit on me again...'

'And you'll turn up with a proper cricket team,' I over spoke.

'Don't be fucking daft. So, ya wanna meet up in the land of plenty? I can you show some real fat sheila.'

'No. This is it, Tommy. Take care of those lovely kids. Hooroo.' I ended the call.

I had staked out the house from the opposite bus-stop for four days consecutive, catching the same bus up the road to my car. The wet weather clothing had helped me conceal who I was. Today, the sun was out. Spring was in the air. Over the top of my newspaper, I watched them both leave in his car. As per usual, the TV went on in the lounge. This time I waved the bus on, much to the bemusement of the driver. I was more nervous than when I had visited my mum, but I needed to do this for closure. Leaving behind the paper, I crossed the road. In a parked car's windows, I made sure I looked presentable in every way. Here goes, I thought. I knocked...

'Johnny,' she gasped.

'Ella, we need to talk.'

I placed my hand on the door that tried to close, but she pushed slightly back on it, then looked at my hand. I stared hard into her frightened eyes.

'I've nothing to say. Go away.'

'Five minutes, and I'm out of your life forever. Please, Ella.'

'My parents are in.'

I smirked. 'Do you think I would be knocking if I hadn't seen them leave?'

Ella released the door.

Following her into the lounge, I was reminded how stunning she was, and how much I missed those wonderful feelings. I sat down on the main recliner. She sat on the other side of the room, defensively. I raised my eyebrows; she wrung her hands together.

'I'm sorry...'

'Would you like a milky coffee?' she interrupted.

'With a caramel slice, like the good old days,' I said jovially. What dumb reply, I thought.

She blushed awkwardly and left the room.

There were no pictures of me or other men, just her and her parents. I wondered what they would say if they knew I was here. It filled me with dread, as if me and Ella were young lovers again. They had never liked me.

Ella handed me the coffee, her hands trembling.

'I know it went tits-up for us, but I'm really, really sorry I never listened to you in the days leading up to Blue Halo.'

'Days? Months,' she blurted. 'Sorry.'

'It's OK. I know you wanted to start a family.'

'Well, that's in the past. What have you been up to?'

That was an abrupt conversation stopper, I thought. 'I'd like to make amends. As you know, I wasn't right after the mission. I'm not sure how much you've heard, or even if from the right person, but I've made some big fuck-ups. I just…'

'No, you haven't,' she said. 'You're still the Johnny Vince I loved back then. It's me that made the mistake of leaving you high and dry, ending up with that prick… him.'

I knew who she had meant and why she couldn't say his name. What had shocked me was her admission for leaving me helpless. I took a gulp of coffee to ease the lump in my throat, so did Ella with her cup.

'If I could turn back the clock for you,' I said.

'You know, don't you.'

'In your own time, Ella. In your own time.'

Tears trickled down her beautiful cheeks. I placed my coffee down and walked over to her, giving her a reassuring and gentle hug. It was amazing to hold her again.

'Thanks, Johnny. It's nice to see you back. Perhaps we could talk more, meet up.'

I knew she had meant back to my former self. 'Now's not the right time for me and you, but we'll meet again one day, when the world is clearer. Perhaps like it was in our new house.'

Ella looked puzzled as I got up to leave. 'Are you staying in Newquay?' she asked.

'Thanks for excepting me back in. I hope you find the strength and love to carry on.'

'Hold on, Johnny.'

I stopped.

She squeezed me from behind. 'Thank you for everything,' she said. 'Please visit again.'

I wanted to turn and hold her, kiss her, but this was not part of my plan. Once she had released, I walked out the door, only wiping my eyes as I crossed the road. Instead of waiting for a bus, I walked the two miles back to my car. I needed to reset my feelings.

Driving past The Whitehouse Inn, I smirked remembering Monkfish throwing the bread rolls. Taking the next bend, at a sensible speed this time, I wondered if the film of me standing in the muddy field aiming a baseball bat like an RPG would ever be made public. I shivered at the thought. Hopefully, those that I now had made peace with understood what had happened to me. Shit, I had not contacted Monkfish's wife. How fucking insensitive.

At the next layby, I parked. On my new phone, I text: 'Hi Christine. Thank you for the relief of any blame. I hope you find fun and love again. Do you know Chris Breedon?'

After waiting five minutes, I continued my journey. Typically, a text came in, so I found another spot to stop: 'Hi Johnny. You've never been to blame. It's funny you mention him. He contacted me unexpectedly a while ago asking for Roy to make contact. Why do you ask?'

I replied: 'I knew his wife and wanted to talk to her about a matter.'

I set off again after getting bored of waiting. This time when the reply text came, I couldn't be bothered to pull over; it's not going to matter if the police stop me. It read: 'I'm so sorry Johnny. She died of cancer two years back. Chris didn't leave a number.' I almost ditched the car, also hearing Chris say, "I have an empty heart with my wife gone". So, he had been telling the truth that his wife had left him. I pictured the wedding ring hanging from his necklace.

At the kiosk, I paid my fee, the bloke studying me. He handed me back the change, purposely looking down the length of my Audi.

'Have we met?' he asked.

'Don't think so.'

'Don't remember wheel spinning around this car park, lad.'

'No, this is my first time here.'

'Hmmmm,' he said, waving me on.

'Wanker, 'I muttered, just enough so he could hear.

I sat on the exact spot, dangling my legs over the edge. The sea was calm. I turned to see if anyone else had decided to take the glorious walk on this beautiful spring day. From my phone, I played out a new song by Coldplay: *Amazing Day*. I had beaten the black dogs. Still in the boulder behind me was the Petzl life anchor. I smirked, knowing I did not need any climbing gear today. I had made the tough decision.

CHAPTER EIGHTEEN

Racing home, but not as crazy as I had with Monkfish, I mulled over what I had written in a leaving note at home. Was it enough? Parking outside my home, I looked at my lovely car, possibly for the last time. Heading inside, I picked up the mail from the mat, opening the important looking letter first. It was what had hoped for, cutting it fine: solicitors letter confirming I had left my unmortgaged house and all possessions to Oliver.

Over the last three months, I had sorted all my documents and cashed in my ISA and savings. I had left some of the cash in an envelope, placing it and photos from my personal locked box in a file organiser. I had kept back one important photo and stashed it in my backpack. Everything that was of no importance to anyone, including the photo of my dad and Steve, had been disposed of. Lastly, I had placed three sealed envelopes on top of the unit. One addressed to Mum & Oliver, the other to Trevor and Simon, and the last, to Ella. I stared at them for a few seconds. This was the new beginning.

Wanting to keep the place immaculate, I started throwing the junk-mail in the bin. I stopped when I came across my name only, hand-written on an envelope. I tried to guess who it was from before I opened it. Firstly, I read who had signed it: Steve Steve.

Johnny,

You have a purpose in life. Do not waste it, use it.

Steve Steve.

P.S. The mobile number Christine gave you will not work. Leave me alone.

Lighting the gas, I set it alight. When the flames got to my fingers, I chucked it in the sink, allowing it to burn out. I imagined Steve posting it through my door. I still looked out the window.

The remaining letter, I opened. I had forgotten to pay my psychologist for the last four sessions. I had been seeing a new professional twice a week on my return. He was ex-military that had seen action on many tours. It was the final nail in the black dogs' coffin; although, he had advised the PTSD would never go, but could be managed. I left the letter on the file, hoping Oliver or Mum would pay it. Whilst I cleaned the sink, a car sounded its horn outside. I checked my new watch, a Rolex Sea-Dweller, a tribute to my dad, then took a last gaze at my lounge.

As we left the town, I looked back, not with sadness, but intrigued to how it would be when I returned. The driver made small talk, asking where I was going, etcetera, but I fed him bullshit.

After he helped me out with my medium-sized rucksack, he made a comment about travelling the world with only one bag. To shut him up, I tipped him generously.

Like before, the near fourteen hours and seven thousand miles of travelling had numbed my arse. Not so much my brain this time, as I had managed to read that book my dad had given me: *How to Stay Safe as an Adventurer*. The argument we'd had in conjunction with this book didn't affect me so much.

There was no apprehension going through passport control, and I strolled outside. Instead of the pure-blue sky of last, there were slight clouds, reckoning the heat was in the early thirties—nice. This time I walked past where I had sat on the small brick wall under the main airport sign, the three red and white flags still fluttered up high on poles. That evil, little, skinny Setiawan came to my mind, being all rude and cocky sat on his junk-heap motorbike. Poor old Gavin getting sucked in, having said Setiawan's name meant faithful, his reliance solid.

Not seeing any obvious taxis, I returned to a man selling food outside the airport's exit and asked about a taxi. He told me to find a Damri bus, pointing in the direction. When I turned back to him, he pleaded for me to buy some food on display. Thinking a seller in the airport had to have good food hygiene to work here, and that I was a bit peckish, I purchased some sort of chicken satay and rice wrapped in a vegetable leaf. Munching on my snacks, I headed in the direction he had showed. Reaching the sign, I was annoyed to see a large coach instead of a minibus, but I joined the queue of sweaty people.

Being the last to board, I asked the driver how much to go to Solok. With the language barrier not helping, we repeated our questions and answers a couple of times. It transpired I did not have a pre-booked ticket. Seeming rather impatient, the driver told me to pay five hundred thousand rupiah, then held out his hand. The driver shoved the cash in his pocket and did not issue me with a ticket, or even acknowledgement. Being the only English person on the coach, I sat on my own at the front.

It wasn't long before I remembered certain sights I had seen before: roads, houses, the way of life. It was better than sitting on the back of that motorbike: back breaking with flies in my hair and teeth. Shutting my eyes, I started to lay out my plan in my mind, ignoring the troubles I previously had here. Hopefully, I would find Nico, and he would help me. After all, I had saved his mate Georges. My gut gargled. I opened my eyes. Small cramps rippled, so to release the pressure I let one rip. It was disgusting, hoping the people behind could not smell it. After taking on some much-needed water, I closed my eyes, starting off where I had left my plan.

The coach door piston sounded, startling me. Not remembering a long dream, I checked the time: 09.17 hrs. I looked at the driver for answers. He pointed at the hotel. Others got in the way as I checked the name, but I could only see one of the cream-coloured walls with orange painted pillars. Grabbing my backpack, still amazed how quick the journey had been, I thanked the driver and stepped out onto the tarmac. The heat hit me. I needed a car to find Gavin's village, but there were no obvious hire cars. The coach pulled off onto the main road, leaving me bewildered to where I exactly was.

After yet more water, which was running empty, I made my way over to a bloke cleaning the bugs off his SUV screen. I assumed that the black car with its orange decals and writing belonged to the hotel. My belly twinged as I reached him.

'Excuse me, can you take me to the mountains in Solok?' I asked.

The bloke just stared at me.

I repeated the question, but he just glared.

By the look of his appearance, I wondered if he had anything to do with the hotel. This time I gestured driving, then money. Half-way through trying to hand sign mountains, along with saying it slowly, he grinned, showing what sparing and brown teeth he had. For fuck's sake, I thought. Just as I was about to head to the reception, he pointed at a car just on the outskirts of the carpark.

'Taxi?' I said.

The screen washer put his thumb up and smiled.

'Hope you get enough tips to sort your toppled gravestone teeth out,' I said.

He kept his thumb up, not having a clue.

I began to stroll towards the silver car, but with every step, I became concerned at the beat-to-fuck motor. There wasn't a panel on the passenger's side that wasn't scratched or dented, including the front. I wasn't even sure what car it was, only an estate model; the grill and badge were missing. A puff of smoke bellowed out from the window. Fucking great, a smoker. Waving his shit away, I tapped on his slightly open window. He looked up from the naked photos on his phone, sweatier than an armpit at an Ibiza rave.

'Taxi?' I said.

'Yes, yes of course, my friend,' he said, in fairly good English.

He dusted his clothes down and cleared the dash of all the shit. I took a step back as he got out, sweat on his face reflecting the sun.

'Are you sure you're ready for hire?'

'Yes, yes,' he said excitedly.

The taxi-driver did up his trousers and opened the rear door. Grabbing a load of what looked like clothes, he rushed around to the rear and threw them in the boot, slamming the tailgate hard after. He came up to me and put his grubby hand on the rucksack straps, touching my hand. I pulled my hand away from him, instinctively wiping it on my trousers.

'I can handle my luggage,' I said.

'OK, sir. Where you go?'

'I just want a quick lift to the Solok mountains. There's a little village on…'

'I take you but cost eight hundred thousand rupiah.'

'That's more than the bloody coach,' I exclaimed.

He held his nicotine-stained hand out.

I quickly tried to work out the currency. 'That's about forty-five quid.'

He smiled.

'How far are they? I'll fucking walk.'

The driver pointed along where the coach had left, showing his sweaty under-arm stains, also appearing smug. 'Seventy kilometres.'

'What the fuck? Are we not in Solok?'

'No. This is Hotel Rasaki.'

An urban cart pulled by a horse raced by. For a moment, I contemplated chasing it for a lift.

'How far are we from the airport?' I asked.

'About twenty kilometres.'

'Fucking coach driver. I paid him to take me to Solok.'

The taxi-driver scowled. 'My brother not rip you off. You said wrong.'

His brother? Oh shit, this gets worse, I thought. I started to count the notes… 'Ok, I have five hundred thousand.'

'Yes, yes get in, my friend.'

He ran around the passenger's side front and opened the door. I got in the rear.

I recognised the Seat brand logo once inside. Like the previous motorbike road trip, this lacked comfort and ran like a log of shit caught in a fan. The window eventually managed to lower, easing the smell of nicotine and BO. Through the stained screen, we were taking a direct road, unlike the back streets Setiawan had led me down. No meter was running. I had read in the inflight information leaflet about avoiding taxi scams. I had to loosen my belt because the stomach cramps had worsened. As we plodded along, the only thing we overtook were animals and people walking. Sure, there was the stunning backdrop and fields to look at, but the lack of speed was doing my nut. Then the worst happened: small talk.

After an hour of hearing in broken English about his life and the rest of his family's life, I wanted to jump out. I thought I would change the subject to the Sumatran tiger and its demise. So far so good, I thought. However, as soon as I mentioned Nico, it was like I had disrespected his mother. The driver started ranting off at speed in his own language. The hand gestures got worse, veering close to oncoming trucks. Then there was silence, followed by another load of abuse. I had no idea what he was on about, and I started to find it funny—it didn't help the matter.

As soon as I got the opportunity, I told him to shut the fuck up, or tell me what the problem was, in English. Many calmer questions from him followed about my involvement with the ominous Nico. Wanting to reach my destination, I went along with it, saying I also hated Nico. For some strange reason, I said I was going to hunt him down—I think I was caught up in the moment. That statement led to more of a farce that I was a hit-man. The driver was in awe of me, and stupidly, I played along.

The driver suddenly veered off the main road. It didn't matter how many times I said to turn back, he didn't listen.

'I have friends you meet,' he said.

'No, no, I need to get to Solok.' I also needed to let rip, wondering if he would even realise the evil odour.

Off the tarmac road and away from civilisation, we stopped at a large wooden house with the typical design, but this property was run-down.

Bits of junk were strewn across the front. It did not appear to be any connecting evidence the farm was agricultural. Perhaps some of the outhouses had animals in. I was instructed to stay whilst he found his friends. As soon as the driver shut the door, a shady bloke appeared from the side of the large shed, carrying a shotgun. Dressed in jeans and a leather jerkin, he spat out what he was chewing. I did up my trousers and belt.

The driver appeared apprehensive as he went over. Like out of some poorly stereotype scripted movie, the armed bloke whistled with his fingers. Worse to come, a bunch of cronies started surfacing. The driver wrestled with his hands, then beckoned them all over to our Seat. Oh fuck. For once, could I not just have a normal fucking holiday? The posse followed the main leader around to my door. Even though they were loaded to the hilt, they were a little uneasy. No time for the grey man here, I thought. Barging the door open quickly, they all jumped back.

'What the actual fuck?' I said.

The main man, perhaps feeling belittled, stepped up close. His breath was like that of a disused fridge. I stared hard into his eyes.

'I haven't got all fucking day.'

'You know Nico?' he throatily said.

'I have good intel on him. Why?'

'Ratu says you going to kill him.'

I narrowed my eyes in distrust at the driver, Ratu.

He looked at the ground.

'I'm not meeting the target for a fucking beer, put it like that,' I said.

The gunman lightly laughed; his posse joined in. When he stopped, they did. Who the fuck is scripting this? Taking a step back, the leader looked me up and down, and then he spotted my rucksack in the footwell. I should have shut the door.

'You carry no gun. What's in the bag?'

Ignoring my gut pains, I stepped up close and snarled at him. 'I don't need to carry a weapon, fuck-face.'

There was a tormenting pause, we locked our steely stares. Now wasn't the time to start to have the sweats from my cramps. The pressure was becoming too much. Releasing my tense muscles, a fart followed. Just for a second, there was an air of disbelief—rank.

'We have guns,' someone said behind him.

Promptly, I barged past the bloke in front of me and went up to the person holding up his battered machinegun, smelling worse than what I had left.

'This isn't the part in the film where I fucking kick the living daylights out of all of you,' I said. 'Leave that to Hollywood. Yeah, fucking kill me, but before nightfall, this place will be wiped off the face of the earth, along with you and your inbred family and the drugs factory.' I nodded at the large shack. Before he had chance to answer, I walked back to the main man. 'My organisation has enough shit on this small-time pikey operation to send in anyone in my line of work, but you're nothing but a sperm dick; tiny.'

'You kill Nico, slowly,' the leader said. 'Nico hire men to kill my cousins, including young boy. He cut them up.'

I tried not to show the shocking revelation he was related to Pepen, Rede, and Wayan. 'Who cut who up?' I asked.

'Nico hire an American assassin, John Vince. He also kill Tirta's English boyfriend.'

I sniggered. 'John Vince? American?'

'Why you laugh?'

Pointing the shotgun at me, he rambled off something in his own language. One of his men grabbed my pack. An image of my passport in the bag passed before my eyes. Shit. Think Johnny, I thought.

'I've ended Johnny Vince's days,' I blurted. 'He'd pissed many people off. It's a shame I never got to him before he killed Tirta's fiancé, Gavin.'

The leader scowled and grunted.

'And obviously your cousins,' I quickly added. 'Oh, and Johnny was English, not American. You need to sort your intel officer out.' I smirked.

The bloke who had rifled through the pack tapped my passport on the main man's shoulder. Without lowering his weapon, he brought it forward, page open on my photo. He read it, then glared at me, fingers tapping his weapon.

'To get back into this country undetected, I've doctored his passport. I have many passports and ID.'

'You are John Vince,' he said, but more probing than an accusation.

'I've killed Johnny Vince. Now I find Nico.'

'What is your name?' someone else said.

I snatched the passport back and, pushing the shotgun aside, got into the leader's face. 'I've got fucking business to attend to.'

'How you kill him?'

'I came in with a nasty Australian friend of mine. We searched the forbidden temple in the mountains. Once...'

'You lie. No one ever comes back from there.'

'Me and Ocker are living proof you do. Now if you want to…'

'Ocker?' one of the cronies interrupted—a slight murmur circled.

'Yeah, Ocker, who would fucking eat you raw. Do you fucking think I would return without this psychopath?' I nodded with a sinister smile, lapping up their concerns. 'Trust me, if I don't get to where I'm going on time, then it's him you will be answering to.'

The leader took a few steps back, one of them raced to put everything back in my rucksack. He swiftly handed it back to me. I snatched his hunting knife out of his side sheath and threw it in my pack, thanking him for his nice gift.

Stomach on fire, I got back into the stained rear seat and closed the door to this farcical scene. One of them cuffed Ratu hard around the head, ranting, probably for bringing me here. The leader leaned in my window, adding to the stench.

'What are tribe like?' he asked.

I leant forward, adding to the tense situation. 'If you have a weak mind, the tiniest doubt, they will turn you into your own worst nightmare. Everything you have ever done wrong, or fear, will haunt you.'

He took a step back, contemplating.

'That's why me and Ocker don't have a conscience, we kill for pleasure.'

Once back on the main highway, to hide my relief, I gave Ratu a bit of the same movie-type assassin shit. Funnily enough, he didn't reply. How fucking close was that situation. I sneered thinking of how I had portrayed Ocker, but then, there must have been some truth for them to believe what they had heard of him. What had Ocker done when he had rescued me? I should have let Ocker tell me, instead of telling him to shut the fuck up. I had been a total bellend in the hospital.

Looking at the enthralling forestation, mountains, and the clouds rolling in reminded that I had been to this spot before. I thought of what I was doing. Would my plan work? Would I ever get to see my family and friends again? I shook the thoughts away. Another thing spoiling this beauty was my rotten guts. I asked Ratu to stop at an approaching junction on the dusty track. Dust bellowed through my open window, clinging to my soaked shirt. Ratu informed me the village was left, and we should go and meet the people. Dread followed, thinking of Gavin's fiancée and the ugly mother-in-law, Zelda. Instead, I ordered him to turn right, he didn't argue.

Keeping one eye on the stunning scenery, the other on the situation,

I ordered Ratu to get a move on or Ocker would be seriously pissed off. The slow speed didn't increase, and I was told we were flat-out. I knew I needed some action, a rush, and for once I wanted it, not worrying that it might have consequences. I was so near to finishing my plan, nothing would stop me.

Double looking, we had passed the turning to the weird cowboy saloon where I had watched Gavin with his lightning and formidable Kung-Fu when he beat-up his three brothers-in-law. I wondered if the barman Ahmad was still serving that brown shit.

A couple of klicks further, I spotted the left turning I needed.

'Stop the car,' I said.

Ratu stopped the car, although it took a fair distance. 'Why here?'

'That's on a need to know basis, and you don't fucking need to know.'

I climbed out of the cess-pit and strode around to the driver's window. Ratu was sweating even more, not from the humidity. I knocked on his window. He gingerly faced me, so I tapped the wedge of notes on the glass. Relief was written on his face, guessing I'd had something nasty in store for him. His dirty fingers came through the two-inch gab, so I fed him the notes; it was comical. Before he had sped off, no, dribble off, I had told him he was never to talk about me, or he would be next. He had got the message.

I waited for the cloud of dust to disappear before I slung my rucksack over my shoulder, and then headed for the junction. I was still laughing with the morning's events. Following the footsteps that me and Gavin had taken, I eventually found the torrent wide river. The edge seemed more volatile than before.

Unbelievably, twenty-five metres or so later, the wire still expanded across the river. However, this time I did not have Gavin's crude wheeled contraption for getting across. I started to suss out the best way to traverse. At least this time I did not have a large Bergen to contend with. Hitching up, I started to get a good motion going across. To take my mind off the swaying, the noise below, and bits of wire poking from the cable, I thought about Gavin's wind-up that Nico loved swearing, and that Nico was Swedish. I still did not get why Ocker had said that me and Nico were like two dingo balls in a sack. And what was that nickname Nico had for me? Thinking on, as I lowered down on the bank, I had not had that typical trait where I would make a nickname for someone who looked like someone famous. I smiled as the different people entered my head from the past.

Further in the forest, once the sound of the river disappeared, like before I sat down and tuned into my surroundings, watching different insects on the trees and floor. Exactly like last time I got a sense of my meagre existence compared to planet Earth's mother nature. How many other people at this moment in time were having the pleasure of sitting in isolation of humans? Had I become a people hater?

The humidity was rising, even though I was in the shade from the large canopies. With a large gulp of water, I swallowed two Paracetamol and loosened my trouser band. Time check: 14.47 hrs. After getting changed into my old Afghanistan tour trousers, shirt, boots, and leg holster, I buried the old clothes. Seeing the photo on the floor, I picked it up and straightened the creases. How fresh and young were me, Planet, Fish, and Shrek back then. I wore the same uniform and boots now as I had in the photo. I took one last look at what I had achieved, knowing it was the life I was going to leave behind. After checking the GPS, I went into the thick forestation.

CHAPTER NINETEEN

The humidity had become stifling, especially making the difficult and most direct route towards the lake. I did not have the exact co-ordinates of Nico's underground stronghold, but I had researched beforehand to where I thought it was. One thing I did curse myself for was not purchasing a machete in one of the local towns, but at least I had a decent hunting knife from one of the crazy folks at the farm. Even though I had seriously physically worked out in the period before for this mission, I was now feverish, giddy, and with my gut spasms increasing, nauseous. The positive side was it made me push on harder to reach the lake for a well-earned rest.

One klick further, wet through, cut, and grazed, I had reached the edge of the lake: again, by luck, missing Nico's traps. Under the shade of a tree, I slumped. I slapped on even more repellent. However, unlike last time, I could not care about the strong smell of it. I knew Nico would disapprove. Beyond the new swarm of insects that were trying their luck, time stood still as I admired the blue Danau Singkarak and its idyllic scenery. As tempting as it was to strip off and go for a swim, I decided to instead take on more fresh water. The problem was, every time I drunk or snacked on an energy bar, my guts did somersaults. I now wish I hadn't purchased the food at the airport.

In the near distance around to my left was the decaying wooden shack. Seeing this prompted me to get off my arse and search for Nico's real dwelling. Even though it was only a few hundred metres, it felt like the journey from hell. Whatever was going on inside, I am sure it wanted to explode out, both ends.

It didn't take me long to find the camouflaged hatch. Lying prone, sweating buckets, I poked my fingers under the lip and carefully lifted an inch. A hum came from below, someone was down there. I took my ear away and tried to see in, but only a dull light shone. Bollocks, I needed to be sick. As silently as possible I crept into the bush. Finding a clearing, I spewed up most of the watery mixed food. After two further heaves, I instantly fumbled to pull down my trousers and pants. The combination and smell were grotesque. Angry, I wanted to go back and kick the shit out of the food trader. I laughed inside at the 'kick the shit out of' part; I had none left. Most of the pains had subsided, but I had a blinding headache. Drawn to look at the mess, I noticed another camouflaged hatch: the other exit. I grinned wide thinking of the trick I had played on Roy back in Afghanistan. My mind worked overtime how to get whoever was below out through the exit. I was that excited prankster kid.

Making as much noise as possible, I returned to the first main hatch and lifted it.

'Come out,' I shouted. 'I have some tiger skins for sale.' Slamming the hatch down, I sat on top and waited.

'I will slit...' Nico stood shocked; a large machete raised.

'My fucking Swedish *Bru*,' I said, knowing he despised swearing.

'Johnny Vince,' he said in his rich South African accent.

'Damn fucking right.'

'I do not like your swearing. It should be only used when appropriate.'

'This is fucking appropriate.'

'Obnoxious twat,' he snapped.

Nico took a large step forward, but his threatening demeanour changed for an open-armed embrace, his huge smile beaming. It wasn't the fact he was slapping on the back with a huge machete that bothered me, but he was covering me in my own vomit and shit. Once he let go of his powerful grip, he held me at arm's length, tears of joy filling his eyes.

'My old *chommie*,' he bellowed.

'You stink worse than before.'

'*Eina*. I don't remember eating that.' Nico wiped the mess down with his grubby hands—the prank had backfired. 'We have so much to catch up on, Tom.'

'Not the old Tom Hardy shit, still. You need to go to Specsavers.'

'You need to stop wearing perfume. You will attract the unwanted. Follow me.'

I followed him down the ladder into the cabin.

Watching his huge stature clear the bed brought back a load of nostalgia. Nico ordered me to sit—somethings never change. The atmosphere was cool and surprisingly fresh, except the odd whiff of my prank. Nothing had altered since I was last here, like being stuck in a time-warp; however, it wasn't like he could pop down to Ikea. I remembered the show he did for me with the snared wire. An air of awkwardness settled as I sat. Where do we start the conversation? What had happened to me? How did I get saved? Where had I been? How was his best mate, Georges? Did he make it back OK?

Nico held back a white can of drink. 'What are your views on the Sumatran Tiger being kept in captivity, you know, zoos in Great Britain?' he asked.

Typical, the tiger was more important than me, I thought.

'Well?' he prompted.

'Yep, I'm thirsty.'

'Always avoiding questions. Just answer the question.'

'No. I know whichever way I reply, you will jump up and down and throw your toys out the pram. I've learnt that much about you.'

'Is the tiger not important to you?' he snapped.

'*Eish*,' I said, imitating his voice.

Nico threw the can at me, rather hard. 'Why have you come back then?'

Straight to the point, I thought, and looked at the labelling of the can: Bintang Pilsner.

'Well?' Nico asked.

'Have you got any tea or coffee?' I held the can out to him.

He sighed, then snatched it. Opening it in his huge hands, he gulped it down. 'No,' he said, and burped.

I quickly thought of when Ocker had said I was just like Nico. 'Your manners are just like Ocker's.'

'That wanker is not *indaba*. Don't tell me you brought that *gogga* back here with you.'

'*Indaba*? *Gogga*? What the fuck does that mean?'

'*Hou jou bek*. I do not like you swearing in my house. Have some respect. I do not want to discuss that insect.' Nico punched the worktop he was leaning on; rows of cans fell over.

'Ocker did save me. What's so bad with that?' I said, floating the baited hook.

'I will tell you why, my *Bru*.' Nico strode over and sat next to me, barging me. 'He came here with his disgusting language and sayings. He said unless I helped him find you, he would drop his entire Special Forces friends into the forest until no stone was unturned. Worse, he didn't give a "crocodile shit" which animal got in his way.' Nico crushed the can.

I was stuck for words.

'He called me an "Abo's Bitza",' Nico continued. 'I did not know what it meant, but he could not stop laughing at me. I could have killed him.'

'Perhaps you should have learnt the Australian pikey language,' I joked—wrong timing.

'Once we had found your first camp in the riverbank, he pulled out an array of weapons from his backpack. The bastard had tricked me. The *siff* vermin killed three poachers, and…'

'What's wrong with that?' I interrupted.

Nico stood up, breathing heavy, almost ready to explode. 'Because you thick bastard, once the locals find out, they will descend on the forest for revenge and kill my rangers. More weapons will be brought in to find Ocker.'

I wished I hadn't interrupted.

Nico kicked a few things on the way to getting himself a beer. With his back to me, he had his hands on the worktop, staring at nothing.

'So,' I said meekly, 'where did you find me?'

'A few days later we found the temple, and…'

'I thought you said you would never go that far.'

'Your best *chommie* said he would set the forest alight if I did not go with him to the sacred grounds. If I'd had a rifle, I would have killed him. He knew it, and he had his pointing at me.'

'You know Ocker wouldn't have brought hell to this beautiful place or shoot you,' I said, doubting it.

'Are you bloody sure, Tom?'

'As sure as I'm not Tom… bloody… Hardy.'

Nico rubbed his chin, smearing the sweat and dirt. 'You still *tune* me too much,' he said.

'Whatever, *ou ballie*. Look, it was all a front. Yes, Ocker was in the SF, but he was a decent solicitor after he'd left.' I thought of Ocker banging his boss' wife on his boss' table—I grimaced.

Nico shooed his hand at me and said, '*Eish*.'

I was desperate to finish the story. 'So, did Ocker and you find me in the temple ruins?'

'No. I would not venture in. It was spooky enough to get to the walls, with unexplainable weather changes, *Tokoloshe* warning us to go back. Ocker said he felt nothing. My mind had started to play tricks on me. I quickly returned.'

'How did Ocker get me back here, then?'

'Let's just say he managed it.'

'Who paid for all my travel and hospital care? Ocker? You? The charity?'

'Johnny, I want to thank you for saving my brother Georges. You are a great warrior,' Nico said.

Nico still had a knack of body swerving questions, like a politician. He almost crushed the oxygen out of me with an embrace. I tried to suck in some air, and then he released me.

'How is Georges?' I said.

'After a short break in his homeland, Georges returned here. He has now taken over Dian as ranger field manager. Dian had disappeared.'

'Disappeared?' I asked.

Nico plugged in the kettle and started to make me a brew. After, he began to collect photos and paperwork. I knew this was going to be the next life story of him, Georges, and the tigers. As much as I found this all genuinely nice and important, I really was itching to move on.

We continued to talk about the tigers and how Ocker had got me back to Great Britain. I didn't disbelieve that Ocker had pissed some locals off, and I didn't tell Nico about those at the farm. Now that I knew how much Ocker had put his life and reputation on the line saving me, I despised what I had said to him. Although we had kind of made up, I had lost a damn fine friend who had my back. I was hoping to change that.

Sipping my coffee, I declined the chicken and rice dish, much to Nico's displeasure. As Nico got into his stride about how the poaching had not declined, I switched the conversation to how I had killed Gavin's in-laws, and how Gavin had met his gruesome death. After, Nico stared, pondering.

'Why are you here?' he asked. 'It is not to see how I and Georges are dealing with the demise of the Sumatran tiger.'

I had not really thought of an excuse. 'I need to go back to the temple.'

Nico coughed on his slurp of beer and then slapped his leg. 'My *bru*, you are funny.'

'It's no fucking joke. I need you to help me find it.'

'*Aikona*.'

'Thanks. Let's get pack…'

'Meaning, not on your life,' Nico said, butting in my sarcasm.

'You don't have to come all the way in. You know, if you're chicken shit.'

Nico went to rage, but he stopped, nodding that he knew he had nearly taken the bait. 'Why me?'

'Why do I need the Anthony Middleton type Nico in Indonesia to help me find this lost city.'

'Who is this person?'

'OK, Bear Grylls, then.'

'Never heard of them.'

'Look, you oversized mountain, I'm trying to pay you a compliment,' I said.

'Why?'

'Because I think you…'

'Stop kissing my arse.' Nico smiled, knowing he had hooked me. 'I meant, why do you want to return to the temple?'

Shit. I didn't really have an answer ready, except the real reason, and I doubted he would buy it.

'Well?'

'I left my dad's watch there,' I said—rubbish.

'Bollocks. And that is necessary. I will cut you a deal. You tell me why you want to return, and I will help you on your journey. My word. Agreed?' Nico held out his hand.

I placed down my mug and shook his hand. Here goes, I thought.

I began to tell of how I had escaped from the poachers and the claws of the tiger. This led the story onto me almost dying on the end of the rope, and how I awoke with the weird tribe transporting me to the temple. The next bit felt tricky, but if he does not believe me, like the others, so be it. It was not going to stop my mission. I told him about going back to 1944. Nico stayed quiet, which was peaceful, but then him thinking and not talking for a few minutes started to get me impatient. Nico went to the fridge. In one hand, he gnawed at a piece of cooked meat, whilst he held onto another beer. The wait whilst he finished the meat and drank the beer done my head in.

'Well?' I burst.

'I remember a Mr Hardy thinking I was an old *domkop* when I had mentioned the tribe, the *Tokoloshe* that would steal your mind.'

'Right, I get it that I was wrong back then, but you said…'

'You have not told me why you want to return to the evil spirits,' Nico interrupted.

My frustration was going beyond boiling, I had to tell him. In my mind, I heard Steve say, "And, Johnny, stop thinking about the past negative. Would you want to return to that bad shit?"

'*Eish*,' he said.

'I want to return to May 2013. I need to go back to the Afghan desert where me and the squad were waiting for the Chinook extraction at the LZ. I want to tell Roy to take a different flight path, to stop the crash. The tribe can take me back there.' I was ready to rage if I saw the slightest piss-take.

Nico contemplated for a while, then said, 'Johnny, I am really sorry for your father's death, but you have to realise what you are saying won't bring him back.'

'I'm fucking going, with or without you.'

'Go home, find a woman, fuck like a Bunyoro rabbit, and then settle down. It is too dangerous for you to go on, even for a warrior like you.'

'I've been through worse battles,' I bragged.

'I meant for your state of mind. I won't allow you to do this to yourself.'

'Tough shit. The plan is in full motion, ending very soon.'

'There is a life here, or at home for you.'

'I'm returning to 2013 to continue with Ella and to be with my dad again,' I said firmly.

'No, I will not help you.'

I exaggerated my sigh. 'You gave me your Africana word that you would help me on my journey. I didn't turn my back on Georges.' Emotional blackmail it had to be.

Nico rapidly started opening the padlocks on a door, the same cupboard that I had wondered what was in there on my last visit. Like last time, he only opened it enough for him to lean in. Even turning the light on did not let me see further. I hoped he was not going to give me an old rucksack full of antiquated adventure travelling paraphernalia, again. He began placing items inside his camouflaged jacket. To my shock, he pulled out an SLR and mags. He then went up the exit ladder.

'Follow me,' he demanded.

Excited to crack on, I was quickly on his heels.

Out in the clearing, the daylight hurt my eyes. Nico thrust the rifle on my chest and, opening my pack at my feet, chucked in the extra ammo and a mid-sized machete. I went to remind him of his morals about bringing weapons into the jungle because of the dangers that poachers could get them, as he had ranted off last time, but decided not to. Nico stomped off to the bushes. Taking the rifle off my chest, I examined the black stock and fore-stock, wondering where it had gotten all its scratches. The sling was missing, so instead I went to pull up the charger handle but stopped when I noticed the engraved crest on the receiver.

Nico was grunting, so I looked to see him hauling the navel kaki Mokai kayak. I smiled thinking of Ocker being proud of his own design. Nico dragged the one-man kayak past me and slammed it into the tranquil water, wading in after it.

'You're not going to bleat on with all the stats again, are you?' I jested.

'*Jou poephol.*'

He pulled on the starter handle from the inside, like that of a chainsaw, then strode back. From the inside his jacket, he pulled out a rolled-up cloth. I placed the rifle between my legs and unravelled the material. The grubby, sandy-coloured beret had the old blue winged dagger badge on, starkly reminding me of Operation Poppy Pride. The connection of the FN FAL rifle and beret connected me to Nico's dad, who had been in the Rhodesian Special Forces.

'Are you not coming with me?' I asked.

'There is enough fuel to get you to the other side and back.'

'You gave me your word you…'

'I have helped you on your journey. Now, go, crazy English man.' He folded his arms, clearly upset.

I passed him the beret and weapon. 'These are your treasured items. I'm not coming back. Thanks…'

'You won't make it without them,' Nico interrupted. 'This weapon will make sure they stay down.'

I took the mags from my backpack and placed them at his feet. Taking off my Rolex, I placed it over his thumb. 'Take this. Sell it on eBay, put the sale towards your invaluable work here.'

Nico looked at the watch, then he grinned.

Wading into the water, I climbed aboard. 'No pikus this time?' I asked, taking the piss.

'That's *Padkos*,' he snapped. 'And the last time I gave you biltong for the journey, you threw it over your shoulder.'

I smirked. 'Not even any of the old rat-packs?' I said in my richest South African voice.

'You left them in the hull last time. And your fucking accent still has not improved, Tom Hardy.'

'Take care, Ulrika Johnson. Give my regards to Sweden.'

'Who is he?' Nico yelled.

'Google her.' I held up my middle finger.

Something hit the back of the Kayak and plopped into the water. I turned to see Nico with his hand up, waving, looking in low spirits. I stuck my thumb up, nodding my appreciation.

CHAPTER TWENTY

Time check: 17.02 hrs. I placed the GPS away and continued to enjoy the mountains and forest covered slopes. Was anyone watching me in this almost silent, modified kayak gliding across this seven-kilometre-wide lake? There wasn't a cloud in the sky. The odd bird soared across the vast openness, whilst fish jumped at the insects. Even though I was in love with this place, I had to remain focused to why I was here. I had not looked back since leaving Nico. At first, I was surprised he had not ventured with me, but then he had too much to lose on his quest to save the critically endangered tiger. I hoped very soon his vision would happen.

It had taken me about an hour to travel the twenty-one-kilometre tranquil waters. As the mass of thick forestation dominated my view, my heckles raised. I wasn't alone. Yes, it was brilliant my sixth sense had returned, but I didn't know what was watching me. Without drawing attention, I slowly undid my rucksack, making sure the machete was ready. A crack from the almost silent forest alerted me. I climbed out and, letting the sound of the ripples diminish, I drew the machete, tuning in, eyes scanning. Standing waist deep in the cool water, I imagined the tiger ready to pounce, so I moved the kayak between me and the bank.

A radio squelch broke the intensity.

'He has made it,' said a deep South African voice.

Out of the bush came Georges carrying a large antenna walkie talkie; my shoulders relaxed.

'Take care of Tom Hardy,' Nico replied on the radio—did Nico know I was listening?

I studied Georges' dusky-blue uniform as I waded forwards, taking his outreached hand. Georges' muscular arms pulled me up and then slapped me on the back. I patted him back. He had physically been working out since I last saw him.

'Great to see you made it back, Georges,' I said.

'Thank you for saving my life from the barbaric poachers.'

'We need to get going,' I ordered. 'Do you remember the way?'

'Where?'

'I don't suffer fools.'

Georges sighed. 'Do you want to go via your previous camps, the way you headed last time?'

'Bollocks. I'm done with nostalgia. Take me the most direct route to the temple.'

Georges knelt, tying off the kayak whilst I hitched my pack over my shoulder. I cut away the first bush to show I meant now. Instead of following my lead, Georges pulled his rucksack out of the nearby bush and opened it. From the top, he drew a clear dry-sack and handed me some clothes. Unravelling them, they were the same uniform as he had on.

'Why the change of clothes?' I asked. 'I've only just got changed.'

'The uniform may help you stay alive.'

I pondered what he had said, but decided to get changed, placing my old clothes in the dry-sack, then back inside my backpack.

'That's better,' he said.

'Why are they blue and not green kaki? Is it because we don't want to be like guerrilla warfare?' I smirked at Georges blank expression. 'Do you get it? Guerrilla, instead of Gorilla; jungle.'

'Nico warned me of your twisted humour.'

'Jesus, this shirt is tight,' I said, tucking in the bagginess. 'About time you went back down the gym.'

Georges took a step closer, fists clenched. 'I could fucking rip you apart like a gorilla.'

I stood there, locked in his menacing glare. My heart began to increase. Guessing this was for real, I dropped my backpack. Unexpectedly, Georges turned and led the way, laughing.

I relaxed. 'South African humour is fucking shit.'

Georges laughed louder.

After about half an hour of trekking through the dense forest, Georges had led me to a track. It was just big enough to take a four by four. The tyre ruts in the road were covered in leaves and vines. Georges explained this had been the main road in and out for the poachers' camp, the one where I had rescued him from Pepen and his gang. I knew it was the track I had crossed last time. A tiny part of me wanted to take the old route, unsure to why. Was it for closure?

Resting on one knee, I checked my GPS: the river was close. I then sipped from my water bottle, knowing I was down to the last few inches. The sun was setting, the area took on a different atmosphere. New sounds of animals came to life. I unclipped the torch.

'We need to make camp and get a fire going,' Georges said.

'No. We need to press on.'

I thought of Sarge saying this back in 1944, but then remembered how the tribe took your thoughts. I had to turn all my memories to Afghanistan 2013, the SBS, and any friends and family from that period. Switching the light on, moths and insects buzzed in the beam. Georges slung down his large rucksack and started to remove the wire snares from the top, pulling out his torch.

'It's too dangerous to head out with the number of traps, let alone the wildlife,' he said.

'It's a risk worth taking. If you don't want to come, like Nico had bottled it, then give me the co-ordinates and I'll go it alone.'

'I have never fucking "bottled" anything,' he retorted.

I grinned.

Georges sighed. 'You cause a lot of problems, Johnny.'

'I bet you now wish you'd pushed harder with that stick into my neck,' I jested.

'*Yebo,*' he muttered.

Georges tied a holster's leather strap over his shoulder, fitted his pistol, and then pushed at a fast pace, his powerful beam lighting the way. I couldn't wait to get to my new life. The more I thought about seeing Ella, dad, and my mates lost in the horrific Chinook crash, the eager I became. Like Georges, I was covered in a mass of different bugs and insects. Occasionally, a pair of eyes would get caught reflecting, but instantly they disappeared. Either side of us was an impenetrable wall of forestation, alive with different weird and wonderful sounds—majestic. Georges kept quiet, even when I had asked questions about his capture by the poachers.

The only thing that had kept the monotony of trekking two hours on the track was trying to imagine the temple and the weird tribe of people who had rescued me. Would they remember me? Would the head of the tribe help me, rather than eat me? I quickly ignored that last dumb question, not wanting trouble to follow me on my final phase. I then realised I had not thought of a mission name.

'This is the edge of the jungle,' Georges said.

'Operation Edge it still is then. Thanks, Georges.'

Georges looked confused as he slung down his huge backpack.

Making the beam as narrow as possible to see further down the track, a wall of vegetation imposed itself, like security gates. I sat down next to him for a well-earned drink and rest. Time check: 20.13 hrs.

Opening my rucksack, under my folded clothes in the dry-sack I pulled out the photo of me and the SBS lads. Georges leant over to look under the light.

'You really need to think about what you are doing,' he said.

'Oh here we go. Nico has twisted your mind into thinking I'm crazy.'

'*Gatvol* with your bull, my *bru*,' he snapped. 'I will take you to the temple walls, but that is as far as I go.'

'In case you go back in time with me,' I joked.

'I would rather kill myself now than spend the rest of my life, no, another day with you.'

After a little more banter, well, I hoped it was, we got our shit together and started to move towards the edge. To my left, a track headed into the darkness. When I asked why we couldn't take that route, Georges explained that way was to the poachers' camp. He had not returned there since his imprisonment and abuse. Instead, the other rangers had destroyed it. With Georges' thousand-mile stare, I wondered if he'd had any counselling for his obvious PTSD. Months of solitary confinement and brutality from those evil poachers must have messed with his mind. Perhaps returning to help the Sumatran tiger was therapy itself. Going to find Roy with Steve and Ant had without doubt secured my mind back to the old me. I had Monkfish to thank for that.

We stopped at the jungle's new beginning. Why couldn't I have taken this easier route before, rather than the arduous journey along the river's edge? It pissed me off, but then, I would not have found the betrayal of Gavin.

After ten metres of hacking away, getting snagged and slipping, both torches stopped working. I tapped mine on my thigh. When I looked up, it was so black I could hardly see Georges. Suddenly, he turned, his face was missing. I had seen similar images in my recent nightmares, so it wasn't a shock, something positive from the PTSD. Then for real, he turned, his face normal. Georges took my forearm and told me it was OK. I wasn't in the least bit worried, knowing this place would try to mess with my mind.

Weirdly, but warming, the sun above the tree's canopy brightened. Different pastels of green descended. The nightlife stopped, leaving pure silence. Stupidly, I checked my GPS for the time: 06.43 hrs. Looking up, I winked at Georges. He grinned back, knowing he had experienced this unexplainable place. He nodded in the direction behind me. Trying not to get concerned at what he was showing me, I turned around: the path we had taken had grown back.

'Fucking freaky,' I said, and laughed exaggerated, deliberately showing no fear.

'Not as much as your looks, Johnny.'

A few metres in, the jungle became easier. We put our machetes away. I ignored the feelings it was a trap, to turn back. I told Georges. He said he felt it as well. Like before, the trees were black and slimy.

At what I guessed to be an hour gone by, a mist came rolling in at our feet. Georges stopped and linked arms with me. A gentle wind blew the mist away. Then a gust of leaves and twigs became so strong, we had to bow to protect ourselves. I could not exactly hear what Georges was shouting, but it had been something like, "keep going and think about it all stopping". Head down, forearm up, we continued through the gale. The sun was wiped out by a black cloud, and then freezing rain punished us. At every swaying tree we huddled for a few seconds, before almost blindly finding the next one. Lightning strikes and thunder added to the cacophony. No wonder it had freaked me out before. The cracking and crashing of nearby trees were intimidating. Georges held on tighter. If only he had been with me the first time, I thought. Negative thoughts tried to trick me, so I began to sing in my mind: '*Pack up your troubles in your old kit bag.*' Shit. Why this song?

Then the storm ceased within a blink of an eye. Soaked to the red-raw and numb skin, I wiped the shit from my eyes. Georges' face was covered in black bits and leaves. We both laughed at each other's appearance, banter followed. He released his grip.

'Forwards,' he said.

Why had he impersonated an officer going over the top? I asked him; he hadn't said it.

He continued to lead. What I thought were a few minutes later, we found a sandy path, our footsteps appeared exaggerated in the quietness. Images of the deathly Enfield head-shot wounds of Wayan and the camp's old man filtered in. '*Threat neutralised.*' Water flowed over the decomposing body of the poacher I had thrown over the edge into the river. I tried to shake the thoughts, flick the positive switch. The roar from the tiger as it had attacked Pepen and Setiawan rang in my ears.

My old wounds started to flare up. Georges was loudly whistling Vera Lynn's 'White Cliffs of Dover'. I grabbed his shoulder, he turned around. The tune whistle continued, but it wasn't Georges.

'Are you OK, Johnny?' Georges slapped me around the cheek.

I shook my head, not realising I had stopped walking; the heat and humidity hit me.

He picked a spot to sit and said, 'Not long to go, Johnny, but I need some rest and *Padkos.*'

'I know that Africana saying, its food for the journey. Bottler barbie and amber fluid would be ace,' I said, impersonating Ocker. Shit, I thought, knowing Georges probably loathed him. I hit my head of the mind tricks. 'I'm sorry.'

'No big deal.'

I knew he was trying to cover the fact this place was getting to my mind. I had to change my thoughts to the friends and family I wanted to return to.

Double-checking the GPS time, it had still not moved. I rejected the rat-packs Georges handed me; my guts were still tender. I let him know that he would need them for his journey home. After a few more probing questions from him about why I wanted to return to the lost city, I told him about waking up in the Cambridge Military Hospital. My story ran away with itself. Weirdly, I found it necessary to finish it, as if my life depended on it. As I got to the part where me and the remaining squad had been barricaded in the German comms room, Georges put one sweaty hand across my mouth, bringing me back to the place we were sat.

Georges took his finger from his lips and lowered the other hand off my mouth. He drew his pistol. I mocked saying it looked like something from World War One, much to his annoyance. Again, he listened into the empty jungle. I thought he had stopped me talking about Operation Poppy Pride as it had been boring him. I tuned in to what had spooked him: a groan filtered from the right. It was the only sound we had heard in a while. A cold feeling came across me.

My curiosity got the better of me, I quickly got to my feet. Georges held my bicep.

'It could be a trap,' he whispered.

'Well, you've got the pistol, that's even if it works.'

I slid out my machete, Georges untied his. Leaving our packs where they were, we headed towards the moaning. Cautiously, Georges moved the branches away with the tip of his blade, pistol slightly raised. The groaning became heightened. Had the person heard us? Georges spoke out, the sound stopped. We looked at each other.

Gripping the handle, I made my way around the right side of the last thick, spikey bush. Georges headed left of it. I first noticed the footprints on the trail; some human, some not. To my shock and then disgust, a naked woman was tied to a crude square made of a thick twine. Behind her was a mass of spiked bushes. The young woman's hands and feet were cover in dry blood; her delicate, brown skin bound tight by a rope. Her body and face had been painted at one time, only the smear marks remained. The woman started to moan; her dry lips cracked. Insects had started to fester on her open wounds. Had she been whipped? Slashed with a blade?

I moved in to cut her down.

'No,' Georges snapped.

I froze.

Georges nodded at my feet.

In front of my boots was what appeared to be slightly disturbed sand, with twigs and leaves scattered. Getting anxious to help her down, I faced Georges who was knelt, prodding with his machete. He glanced up and then chucked me the pistol, telling me to stay still and keep watch. Once he had disappeared, I studied the pistol's black handle with the lug on the bottom. It had a stamp brand: 'Webber'. Pulling open the black barrel, like that of a cowboy's pistol, I checked to see if was fully loaded—it was.

Quickly, I closed the barrel as Georges had returned with two fallen thick branches. He laid one at his feet, then started to smash around the edges with the other. To my shock, the sand and leaves easily fell in. I peeked over: at the bottom of the six feet pit was a layer of nasty sharpened sticks covered in an orange goo. I looked back at Georges. He smiled, most probably at my drained colour.

Georges placed the two branches over the death pit and forcefully trod them down.

'Throw me the pistol.'

I did.

'Now cut her down,' he said.

'Fuck off. Why me?'

'Because I need to keep guard.' Georges waved the pistol.

Bollocks, I thought, knowing I'd fallen for it.

Even though I did not want to fall for any more traps, I delicately stepped onto the logs. Reaching down to her ankles, maggots were in amongst the flies. I cut the rope on the frame; her spread legs fell inwards. She hadn't made a sound. Respectfully, I kept in the urge to comment on her putrid smell. Standing tall, butt cheeks tightening as I wobbled on the logs, I cut one of her wrist bounds, immediately flopping forward. Quickly, I put up my forearm to hold her limp, greasy body against the frame. With the tip of the blade on the other rope, I paused. How was I going to get her down and across to Georges? Suddenly, the logs below moved a little. My heart skipped a beat. A strange howl came from deep in the forest. Georges told me to hurry. I hissed at him to shut the fuck up.

Pushing my face into her oily chest, I thrust the knife through the rope. Even though she was skinny, her limp body's momentum made me stagger back. Rather than fight the situation, most probably slipping to my death, I fell backwards into the spiked bush. Lying there, seething in pain, trying to stop any further anguish, I asked Georges to stop laughing, and help.

'I've heard you Brits are kinky fuckers, but this is a whole new level,' Georges said.

'Fuck off. Get her off me and help me the fuck up.'

Georges picked the naked woman from me but left me lying on my back. His patronising pitiful look did not help. The bush would not let go of me, so I let out expletives.

On the way back to our kit, I plucked out the thorns. I was just in time to see Georges giving the lying woman some water, then he gently laid her head back on the soil. He started rifling through his rucksack. It was enjoyable to see this rugged giant take so much tender care. Georges threw me the med-kit. Placing it at my feet, I started to take off my shirt.

'What the fuck do you think you are doing?' he asked.

'Using the med-kit for my wounds.'

Georges shook his head in disbelief, and then pointed at her.

'Only joking. I was just getting too warm,' I wretchedly lied.

Under a shade made from his poncho, I cleaned her injuries and then bandaged her wrists and ankles. Because we did not have an intravenous drip, I instructed Georges to wake her for regular sips. At least the woman was taking some water, but she was still seriously dehydrated. The rest of her cuts I washed out with a disinfectant and added a few steri-strips on the deeper ones. The suffering woman had multiple bruising over her body. Why had she been hung up and left to die of her injuries, or the pain from dehydration? Who could have done such a heinous thing?

When I had finished, Georges patted me on the back. He then wrapped her body in a green and black khaki blanket. I sat back, slid down my trousers, and picked the spikes that I had missed. Georges came around the rear and attended to my back.

'We need to get her back home, Johnny, for some proper medical attention.'

It had put me in a dilemma. He was right, but I needed to get to the temple. I had come so far. I flinched as he uncaringly slapped some cream on my wounds.

'I can't go back,' I said.

'I don't mean home, as in our home. Can you not see where she is from? You should know.'

Staring at her, I began to remember the tribe I had encountered before: piercings, tribal paint, the same haircut, possibly all inbred. I was relieved that we were going to take her back to her people.

'Who would do such a horrible thing to her?' I asked.

'I think the tiger trap below should give you the answer.'

'You mean she was bait?' I said, thinking of Gavin.

'Let me meet the fuckers, and they'll be great white shark bait for my next homeland trip.'

Georges heaved on his over-laden backpack and then placed her over his shoulder and Bergan. She slightly moaned. Georges cocked the pistol and squatted to pick up his machete. Like a man mountain on a mission, I followed him into the jungle on the trail we had found her on.

We had been on the go for about forty-five minutes. Again, a roll of mist swirled around our feet. The trail was hard to see, especially for any traps. Georges gently laid her down, stood, then twisted his neck muscles. I leant down and put the water to her lips. Weirdly, the rain started to fall, but I couldn't see the cloud.

'It's a monkey's wedding,' he said.

'A what?'

'A rain shower when the sun is out. You really ought to learn the dialogue.'

'Yeah, like that's any good in the jungles of Indonesia.'

Strangely, Georges made a sudden body swerve and then charged into a nearest bush. Standing quick, my machete in hand, he hit aside what appeared to be a branch, and then piled in with his fist. Georges dragged out a near-naked man, the victim's face blooded. Eerily from nowhere, more of his tribe appeared. Georges grabbed the beaten man to his feet and put the pistol at the tribesman's head and a blade under his throat. Further people appeared; familiar head masks worn backwards. A few had their blowpipes aimed at us.

'Fuck,' I muttered.

CHAPTER TWENTY-ONE

Georges was rapidly searching from left to right, pressing harder on the neck of the person he grasped. The tribe circled us with hate and suspicion.

'Carefully put the lad down, and your weapons,' I calmly ordered.

'Bollocks.'

I gradually bent down and placed my machete on the floor. Even slower, I unclipped my knife and placed it next to it. A row of blowpipes followed me. As I raised my hands above my head, Georges cursed and tutted, then let the lad go, eventually laying his weapons. One of the tribe started to chatter. The blowpipes came forward, I swallowed hard.

'Hold on,' I softly pleaded, then slowly pointed. 'Look.'

Without taking my eyes from them, I carefully moved towards the woman wrapped in the blanket. Turning my back, gritting my teeth from fearing what might come, I unravelled the khaki cover. A shocking sigh went around. An older man came over and started to check her. I hoped she was alive. This short, wrinkled man turned to me and began rambling, appearing stressed.

'Georges, show them the med-kit. Tell them it was us who saved her.'

Georges, a bit too quickly for my liking, grabbed the med-kit. A few threatened him with their weapons. Georges showed the same bandages from the kit as the ones her ankles and wrists.

'We helped save her,' he said.

The tribe suddenly took a few steps back. Lowering their arms, they parted to each side. A woman began to chant. Another small tribesman walked in, with the same haircut and looks; also, clean-shaven. The only difference was he had many bone piercings on his face and body. I am so glad Ocker wasn't here to mention the thinkable. The elder studied the girl on the floor. Guessing he had asked for her to be taken away, she was moved. He came up to me and squeezed my shoulder, arm, and leg. A thought flashed through my mind about siting in a cauldron. His eyes narrowed. Shit, could he read my mind? Up close he touched my face, then lifted my lips and peered into my mouth. What was he doing?

After he had said something, I was surrounded and held. My backpack was harshly removed and then I was marched away. I didn't put up any resistance, believing I was safe as they could have killed me there and then. But what about Georges? Twisting my head around, I got a glimpse of the elder standing in front of Georges.

Now out of my view, I turned back to see where I was going. The white wooden masks on the blokes in front reminded of when I had awoken, being bound, and transported on a pole. Was this why the elder was checking the injuries I'd had when they first saved me? Every now and then I searched back for Georges, but worryingly, he did not appear. Without warning, some sort of basket was placed over my head, light barely visible through the weaving. At least this time I wasn't induced into a zombified state.

The marching went on for about ten minutes, with no one saying a word in the eerie calm. Abruptly halted, the grasping hands left me. A strange creaking noise happened and, even more weird, new sounds and smells wafted through whatever had been opened. Jungle life had retuned. A push thrust me forwards.

After ten strides, something warm on my chest stopped me. The basket was whipped off, the light taking a few seconds to adjust to. With everything coming into view, it felt like I was standing on a stage with the world watching as if I had lost my words. It appeared the whole tribe was in front, just staring, at least a hundred of different sex and ages. Insects buzzed around me, monkeys laughed deep from somewhere near, adding to the tension. At least the jungle's normal humidity and ambiance had returned. I smiled, but there wasn't a single expression, and they already looked uniquely the same. It was unnerving.

Behind me was a vast wall of branches and vines, all interwoven, at least thirty metres high. How did I get through that? Where was the elder and Georges? Not knowing what to do next, as I was left alone in front of this growing crowd, I started taking in the main structure in the background: an entrance led into the damp-green stone building. The biggest tree roots I had ever seen splayed down the front of the temple, gripping on for dear life. The humongous main tree above was still living, with various vines dangling. At the rear was a crudely made bridge that went to one of the towers. Stones and gargoyles lay scattered on the floor. Some of the moss-covered walls had carvings displaying animals interwoven with women. Special elaborate stone peers held up the next level of this magnificent structure. In arched gaps way up high stood young children, alone. I couldn't see beyond the structure, except the blue sky. I was captivated when a flock of colourful birds flew by.

When my eyes returned to the immediate front, I flinched backwards. Two tribesmen stood, the size of sumo wrestlers. I wondered why these two were fatter. Anxiety followed about them being possible cooks. They chanted something at me, then pointed with their staffs towards the temple's darkened entrance. As Sumo-1 led the way, I noticed his hair looked odd. Was that a wig? Is that why the tribe all had the same hair? But why would they shave their heads and wear toupees? If they were cannibals and used the hair of their victims, then why was I spared last time?

Trepidation set in as I tried to make my way across the fallen ornaments and building stones. A cool but damp air drifted up from the darken steps below me. Out of the gloom came a light. A woman, in just a leather thong, handed one of the sumo men a lit twine and oil-soaked staff. This was getting more bizarre. I couldn't help noticing her firm breasts. Nico was right, it been ages since I last had sex or a relationship. A sharp prod in the back ruined the feeling. I turned to give Sumo-2 a warning, but I spotted Georges being led through a secret door in the woven wall. I tried to wave, but I was poked hard in the ribs.

'Listen you oversized chubby baby, you do that again and I'll make sure you fucking pole-vault from your arse. Cappeech?' I smiled, knowing he did not have a clue.

Sumo-2 moved into the doorway so I could not see Georges.

The blazing torch lit up the walls. I recollected the strange lights and shadows that had danced on my eyelids previously, as did the oily smoke on my nostrils. Deeper and deeper, we stepped; the cold walls radiated. Beyond the hairpiece in front was an orange glow emitting from a corridor at the base of our stairs. As he entered the corridor, the flames on the staff flickered in the refreshingly cool breeze. Thinking of what might lie ahead, I planned which one I would attack first. Again, the brute behind prodded me. It was starting to piss me off. Shit, could he see my mental images? I half-turned and smiled. Sumo-2 just glared. I needed to keep my mind pure.

Sumo-1 stopped, bowed, then took a step back behind me. The long corridor was aligned each side with arches with pillars. On each corner of the stone architecture wall was a stone cup with a burning oil. The smell pacified me, until I was harshly shoved forward. I sharply spun, but two curved daggers pointed in my direction. Where did they get them from? I now had another weapon to seize and use against if the time arose. Sumo-2 nodded at my boots and then gestured forwards. I guessed he wanted me to go down the long hall of lights barefoot. I undid the laces and handed him my stinking boots and damp socks—he was still expressionless.

'Look after those boots, they've done a lot of mileage,' I warned.

The sandy floor stuck to my sweaty skin, cooling the soles. Slightly backlit in the alcoves was some sort of stone tomb, but it was too shady to read the inscription on top. Concerns dissipated, knowing that Operation Edge was nearly over; at last, I would return to my previous life. The perfumed joss-sticks were helping me relax as I walked further in, each alcove having the same tomb. Tempted, I wanted to see what was written on one, so I checked behind me to see what the sumo team were doing, but strangely the entrance had replaced with a stone wall.

The lights started to dwindle one by one at that end, as if following me. A chill ran across my feet, like water. A frightening memory came of being locked in the water tank by the German tank drivers. I had been confined in many other different situations, so why was I thinking of this episode? Turn your mindset, I thought, and tried to envisage stuck in the helicopters fuselage—blank.

A weak voice came from the other end. Trying to shade the oil lights with my hand, I moved forwards, hesitant at first, but then I chose to walk boldly. Sitting in a circle of artfully arranged candles was an incredibly old man, so old that he looked like old leather on a skeleton. OK, this was the weirdest shit I had ever been in, something like the film of *Indiana Jones*. He stopped mumbling and rocking, then looked up. Frail, he picked up one of the candles and handed it to me. He then pointed to the alcove to his left. I guessed he wanted me to take the candle over to the tomb. I was getting good at charades.

I held it in front to see what he wanted me to see. The stone slab lid was laying against the side. I hoped some mummy wasn't going to sit up. I sneered at my stupidity. Inside the coffin was nothing but dust. Returning to the old man, a tiny object just under the surface reflected. I brushed the grit aside, picked it up and placed it to the candle: a tiny badge. Cleaning the front with my thumb revealed two white elongated 'S' letters on a black background. I had seen them before somewhere.

Clumsily, I dropped the badge. On my hands and knees, I searched, but couldn't find it. On the way up to my feet, I froze. I read it again, my heart fluttered. The tomb's lid read: Johnny Vince.

Taken aback, I almost dropped the candle. Is this where Ocker had found me? Hastily, I returned to the old man. Inexplicably, the woman who we had found in the jungle was kneeling next to him. I checked the long, dark corridor for any further surprises. The old man waved me to sit, so I did, placing down the candle. She had black and orange stripes painted on her torso, with thin red swirls painted on her face. Her bandages had been removed and exchanged with a thin layer of green wax. Her deep brown eyes stared at me. I had not realised till now how beautiful she was.

'I need to cut to the chase,' I said.

The stunning woman gently took my hands and placed some items in, cupping them after. I counted three contorted rounds, guessing double the used shells. It dawned me that these 5.56 ammunition were from something modern. Cringingly, I looked at her.

'Ocker, right?' I said. 'He only came to save me. He's a good...'

'Death,' the woman said.

'I'm really sorry if he's killed some of your tribe.'

No reply followed.

'Look, forget that incident for a now, I need to get back to 2013.'

The woman bowed her head at the old man, then mumbled something in her native tongue.

'Do you speak English?' I asked.

She just glared at me, deadpan.

For fuck's sake, I thought, and stood up. 'Right, I want to go back like last time, but this time I want to go back to the desert.' I picked up a handful of sand and pointed at it, then fanned myself as if under the baking sun. 'Desert. Hot,' I continued.

If only I had my rucksack, I could show them my uniform and photo. The woman started speaking to him in a low voice. She must have understood, she was my ticket out of here. I nodded my agreement and put my thumb up.

'Yes. I was in the desert fighting the terrorists, erm... baddies... evil.' I got down on one knee and played out shooting. 'Then a helicopter... err...' How the fuck am I going to explain this? 'A big aircraft, like a bird, came into land.' I did a twirl finger above my head, then simulated an aircraft flying and landing.

The woman and old man looked at each other, then back at me.

I pointed to where the forest was outside and said, 'My squad and I crashed in a forest. They were killed.' I laid on the floor and pretend to die.

The woman muttered a few words.

'I need to return back to the war, the desert, that point when the Chinook came in, so I can redirect the flight path and miss the barrage of fire.'

I tried to do a visual impersonation of an AA gun, but I felt more stupid than ever. Was I wasting my time? After the lady finished softly talking, the chief said one inaudible word back to her. Was that it? All that fucking drama for one word. My frustration levels were rising. The woman got up, bowed, and went over to the wall to my right. Like something out of a movie, the stonewall slid open and she went through. Twisting my neck to get a better look what was inside, the wall slid back. Typical, I thought.

'Do you understand me?' I pleaded.

He stayed pokerfaced.

'Last time you sent me back to the Germans.'

He half-smiled.

'Yes. Yes. The Germans. Remember?' I marched around like the Germans did and then did the infamous hail Hitler. I pointed at the tomb. 'I'm Johnny Vince. Remember? I want to go back in time, forever.'

The elder nodded.

At fucking last, I thought.

The woman appeared through the sliding wall, followed by a swirl of mist. The odd smell toyed with my nostalgia, like *déjà vu*; you know you have been somewhere before but cannot explain when. In her hand were two objects: a stone bowl and a pistol. She handed both to me. Worryingly, the pistol was the same as Georges. Was it his? What had they done to him?

I put the weapon to my head. 'Were my charades that bad?' I joked—pointless humour. 'What have you done with Georges Demblon?'

Their lifeless expressions were annoying me. I wasn't sure what I was supposed to do with the pistol, and with no help from the numb-nuts next to me, I placed the weapon on the floor. Smelling the black liquid, I alarmingly turned away.

'Fuck me,' I said. 'Don't tell me I have to drink that.'

The woman pushed it to my lips.

'Can't you just inject me with some shit instead?'

She softly brought the bowl further until it touched my lips. The fumes stung my eyes. I pushed her hand away, showing I had this. Whilst I grew some bollocks, doubt crept in. If I didn't die from this toxic shit, would I genuinely go back to 2013? What about all the people I had met on PMC missions? I slightly lowered the bowl. Could me and Roy relive that bond away from our miracle escape? Would we continue to hate each other like before the crash? Would I know that I could change the Chinook's flight path, or worse, I can but the pilots do not listen? If we crashed again, I would know what lies ahead. I could not go through all that torment, again. I thought about the notes I had left for my family and friends, and all the stuff I had sold before coming here. How could I return if I decided not to take it, or if this weird drink did not work?

Placing the bowl on my lap, I searched them for some help, but it was pointless. I closed my eyes, trying to think about meeting my squad: Robert, Tony, and Gary, but only their relations from 1944 came.

'Make a fucking decision, Johnny,' I said.

I had come this far, desperately wanting to see my dad again. Instantly, I opened my eyes and rushed the bowl to my open mouth. Without any hesitation, I gulped down the liquid, gritting my teeth after. My mind sent out loads of warnings on the smell and taste. I couldn't explain how vile it was. The burning from my chest radiated through my whole body. Pain like nothing before crippled me into a mess on my side. The screams echoed back at me. Through blurred vision, many feet surrounded me. Just as I wanted to give up on life, a glowing feeling empathised my suffering. As if floating on a cloud of joy, the people around me were touching me with cold objects. Weird but wonderfully hypnotic chanting engulfed the colourful lights and shadows. Then... all went black.

I wondered how long I had been zombified. Half-opening my tired eyes, new senses smacked me: wet, cold, and laying awkwardly in a confined space. In the gloom I touched the soft, sticky surface. With my hand up close, I tried to examine the black stuff. Either it did not have an odour, or my smell had not returned. In the deafness, I poked the tip of my tongue on the stuff. As I registered the earthy taste, along with a chemical, a waft of something strong whacked my nostrils. Was that acid? What was the other decomposing scent?

With the cold and cramp settling in fast, I pushed away from the slippery ground, but hit my head on something only a few feet above me; my pain receptacles were working.

CHAPTER TWENTY-ONE

'Bollocks,' I said, but couldn't hear my voice.

Touching the cold surface above revealed more sticky mud, so I clawed it off to expose a hard exterior. Running my hands further along produced teasing bumps, like large rivet heads. Further on, I held a thick chain. Where was I in 2013? I tried to remember something similar in Operation Blue Halo, but nothing immediate sprung to mind. Was I in a wadi? If so, what was above me? A worrying thought crossed my mind: the Toyota I had crashed into the wadi. No, that event was after the helicopter crash. I was supposed to be before the second extraction.

I was still in the same clothes Georges had given me, but they reeked of chemicals, and they had started to burn me. Continuing to feel the object above, I knew it was some sort of vehicle. Anxiety flooded me as I thought I might be under the Chinook. I didn't want to be burnt alive. My rational mind told me that the pilots Roy and Ashley would have dumped most of the thousand gallons of fuel. However, the skin irritation and fumes, along with the Roy's story that the Chinook had burst into flames, spurred me on to get out.

Frantically rolling onto my front, I spotted bright daylight a few metres in front. Unidentifiable objects poking out of the mud got in the way as I heaved to the exit, sending up putrid invisible gases. I still could not hear anything. The low-light was no more than the size of a golf ball, so I punched my fist through; the fresh air, satisfying. I continued to take deep breaths as I pushed through. My eyes shut because of the desert's stark light difference. The warm Afghan sun glared at my eyelids. So, Operation Poppy Pride was true, I could go back in time. A mass of relief hit me, then anger against all those who had doubted me, even my own complex mind, sometimes.

Just as I pulled my bare feet out, I knew I was rolling down a bank. On my back in the wetness, I looked at the dull light on my eyelids. Even though I began to slightly shiver, I knew the sun was rising. I kept my eyes shut, enjoying it. The only thing that had not changed was the stench of some sort of chemical, like grease, and something familiar, but I just couldn't fathom. Getting my shirt off relieved some of the stinging. I touched my soiled clogged feet, remembering I had no boots and socks on.

A howl of wind floated over the top of me. Even though it had been slight, I realised all my senses had returned. Then, someone close shouted, a thumping also filtering in. I opened my eyes to a dusky-red sky. The yelling continued. I sat bolt upright and immediately scrambled up the dirt bank to find my SBS mates in the wadi. On the ridge, looking down into the next hole, confused me. Then, the horror of what I was witnessing: a man in an out of date muddy, green uniform and helmet was continuously punching another bloke in the face, constantly shouting abuse. The poor blooded sod in the filthy, torn, grey military uniform was not putting up a fight. Sickeningly, the soldier taking the pummelling had no lower half, carnage strewn everywhere. I staggered back, gagging. The attacker stopped hitting and looked at me, contorted with anger and pain. He stared at his actions, continuing his eyesight at the missing lower limbs. I didn't know what to say as he faced me full of remorse. The saddened man stared at the other twisted bodies and dismembered limbs around him, then took out his revolver and placed it to the side of this head.

Bang!

Incensed at what I had witnessed, I shifted back on my arse. Falling off an edge, I landed on my back. Something cushioned the large drop, but it had still winded me. Sucking in air, a sharp steel object poked out of my trousers at shin level. Already sitting half-up against a timber post supporting a corrugated sheet, I slowly lifted my leg off the thing to reveal a serrated bayonet, the rifle below ground. Rolling up my trouser leg showed it had missed, but red liquid dripped from my soaked trousers. Disturbingly, I started to take note of the blood mixed mud and remnants I was covered in. In disgust, I raced to get my trousers off.

After getting my breathing and emotions under control, I looked at the smashed trench I was in. Most of it was covered by soil, only exposing fragments of splintered wood and barbed wire.

'Where the fuck am I?' I muttered. Find the helicopter you were under, I thought.

Clambering up, I noticed another piece of dusky-blue uniform under me, but I kept moving through the clogging soil to the end of the trench and then climbed the mud bank. Nothing could comprehend the enormity that smacked me; I had sunk to my knees. As far as I could see in every direction as the sun rose was a landscape of broken trees, craters, twisted fences, barbed wire, and a haze of flies. Strewn on the ground were dead bodies and unidentifiable macabre parts. Sections of the area had piles of sandbags and weapons scattered. Many soldiers in different uniforms laid by their weapons in shallow scraps. Some as if they were sleeping, some not so fortunate, all facing different directions of the recent battle. It frightened me to what was in the other craters, including the one I had first fallen in. I looked at the red stains on my body.

Slightly cocking my head to get a better angle, I worked out someone who was trapped under a horse. Part of his face was missing, even though he still had his hat on. The horse was riddled with puncture rounds. Looking beyond this grave scene, I gave up counting the other horses and bodies. Hundreds of crows were busy having a feast. Was this hell?

Mist filtered from the earth; I got the distinctive smell of cordite. The original decomposing smell I was unsure of before, was death. I turned back to what I thought was the helicopter, only to see an old, huge artillery cannon. Its half-sunk steel wheels had been shredded, along with the main cannon. Spread around the misshapen wreckage were huge craters with used and unused shells. Bodies with slightly different uniforms and weapons were littered. Two of the mangled dead had single-filtered beige gas masks on. I bowed forwards and placed my face in my hands. Something tickled my ear and, swiping it away, a small feather floated to the ground.

'Arghhhhhhhh.'

I looked up to see someone charging towards me with full on aggression, holding a bayonet charged rifle. Quickly, I scuffled back and held up my hands.

CHAPTER TWENTY-TWO

The youngster stopped within about a metre, just as I was about to try to side-swipe the bayonet, most probably without luck. My heart was coming out of my chest. He was also breathing rapidly, and not just from the five-metre dash that I had first spotted him. Where had he come from? More importantly, what were his intentions as he studied me? I started to lower my hands, but he regripped his Lee-Enfield rifle, stepping up his threat.

'Do you speak English?' he nervously asked, his feet shuffling.

I slowly stood to my feet. 'I am English,' I retorted. 'I know London,' I continued, trying to appease to his accent.

The skinny lad, looking just out of school, slightly lowered his rifle and then loosened the helmet strap off his chin. Tipping the hat back, he narrowed his eyes. He appeared restless, but then his focus was taken by a pigeon high in the sky.

'If you are not Fritz, who was on the front of last month's *Boys Own Paper*?' he asked.

'I don't know. I'm not supposed to be here.'

'Where have you come from?'

I turned to the huge artillery weapon. 'From under that.'

'Where were you born?'

'Cornwall, from the future. I know it...'

'How did you survive and none of the other Fritz?' he interrupted.

I went to answer, but he wasn't paying attention, so I stopped. The young lad undone a few buttons on his grubby uniform jacket. Keeping his rifle raised, he swiftly walked over to the cannon. I kept my eyes on his bayonet as he returned. He handed me a soil-covered pistol.

'You could be shot for leaving this behind,' he said. 'Or worse, receive orders to clean the latrine.'

Bizarrely, he then started acting he was digging a hole, and then what appeared to be squat shitting over it, with all the noises. He put his fingers to his head and mimicked squeezing the trigger. I wasn't sure what shocked me the most: the pistol I was holding was the one the temple's old man had given me, or this lad's antics. Brushing the grit from his arse, he then raised his rifle at me.

'What model is the revolver?' he asked.

I was getting pissed off trying to tell him who I was, and I was not enjoying the threat. I put my hands on my hips, frowning at him, letting him read my body language, but he didn't seem to understand my feelings.

'Why did you stop your bayonet charge?' I asked.

'Because you looked queer just in your underwear.' Immaturely giggling, he begun rubbing his thumb and forefinger on his collar, going slightly red-cheeked.

I looked down at myself and smiled. 'I suppose it does look odd, but I...'

'Where is your uniform?' he over-spoke, then started to pace around.

'I took it off because...'

'Where is your rifle?' he butted in, again.

'For fuck's sake, will you let me finish the first question.'

The lad became uncomfortable.

'I was covered in chemicals,' I said, at last, 'so I took my shirt off in that crater over there.'

The lad looked in the direction.

'And I never had a weapon...'

He had stopped listening to me; instead, walking over to the large crater. He looked in.

If I had been the enemy, I could have rushed him; what a fool. Standing here near-naked, I felt like a primitive man, and a little humiliated. The lad came wandering back.

'I can only see a Fritz blue jacket amongst the dead,' he said. 'Where is yours?'

I had to think fast to why my dusky-blue jacket was like the enemy. 'It must be in one of the other craters.'

'But then again, it could be French, Belgium, Hungarian, or even Portuguese,' he stated, as if he had not heard my answer. 'It is full of jam in there.'

'What do you mean, "Jam"?'

'Like what my mummy and daddy spread on my toast as a kid,' he sombrely said, staring at the far distance view, eyes watery. 'Except it is not jam, but gore,' he muttered.

It wasn't the time to take the piss out of his childish ways; instead, I had to get him on my side. I slowly walked up to him and placed my hand on his shoulder, his satchel under his lapel. He pulled away, not liking to be touched.

'What's your name?' I asked.

'Private Adrian L'Estrange.'

'French then?' I joked.

'No. Bugger that,' he snapped. 'I am Second Battalion, Green Hornets.'

Adrian adjusted his collars again. Lowering his Enfield onto the stock-butt, he swung around his satchel and, offering me an apple from it, I noticed his dirt engrained nails. Perplexed at such an odd thing to do, the hunger hit me.

'Thanks,' I said.

After dropping his rifle, he picked it up. Leaving me with my apple, he took a few springing steps towards the damaged artillery cannon. I bit into the sweet, rosy apple as he leant against a spoked wheel, next to one of the draped deceased.

'Bloody lucky, chum, you had found this Fritz Mörser-10 heavy field gun to hide under,' he said.

'I wasn't hiding, I...'

'You must have had a decent upbringing,' he said. 'No humpback, bow legged, or knocked kneed. What battalion are you from? What is your name?'

Suddenly, huge explosions rocked into life in the distance, the vibrations went through my bare feet. Adrian energetically stood to. After fidgeting with his bag and rifle, he adjusted his jacket and then looked at his watch.

'Bugger. I'm late for roll call. Sergeant Rowe is going to have my guts for garters.'

'Who?'

'You know.' Adrian did an unorthodox impersonation of some sort of monster. 'This is my hundred-metre frontline,' he bellowed in a deep, husky voice, continuing the act.

'What time is it?' I asked.

'Hold on.' Adrian leant the rifle on his chest, checking the wrong wrist first.

I frowned, puzzled as he had just looked at the time less than a minute ago.

'Seven o'clock.'

I had a feeling it would be close to what the GPS had last showed, the point where we had entered the strange tribal wall. The same had happened in 1944.

Adrian had started to jog towards the explosions. Then he must have realised he had left me standing, as he came running back.

'We need to skedaddle and get back to the trenches,' he said.

Already looking a little like the comedian Lee Evans, he pulled a crazy face like him. Then he continued to giggle as he headed back, but he stopped. After a short pause, he faced me and trotted towards where I stood.

'Your revolver is a Webley Mark five .455.'

'Oh... right,' I said. 'Where're we heading?'

'To the Western Front, chum.'

It filled me with dread. What the fuck was I doing in World War One?

We had only been jogging for about one and a half klicks. The landscape had improved slightly; however, I had passed many hundreds of corpses, smashed trees with bits hanging from them, flattened trench systems, sandbags, corrugated sheets, and weapons. At the same time, I had tried to ignore all the personal items: billy-cans, mugs, etc. It did not matter how far I had looked in any direction, it was like a blanket of death and destruction, unparalleled to anything I had ever witnessed before. I had a bad feeling the month and year I was in.

Keeping up with Adrian's energy as he kept out of the craters was difficult enough, but without shoes on, I was very watchful of bits of shrapnel and barbed wire, but at least it kept my mind from asking so many questions. In the end, I told Adrian to stop and that I needed some clothing and shoes. In an instant, he gave me his rifle. Running parallel, about thirty metres in, he dropped into one of the craters. Standing out in the open in just my boxer-shorts holding a Lee Enfield was weird, to say the least.

I laid his rifle across both hands and, lifting it up and down respectively in short bursts, I guessed it to weigh around four kilograms. Adrian's wooden rifle was immaculate, bayonet gleaming. I wanted to test it. Checking Adrian wasn't watching, I pulled back the bolt-action leaver. Firmly in my shoulder, I lifted the middle metal sight. Feeling the pit of my stomach knot, I lowered it as I had zeroed-in on a body impaled on a sheered tree trunk. Out of the crater next to this single smashed tree was the tail of a plane; the red, white, and blue rudder had a part missing. Parallel to its angle, amongst the bullet holes, was red lettering: 'O'. Just before the damned plane disappeared out of sight was another symbol: a horse and white shield on its side. A piece of metal creaked and flapped against the frame. How long had it been there? Was the pilot still in it? Had he survived? No flames or smoke were evident.

'Here we go, chum,' Adrian said.

Adrian threw the clothes at my chest and, snatching back his Enfield, he held it close to his chest. I unravelled my new damp clothes, accidently dropping the boots.

'I am in disbelief you survived the bombs and machinegun bullets,' he said.

'I've survived many war zones. I find it hard to believe it myself sometimes. How the hell did *you* survive that onslaught?'

'Touché.'

'So, you *are* French,' I jested.

'That is bloody offensive. I speak many languages, but I am true British,' he said patriotically. 'Now hurry up, chum, before we are shot.'

I searched in all directions looking for the enemy, but he did not get my sarcasm.

My mucky, green shirt had the sleeves rolled back and buttoned. Sliding my arms through the thick, green jacket, a plume of dust filled the sun's rays. The smell was awful. Adrian coyly looked around as I picked up the sodden trousers. Holding them up, I looked at him with despair. One of the legs had been shredded at the knee, still stained with blood. Adrian looked mournful. I sighed, then started to put my leg into the good side, grimacingly.

Adrian started to hop around on one leg. Trying not to show my bewilderment, I pulled the other trouser leg over my foot. Glancing up at him, he now stood still. He saluted me whilst I did up my button. Arm back by his side, he started to walk around like a robot.

'Officer Tin Woodman reporting for duty,' he yelled.

'What the fuck are you doing?'

'I am the Tin Man from *Wizard of Oz*. Blimey, did your mummy and daddy never read to you as a child?'

Sitting down, I put on a boot over the warm woollen sock and then did up the blood crusted laces. Adrian was still marching.

'Stop twatting around,' I said.

CHAPTER TWENTY-TWO

Adrian stopped, confused.

'Of course, you wouldn't know what that meant, would you,' I muttered.

'*Matar o diabo, ou ser morto pelo diabo.*'

'What's that?'

Adrian fidgeted, putting his uniform and kit straight. 'Kill like the devil, or be killed by the devil. It is Portuguese.'

'Not that. Why have you given me two fucking right-hand boots?'

'I could not find the poor bugger's leg, and the next dead bloke only had the same boot.'

I wished I hadn't asked.

Apart from two right boots and the missing lower trouser leg, I felt as if I was rein-acting World War One. On both arms I had twin stripes woven in. I looked at Adrian's ammo belt around his waist and chest. Walking around the rear of him, he had a water bottle, small rucksack, and spade. As I came around the front, Adrian appeared a little uneasy, but saluted.

'Private Adrian L'Estrange, Corporal...' He paused.

I smirked. 'Don't salute, you fool. You made me a corp...'

Abruptly, Adrian grabbed my shirt, putting his face right up close, gritting his teeth. His breath and spit from his yellow teeth showered my chin.

'Do not name me a fool again.'

My driven instincts were to use my close hand combat and put this fucker on his back, but there was something innocent about him. 'I'm sorry, Adrian. No malice intended.'

Slightly taken aback, he said, 'Oh, you apologised.' Adrian let go and began to rub his collar again, sheepishly looking in all directions.

'Why do you keep rubbing...'

'What does "malice" mean?' he interrupted.

'And why do you never let me finish?'

He didn't reply.

I had to play him on his own level, I thought. 'Right, Private L'Estrange, my kit appears to have gone missing.'

Adrian stood to attention to my stiff upper lip accent.

'Now off you pop, dear boy, and find me some kit. We don't want Sergeant...' Shit, I had forgotten the officer's name.

'Sergeant Sean Rowe,' he whispered.

'We don't want Sergeant Rowe to beast me for losing my kit.'

Adrian's proud face disappeared, instead, looking panicked.

Was it something I had said?

This time, even though I wondered where such a wiry lad got his energy levels from, it was easier to keep up with Adrian as we headed towards the Western Front. With my mind working overtime, I had asked him the date: June 1916. The actual day and date eluded him; yet it was confusing to how he knew so many facts about weaponry. Even though we had found a hard-baked rutted track through the main battlefield, caused by many feet, horses, and wheels, he continued to name weapons that were laying without their operators. I did think, not another bloody egghead like Fish, but then Fish would have known the exact date, time, and longitude and latitude. I smiled, thinking of him and my other SBS mates, but then I became angry and frustrated at the old man in the temple. Maybe he was so ancient that he had not heard my plea.

As we tabbed, I kept my head down, trying to disregard the carnage and not worry where we were heading. Eventually, I reverted to looking at the destruction. Behind a thick steel plate with a slot in, a body lay decomposing. What was weird was that he lay face down, still with his scoped rifle just poking through the slot, whereas everything around him was obliterated. His helmet had a gold symbol and point on the top. A swarm of flies engulfed him.

I slowed my jog to a walk, taking in the sheer number of smashed trenches, most filled with soil. A hand poked from a crater's rim, still holding a revolver. I averted my eyes forwards; again, I had seen enough. It then dawned on me as I looked down at the pistol in my hand: is this why I was back here because it was given to me? An image filtered in of the little SS badge I had found in my tomb, being from the World War Two German Secret Service. Is this how I ended up in that era last time? Do the tribe read my mind in the jungle and then add an object relating to the year? If only I had given my SBS photo to him. I had talked about Operation Poppy Pride, but also, I had taken the piss out of Georges for owning a pistol that looked like it was from World War One. What else had I mentioned as we had hacked our way into their weird world? I thought the Vera Lynn song that I had thought Georges was whistling was a World War Two song. Why did I think I had heard Georges say "forwards" when he hadn't? I can't remember thinking of an officer going over the top.

The worrying led me to think about my attempted charades when trying to explain that I wanted to return to 2013. Had they assumed the helicopter was an artillery field gun? How fucking dumb. And were my shooting actions meant to be the Germans? Oh shit, I had mentioned Germans, but that was supposed to be related to the last time they had sent me back to 1944. Oh bollocks, I had marched around and did a hail Hitler. I hit the side of my head. Oh Fuck. I stopped walking. I had told the old man "I want to go back in time, forever".

Breathing heavily, almost hyperventilating, I looked up at the blue sky, trying to get more air in to calm my tense stomach and nausea. Too late, I arched forwards, retching like a dog. A few laughs made me half-look up: a group of six soldiers. I stood tall.

'He is dandy,' Adrian said to them, and hid the apple sick into the dust with his boot.

'Cheers, Adrian,' I muttered.

'Just ignore their guffawing,' he whispered.

Three of the men had wooden poles tied together, slung over their shoulders. The bloke at the rear also had a shredded white flag with the Red Cross, all mounted on a thin stick. The soldier without the helmet, a kind of Pakol type beret, stepped forward. He was broad and tall, the only one not wearing a Red Cross armband.

'Got any apples for me?' he said, in a strong Liverpudlian accent.

Adrian nervously shuffled his hand over his side satchel. 'No, Spencer.'

'That's Second Lieutenant Spencer Bridge,' he retorted.

Bridge thrust Adrian's hand away and started undoing the strap, smugly grinning as he did. He showed Adrian the apple and then lobbed it over his shoulder into one of the damp pot-holes.

'Not going to fetch it, boy?' Bridge laughed—the others joined in, but it was fake.

Annoyingly, Adrian let this bully tip the rest of the contents out.

'Oh, by Jove, no gas-mask,' Bridge patronised. 'That is a direct order disobeyed from…'

'He's not a fucking dog, you twat,' I butted in, thrusting Bridge's hand off the satchel.

Adrian's lip quivered.

'You want to watch your ruddy manners, sunshine, or I will give you such a wallop,' Bridge said.

'And you can pick the fucking apples up and clean them on your overrated ego, you fuckwit,' I said.

Adrian put his hand over his mouth, but we both heard him snigger.

Bridge threw a swinging punch. Having expected it, I blocked it, then followed up with a sharp round elbow strike to his jaw. He staggered slightly back, holding his cheek. Watching him like a hawk, I front kicked him as soon as he had retaliated. I had forgotten how sharp I could be. One of the other stretcher-bearers ran over to see if he was all right. Wheezing and gasping, Bridge told him to get lost, then he got to his feet.

'Now you have ruddy gone and done it,' Bridge huffed.

Adrian was squirming.

'You upset my mate Adrian again, and you will be on that stretcher. Fucking permanently,' I said.

'You wait till I tell Lieutenant Taylor of your insubordinate behaviour...' He looked at my stripes.

'Corporal Johnny Vince,' I gave him the answer, then immaturely showed my arm.

Bridge picked up his hat, returning it to his head, red in the face. Perhaps it was because the others had begun to find it as amusing as me.

'You do not know the clout I have with the officers. You are going to spend many hours incarcerated,' he said.

'I have all the time in the world. In fact, I have till 2013.'

He ordered the group to follow him.

After I had got a few smiles and winks as they went past, I started to pick up the apples. I then manhandled them in my shirt over to Adrian.

'What a prize cock,' I said.

Adrian frowned. 'He is not a hen.'

'Let's hope we don't meet him again.'

'I do not want them now they are dirty.'

'But your hands are dirtier than the...' I stopped; it was pointless.

However, Adrian snatched them one by one and put them back in his gas mask satchel. Finishing the strap, he stomped off, wiping his eyes.

'Some thanks for sticking up for you would be nice,' I muttered.

After walking about a klick, the hell we had left behind now became rolling fields of grass, trees, and the odd fence. We had even crossed something of normality: a tarmac single-road. Small flocks of birds flew across, not the horrible black squawking ones like before. The sun was making the experience even nicer. For some reason Adrian kept his distance in front, not wanting to chat, constantly itching his nose and sneezing. During the walk, I had heard a few nearby explosions and shots; also, some far away.

As we neared a treeline on the top of a gradual low hill, Adrian stopped and adjusted his clothes and gear. About three hundred yards to our right was a long line of army lads carrying equipment, riders on horseback, and carts being hauled. A few were looking over at us. Obviously, it went down the line as one of the riders had begun to look through binos. I waved—no one waved back. Adrian whistled through his fingers. As I looked at him, he turned his back to the watching binos and then waved a yellow cloth over his shoulder and onto his backpack.

'What are you doing?' I asked.

'The Manchester Regiment gave it to me.'

'I thought you said you were Green Hornets?'

'I am. A few of the Manchester's said I should wear it so they could recognise me, so as not to shoot me accidently. They use them on their packs to differentiate each other.'

'Accidently?' I mocked. 'Did everyone get one?'

'No, just me,' he said proudly.

I smirked. 'Was that because you were the only southerner?' I asked, trying to show him the Manchester's stigma.

'No, there are plenty of us. They just told me to stay out of their way or they would shoot me.'

I shook my head in dismay, realising he was not able to read certain situations.

We had reached the treeline before the convoy had. As we went through the sparse trees, a highly sandbagged entrance appeared. Rows of barbed wire held up by posts led in both directions through the trees, as far as I could see. A huge concave trench about ten metres wide had been dug. I paused, watching a group of men sitting on one bank, all smoking, but no chatter. A few others were loading boxes next to six small artillery cannons. At the furthest end, soldiers picked up laden stretchers from rows and rows on the floor. There were not enough horse-pulled carts, or vehicles. Some of the casualties were being taken off the stretchers and then manhandled into another area. A padre was kneeling to one man. Refreshed soldiers were being led in. I suppose it was out with the injured and dead, and in with the new battalion that I had earlier seen.

Scottish voices came from behind me. A group of five men strolled out from behind a stack of wooden crates under a tarpaulin. All were laden with military gear and weapons, wearing green and red with white inlay tartan kilts. I smirked, imagining if Adrian had come back with a kilt for me. I looked at my two right boots and one shredded trouser leg.

The hairs on my arms rose as a set of bagpipes had started; the centre guy was playing.

'Johnny, we need to get back to the trench, sharpish,' Adrian said.

'Because Sarge is going to have a hissy-fit?' I chuckled.

'I am not sure what that is, but worse, the Seaforth Highlanders hate us English. I have heard that in their homeland they turn any English who trespass into some sort of meat dish.'

I laughed at his silly humour—he stayed straight-faced. 'You know haggis is made from sheep's stomach and stuff, not the English,' I said.

He inquisitively frowned, then walked off in a hurry.

I followed Adrian up to the heavy-timbered entrance that was cut into the low-rise hill. It was pitch-black inside. Sounds of horses filtered in from my right.

'I hope you have not forgotten the password,' Adrian said nervously.

'What password? For what?'

'Bugger. So have I again.' He hit the top of his helmet and then searched his pockets. 'We don't want to brown these chaps off. Have you any shillings?'

I checked my pockets; well, not mine, but whoever had owned them. Only a crumpled packet of Wills Woodbine Cigarettes was in them.

'Dandy,' he said. 'Get jovially drunk on one of these.' Adrian held up a shilling, then went down the muddy steps.

Do I follow? I knew I was supposed to be back here for a purpose, to meet someone perhaps that was linked to the future, but what about me being in a desert, like I had pleaded? Is Adrian the sign? I stayed close by, wondering what was install for me.

CHAPTER TWENTY-THREE

'Halt,' someone shouted from the shadows.

A guard came forward with a lantern. The sentry behind the guard lowered his rifle. Holding up the light, the guard's eyes were whiter against his dirty complexion.

'Who goes there?' the guard asked.

'Cecil, it is me Private Adrian L'Estrange.'

'Forgotten your password again, Adrian?' Cecil said.

'Afraid so.' Adrian proudly held up the shilling.

Cecil snatched it. 'Once you have loaded one in the spout, on you go,' Cecil said.

Adrian made ready his rifle.

'Oh, by the way, Rowe is having a few guts for garters; be warned. Seventeen dead since the last roll call,' the sentry said.

'How many injured, Frank?' Adrian asked.

'The big medic says forty-one. Not sure how many are Blighty,' Frank said.

'How many Germans?'

Cecil and Frank, perplexed at Adrian's question, shoved him on.

As I shuffled behind Adrian through the damp, dark, and timber held earth walls, Cecil poked something hard in my gut. I looked down to see a Hickory handle with a lump of metal on the end, all wrapped with barbed wired.

'Halt. And who goes there?' Cecil bellowed.

'I'm with him,' I said.

'I do not recognise you, sonny. Name?'

'Johnny Vince.'

Cecil pushed the club.

I rapidly held up the fags.

Cecil smiled. 'Ah, only if they have the card inside.'

Cecil handed his weapon to Frank and then whipped the packet from me. His mate looked on with envy as Cecil checked under the light. Where had Adrian gone? Thanks for leaving me in the shit, I thought. Cecil held up a card to the lantern, showing a picture of old biplane. I leant forward to take a better look, but he quickly put it in his pocket.

'Cheerio, sonny,' Cecil said, and stepped out of my way.

Frank showed me his bayonet. 'Where is your rifle, man? You know the rules of making your weapon ready before entering the trenches.'

I cocked my pistol, hoping it was enough.

Frank stood aside.

Unnerved by where I was heading, I looked behind me for the last time. A wind whipped through, bringing a strange new odour.

'I was supposed to be in the desert in 2013,' I quietly remarked.

'I have not come across this regiment, but even our darkey friends the Fifteenth Sikh Regiment have had to stop fighting in the deserts of Burma to join the frontline,' Frank said.

They both laughed. Cecil pushed me in the same direction as Adrian had gone. I was going to kick off about their choice of words, but I suppose it was deemed as all right in this era.

The boards underfoot squelched up water in places. Adrian was "flabbergasted" that I could not remember the recent downpour for three days. The trenches were wide enough for three people to pass. Occasionally, an alcove had been dug out, being fortified with timber and a crude wooden door. Inquisitively, I went to look inside, but Adrian yanked me back, saying that "I should know better than to disturb the higher-ups". Zig-zagging trenches woven into the maze didn't help me follow Adrian's hasty pace. I did not even get to see ranks and regiments of those we had passed. I am sure Adrian had forgotten the way, as he had looked baffled at times; also, embarrassed.

Taking a right into another trench, the floorboards stopped, mud clogging our feet. Adrian was halted with weapons. He gave one of the guards a small tin, the other a packet, like an old ration packet of biscuits. They let him through, whereas I was stopped in a threatening manner. With nothing to offer and with no help from Adrian, I had to watch from the side-lines as he had entered this five-metre-squared pit. Ten war-torn soldiers were huddled. Some were being dressed by a medic. I realised they were Germans. Seeing them nod and thank Adrian as he gave out the apples was humbling. They appeared dehydrated and hungry as they devoured the apples, but had a different look in their eye: content? Relief? Staring at me with pity? Why? Adrian had started handing out packets of cigarettes; the happy smoke wafted up.

On the way out, I caught Adrian and pulled him to the side of the earth wall. Again, he did not like to be touched. I waited till a few soldiers went by.

'Why did you do that?' I asked.

'They are just men, like us.'

'Were you giving them their last meal? You know… shot at dawn?'

'By God, Johnny, we do not give them to the firing squad. These poor beggars have an exceptionally long slog back to Marseilles, to be put to work on the dockside.' Grabbing me, he came up close, eye to eye. 'Are you sure you are not Fritz?' he insinuated. 'It is like this is your first time in a trench.'

'It is. Like I said, I'm from the future.'

'Shhh. I am not sure what part of Cornwall that is, but you had best remember your trench training.'

'Cornwall? No, the future, as in…'

'By Jove,' he interrupted. 'I could be your guide. Just between me and you, though.' Adrian let go of my shirt and then did a little dancing jig on the spot. 'Follow me.'

Instead of moaning that he had stopped me finishing my sentence, yet again, and not to ruin his now ecstatic new role, I jogged after him. I could not wait to find our sleeping quarters so I could get these itchy trousers off; they were driving me insane.

Adrian explained the basics of why the trenches were zig-zagged, traversed, and with dugouts; mainly to "increase life expectancy when the shells came pounding in". He also taught me that the "narrower trenchers were communications, their design harder to destroy by the Fritz". Adrian was enjoying his new job so much that he showed me each officer's and news reporter's quarters, including what battalion each soldier was from that we had passed. A lot of blokes said hello or tipped their tin-hat at him; I was just blanked.

Just as we entered the new trench to the right, Adrian stopped me by holding my wrist.

'This is it, the frontline, chum. Do not show your nerves, even though it is understandably your first time. You will be fine. Three things: do not brown off Sergeant Rowe. No Blighty wounds. And lastly, when the shells come in, drop onto your front and cover your head.'

'Cheers, Private,' I said.

Adrian frowned, briskly taking back his hand.

Had he forgotten his little private versus corporal game earlier?

For some reason, the atmosphere changed as I walked into this newly dug six-feet deep trench. Most of the dishevelled soldiers, made up of different units, were doing nothing but sitting on piled crates, scrapes in the wall, or standing chatting. A few were having a shave from a billycan holding what looked like a small amount of tea. Or was that muddy water?

The first bloke that I drew level with I said hello to. He didn't look up from what he was writing. Most of the others that I trod around did not acknowledge me either. One bloke was repositioning sandbags on the soil parapet. His mate pulled out the long weeds. Both ignored my greeting. It was like joining the British Army for the first time, but then I told myself not to be such a twat as I had served with the Elite. A pigeon flew up into the pure-blue sky. I watched as far as I could; lonesome, free.

Someone speaking with a raised gruff voice broke my stare. I looked down: a tall, broad man was giving a lot of the men a grilling in a large dugout. Most around me put away their notepaper and craftwork, then started checking their uniform and weapons. This big stature had a Kent or an East London accent. He had now spotted me. I seem to straighten up, puffing out my chest. He stood there staring at me. I glared back.

After taking a big sniff and spitting to the side, he strode over with his metal ended club resting on his shoulder. His glowering sinister eyes were still burning. As he came nearer, he looked down at my boots, then worked his way up. He reached the side of my face, pausing, and then walked around the back of me.

'Brawnier than most,' he grumbled in a low voice, his breath on the back of my neck.

I didn't reply.

He started feeling my shoulders, working down my arms, making me uncomfortable. He then moved to the side of me, two inches from my face.

'I am Sergeant Sean Rowe. This is my hundred-metre frontline,' he said deep, husky. Adrian had done the same line in the same voice earlier.

Again, I didn't reply.

'Where's your kit, laddie?' Spit landed on my ear.

I thought quickly. 'Dropped it.'

Rowe came back around to the front, lowering his club, showing off two medals on his jacket.

Thud!

I couldn't keep my balance. My heal must have gone through one of the wooden trench slats. In my wake as I rubbed where he had prodded hard, the reeking water seeped into my arse and elbow. He stroked his large black sideburns. Again, he poked me with the metal tip.

'Where's your puttees?' he hushed. 'Quiet type, are we? Soon have you screaming at night.' He rubbed the blue-stain stubble that was over his lip and chin.

I knew I was going to kick off; the countdown was ticking…

Five…

'Have you seen the state of yourself?' He smacked down the hand that I had up.

Four…

'Where's your fucking rifle?' He raised the weapon.

Three…

Zip… ping!

The blood sprayed everywhere. The soldier who had been looking over the parapet timbered back like a falling tree. Rowe slowly turned and looked behind him. I scrambled to my feet. The sniper had a hole in his helmet. Gore ran down his face, his open eyes collecting it.

'Stretcher,' Rowe yelled. 'Stretcher-bearer.'

Two blokes from the other far end of the trench came running down. The onlookers closed in behind as they sprinted past. Rowe undid the dead man's chin strap and, taking off the helmet, shook the contents to the ground. Strangely, he put a helmet on the end of his club and stood where the sniper was. The two medics arrived.

'No need for aid,' Rowe said. 'Note who he was and put him with the others.'

They started loading his lifeless body on the stretcher.

A lot of the men turned away and got on with their own business. Rowe held the messy helmet on his club just above the parapet and pulled down tight on the strap.

Zip… ping!

He then lowered the helmet and began to work out the direction the round had travelled.

'Runner,' he hollered.

The stretcher-bearers had covered the soldier with a grey blanket and were now plodding back. Rowe shouted again for a runner—nothing. He waited for a while, then he loudly growled in his throat.

'Private L'Estrange,' he bellowed. Still annoyed, Rowe turned to me, loured.

Adrian came skidding to a halt, spotting me, then the gory mess. 'Yes, sir.'

'Get me a sniper, now,' Rowe said, through gritted teeth. 'And don't call me sir.'

'Yes, sir... sergeant, I mean,' Adrian said, but just stood there.

I wished him to go find a sniper.

'Go then, laddie,' Rowe shouted. 'Unless you want to feel my cudgel.'

'What was it again?' Adrian said, and banged his hat. 'Oh, yes, a sniper.' Adrian ran like the wind up the trenches.

'Start clearing your shit up, gentlemen,' Rowe barked. 'This is not the time to get bored and start sending fancy letters home to your loved one and French whores. If I see as much as one brass or wooden model, I'll shoot you there and then.'

Everyone in the trenches started hiding stuff—indiscreetly. Some of the infantry lads began to reinforce the parapet. Rowe checked the time and then replaced the leather cover over his watch. I wasn't sure if he was timing the men. He took a stride my way. I was ready to whack away his club.

'Won't be long before the Boche return,' he harshly whispered. 'Name? Unit?'

'Corporal Johnny Vince.' Shit, what era unit?

'Don't start a quarrel with me, laddie. Unit?'

'He is from Duke of Cornwall Light Infantry, sir,' Adrian blurted, after running into him.

'Clumsy, lad,' Rowe fumed. 'Is he suddenly a mute, Private?'

'Suffering from shock, sir, I mean, Sergeant Rowe. Corporal Vince saved quite a few chaps back there.' Adrian kept his hands tight together, but his lack of eye contact made it plain obvious he was lying.

Rowe faced me. 'Is that right, Corporal Mince?'

I went to retort it was Vince but wondered if it was a trap to see if I was really suffering from shock; I vacantly nodded. 'Yes,' I muttered.

'Yes, *Sergeant Rowe*,' he said. 'Why have you two right boots and missing half a trouser leg?'

I glanced at Adrian.

'Because he cut off his clothes to plug the gun shots and blast wounds of another man,' Adrian said. 'He mislaid his boots in doing so. It is a miracle he survived the onslaught, sir.'

Rowe sighed. 'Yes, yes, I get the gist. What battalion, Corporal Vince?'

'This is the sniper, Bombardier Mark Morrison,' Adrian butted in.

Rowe's beady attention lifted off me to the sniper.

Adrian sneakily held one finger up to me; I understood why he had.

'Well, Vince?' Rowe said.

'First battalion,' I exclaimed.

Mark saluted, showing his large biceps, and said, 'Bombardier Morrison of...'

Rowe put his finger on Mark's mouth. 'You are the bloody Royal Artillery Brigade.'

'Yes, Sergeant. 113 Brigade. A-Battery. Orders sent me from the Howitzer to man the...'

'I do not give a fucking flying hoot, laddie. I ordered a sniper,' Rowe said threateningly.

Mark crooked his neck, seeming not to enjoy Rowe's remarks.

'Private L'Estrange,' Rowe blustered, 'when I give you an order to find me a sniper, you fucking...'

'Sir...'

'For the love of God,' Rowe interrupted Adrian.

Adrian began to jig slightly and rub his collar. 'Sorry, I meant Sergeant. We have no more snipers left. They have all been killed or are somewhere hiding in no man's land. Mark Morrison is the best shot we have.'

'I am better than any sniper you have,' Mark said. 'That's when I am not landing our shells on the bastard Jerries.'

'You had better be, Bombardier, or I'll have your bollocks with my fried herring for breakfast. And shave your facial hair. I do not want any more lice infestation.'

'Yes, Sergeant.' Mark itched his stubble.

Rowe hit both Mark and Adrian on their tin hat and said, 'L'Estrange, take this babbling wreck Vince and get him fit for duty again.' Rowe went to hit me, but I grabbed the club, holding it firm. 'Tough as coalminers fingers, hey?' he said. 'I'll see you in my quarters this late evening.'

We made a hastily retreat as Rowe was handing over the dead sniper's rifle over to Mark, still giving him a hard time in his kind of old London growling voice. One young pale-faced soldier who was sharpening his bayonet looked up, giving me a half-smile, trying to hide his fear. At last, someone new I could connect with. I winked at him and tapped his helmet for reassurance. Little boosts like that can mean so much. Adrian was sniggering to himself. I asked what he found funny.

'The word, bombardier,' he replied.

Nearing the traverse, I looked down at a trail of blood on the slats. Even though I knew who it was from, I still turned to see the rest of it. I wished I hadn't, Rowe was marching at pace towards us, swinging his club.

BOOOM!

Face down in the dirt, more earth landed on me. Vibrations shook my spine as another one had exploded in the field. In between another bombardment and heavy-machinegun fire, I heard a few laughs. How could they be finding this funny? I shook the shit from my hair and peeked to see Adrian with a few others taking the piss. One said all the new boys did the same. Adrian exaggerated his laugh. It had been Adrian who had instructed me to do this. The bastard had tricked me.

I stood up, shaking the debris. Another two explosions impacted in the trenches that we had entered earlier. The wreckage went high, along with what I thought were human remains. Pulling my neck from out of my shoulders, Rowe was barking orders, but became drowned out by our heavy-machinegun. Groups of soldiers were speedily taking their orders; the surging crowds were not clamouring in panic. Some tucked in tight to the wall. The braver men stood on wooden steps, taking aim through cut outs in the ramparts. The noise was frenetic, but Rowe was still cursing orders.

Adrian grabbed my arm and ran in the direction a few men were grappling with a mound of soil that blocked the trench, the exact place was where I had tapped the young lad on the helmet for reassurance. The rear bank had been blown apart. I joined in the digging. Further thuds echoed through the earth; bits of dirt flew up from the parapet. Suddenly, I found a boot and I started heaving. Because of the noisy battle, Rowe came up close and told me to stop pulling or I would choke the man; I didn't understand.

Without warning, the soldier's boot came free, and I fell back onto my arse. Shocked, gut wrenching, I threw the boot and half-lower limb to my side. The soldier to my right toppled off the step and landed on me. The dead weight was too heavy to lift. Rowe lifted the lifeless soldier off me, ignoring the shit that landed on him from another mortar attack.

'This fuckery stops now, laddie,' he bellowed.

I turned the soldier over, trying to do something to help, but his jaw and cheek were missing. Through the blood I felt for a pulse. Dirt fell into the young lad's open eyes.

'Medic,' I yelled.

Rowe pulled me off from sheltering him and said, 'He's gone, laddie. Now fucking help find Bombardier Morrison.'

'Where is he?' I yelled.

'Somewhere on the other side.'

By now there were a lot of men digging with their spades and hands. Fuck it, I thought. I burst my way through those frantically helping and hitched up onto the rear ground level. In the haze of cordite smoke and the consent barrage of incoming shells throwing up their wake, I squat-ran along the top of the ground. I didn't want to add any further pressure on top of the fresh mound because of Mark. A few zips whipped around me, somewhere out there many heavy-machineguns fired. A nudge from behind revealed Adrian. A round sparked off his spade. I threw myself down the trench wall, landing on two men digging. They were perplexed from where I had come from. Suddenly, Adrian landed in a heap next to me. I wasn't sure if he was crying or laughing.

'Found 'im,' one of the men digging yelled.

I started to pull at the Mark's trouser waist band. Rowe was yelling and cursing at me to stop. Astonishingly, once the smoke had cleared, Rowe was stood on top of the mound. Was he brave, or a fucking lunatic? How were all the incoming missing him?

'Johnny… Johnny. Let go,' Adrian cried. 'If Mark's chin-strap is on his throat, you will choke him to death. Just dig in.'

Digging around the arched-over body like a man possessed, the four of us managed to find mark's shoulders. Adrian shoved his hand in, saying his helmet wasn't there. Did he mean head as well? Once we had heaved him out, Rowe shouted for a medic. I hadn't realised the battle had stopped. As Adrian cleared Mark's airwaves, I yelled at Rowe to get down before he was taken out by a sniper. He looked defiantly at me.

'I don't take fucking orders from you; remember who you are,' he said.

'Bollocks to you,' I muttered.

Mark started to choke and panic.

Rowe jumped in and said, 'Great work, men, but clear this mound so we can get the medics and stretcher-bearers through.'

I looked in the same direction as Rowe, whilst Adrian held onto Mark's hands. Many bodies littered the floor, smashed parapets, and the walls.

8 dead. 13 injured. 1 MIA.

CHAPTER TWENTY-FOUR

Once the soil, timber, and gore had been removed, normality started to return. Rowe ordered Mark that he was fit to continue. A military padre was praying where the young lad sat before the German artillery shell had hit. I was given some new duckboards, as they were called, and proceeded to lay them to the misshapen floor—that was all that was left of the lad. Adrian came up to me and handed me a piece of something in a white cloth. Wiping my dirty hands on my filthy trousers, I unwrapped it: cheese. I was so hungry, I started to cram it in, chomping at it. The flavour awoke my dead taste buds. Adrian looked on with a frown.

'Do ya wanna bit,' I garbled.

Adrian pulled a disgusted face. 'Oh, relish the thought,' he said in a fine English accent.

'Bollocks then.' I stuffed the rest in.

Adrian grimaced.

'Where did you get this?' I asked, distorted.

'Sergeant Rowe wants us to meet him in his quarters at ten sharpish. But first, he wants you all spick and span. Follow me.'

Adrian squeezed past the soldiers that were leaning against the wall for another attack. I stopped following and watched one bloke handing out four wooden contraptions. One soldier had it laying on the parapet and was viewing into the timber made device. I asked him what it was, only to be frostily told "it was the latest periscope". I stopped myself going into what the British Army really needed from my era, which started me reminiscing my old life.

Leaving them with their antiquated weapons, Adrian had disappeared, so I muddled my way through the maze of interwoven trenches. Turning right the walls became narrower. A disgusting smell tore my senses. Cut neatly into the sides, the trench grew in width to about ten feet. The ground below became softer. I wondered if it had recently been hit by the barrage. The air had now become a putrid invisible gas, so I placed my forearm over my nose and mouth. At the furthest end, about thirty metres, three lads were placing something in the ground. They weren't making a fuss about the smell. Inquisitively, I moved to one side of the trench and walked along the planks. A pile of grey blankets and stretchers were piled high. On a large coach-bolt hung a collection of small brown books wrapped in string and tags. The first bloke leaning on a long-handled shovel grinned at me; front teeth missing.

'You come to relieve me, chum?' he said.

Peering over at what was in the hole, I expected a cess-pit. Shocked, I took a few steps back, realising why the way in had been stinking and soft.

'If we keep digging graves at this rate, reckon we might get back to Le Havre by the end of the year,' he said.

'Unless we bury them ten high, instead of six,' the other digger said.

'Johnny, this way,' Adrian shouted from the entrance.

With questions buzzing around my mind, and without wanting to tread on the graves, I hurriedly tiptoed back on the planks. Ignoring Adrian's comment about getting used to the smell, I shoved him out of the way and headed back into the main trench, spitting out the taste. Even the close by sporadic gun-fire didn't bother me as much.

Getting away from the stench, even though it seemed to be on my already rank uniform, I stomped into four soldiers. They were setting up soil around three wooden crates that went through the bank on the trench's edge. One soldier loaded a machinegun into the square aperture. I stood watching, taking my mind off the grave diggers.

'What are you doing?' I asked.

Their look of what they thought of my stupid question was said in their expressions, perhaps even at my mishmash of uniform.

'You been at the SRD ceramic jar, chap?' the young soldier said.

'A what?'

'Obviously, he's had the 'service rum depot' instead of our 'service rum diluted,' another one said, all finding it amusing.

'Must have spent a night with the sergeant,' the first said; again, chuckling to themselves. 'Can you remember where you are billeted?'

The soldier slapped on the round top magazine on the last of the three weapons. I had to clench my teeth as the jesting continued, me being the centre of the piss-taking. As my frustration grew, I had to keep a lid on it, needing to make as many new friends as possible in this world I had no idea about.

'What I do fucking know is there's more IQ from a curried goat's brain than you lot,' I said—the piss-taking stopped. 'For a suppressed defence, who the fuck would put all three weapons within a metre of each other? Especially from one enemy direct shelling, grenades, heavy-machinegun post, or a sniper.'

They all looked at each other.

Adrian grabbed my arm and pulled me away.

'With the lack of your weapon arc, let's hope they don't attack you at thirty degrees,' I yelled. 'Or you'll all die, very soon.'

There were a few choice words from them about me and the fool, but I left my new friends.

On the way to our new bunk-house, letting off some frustration in the way of cursing, I became very heavy to why I was here. What was the link for me being here? Who was I supposed to meet? How was I supposed to get back? Would Georges, or anyone, come and rescue me from the weird tribal ruins?

Stroppy at not being back in 2013 as I had besought, I kicked a large tin on a box, knocking over a pan on a stove. Adrian dragged me along, as those in the dugout furiously vented, but I wanted a fight. Adrian's grip increased on my already tensed forearm. Once I had been pulled into a smaller width trench, Adrian let go, but he continued to walk at pace. On each side were entrances with stairs going down through heavy timber-framed apertures. Some had a hessian cloth hung, a few had wooden doors. Engraved wooden signs, or brass plaques made from artillery shells, were nailed above each entrance. It was like what we had used to do back in Afghanistan to mark your five-star FOB apartment. I smirked at the positive memory.

Adrian turned right. At the top of the crude timber-floored stairs he asked me to wait a while. The hessian swished back; insects scattered. Whilst waiting, mutts faintly barked in the far distance. In concession, single gun-fire started to echo nearby. The mutts fell silent. Adrian, with a smile like a split watermelon, signalled for me to come in. A waft of burnt matches greeted me in the gloom. Adrian quickly climbed onto the top bunk; candle flames moved in the wall lanterns. He didn't stop fidgeting. I half-grimaced at the rudimentary thick timbered post that held up oak beams supporting reclaimed floorboards. In fact, almost everything was made of wood. The only thing that wasn't was a rusty, bending RSJ that interlinked the wooden ceiling beams. Was it an old railway track being used?

'Let's hope it's all flame resistant,' I said.

'We have sentries positioned to halt any Fritz flamethrowers.'

I shook my head in disbelief. 'Oh, that's good to know.'

'And if they are unsuccessful, we have trench guards.'

'With fire extinguishers? Jesus.' I sat on the bottom bunk.

'That is Mark's new bunk when he returns from sniper duty.'

Annoyed that I had already squeezed in, I moved to the opposite uncomfortable lower bunk, with its itchy brown blanket.

'Take the top one opposite me,' he said.

'Why not this one?'

'Henry Bellchamber is under guard, on suspicion of his own Blighty wound.'

'A what?' I asked.

'You know, you get sent home to Blighty if injured bad enough. Second time he has shot himself. The first in the thumb, now his little piggy.'

'Piggy.'

'This little piggy went…'

'Shut up, Adrian, I know what it means.'

'Oh,' he said. 'Sergeant Rowe does not believe Henry again. And worse, Henry tried to make an excuse when Rowe found his boot without a bullet hole.'

I laughed. 'What a bellend, not just because of the boot, but to shoot yourself. Why not just throw a sickie.'

I climbed up to the top bunk, hitting my head on the low ceiling timber boards, and then pulled back the thick, dusty brown blanket to reveal wire mesh, like chicken wire. I looked back at Adrian who was frowning, contemplating.

'Throw a sickie?' Adrian asked. 'You mean a bomb wound? Yes, throw a bomb and lose a body part would count as a Blighty wound, but a bit dangerous, as you could be killed.'

'No. Throw a sick…'

'It will not mater this time,' he interrupted.

'Why? Because Henry has nine fingers and toes left? You know, nine lives.' I sniggered.

Adrian threw a blanket bundle at me. 'Corporal Vince, you are ruddy heartless.'

'Why? What have I said?' I asked, trying to stop more items falling to the floor that had been wrapped inside.

'I will wait outside whilst you change,' he harshly said. 'Put your old kit on the rack under the bottom bunk and leave any food in the sack nailed to the ceiling.' Adrian huffed out of our tiny dormitory.

Jesus. Adrian was harder to read than Nico.

Not wanting to hold onto the bed's end pillar that had a wooden chock wedged to support the ceiling, I shimmied down. I picked up the tin mug and toothbrush. Leaning further under the bed, I found a large brown material wallet. Under the nearest lantern, I undid the tie and popper, revealing a secured shaving kit. Placing the brown blanket of goods on the lower bunk, I made my frugal wire bed of a top blanket and a folded blanket as a pillow; all smelling old. In a neat row, I placed the dropped items and then unfolded the rest of the blanket bundle.

Happy to get out of these battle-worn itchy mishmashes, including two right-handed boots, I stripped off quickly to don the new uniform. Little red spots lined the inside of my legs. Further inspection in the small mirror that was nailed to the post exposed the irritations on my neck. Whilst wondering if the rash was either from mosquitos or from the chemical grease under the artillery cannon, I started to unfold the neatly unused clothes. At last, some good fortune: the brand-new clothes fitted. Even the boots, although not worn in, sort of fitted. Perhaps I should piss in them to soften them up, like stories of old.

Morale up, I shoved the old clothes under the opposite bunk and then proudly strode outside.

'You're late, laddie,' Adrian said in a decent impersonation of Rowe. 'Private, follow me.'

'Cheeky bastard. That's Corporal,' I said.

Adrian strutted off in a caricature of Rowe.

There were a few wolf-whistles and banter as I walked through the new part of the trench. Admittedly, I looked sparklingly clean compared. Adrian was lapping up this new 'I'm the sergeant in charge' role. As the men laughed and clapped his performance, he became more into the character; no, exaggerating the fact.

In one alcove, a huddle of five soldiers were cooking what smelt like fried corned beef. Adrian ordered me to halt and, delving into his ammo pouch, he handed two eggs to them. The messy bunch handed back something in a cloth. Adrian quickly stashed it away. This little area they had was the best I had seen, with all sorts of weapons, tins, rations, cooking paraphernalia, seats, and a locked trunk, like a pirate would own. A sign above their dormer read: 'Ratten Koch Haus'. Poking from under an oily tarpaulin was a metal basket, like what you would fry chips in.

The eggs were added to the beef-type meat in the billycan. My guts rumbled with hunger. Slightly ducking under the poles that spread from side to side, I moved in. As if reading my mind, or perhaps seeing the drool, the group circled in front of their cooking, menacingly. Adrian quickly said his goodbyes and barked at me to march behind him.

Further down the trench, Adrian stopped and took something from a dugout wall. He kept it in front of him. From time to time, he was cleaning whatever it was with his spit and his sleeve. Once he had stopped outside a sandbagged staircase, which led down deep to a timber-framed door, Adrian came in close, keeping his hands behind his back.

'They were the Twelfth Battalion London Regiment. A bunch of dogs,' he whispered.

'More like Mary Poppins and the cast.'

'Is Mary a savage?'

'Oh yeah.' I sighed. 'I've noticed you have this trait of rubbing your collars. You did it back there in front of them. What's that all about?'

Adrian shielded eye contact. 'Here, Private Vince, take this.' He handed me a tin hat.

I was about to tell him I was a corporal when I noticed the hole in the front. Dirt had stuck to the inside remains. I poked my finger through.

'Knock before you enter,' he said. 'Don't brown him off. I have some errands to do. Goodbye.'

'You gonna grab me some of that fried beef,' I asked. 'I know back in these days they used bully beef.'

'These days?' Adrian tilted his head trying to work me out—I hope he wasn't thinking I was a German, again. 'And that wasn't beef those dogs were cooking.'

'What was it?' I asked.

'Time is ticking for you.' Adrian pointed at the door.

As I turned back to tell him not to be so anxious about a few seconds late, he was already making a paced getaway, still fiddling with his uniform and kit. There was something endearingly odd about Adrian.

Treading carefully down the damaged stairs, I wondered what type of person would want their quarters right on the frontline. I knocked on the door. Scuffling and voices came from inside. Then the door was sharply pulled open, and a young lad hurried out, still doing up his trousers under his pulled-out shirt. He kept his face away from me as he barged past. I ducked under the oak beam, entering the musty atmosphere. Laid on his bed was Rowe in his grubby white vest and pants. His clothes were hung neatly on a rack. The only difference between our quarters and his were the desk, writing paper and pen, and a wooden box with its lid closed. Rowe was still writing something on his leather-bound notepad. What had been going on with the lad? Was he waiting for me to say something?

Taking my stare off all his scars, I inquisitively looked back at the box. It had got the better of me. Shiftily, I made the short distance over to it and slyly lifted the lid. As soon as I saw the two round bell tops and receiver, Rowe made a cough. I immediately shut the lid and stared back at his menacing glower. Rowe swept back his black, messy hair and then swung his legs over the side, putting his hand on his club; white powder floated to the floor.

'This darling Duke of Cornwall, did he not teach you how to salute?' he grumbled.

'Yes, *sir*,' I sharply said, and saluted.

'Laddie, you have been hanging around with that fool too long.'

Calling him "sir" had worked. I hadn't forgotten the thump from him earlier. It came to me who he was the perfect likeness to, and in mannerisms: Bill Sikes from the Dickens novel, *Oliver Twist*.

'Where's Bull's Eye?' I asked, not being able to resist.

'Laddie, your ill-discipline is rife. You need to learn some manners.' His London gruff voice had thickened more than ever. He stood tall, club in hand.

I got ready to attack this bully. 'I'll take my chance, and then beat you with your club,' I dared.

Rowe ran his fingers through his large sideburns, eyes ablaze. Half-smiling, he slowly handed the club over to me. I curiously took it from him, then Rowe started to get dressed.

Almost fully kitted, he done up his last jacket button to the neck. Once he had positioned his medals perfectly, he placed his cap on. Unexpectedly, Rowe un-holstered his pistol and pointed at my face, cocking the hammer.

'Deranged,' he said. 'Suffering from shellshock. Come to my quarters to kill me. That is good enough reason to shoot you dead.'

Fuck. Further thoughts flashed through: would he really do it? Would I die and never wake up in the tomb? If I did return, was the stone lid secured? Would I be able to lift it? Not knowing any of the answers, I lowered his club onto the table, the metal end clunking. However, he didn't lower his weapon. In his eyes, I could almost see the pleasure of him squeezing the trigger.

'I have a mission for the Twelfth Battalion London Regiment,' he said. 'But instead, I'm giving you a choice. Either I shoot you now, or you take the mission directives?'

'No brainer.' I smirked at my own quip.

'Shame, as I really wanted to see your brains come out the back of your head. Pass the club to me, Private.'

'What's the crack with the "Private"?'

He didn't reply.

I leant to pick up his club. Rowe took off his peaked cap and he placed it on the bed. As he took it from me, he put his hand out to shake. At last, some respect both ways, a new beginning, I thought. As soon as I grasped his hand, he squeezed hard. Striking me with the melee weapon on my forearm caused me to come in with his pulling pressure. He violently headbutted me in the face. I was still dazed when he swung the club end into my gut. Before I could react, he hit the other end round into my jaw. After staggering back, I landed on my arse at the base of the way I had entered. Shaking my head, I got ready to defend the onslaught, but was surprised to see Rowe with his back to me, adjusting his tin hat in the mirror. Rage flooded me, and I had visions of me sorting Rowe. I spotted a ceramic jar under his bunk, then remembered smelling alcohol on his breath after he had butted me.

'Stand to,' Rowe ordered, 'and listen to your mission directives.'

I clambered up and made my uniform more respectful, the counterattack moment had dispersed. Rowe handed me a clean white hankie with 'Selfridges' embroidered in the corner and then nodded at my face. I wiped the blood.

'Before dawn, I want you, Lance Corporal Bentley, Bombardier Morrison, and Private L'Estrange to make your way across no man's land towards the wire.'

'Who's in charge?'

Rowe sighed. 'You maybe in Private Henry Bellchamber's uniform, but you are still a corporal.'

I got the joke about calling me "Private".

'On your way in and out of the shell-holes, I want you to tape a route to the Boche wire. Once you reach the wire, I want you to lay Bangalores. You are to cut a way through to the trenches and take two of them prisoner. Always two, just in case one of them is mute.' Rowe's sinister smile lit up, then he continued, 'All before the big event, laddie. And try not to fall on your face when you hear enemy heavy-machinegun fire. You know what is sounds like now.'

'The "big event"? You mean…'

'Yes, laddie. In a couple days we'll be pounding the Boche, ready for an onslaught of everyone going over the top to finish them off.'

I knew what he had meant, and it now filled me with even more horror, a challenge too far. 'Why do we have to risk our lives to snatch two Germans?'

'The darlings want to know what offensive they are preparing. I have been ordered to get information from them.'

'Darlings?'

'Officers.' Rowe snorted in and then spat on the floor.

I had a quick thought of Sergeant Andrew Graham's dislike for officers. Perhaps Rowe was the link back to 2013.

'Well?' he asked.

'You don't have any Graham's in your family tree, do you?'

'Now, Corporal Vince, I suggest you find a rifle. You know it's two warnings, then I will have you marched by the MPs to the firing squad.'

I studied him to see if he was joking—he wasn't.

'Get L'Estrange to take you rabble to the quarter-master to get kitted up,' Rowe ordered.

'What about Private Henry's stuff?'

A wry smile followed. 'Oh, he won't be participating in this war any further. Make sure you get a good night sleep, laddie.'

Suddenly, our heavy-machinegun opened fire. A few men started shouting. The door flung open, and a lad told Sergeant Rowe he had to come and see. Quickly, I placed on my tin hat and ran after Rowe.

The noise was frenetic with incoming rounds. Mostly every man was on his fire-step or hunkered behind their Vickers and Lewis. One soldier started shouting the direction of the incoming mortars. Anyone close to the direction laid flat until it exploded, then that person got up and returned fire—if not blown to bits. Even though I knew where this tin hat came from, I was glad I had it, as debris was flying around all over the place. Some of the soldiers were falling back in the trench, some unlucky were dead, some even worse were screaming with horrific wounds.

It was instinct to flinch or duck, but Rowe just marched on, only stopping to check on those lying face down. He would bark orders or yell for a medic. As we reached the spot where the Vickers operators had been giving me jip earlier, it was good to see they had taken my advice. An officer was standing behind two guys that were blasting the hell out of the Vickers. Rowe grabbed the young lad off the trigger and bollocked him for not giving short bursts, reminding the lad about its over-heating. The crazy-eyed lad came around to his senses and said something in Rowe's ear. Stupidly, Rowe poked his head above the sandbags. Stepping down, Rowe blew his whistle. Soon, the shouting went down the trenches to "ceasefire". Strangely, once our last shot had fired, the Germans stopped.

4 dead. 6 injured.

In the cordite haze and my ringing ears, Rowe squared up to the officer. Both glared with hatred.

'Why the fuck have you sent a man out into no-man's land on his own in broad daylight?' Rowe said.

'How dare you swear at me. I warned you last time.'

Rowe gripped his club and pushed his nose on the officer's, snarling. 'Listen, Lady Muck, I fucking warned you the last three times not to send a man out without my say so. The same fate by the looks of it, you miserable traitorous swine.'

'You went against my direct orders and had these gun positions changed,' the officer said.

Shit. That was me, I thought.

One of the gunners spoke behind the officer, obviously telling him it was me that had told them.

'You. What is your name and unit?' the officer asked.

'Corporal Johnny Vince.'

'And your unit and commanding officer?'

I looked at Rowe, who was removing his holster.

'I am talking to you,' the officer said.

Rowe took off his hat and handed it all to one of the soldiers, along with his club. Shockingly, Rowe started to climb the sandbags. No one questioned his actions.

'Where is your rifle, Vince?' the officer barked.

'Sergeant, what the fuck are you doing?' I yelled.

CHAPTER TWENTY-FIVE

Whilst the soldiers were peeking through their periscopes, I almost knocked the officer off his feet as I sprinted to the Vickers.

'Get on the other machinegun posts,' I yelled—none of them moved. 'Pass the word to the snipers to take out anyone that pops their head up.'

'The Jerries won't shoot him, pal,' the soldier on the periscope said. 'This is the fourth time Rowe has gone out.'

'Reckon the Jerries fear him,' someone else said.

I shoved him off the periscope and searched no man's land, eventually spotting Rowe. 'You crazy fuck,' I muttered. 'What the hell are you doing?'

'I want you in my quarters at midnight on the dot,' the officer whispered weirdly in my ear.

Too transfixed to be bothered with him, Rowe was striding towards the wire. He wasn't even holding his hands up or sneaking in and out of the shell-holes. Was he drunk? Insane? Fearless? More to the point, why weren't the Germans firing at him?

Within about three hundred yards, he started to work on something in front of him. I asked for a pair of binos, but no one handed them over. I turned to the officer, but he had gone. Running a little further down the trench to a sniper post, I snatched a pair off the sniper who was looking through them instead of his weapon. In fact, no one was aiming down their sights. After a little scuffle to get them back, I harshly pushed him away.

Through the slot in the steel plate, I focused in on where I had last seen Rowe. He was cutting barbed wire. Finally, he picked up a body of a soldier and placed him over his shoulder. As if all the time in the world, he started trudging back. My nerves were on end, thinking he may get a round in his back. Switching my view beyond him to about another a hundred yards, I could just make out a long row of what looked like pots; then, I realised they were German helmets. Jesus, how many were there?

To the right on the sandbags that surrounded their heavy-machinegun stood one large man. He was watching Rowe, tapping a club on his leg.

'Keep your weapon on that fucking German,' I said to the sniper. 'If he shouts any orders, take him out.'

'Listen, chap, I do not take orders from a private.'

'I don't give a fuck if I was in the Girl Guides, it's your job, your fucking duty to protect the sarge. If he gets shot, I'll make sure you fucking carry him back.'

On my return down the trench, still fearing the dreaded attack from the Germans, I glanced back to see the sniper had his weapon aimed. This time the bloke holding the periscope did not give it to me; yet, looking at the rest of the infantry with their heads above the parapet, I didn't need it. But I still crept my eyeline to the max.

Rowe stumbled a few times. I decided to go and help but was abruptly pulled back and thrust down onto the fire-step.

'Hey, pal, I would not advise that,' someone said.

I tried to pull this giant's grip from my chest ammo belt, but he was too strong. 'Why's that?'

'Because I am the poor bugger that has to go out and plug the holes,' he said slowly and calmly.

I glanced back from his medic band stretched over his bear-like arms. He was the first bloke I had seen with a full beard. I glared at his big fist, then back at him, letting him know he had better fucking let go—he didn't. His eyes gazed at the hole in my helmet.

'Listen, man mountain, you best...' I paused as a thought of Planet popped into my head. 'You're not related to the Archibald's, are you?' I said excitedly.

'No. Jason Bentley is the name I was given.'

'Bollocks. Thought I'd found the reason I was back in World War One.'

'There is a battalion of Royal Scots back there if you want to find a few Archibald's, but be warned, they are all in dresses. I will admit, it is easier to treat their genitals for shrapnel wounds.'

A few soldiers started to run to towards us, but instead of helping to get Jason off me as I had thought, they began to take something from above. Jason let go and took the wounded soldier from Rowe, blood dropped onto my face.

'Lance Corporal Bentley, why are you still wearing that monstrosity?' Rowe asked.

'You know what it is like, Sergeant, cannot put down your cut-throat razor for one minute before some toe-rag steals it.'

With no stretcher-bearers available, Jason strode off up the trench with the casualty. I turned to see Rowe standing on the edge, waving at the Germans, then he jumped down. Grabbing my hand, he heaved me up and tasted the blood off my face with his finger.

'This fuckery stops now,' he grumbled.

'*Minenwerfer*,' someone yelled.

BOOOM!

Like frantic ants that had had their nest disturbed, we all scurried into position and started to return fire, including me with the rifle that Rowe quickly had handed to me. Obviously, it had belonged to the injured soldier that he had bravely helped.

And so, it continued with mortar strikes, shelling, sniper shots, heavy-machineguns, infantry with rifles, all from both sides. Occasionally, someone shouted they had got one. Again, we took many injured and losses. I had not seen if I had dropped any enemy, and I never again saw Jason. Had he been injured or killed? It was total chaos, but weirdly in control. And then, it just stopped, just as I was searching for another magazine. I had not heard a whistle or the order to ceasefire.

Looking around, soldiers stood in their positions re-loading or servicing their main weapons. Others strolled back to their dugouts. It was time to restock my ammo, I thought. Two pigeons caught my eye. A shot from the Germans zipped by. I readied myself, waiting for the barrage to start again. A single shot was fired from our side, sounding from way behind us. The young lad by my side told me he would take first watch whilst I went and got some scoff; also, reminding me to keep the bayonet fixed.

On the lonesome trudge back to my quarters, there were many bodies that lay down covered in blood and soil. I wasn't sure if the ones facing up had been checked. The atrocities stained my mind as I walked by the medics. One screaming soldier was being comforted by a padre, but the seriously injured man started telling the man of cloth to leave him. No more than five metres away, some lads had started frying their lunch; it was surreal. It had confused me so much that I had walked over a mound of earth with my upper torso above the parapet and then down the other side before I had realised. Lucky? Or was it the Germans had stopped for lunch? Was this the rule?

23 dead. 29 injured. 2 MIA.

The tip of my bayonet hit something above my head, and something fell on my shoulders. I flinched.

'Oi, ya ruddy fool.'

I swung around to see one of the London Dogs get up from his one-man dugout in the main dugout. I presumed he was the boss-man. At my feet were bits of brown biscuit. As he came thundering over, pistol in hand, he ducked under further poles lined with biscuit on top.

Bang!

Having shot at my feet, I had raised my Enfield. However, he swatted it away and picked up something. Stepping back, he held onto a silky-black rat. It was the largest I had ever seen, being the size of a puppy Jack Russel. Inexplicably, he kissed it and grinned, teeth as rank as the rat. Suddenly, the other Dogs started running in, stamping, swinging clubs, and axes. I stood rooted to the ground. A few rats managed to scurry away with the meal that I had knocked off. The boss-man held the rat up again.

'Best catch ever that, mate,' he said.

'You ain't that piped piper chap, are ya?' another Dog asked.

'No, or the chimney sweep in Mary...'

'I fought the rat catcha wiv the flute was German?' the boss-man interrupted me.

I looked on at the others.

They stared back, even though they were dicing and slicing.

One of the rats in the wire basket, still alive, was placed over a flame in a bucket. Finally, the burnt mass stopped squealing. One Dog tested his tongue on the axe that he had just sharpened.

'Fancy a full London breakfast?' the boss-man asked.

'Be ruddy rude not to accept,' another added.

'Set the table,' I said. 'I've just got orders to see Rowe,' I lied.

They all sneered and grumbled.

Not realising I had missed the trench to my quarters, by fortune I was in sight of Rowe's. I hastily made my way over to his stairs whilst the Dogs observed. What excuse can I make? Once I knocked, I was told to enter. Again, Rowe was sat in his pants, a mug in his hand. A spare one was next to a large ceramic bottle on the table. He lowered his mug, surprised to see me, hands slightly timorous.

'What the blazing do you want?' he said.

'If we are to lead the mission just before dawn, can we be excused from night duty, and perhaps some extra food and drinks?' I brazenly asked.

'A fair request. I will see to it. Now leave.'

A shadow appeared behind me from the door I had left open. I moved out the way as a man in a suit walked by, but still with a tin hat on and a gasmask satchel. This wiry guy stared at me, then held out his delicate hand.

'Good day. I am Mr Pickard from the Daily Chronical. Your name?'

'Johnny Vince.'

Rowe sighed and then muttered something about reporting being outlawed.

'Can I have a photo?' Pickard asked.

'Yeah, sure, a photo sounds cool.'

He frowned. 'Cool?' he asked—I couldn't be bothered.

The reporter placed me next to Rowe, but Sarge pulled out his pistol, threatening to shoot the camera. I was positioned next to the rum on the table, then told to smile with the empty mug. I started to feel dehydrated, again. The camera seemed to take ages to take a photo. Once the contraption had, I couldn't see for a little while because of the flash. Whilst I rubbed my eyes, the journalist started asking my unit. As soon as I had given it, the notepad was placed away.

'Are you not going to want to know about my time here, especially the last battle?' I asked.

The reporter pulled out his note pad and read, 'Germans received a good thrashing, with no loss of life of the King's men.'

I went to speak, but Rowe shouted at me to leave. With his pistol in his hand and the rum taking effect, I decided not to provoke the situation.

On the way back, I quickly passed the Dogs enjoying their meal, shuddering at the thought of it not being bully beef. Just as I found the trench entrance to where my abode was situated, I spotted Second Lieutenant Spencer Bridge standing at the entrance, looking shifty. I finished sizing him up for round two, when out came the officer that had given me a hard time earlier. Bridge spitefully pointed at me.

'That is the scoundrel,' he said.

'There's the bully,' I countered, stopping my stomp.

The officer stood in front of Bridge. 'You just cannot cut the muster, Private, can you, dear boy,' he said.

'Isn't that mustard?'

'Quite frankly, no.'

'I guess you're Lieutenant Taylor,' I said.

'Yes, Spencer informs me of your insubordinate behaviour with the apples, and that fool LeString.'

CHAPTER TWENTY-FIVE

'That's L'Estrange. And he's no fool.'

Taylor smugly took off his slender brown leather gloves, as if he knew I would react like that.

'Bridge tells me how far his nose is up your arse,' I added.

Bridge looked ready to explode and pulled around his rifle; a new type I had not seen before. Taylor waved it down.

'I'm tickled pink by your courageousness,' Taylor said. 'However, I could by order have you cleaning the latrines, digging graves, or sand-bagging the unwanted scraps of food, for your entire stay. Until you die, that is.'

I sighed.

Both smiled. 'There are two other options,' Taylor continued.

'Let's hear them,' I said, dreading.

'Before you hear the choices, how about stand to attention and salute an officer,' Bridge said.

Taylor nodded his appreciation.

Loathingly, I stood to and saluted, quickly whipping my hand down.

'Good boy,' Taylor said patronisingly. 'First, you can either be my billeted servant, starting at midnight tonight, or...'

I waited, and waited, then I looked at Bridge to fill in the blanks. 'Or?' I blurted.

'Or, I will have you shot at dawn for striking an officer,' Taylor said complacently.

I wanted to tell him that if did hit him, he would never get up to make the order, but I said, 'I suppose Bridge here would lie that I thumped you.'

'Oh yes. Just a little bump from Spencer would be sufficing.'

'Then, Lieutenant Taylor, I'll clean the latrines for the rest of my stay,' I said. Side-stepping them, I made my way down the timber stairs.

'My dear boy,' Taylor said, 'I am afraid those options are now invalid. See you at midnight. I will send Spencer to fetch you.'

I whipped the hessian back, letting it fall behind me as I went inside. 'Cunts,' I shouted.

I waited till their chat outside faded into the distance, then took out my anger on the timber wall. After a few good thumps, I slung my rifle around and lent it against the table.

'You have met Bridge and Taylor then.'

Startled, I looked under the bottom bunk: Mark had his hands behind his head, the itchy brown cover pulled up to his chin, beaming a smile.

Opposite was Jason, looking stupidly too big for his bed. Both boots were sat on a makeshift plank shelf. Jason's feet must be fucking huge.

In a mood, I first took off my boots and then started removing the kit. Once I had stripped down to my vest and shorts, I made my way over to my bunk to sulk it off, ignoring the itchy bites on my body.

'I would keep your uniform on, fella. Bastard Jerries might start another attack,' Mark said.

'Bollocks,' I ranted—a chuckle went between them.

'You know the Jerries like to bugger new British recruits,' Mark said.

'The Kaiser up the Khyber Pass,' Jason added, his low, deep laugh seem to shake the walls.

I smirked as I climbed up, stopping at something under my cover. Underneath revealed a half-bottle of red wine, cheese, and a crusty baguette, smelling amazing. First, I sneakily checked out the label on the half-bottle of French wine. Then as carefully as possible, I slid out the cork, secretly taking a sniff—unbelievable. I climbed in and snatched the brown cover over me.

'Are you all right, fella?' Mark asked.

'Never been better,' I said.

'Me and Jason have not even had lunch yet. How about you?'

'Starving and thirsty I am,' Jason said.

Fuck. I now had a mouthful of the bread and was just fingering the soft cheese. Instead of wanting to let the cat out of the bag, potentially sharing my food that I guessed Rowe had sorted, I swigged the wine to wash it down. It had been ages since I'd had alcohol. Worryingly, the bread got stuck in my throat. Shit. The pair started to laugh as I coughed, worsening as I began to choke. The bunk started to rock. Jason stood up and then tipped me forwards, whacking me on the back. Breathing erratically as I had coughed up the red wine, bread, and cheese mix, both went into a fit of laughter. I wiped my eyes to give them both a verbal lashing, stopping when they both held up the same food, but a bottle white wine instead. Wankers.

Once we had settled on our bunks, there was no talking whilst we feasted. Being so hungry and thirsty, I wanted to stuff it all in, but decided to enjoy the moment, especially with the peace. Jason handed out oranges and apples, which got the conversation started about Adrian. These delights had not been from Rowe. No one knew where Adrian kept getting his stash, but he would always sneak back before light with his hoard. A few called him a jester, fool, dim, and the like, but in truth to those who knew him, he was trading anything for everything. Most of the loot and trade-offs were given to the men who needed it, including the German prisoners.

When Adrian would run out of provisions, he would always get the men together and make them laugh. According to Adrian, he had worked behind the scenes as a cleaner in a theatre. The incredibly sad part was he had been abandoned by his parents when he was ten years old, leaving him in a side street in London. I imagined my parents doing that to me—awful. In later years, he returned to his hometown of Portsmouth, but his family had moved on without him. Incredibly, Adrian returned to London and made it on his own.

He never went to school, learning most from theatre shows. Volunteering since the war had started in 1914, Adrian had learnt many languages, baffling everyone. Most have guessed he spoke good German whilst he had to guard two prisoners for a couple of weeks. The first had been shot dead by Rowe for not complying with Rowe's questions. However, the dead prisoner turned out to be a mute. This must be why Rowe had a wry smile after saying, "Always two, just in case one of them is mute". After another week of interrogation, the second German had escaped. Adrian was nearly shot for the mistake of leaving his post. It had been the other soldiers that had begged Rowe not to. Apart from my good old mate Shrek, I have never met someone more blood thirsty until meeting Rowe.

With the contented feeling of chilling with our bellies full, the chatting continued; however, I had the urge to take a first dump. I asked them where the toilet block was, much to their amusement for some reason. Jason said he had to take stock of the medical supplies, so would show me on the way. I began to urgently get dressed. It turned out that the clothes I was wearing were of Henry Bellchamber's. He was going to be shot at first light. Also, the soldier that Rowe had saved on the wire, died shortly after. I held on tight to the dead man's rifle. Ready to do battle with what felt like the biggest turd of all time, we left.

Jason had taken me the long way to the toilets. I knew this, not only by his banter and chuckling, but we had passed the same trenches. I had become desperate. After we had said our goodbyes, I awkwardly ran down a narrow side trench; so thin, I had to turn side-on. Cramps had started to become painful. I hoped nobody was coming the other way. Without warning, the trench stopped, but it went up out onto the main battlefield. Had I missed a turning? There was no way I could make it back, so I slowly ventured up the slope, trying to keep my expletives and face pulling down to a controlled level. The only identifiable objects were a cluster of trees. Where were the toilets? Then it dawned on me: this was a wind-up.

I didn't find the funny side of it because I was now out in the open, and squatting low was not an option. I literally had to go. The only comfort mincing to the trees was I was a long way back from the German lines, and British, for that fact. I doubted any sniper could hit me from here, but I knew an artillery shell could. Ungracefully, I found the nearest tree, appearing dead anyway. Fumbling to get everything down and out of the way, I let it all go, including the panic. Relaxing, I found a little humour in what Jason and Mark had set me up for. My thoughts turned to the Delhi-belly I'd had in Indonesia, and how my prank against Nico had turned against me. I am not sure why this time I had the shits. Maybe it was because it was my first alcoholic drink in a long time. Perhaps it was because of the evil goo that tribe got me to swallow.

Apprehension set in, wondering if this were the life that I would be stuck in. I made the best to clean myself up and re-dress. In the pure quietness, I sat between some trees a little away from my deposit and contemplated what to do. On my last visit back in time, at least I had the music and beeping playing. Although at the time I had been confused, and began to get irritated by it, I missed it now. It had been something significance to my era. So far, I had not met anyone for the reason I was here, and more importantly, how I was going to get back to Afghanistan 2013. It filled me with anxiety. Had my letters been found at home? Perhaps a full-scale search would take place. Would Nico or Georges find the tomb? A complex question popped up, even complex for me: if I had ended up in 2013 at the LZ, would the previous life I'd had after the crash be erased? I thought about all the parallel universe lives that could go on, but it was too much for a non-believer, and I binned the thoughts.

The biggest concern as I looked across the whole baron wilderness was that, although it was a stunning tranquil day, the storm that was coming was unprecedented to anything I have been through before: over the top. I remember reading stats for the losses on both sides leading up to the Battle of the Somme, and when those poor bastards were ordered to attack on the 1st July 1916. Even if I did survive the first attack wave, would I become one of the mass of casualties in the battles that continued after? I scoffed thinking of how Adrian was dealing with it all, bearing in mind he had been fighting for nearly two years. How many atrocities had he seen? Is it fair he fights on for another two years? Would he just end up being "jam"?

To think back less than half a year ago I had been precariously on the edge of life, and how I had pulled through with the help of Ant, Steve, and dare I say Monkfish. I looked at the treeline way back where I had first entered the underground passage to hell. I had a choice: to leave as a deserter and find another way back to my destination, and who could blame me, or to go back and fight in squalid conditions with comrades that I did not know; perhaps to the death.

CHAPTER TWENTY-SIX

That afternoon began peacefully on my return to the main frontline trench. Funnily enough, by smell alone, I had found the main toilet area. It was a zig-zag of trenches half-covered by timber roofs with sandbags on top to allow the pungent smells to evaporate. Inside, running down the centre was a very deep ditch. The support holding the roof was angled into the wall; you had to be careful not to fall in as you crouched by. Attached to the bottom of the timber support was a rope with a short wooden pole through it. As if skiing behind a boat, you would hold on and squat into the ditch. If you were lucky enough, through streaming eyes, you would find some bog paper. If not, you would have to ask the bloke right next to you; there were no partitions. Apparently, the Royal Engineers had copied this better design from the Germans.

From nowhere, a wave of destruction pounded. I gathered some saliva from my parched mouth and started to make my way to the frontline. Soldiers were running to their duty posts. I did not know how or why, but I had managed to miss some of the incoming bombardment, literally blowing poor fuckers into the air as I had gone by. At the main trench were two dead soldiers crumpled on a fire-step. The parapet that they had fired the heavy-machinegun from had been obliterated. I prised the main weapon from the dead and ran right up the trench for about fifty metres, ignoring the carnage and incoming. Through a small gap in the mound of dirt, I tucked in hard to the wall. I then aimed the Lewis gun at the German sandbagged heavy-machinegun area. At approximately four hundred yards, I could not see any enemy, but the stream of incoming was furious.

By the time I had become used to it, I had run out of ammo. Like a brother watching your back, a dirty faced soldier stood up on the fire-step and slapped on another ammunition drum, quickly ducking before his head was nearly taken off. Through the bits of dirt flying up and rounds zipping remarkably close by, I continued to suppress the enemy dugout. They suppressed back. Groups of British soldiers pushing forwards on no man's land were mown down. Then, the dreaded click: a stoppage. Looking dumbfounded, but trying to sort the problem, my young oppo next to me handed me his rifle. Whilst I kept up the fight, he sorted the matter. We then exchanged weapons, with no words. Every time we had ducked from the incoming bombardment, he would tap me on the shoulder for morale. Weirdly, I was beginning to enjoy the battle, emphasized by my swearing. My oppo joined in cursing. This bond went on for what seemed hours.

From way back, Sarge was shouting; it boosted me. As the voice became clearer, so did his cries for my name. Fuck. What had I done wrong now? My oppo pulled me down and pointed at Sarge who was strutting down the trench. I shook this young lad's hand and then brought him in for slap on the back, thanking him. A little surprised, or maybe humbled, he half-smiled and nodded.

'You, laddie,' Rowe said, 'relieve Corporal Vince of the Lewis.'

Rowe was patting another fighter on the shoulder with his club. I wasn't sure if it was nerves or enthusiasm in the soldier's eyes, but he sharply saluted to Rowe and then sprinted to me. Rowe strode behind. Reluctantly, I stepped down and handed the position to the new soldier, telling him where the main heavy barrage was situated. The bombardment and heavy and small arms fire increased as the soldier readied the machinegun, and my old oppo readied the ammo.

'Your orders are to help Lance Corporal Bentley at the CCS,' Rowe yelled.

'What?' I shouted, cupping my ear.

'The CCS.'

There was a gap in the firing from the Lewis, so I said, 'I heard that, but what is the CCS?'

'My God, man. Who have they sent? The casualty clearing station.'

I shrugged, letting Rowe realise I had no idea where it was.

For a moment, I thought he was going give me a whack, but he growled at me to head down the trench. I wasn't sure why I was going there as he didn't know of my medic training in the Elite. Perhaps he wanted me off the frontline to survive for the morning's raid. Was this shallow? However, I did what I was ordered, weaving through the many who lined the walls.

This time, just before the shout, I heard the whistling mortar. Sarge must have pushed me, as face down between the duckboards and filth he was on top of me. A series of three sonic booms, almost above us, rippled through me. Rowe clambered off, but his shouting between my ringing ears was muffled. For once he appeared shocked as he helped me up. Was it fear or pain? Face to face, he tried to stop me looking over his shoulder. As he twisted me around the way we had been heading, I quickly looked back over his shoulder, wishing I hadn't. Shredded, beyond almost recognition, was the soldier who had been manning the Lewis. Also was his number two, the young brother, my oppo who I had bonded with. Almost at my feet were two other soldiers ripped apart by air burst; possibly the bloke who had originally warned of the incoming. Where were the stretcher-bearers? Why were they so late?

Mixed emotions, not felt since Poppy Pride, surged through me. Rowe was having difficulty holding me back. I knew they were dead, and that it was futile trying to convince myself I could help. Enraged, I stomped off, not really knowing where I was heading. On the way I stopped at every man firing, telling them to mallet the motherfuckers.

With the battle a little way back, having passed hordes of men carrying resupplies, I reached the reserve trench. The reporter was taking photos of soldiers cleaning their weapons. I could have punched his lights out. Rowe had caught me up. He ordered the new recruits to get to the frontline. Like lambs to the slaughter, these young men sprinted off the way we had come, no fear and no excitement on their faces. Seeing the reporter, Rowe thumped him in the gut, pushing him to the ground.

'You can grab a rifle, or fuck off to Blighty,' Rowe said.

I smirked at the reporter's shit-scared expression.

'Private L'Estrange,' Rowe boomed—four times in total.

Adrian beamed as soon as he had seen me. 'Yes, sir,' Adrian said.

'You, laddie, need to stop calling…' Rowe paused, then sighed, defeated. 'You two, follow me now.' Rowe nodded in the direction, then marched passed me and Adrian.

'You are injured?' Adrian exclaimed.

I hadn't seen Rowe's blood-soaked jacket on his back, and it was getting worse.

Rowe marched off. 'Shut your fucking trap,' he grumbled.

In a cleared section of ground, approximately five metres by five, was an artillery cannon. Shells were stacked against the back wall with a sheltered roof.

'You four layabouts stop polishing your knobs and push this fucking cannon up the slope, sharpish,' Rowe yelled at a group of soldiers. 'L'Estrange, retrieve Bombardier Morrison from the tree hideout and get him on this fucking cannon.'

'Yes, Sergeant,' Adrian said, and he jogged away.

Rowe was redder in the face than his back, but he closed his mouth.

Was Adrian calling Rowe "Sergeant", at last, Adrian's humour? I moved aside for two stretcher-bearers coming through: gaunt faces telling the story.

'Vince, follow those chaps.'

'Sarge, let's get you seen to.' I tried to turn him around to look at his injuries.

'Bugger off, Corporal.'

Rowe hit my arm with his club and, walking backwards, he eventually took his icy stare from me. He then helped push this cannon up the wooden planked slope to the fortified sand bagged defence, amidst the firefight.

It felt good to be leaving the battle behind, that was until I walked into a heavily fortified area from what appeared a zombie movie; except, this was real. There were many medics, some with arm-bands, seeing to the fifty or so injured. Not even the guards had stopped me as they were helping one hobbling soldier, having lost a foot. Once they had seen me, they bullied me back. I gave the guards verbal that I was under the orders of Rowe to help Jason Bentley. They took a few steps back, making their excuses this area was restricted to prying eyes. I could see why.

I left alone the injured that had been already attended to. Some of these soldiers were standing or lying on stretchers, all smoking. Even with my ears still ringing, the moaning, coughing, and wailing was awful. The ones most serious, those casualties with evident missing limbs, were being loaded onto a horse pulled cart. Brown blankets were being brought in. Were these our bunk blankets? Had they run out of grey? One uninjured soldier was searching a dead colleague who was completely covered. He pulled out a packet of fags, then the cigarette cards. I raced over, whipping back the cover: Cecil. The soldier offered me a smoke. Was this the norm?

A new cart came in, letting the already loaded one leave, casualties being extensively jolted around in the rutted wide trench—ridiculous. Curiously, I stepped up on two labelled boxes to watch the dust trail. Then, about forty metres in, the vehicle came up the slope and started to make their escape. Bits of the dead tree trunk exploded near to the cart. I quickly ducked. Training kicked in and I quickly made my way into a huge canvas tent with the medic cross on a flag on each corner. Perhaps if the Germans raided, they would not attack this area.

Inside, trying not to look stunned at the amount of injured lined up, the smell of chemicals hit me. Jason was covered in an enormous amount of blood. He came over and shook my hand, not releasing his poignant grip, such sadness in his eyes.

'We could do with the help,' he said. 'How much do you know?'

'I've done a fair bit, but I'll followed your lead.'

I knew my boasting about my medical experience from my era on the battlefield and in hospitals was pointless. After putting on a simple apron, I washed my hands in a carbolic location, as it had said on the bottle. I started to watch the other medics treat the injured. The less horrific were moved to another part of the marquee, with a simple field dressing to hold.

The enormity of the task ahead subsided, along with the wails and screams. As I stood opposite Jason, the first casualty was laid out. Jason showed me the exercise of something he called "debridement", whereby the injured skin tissue around the wound was cut away, then sealed to prevent infection. Jason used carbolic lotion to flush the wounds and then the soldier was wrapped in gauze. For good measure, the gauze was soaked in the same solution. As soon as he was done, two specific porters stretchered the soldier outside to the 'taxi-rank'. There were no sulphonamides or antibiotics given. Those who were lucky enough could enjoy a cigarette or a mug of tea.

Like the injuries sustained by the poor bastards who had died by the shrapnel from an airburst mortar, the next young soldier had the same injuries. He growled through his teeth. Whilst we took his clothes off, I gripped his hand. Inspecting his multiple wounds, I told him his love making gear was still there. This brought a smile and a bit of relief to him. Jason listened to the further banter, then nodded at me, as if he had learnt something. I must admit, there wasn't much talking to the patients from the medics. Some of the shrapnel was too deep, and Jason had said, "it was not worthwhile to remove here". Whilst holding the soldier's blooded hand, Jason ordered someone to fetch him some 'Bipp'. I helped Jason smear it over the wounds, smelling a little like paraffin. There was no time for gratitude, and a blanket was placed on him.

'Next,' Jason shouted.

The sight of a pale-faced officer with his leg missing wasn't good. The use of a respirator string from the battlefield wasn't stopping the blood flow. This time Jason started to chat to the delirious officer about how the horse was feeling. You could see the officer thinking about his best friend. More banter followed; the officer even garbled some back. Another tourniquet was added. Jason then reached in his red-stained side satchel.

'That is all we can do for this chap. I doubt he will last the journey back,' Jason said.

The officer looked scared and closed his eyes.

I vigorously shook my head at Jason, but he frowned in confusion. 'He's just joking, sir,' I said to the officer.

Jason placed a hideously large syringe, although small in his hands, in the casualty's arm and squeezed off a little of the liquid. Placing it back in his side satchel, the officer was taken outside.

'God bless,' Jason said.

As the next was placed on the table, Jason shook his head whilst feeling the casualty's body. This soldier, although no obvious signs of bleeding, except some dried around his ear and neck, had been blown off his feet from a shell that went under the soil in front of him. According to the stretcher-bearers, this medic was running to attend to a soldier, when he flew five metres back into another trench. The other injured soldier still lays in bits on the ground above. Jason made the decision to "take him out the back". I had noticed before this that many other soldiers had been carried out the same way. Jason told me it was where the "imminent death, or dead, were taken, as not to let any further morale slip from the others".

Jason used the syringe on another soldier in a serious condition who had been brought in.

'What's in that?' I asked.

A large boom shook objects on the small table next to us, silence fell. For some reason, I looked at the canvas above our heads, wondering if something big was on its way. Then another tremor quaked, and I realised what it was: Mark on the artillery cannon. Jason raised his look at me whilst he attended another casualty, then smiled; he knew. I had not even seen this new soldier being brought in.

'Heroin,' he answered—the ambience returned to normal.

I laughed, thinking he had the idea of humour in certain situations. He remained straight-faced.

'You're not joking, are you?' I asked.

'Ironically, the Kaiser recently invented the medicine back in 1898. It just helps those who are in serious pain. And now that Absinthe has been outlawed, it is readily available.'

And if they do survive, they could die of addiction, I thought, but stayed tight-lipped.

The concoction of the battle continued, including the nearby artillery cannon. The casualty's pleas for help, the smells, the grime, and re-stocking all the supplies all became the norm. However, the rate of victims affected by gas had increased. Whilst we worked, Jason told me that he had studied at the Royal College of Surgeons. After seeing a poster of Lord Kitchener, he could not wait to get to war to help. Before Jason's frontline duty, he had worked in large mansion that had been turned into a hospital in Rouen. He had to deal with everything from disinfestation, to using a French guillotine to amputate those lucky enough to survive the trip back with gangrene. However, many did not make it back, even after the medics had done the best they could on the frontline. Incredibly, knowing the severity of the conditions, he had pleaded with his CO to be sent to the Somme. Now, Jason oversaw this CCS, the only one in Rowe's one hundred metre domain, one of hundreds along the fourteen-mile line.

Jason had learnt that eighty per cent of those shot in the femur would not survive. One of the main attributes to this was when the stretcher-bearers and comrades had moved the casualty away. Broken bones would tear the muscles, possibly puncturing an artery, causing a second wound shock, ending in a rapid loss of blood. Also, on moving those men, if the shattered bone end protruded through the skin in the trench conditions, or if not cleaned, infection would set in. Right from the beginning, Jason had instructed the top-ranking bearer soldier to invent something that would keep the leg or arm perfectly still whilst moving the casualty. A simple splint was the invention. Even though Jason had transformed this station, his vision, he had never realised the casualty and death rate would be so high, losing count moons ago. He was a giant man, with a larger heart.

With the lack of modern medicines, fluids, instruments, equipment, and the conditions on the battlefield, I was surprised the number that had made it. There was no 'golden hour' here to get the casualties stable. We didn't even have sterile conditions, but they just kept coming. When the high priority casualties and had stopped being brought in, it was only then I noticed the peace and quiet from outside. I was mentally exhausted. Yet, the backlog of the minor injuries had to be seen, from those who were temporally blinded, to fingers and ears being shot off. They had been waiting hours. I treated one guy who was still in spirits. He had a round go through his knuckle, right up through and out his elbow, still thanking me for seeing to him. I smirked at those of my generation in doctor and hospital waiting rooms, all moaning and getting aggressive about waiting times.

Once we had finished treating, a man of the cloth went through to the back. Even though I was hungry and thirsty, we had to sterile everything the best we could, ready for the next wave. All the staff had that glazed look. The old men looked older, and the young looked worse. I was glad to get outside for some fresh air, and so was Jason.

Roll-call: 68 dead. 89 injured. 12 MIA.

Many of those still sitting around tipped their hat or head at us. I left Jason as he spoke to the fresh 'handover' staff, wearily making my way back to my dormer; a wash and a rest that I needed so desperately. I was amazed at how clean and repaired the trenches and dugouts were. I asked one soldier, who was cooking, for the time. He told me to "bugger off". Not knowing if it was because I still wore the lowest ranked stripes, or perhaps that I was covered in blood, or even he may have thought I was poncing for food, I was too tired to kick off. Maybe it was his way of dealing with the stresses.

As I turned the corner to our trench, Mark was banging out his dusty clothes, then his muscular physic went back inside.

'Mark,' I shouted.

He didn't stop, so I followed. Entering the hessian, Mark was down to his shorts, and he had his back to me, nursing each shoulder that were blistered raw.

'All right?' I said.

Again, he didn't acknowledge.

I placed a hand on his back.

Suddenly, he sharply turned with a cut-throat razor.

'Whoa,' I said.

'You should not creep up on me like that, fella,' he bellowed.

'Jesus. Why are you shouting?'

'What?' he yelled.

Then I realised why he couldn't hear me. 'What's happened to your shoulders.'

'No blooming sandbags for me to carry the shells on.'

'And no ear-plugs?' I jested.

'Pardon?'

Mark climbed onto his bed. I waited till he faced me and then gestured him to shut up as he had been too loud. He acknowledged that he had understood.

Looking in the bowl after a cold wash and shave, the water had turned red. In the small mirror, I caught a glimpse of Mark blowing on his blisters. Jason came through the opening, blocking out what little light there was.

'Too many groups sent out into no man's land this time,' Jason said moodily.

'Mark needs some soothing cream,' I said.

'How was I supposed to know?' Jason snapped.

'It's times like this you should have had your mobile on at work,' I jested.

'Mobile what?'

I laughed. 'Smart phone. I could have texted you or WhatsApp you.' I wasn't sure where I was going with this, but it was amusing me; something had to.

'Only Sergeant Rowe and the officers have comms,' he said, then barged me out of the way to use my bowl of manky water.

Once we were spaced-out on our bunks, Adrian darted in and greeted us.

'Eh hem,' he said, again.

I still didn't open my eyes. Mark and Jason started applauding. Inquisitively, I arched my neck to see Adrian dressed in a bowler hat and a cane under his arm, juggling oranges. Between the three oranges spinning, I noticed he had a black mark under his nose: a fake moustache. He threw the fruit one by one at us and then started to do the famous Chaplin walk, twirling the cane.

'You're not Hitler then,' I mocked.

Adrian stopped and took a bow.

Mark and Jason clapped.

'Who?' Adrian said. 'I am Charlie Chaplin. Have you heard of him?'

'Yes, many a time, and you're nothing like him,' I replied.

Adrian looked disgruntled.

I knew the game was to make him feel important again. 'Have you got any food stashed?' I asked. 'You know you're the best at sourcing it.'

Adrian fumbled with his hat but dropped it. He quickly placed it and the cane under Mark's bed and then hauled out a kit bag. Unbelievably, Adrian handed out an Imperial Moet and Chandon Brute. I wondered what this would be worth when I got back to my era.

Even though my thirst had got the better of me, I knew we had to remain clear headed for the dawn raid. I ordered the rest not to open theirs. Adrian clumsily took the bottles back, still filled with joy, unlike Jason and Mark. Adrian handed over bottles of still lemonade. It was beautifully refreshing. He then pulled out a metal tin and, wiping rodent droppings off it, opened the lid. He continued to impress us further with cheese, cured meats, pickles, and chutney. The only thing missing was the camaraderie and the talk about boobs and sex.

'Not only do you guys need to enhance your camaraderie and banter, but I think we need some nicknames,' I said, and loudly burped.

'Guttersnipe,' Jason said.

'That's a bit strong. Nothing wrong with nicknames,' I said, with a mouthful of meat.

'I meant your manners.'

Tutting, I said, 'I know, Jason. Anyway, let's start with you.'

'The Iron Master,' Jason said proudly.

'Who?' Mark asked.

'Author Saxton. The circus strongman who…'

'He was German,' Adrian interrupted.

Mark went into hysterics.

'That's a bit try-hard, Jason, and too long,' I said. As much he was built like my old mate Robert, I couldn't call him Planet, I thought. 'How about tiny, after your dick?' I bantered.

'My what?'

I chuckled. 'Your teeny todger… little knob… miniscule winky… bitsy bone?' It was becoming too difficult to stop giggling, and to think of more names he wouldn't understand.

'What the blazing are you laughing at, Adrian?' Jason boomed.

Adrian's laughter turned nervous.

'Get to the point, Vince,' Jason demand.

'Your micro penis.'

Mark sprayed his drink.

'I would rather not have my personal problem brought into my nickname,' Jason said sadly.

We fell silent with guilt. Adrian gulped down his lemonade.

Jason roared with laughter, then blurted, 'You can call me titanic penis.'

'As in the ship?' Adrian asked.

'Largest ever,' Jason said.

'We'll shorten it to Titan,' I said.

'And what about me?' Mark asked.

'Morri,' Adrian said.

'Blister,' Jason added.

'No thanks, Titan,' Mark said.

'Blister it is then,' I said, much to Mark's annoyance. 'Now, Adrian… hmm… let me think.'

I laid back with the empty bottle on my chest and closed my eyes. With the all the food and tangy drink, and feeling drained, the ideas weren't coming, and not just from me.

'Any idea, lads?'

With no one replying, I lifted to check: all asleep. Mark was holding a black and white photo of his wife and a dog. Great idea, I thought, and shut my eyes.

CHAPTER TWENTY-SEVEN

My nightmare had been full of today's horrors. Every time I had flipped over on my side, I had tried to think of positive memories, but it became impossible. The explosions and screaming in my dream had been so lifelike. I really hoped any PTSD would not return. This had not come into my plan when leaving Newquay. Steve and Ant had helped me beat those demons, the "black dogs" as they had called it.

Suddenly, I opened my eyes as something was on my face.

'Arhhh,' I yelled.

Swiping it off, I sat bolt upright in the near-dark, throwing the approximate dozen rats off me. This caused Mark and Jason to start yelling at me to pack it up. When the rats had gone, something else was in my fingers. From the sunset outside, a figure was silhouetted against the pulled back hessian.

'What's going on?' I asked.

'Be quiet,' Adrian whispered.

An order was shouted to "stand down" from outside. It had been Rowe. Adrian sighed with relief. He let the door curtain go and started to move nosily about. Once the lamps and candles were lit, he falsely started to check his pistol and rifle, as if proving a point that he was up and ready whilst we had been asleep. Mark was the first out of bed to stretch, his empty lemonade bottle clunking on the floor. He nodded at my hand.

'That hungry are you, Johnny?' Mark said.

'What the heck?' I replied.

I threw the large worm I still had in my fingers, and then brushed the rest and the soil off my blanket. Jason stood up to join in Mark's amusement. I looked above at the timber joins: worms were still trying to get through.

'Did they not tell you if you sleep in the top bunk, you have to share with Mother Nature?' Jason said. 'As a medic, I would strongly advise you do not eat them.'

'Perhaps that is why he had diarrhoea,' Mark added.

'Enough to compost those group of trees up on top,' Adrian chipped in. He started chuckling, but it was inflated.

'And the French ploughed fields,' Jason quipped.

I had forgotten about them sending me up the wrong trench for the toilets. 'Piss off,' I said. 'Were you weirdo's watching me then?'

This started them laughing again.

'You remember that old dead tree?' Mark asked.

'Yeah, why?'

'That was my sniper observation post.'

'Bollocks. I would have seen you up it.'

'I was not up it, but inside.'

'Latest British invention,' Adrian boasted. 'A real tree that has been hollowed out with a steel insert.'

Mark pretended to hold a rifle at my nuts, then said, 'I am sure you gave those Jerries a little target.' Mark fired his imaginary gun at my groin.

I covered my nuts.

They all found it funny.

Jason climbed awkwardly back on his bunk. 'I doubt the Kaiser could even hit his puny balls at one yard.'

Even I laughed.

'Yet, my penis could be ranged at a thousand yards,' he continued.

We all groaned, and I threw a worm at him.

How lucky, though, had I been not to be killed by an enemy sniper. Not only had Adrian appeared to go bashful when we had spoken about our body parts, but he did not seem himself. I laid back and got comfortable, but his mood was niggling me.

'What's up, Adrian?' I asked.

'You lot could have thanked me for keeping guard.'

'From those kitten-sized rats?' Jason said.

'Do you mean those Jerry spy worms?' Mark bantered.

'Did a shit sentry job then, Adrian,' I added.

Adrian frowned and huffed. 'Did you not hear the trench raid?' he said, heightened. 'The Fritz broke our wire and made it back into the reserve trench. I thought they were coming for us.'

We stopped larking around at his too emotional state.

'Cheers, Adrian,' I said—Mark and Jason apologised.

'Sorry about the rats,' Adrian said, 'but I had to extinguish the candles when the Fritz entered. The rats only come in when it is dark, so I leave the lights on when I go to bed.' Adrian had tears in his eyes, guessing he had always slept with the light on since his parents abandoned him.

'What are the losses?' Jason asked, perhaps to change the subject for Adrian.

'I do not know as I have not been out there yet.'

'You best get some sleep, Adrian,' I said. 'We'll keep watch.'

'He does not sleep, do you Adrian?' Jason said solemnly.

'What, ever?' I asked.

'I do, sometimes. A few hours, perhaps.'

'Always sneaking out,' Mark added.

'Where do you go?' I asked.

Adrian climbed into his bunk and began to fidget; also, continuingly to adjust his pillow and blanket. 'So, what is my nickname then?' he said, upbeat.

'Fool,' Jason said.

Adrian jumped out of bed and grabbed Jason, snarling. 'I will shoot you.'

Mark leapt out of bed and tried to pull Adrian off, before I had the chance to. I went to stop Jason thumping Adrian, but Jason hadn't even raised his defence. Adrian turned and grabbed Blister's wrists; both were tussling. I came between them to break it up. With the bind broken, Adrian aggressively leant back into Titan's space—it was getting ridiculous.

'Have you ever killed anyone, Adrian?' Titan ribbed.

'No. Have you?'

'No. I save people.'

'Lads, chill out,' I barked.

'What about you, Mark?' Adrian snapped.

'Not that I know of. Unless one of my shells landed one of the bastard Jerries. Oh, but I have killed a Jerry messenger dog.'

Adrian shoved Blister out of the way and gave me a harsh glare, before climbing up to his bunk.

Me and Blister returned to our sanctuary.

As we all made ourselves comfortable, there was a thick tension.

'You killed a messenger mutt, Blister?' I asked.

'Yes, fella. Do you not remember your training to kill any dog that might be taking messages from the Jerries frontline?'

'Is that why they shoot our pigeons?'

It was an obvious question he didn't answer.

Adrian had turned over on his side. Occasionally he would sniff. Had the aggressive mood change been too much for his childish ways?

'Hey, Adrian, how about fearless feisty fucker as a nickname?' I said.

'I will second that, but it's a bit too long,' Blister added.

'True,' I said.

'Triple F,' Blister said.

'That means everyone is going to ask what the three F's stand for?' Titan remarked.

'So,' I said.

'I do not think that is wise in front of any ladies, Johnny,' Titan said.

'Hey, I got it: Bruce,' I exclaimed.

'Bruce?' they said simultaneously.

'Yeah, as in Bruce Lee from my era. He's the only fearless feisty fucker I can think of right now.'

No interest came forward.

'Anyway, Bruce it is. And that's an order,' I said. 'So, from now on, it's Bruce, Titan, and Blister.'

'What about you?' Blister asked.

'Cad? Reprobate? Debauched?' Titan said.

'I've no idea what they mean, and that you even knew such words from being a farmer's ox,' I countered.

'I was not a farmer or an ox, but I did go to school.'

'I was a blacksmith,' Blister said.

'I worked as an actor,' Bruce replied, in a 'lovey's' voice.

'No you were not. You were a sweeper. I heard…'

'You can call me Vinnie, or boss,' I interrupted Blister, who was upsetting the vibe.

'Vinnie, it is then,' Bruce said.

Bruce, now happy again, chucked us all a plum. Even though it wasn't ripe, I kept eating it, inquisitive to where he was getting all this loot. Bruce offered us a packet of cigarettes, but fortunately none of us smoked.

'What shall we call Sergeant Sean Rowe?' Titan asked.

'Not to his face,' Bruce said nervously, and fiddled with his blanket.

'That's easy: Sikes,' I said.

'Who?' Blister asked.

'Sikes was from the future. Rowe looks, sounds, and acts like the character called Bill Sikes, played by the actor Oliver Reed. Like Rowe, Sikes even carried a club.'

'I have never heard of this actor?' Bruce said.

'Way after your time,' I said. 'Sikes did drink a lot like Rowe, but Sikes wasn't a homosexual.'

'Why do you say that?' Bruce said quickly.

'Just a few things I've noted. Rowe weirdly felt my muscles when I had first met him. Plus, he had strangely said something like, "I'll see you in my quarters this evening". And that's not all. He had said, "Soon have you screaming at night".'

'You are mistaken,' Bruce blurted.

'What about when he said to you, "Unless you want to feel my cudgel".'

'A cudgel is a weighted club, Vinnie,' Blister said.

'Stay out of this, Mark,' I said.

Bruce whipped back his cover and climbed down. He began rushing to put on his clothes. What had rattled him?

'How do you explain a young soldier coming out of his room, frantically doing up his trousers? And Sarge in his pants?' I continued.

'Sergeant always rests in his underwear,' Bruce said anxiously. 'The young soldier, Wilfred, has had problems with lice in his privates.' Bruce kept his eye contact from me.

Titan threw me a small tin of Keating Powder, which read: 'Killed fleas and insects.' I remembered seeing powder on the floor.

'Have you not been using it?' Titan asked. 'You should be checking the seams of your trousers and around your collars. Pop the eggs or burn them on a candle flame. Remember?'

'You could be like the London Dogs, and bite them in your teeth,' Blister added.

I was still giving Adrian a steely glare, waiting for him to make eye contact. He seemed he was hiding something. I pulled back my itchy brown cover.

'I'm going to confront Rowe,' I said.

'No. You cannot. It… it… it is not him doing the abuse.'

'Who then, Adrian?' I asked.

Adrian sat on the edge of Blister's bed and sobbed; tears hit the dusty boards. 'Lieutenant Taylor and Second Lieutenant Bridge,' he muttered. 'Taylor orders the new lads one at a time into his quarters, where he gives them brandy. When they are drunk enough, he forces them to bugger Bridge. If not carried out, Taylor will shoot the poor beggar.'

'Slow down, Adrian, you're getting too worked up,' I said.

I jumped down off the bed and knelt in front of him, candles flickering, making weird patterns. I slowly breathed in and out, getting Bruce to do the same; Blister doing it as well to calm himself.

Bruce, a little more composed, continued, 'Once Bridge has been done, Taylor tells the lad he must take buggery. If the lad dose not, Taylor will have him shot at dawn for buggery whilst Bridge had been asleep, under the influence of brandy. Once Taylor has finished the act, he orders the lad to come back every other night for the same.'

Adrian had started breathing erratically and crying. Blister was almost on the verge of patting him on the back for comfort, but he pulled his hand back at the last second. Even when Titan came over, Titan seemed unsure what to do. I placed my hand around Adrian's shoulder and squeezed.

'It is not like they were in love,' Adrian sobbed. 'That would be different. It is abuse.'

'That was a brave thing to not only get off your chest, but to keep it in,' I said. 'How do you know all this?'

'My best friend, my only real friend, Victor, the one I had spent the long journey here from Southampton had broken down and told me. The next day, when Victor did not turn up to Taylor's quarters, Taylor ordered him out into no man's land as a punishment. I also knew the other two soldiers that Taylor had sent to mark a safe route to the Fritz wire. They had also been abused. They all died. I am not sure why Fritz let Sergeant Rowe cross and collect their bodies.'

'I am going to gut the bastard officers,' Blister said.

Bruce started to cry again. My stomach was in knots, the anger forcing the bitter acid into my throat. I held his cheeks and turned his head to make eye contact with me.

'I miss my best friend Victor,' he said.

'Has he touched you, Adrian?' I asked.

Bruce sniffed. 'No. I disobeyed his orders to go to his dormer. I hide at night, or stay around Sergeant Rowe for protection, as they loathe each other.'

'Good evening, laddies,' Rowe said.

With his club, Rowe let the hessian go behind him. Fuck, how long had he been outside?

The three of us must have looked like rabbits in the headlights. Bruce gulped; not so fearless and feisty now. As Rowe came out of the gloom, he appeared more haggard than ever. His eyes were bloodshot, making him look even madder. Was he pissed? We all stood to.

'Cat got your tongue?' he said huskily. 'Just wanted to make sure you were ready for the dawn raid, bearing in mind you just missed the Boche raid.'

'How did it go?' I cringed at my words.

'Only five Boche dead, but one got away, a bit blooded though.'

'Any casualties on our side?' Titan asked.

'Two Northumberland Fusiliers dead. Three Lancashire Regiment lads injured, but all are ready for duty. Here, compliments of my stock.' Rowe passed me a ceramic jar.

We stayed silent.

'That's the good stuff,' he said. 'Double ration tonight.' Rowe's smiled sinisterly and then turned to leave. 'See you before stand to.'

'We've decided not to go at dawn, Sergeant,' I said.

'You can forget the "we" shit,' Blister whispered.

Rowe sharply turned, hand on his holster, eyeing me. 'What did you say?' he grumbled.

My squad stood behind me, almost pushing me forward. I nearly dropped the jar but fumbled it back.

'If our trench attacks are always between stand down at dusk and dawn, they will be ready for us. I was thinking, if you don't mind, if we head out in the early hours. Bruce, I mean, Adrian, what time are the soldiers most tired?'

'Erm... well...' Bruce was looking at the ceiling, squirming.

Rowe crooked his neck and tapped his fingers on his sidearm.

Blister elbowed Bruce in the ribs.

'Not that ours fall asleep on duty, sir, Sergeant Rowe,' Bruce said, 'but most are dog-tired about three AM.'

'Well, you best get down to the Quartermaster and get kitted. Sharpish.'

All four of us, as if been let off by the headmaster after doing something bad, rushed to get dressed—pathetic.

'Private L'Estrange,' Rowe barked, 'tell QM Davis that my orders are you can take what you want. You have definitely fucking earned it. Perhaps a fucking promotion if you return from the dawn raid would be fitting.'

Even when Rowe was giving compliments, he sounded threatening.

As the other three squeezed past Rowe, he made sure they were dressed respectfully, and weapons loaded. I was a bit annoyed, or was it envious, that my squad would get to the armoury first.

'Come on, laddie,' he barked.

Rowe grabbed my forearm as I drew level with him, and then pushed me into the side bunk. Eye to eye, he stunk of booze. I had seen the persona before, that look in someone's eye, including my own mirror.

'I will make sure the lads are out of their funk-hole and…'

'A what?' I asked.

'You can't get to me,' he said scathing.

'I'm not. I just don't know what a "funk-hole" is.'

Rowe rubbed his overgrown stubble, which was unlike him to have let it get so messy. 'I'll have every available man lined up as you leave,' he said.

'No, don't do anything different, especially manning up the guards and defence. Just another normal night.'

'Do not fucking balls this up,' he said, spit coming through his gritted teeth. 'We don't want the fucking cowedly Boche laughing and drinking more rum when they've killed the likes of our brave soldiers.'

'Are you OK, Sean?' I asked sympathetically—his scowl dropped. 'When was the last good night's sleep you had without the nightmares?'

'Shut up, laddie.'

'When was the last time you took R&R?'

Rowe glowered at me as if I were trying to trick him with words.

'How long have you been here without a day off?' I asked.

'I'll have a day off when I am dead. Now clear off.'

I went to touch his chest medals, but he grabbed my hand. 'Probably had it from the Boer War, Sean. I'd had enough once; I know the signs. You need to talk to someone about the horrors you've seen, your demons. I'm happy to listen.'

Rowe held his lips tighter, his eyes filling.

I took my hand from his grasp and placed it on his shoulder, waiting. I knew he was contemplating my words, almost admitting he had issues as he stared into nothing, but then he slyly grinned, tearing my hand away.

'Leave the problem to me. This fuckery stops now,' he said throatily. 'Get kitted up.'

It had taken me ages to find the armoury, having to also ask a soldier at every junction. The sandbagged entrance was guarded by one man who was having a sneaky cigarette. I went through the "who goes there" saga, and when I told him I could not remember the password, he told me there wasn't one. Elaborating further about when me and Adrian had to use passwords, the guard told me they never used them. Did Adrian know? Was Adrian just passing out his loot to make friends? Or was it the guards were tricking him? Eventually, after a bit of lame arguing, telling him who had sent me, the guard let me in. As I went by, I told him his cigarette glow could make a good target for a sniper.

Inside the large room, I became concerned that everything in there was made of wood, including the walls and ceiling. Below one set of stacked boxes, the QM Sergeant was sat in a chair reading. Davis pushed up his round glasses. The sergeant was the perfect likeness to Charles Hawtrey.

'Just come to get kitted up,' I said. 'Rowe sent me.'

'Carry on,' he squeaked.

'Literally,' I said, and scoffed. 'Thanks, Hawtrey.'

'It is QM Sergeant Davis.'

'I need four of the following: night-vision goggles, the ones also you can use thermal imaging on, listening devices, ear-pieces with whisper-mics, and back-up walkie-talkies. Oh, and those latest door-entry cards, spyhole view-finder gadgets, and mobile-phones that can see the German's texts. I'm sure somewhere you have some eclipse grenades and electronic countermeasures. Is that OK?'

'I really am flummoxed there, Private…'

'Ignore the fucking, stripes. It's Corporal Johnny Vince.'

'I am sure…'

'OK, Hawtrey, do you have at least some flash-bangs, phos and frag grenades, two Ultra-Compact Individual Weapons with silencers, two Heckler assault rifles with grenade launcher, and something with a heavy mag, like an MG4?'

I lifted one of the crate lids, and when he didn't answer, I turned to see him lighting a fag. Quickly, I closed the lid on the pineapple-effect grenades.

'I am really sorry, but…'

'Not even a black-ops kit or an armour vest?' I interrupted.

'Ah, yes. We have the latest a Franco-British Cuirass.'

'Really? So why aren't the men out there wearing them?' I followed his wiry frame through the racks, keeping my distance from his smoke.

'Because they were meant for the artillery soldier, but they have been commandeered for officers.'

'Are they fuck, Hawtrey. I'll take four.'

'I am afraid, old bean, I am under strict orders from Lieutenant

Taylor. He has already been in asking questions about the dawn raid.'

'I hope you didn't tell him it's been re-scheduled for two-thirty AM?' I could tell by his reaction that he had; hopefully, this would not come back to haunt me. 'I bet those creeps Taylor and Bridge have one.'

'Of course. They are officers.'

'But they don't even go on the…'

'Look, I am off duty in a minute,' he interrupted, 'so I can give you one for your mission, as I doubt you will return. Then you need to leave, or I will call the guard and have you marched to Lieutenant Taylor's quarters.'

I shuddered at the thought. 'Cheers, Hawtrey,' I said sarcastically.

'It is QM Sergeant Davis,' he snapped.

'That's it, Hawtrey, keep growing your balls.'

Once Hawtrey had struggled lifting the heavy armoured vest, I went into a fit of laughter, but had to reconcile him not putting it back. The front and rear were fitted with square enamelled steel plates that were welded together by small rings, and consequently riveted to a green fabric. Still astonished by the design, Hawtrey had the proud pleasure of fitting it to me, the front being recognisable as the plates hung lower than the rear. Once he had done up the popper fasteners on the shoulders, he tied up the side top and bottom material ties. Finally, he wrapped a long belt like tie around the vest, just under my ribcage. At last, when he was done, I made a point about the weight and time to put it on, and the fact there was no way I was wearing it. His tiny face screwed up with disgust.

CHAPTER TWENTY-EIGHT

Apart from the extra ammo stuffed in Bellchamber's haversack, I had picked up a grenade launching cartridge and cup-discharger to fit my Enfield. Also, desperately needing to keep track of time as I had used to do, a wrist-watch. Time check: 22.07 hrs. I could not wait to boast to the squad.

Boldly walking into our den, sleeves rolled up and ready to show-off, I coughed to get their attention. They didn't acknowledge. The table was already piled high of ammo and grenades.

'Right, before we get down to the plan, let's see what you got,' I said. 'I hope you're armed to the fucking teeth.' I brought around the grenade launcher.

Bruce sat up first. 'You have obviously forgotten how to use it, chum.'

'Can't be any different from using the grenade launcher of my day,' I countered.

'Grenade launcher? Don't you mean Mills Bomb launcher,' Blister said.

'A what?'

They all looked at each other.

'You cannot use it anyway, unless your rifle has been reinforced with soldered wire and bolt-pinned,' Bruce said.

'Why?'

'It will shatter the stock. Did you not pick up a new Enfield with the stamp GF on the receiver?'

'GF?' I asked.

'Grenade firer,' Bruce said smugly.

'I thought Blister had said "Mills-Bomb"?' I quizzed.

'Did you not bring the adapter to take the bomb?'

'What? Oh shut the fuck up, Adrian,' I said—they all sniggered.

Frustrated at the lack of enthusiasm in my find, I chucked the contraption on the table behind me and made the point of letting them see my new watch.

'Nice watch,' Titan said. 'Get it in *Le Bon Marche*?'

'Along with your lacy underwear?' Blister bantered—Adrian blushed.

'You're just jealous it's made of silver and has a protective glass cover,' I said.

'No good out here, fella. You need a decent trench-watch with a leather cover to stop the shit getting in.' Titan showed me his.

'Bollocks, Jason.' I might as well bring out the terrible vest, I thought, and heaved the two parts out of the bag. 'Hey, lads, look at this body-armour, it's fucking useless.'

'God blind me,' Blister said.

'Smashing,' Titan added.

All three enthusiastically raced from their pits to look at it. It was at that moment I could have banged my face into the wall. I pulled it away from them.

'Stop. It's no good,' I said.

'Why?' Bruce asked.

'Because not only does it weigh a tonne, but it also takes ages to get on and off. Wearing it, you would be seen at night from Britain, let alone the Germans.' I threw it behind me—the lads craving.

'I hope you got me one,' Titan said.

I sneered. 'I think you would just about fit in an armoured tank.'

'A what?'

I raised my eyes to the heavens and sighed. 'Right, what have you all brought to the table?'

'It is all on the table,' Blister said seriously.

'It's a figurative of speech,' I snapped.

Both Bruce and Blister looked at the educated Titan, but he shrugged.

After holding it for a few seconds, I breathed out, then said, 'So, what main weapons have you got?'

'I have managed to get an Italian sub-machinegun,' Blister boasted.

'Have you fuck, Mark,' I said.

'Back to first names are we, Private Vince?' he retorted.

'Only when he is annoyed,' Bruce said.

Whilst Blister rummaged under his bunk, Bruce showed me his new serrated bayonet. 'If you do not turn the standard British bayonet, the wound heals, but with this…'

'Here we go, the nerdy bollocks,' I interrupted Bruce. 'Hallow. I know everything about weapons,' I said in a nerdy voice.

No one got my humour.

'Oh, by the way, Bruce, make sure you scream louder and have the bottle to finish the charge next time,' I said.

Whilst we all found it amusing, except the sulking Bruce, Blister started to unwrap mechanical items from what looked like a backpack. Once it was put together, Blister proudly told me it was the Villar Perosa 9-mm sub-machine gun. I made out I was bored, stopping him waffle-on after telling me about its fourteen-pound weight and two barrels that fired twenty-five rounds each. However, it had made my non-use grenade launcher even more pitiful. Deep down, I rather they had acquired more rifles and a Lewis. At least they had extra ammo, grenades, and even a flare-gun, which I quizzed Bruce why. Titan had stayed quiet.

'Titan, you're not one of those do-gooder medics who won't fight, but only heal?' I asked patronisingly.

He just smiled.

'Perhaps one of those gentle giants that wants to protect, rather than kill?' I continued. 'Are you going to react when your piss has boiled over, or when your bollocks are getting bashed?'

Titan shrugged his shoulders, then un-corked the rum.

Quickly snatching it from him, I threw it out of the door; the smash seemed loud. 'No alcohol,' I rebuked. 'You need to fucking switch on, or you will die.'

'Sorry, boss,' Titan said.

'We need to go over the operation basics,' I said.

The jovial mood had stopped as I climbed into bed. I guessed they had the same apprehensive thoughts as me, but at least I was the only one that knew grabbing two Germans would not make a difference when we had to go over the top. Images of black and white films filtered in.

There were no detailed maps and reconnaissance photos to study, even though from time to time those daring British pilots could be heard flying in their highly combustible wood and lacquered fabric planes along the length of the frontline, coming under intense enemy firing. Many pilots, if not shot first, went down burning to death in the flames. Some unlucky had to make the decision to jump many thousands of feet. They didn't have parachutes, according to Bruce, and my squad had not even heard of the life-saving kit. Bruce had informed me that when the British frontline infantry heard the planes, they had to light flares, so aerial photos could show how far they had advanced. It also helped the fighter pilots where not to attack. Worryingly, most of the soldiers never lit the flares as they were easy to spot for a German kill.

I puffed my pillow up and leant back against the wall. Staring at the flickering light, I contemplated where to start our task details. Unlike previous missions, we had no time beforehand to recce, prepare, or act out what lie ahead. One foremost detail I had to concentrate on was I was leading an inexperienced squad across no man's land to the enemy stronghold.

With my squad intently listening, I began with the main objective, and who had which role in the squad. Between us we discussed what the German trenches might be like, including approximate men and weapons. We deliberated the approach across no man's land, how we would enter the enemy trench, and each individual movement technique to snatch two Germans. Stealth was critical on this mission.

After, I threw in different scenarios if the plan goes tits-up. For example: if any flares are deployed, you do not move unless the situation goes noisy. With different circumstances discussed, then planned, I also instructed when SOPs had to be ignored. Against what I never wanted to use when assaulting a bunker or clearing a room, I said we all had to carry a knife in a secure sheath, attaching it by a wire or cord. The bayonet had to be fixed, always, and grenades are not to be used unless we are compromised. The pistol was the last means of attack of defence. Again, I wanted the pistol secured to the person using it in case it came down to a violent fist fight. I instructed them how to sneak up on the target and man-handle him away, even if it means unconscious. If a struggle happened, I told them that they had to effectively kill the enemy with a knife, much to Blister's pleasure.

The last part, the extraction with or without the targets under fire or not, prompted quite a few questions. After we discussed the diverse options, even if we had wounded members, I set the distances for the ERV and the RV, including the length of time each person had to stay there. I made sure they knew their life was more important than the enemy and of any captured German. Adrian seemed a little agitated by the remark.

Jumping down into the middle, I showed them the basic hand signals that we had to use when not being able to whisper in the person's ear. And, when we have reached the enemy wire, how to show orders and enemy positions. Once they had grasped them, I climbed back up.

Even though a few yawns started, I knew they would not get much sleep, but a little was better than none. Everyone agreed that they were clear on the plan, so I ordered them to get some shut-eye. I was drained from discussing the mission details as I'd had to reiterate what each acronym and my era's terminology had meant. It wasn't only Bruce who wanted the candles left on, no one wanted the rats to return.

Time check: 02.35 hrs. I had been up and ready for about forty minutes, checking the weather and viewing no man's land from the main trench. I kicked the bottom bunk snorers and then whacked Bruce. He rolled over with his eyes open, as if he had not slept. With everyone scratching their bits and bobs, stretching, yawning, I handed each of them a tin mug of strong black coffee, courtesy of some of the lads on stag I had visited earlier. A few jokes went around about Bruce losing his touch for not providing the drinks from wherever he used to visit. Bruce was still moping that he was not allowed to leave on his midnight journey.

I started checking my main weapon and pistol, but I had no wire or string to tie it to me. Making more room for grenades and ammo by leaving water and food rations behind, I started to load up; the electric buzz flowed through me. Once we were all ready, I leant against the table and looked at their pale faces.

'Right, listen in and do not interrupt,' I said. 'I want your ammo secured. Make sure all your poppers, slings, and buckles are fastened tight. Anything that clatters out there will be heard. Sound travels further at night. We must be silent. Any shiny objects will reflect the moon, so remove. Before…'

'What about our brass jacket buttons and belt buckles?' Bruce interrupted.

'Like I said, take them off or cover them. It's a cool morning, so go in your shirt. Before…'

'What about my tin hat?'

I sighed. 'You're interrupting me again, Adrian. Leave the tin hat. As I was saying for the third time, before we head out to the objective, we need to blacken up…'

'What does that mean?' Blister asked.

'Cover our skin with cam-cream. But as we haven't any, use charcoal, mud, anything that conceals your white skin. Don't forget your eyes will stick out like a diamond in a baboon's arse, so think of some sort of netted vail.'

'We could be the Golliwogs from the book my mummy and daddy used to read to me as a child.'

'For fuck's sake, Adrian, get focused,' I said. 'I can see why Rowe carries a club.'

'Yes, Vinnie,' he said, rubbing his collar.

'Remember, we are the black shadow. You need to blend into your surroundings. If it takes an hour to get to their wire, that's what it takes. Got that?'

'Yes, Vinnie, but you have said all that,' Bruce answered.

'You will succeed this task. No doubts. No fucker is going to stop us. Don't carry the stress and fear with you. Switch it on and turn into aggression. However, never underestimate the enemy. If it goes noisy, get good cover, think about the situation, stay calm, then unleash hell, but watch your ammo levels. We are heavily outnumbered, so it's OK to be scared. I'm sure as we retreat together, our lads will lay down covering suppression.'

The three of them were nodding, their demeanour had changed. Wanting to strike more into them, I narrowed my eyes menacingly.

'Who dares win. By strength and guile,' I said gruffly.

Titan pulled out a decorative oblong wooden case from under his bed. Gold initials B.W.B were stamped on the front. Undoing the clips and lifting the lid produced a velvet lined inner, holding a double-barrelled shotgun. Titan ran his hand across the grained polished walnut and then onto the impressively detailed metalwork, depicting elephants ridden by hunters and being attacked by tigers. I came in closer to see little jewels were set in the elephant. The engraving down the barrel was stunning, and the hammer was that of a tiger's head. As Titan reached under his bunk again, I leant over and read the engraved brand: 'Westly Richards'. Titan placed another heavy box on his bed and then looked at me.

'This was my father's gun before you say anything,' he said.

'Fine shotgun, but no good for long range or suppressing. Get loaded, we need to move out.'

The trenches were different at night, eerie, even with the moon and stars so bright. Mist reaching the tops of the trench spilled over, but soon evaporated. The duckboards sloshed in the mud underneath, seeming very loud. In a gap where the planks met, I bent down and dug into the wet soil, pulling out a handful. I nodded at the others to do the same. Reaching the London Dogs dugout, two of them were sleeping it rough. Scrapping the fat from their large cooking pans, I mixed it with the dirt and started camming up; it stunk. For some reason, the Dogs had not objected to us using their used cooking fat, but weirdly smiled.

Those we passed on guard poignantly winked or nodded. Some looked pitifully at us. The remaining that was huddled in their funk-holes sneakily opened an eye, watching us silently walk by. Everyone knew what we were heading into. Coming out from a dugout's shadow was Taylor. I held back Blister's arm.

'By Jove, you look queer,' Taylor said. 'I hope the Germans aren't ready for you, dear boy.'

I snarled. 'Rowe was fucking right about you. You're just another yellow belly darling who's never done much time in the trench, but you wear the pips.' It was so hard not to beat the shit of him; instead, I turned my back on him in contempt.

Against the main wall, many soldiers were hunkered down, armed to the teeth. I grinned at Rowe's back-up plan; also, glad for his presence. He placed a hand on my shoulder.

'I want you four reminiscing in years to come. Do not balls this up,' he whispered in my ear, rum breath flaring my nostrils.

'Sean, you need help,' I said. 'You need to be able to put the black dogs back in the kennel.'

Angered, he looked at the other three, slightly confused to the muddy and fat smearing, but his shoulders dropped. He placed a tape-reel in each of the other's hand.

'Engineers Corporal Denis Goodinson and Private Paul Roberts will accompany you. They will tape a safe route through no man's land, right up until the Boche main wire. There, Goodinson and Roberts will lay the bangers, ready for the big push. And with God watching, they return safely.'

'What?' I said.

'Stop the fucking jollification now. You know I mean Bangalore Torpedoes.'

'No, I mean, nobody told me they would be joining. Are they…'

'Good luck, lads,' he interrupted.

There was no point arguing with Rowe, so I went to sarcastically say that is the first kind thing he had said, but he already appeared troubled.

Leaving him, we made our way up to the fire-step. I quickly shook the hand of Roberts and Goodinson, then ordered them to follow, remaining quiet and unseen. A young soldier handed me some wire-cutters, informing me a cut-out had been made through our wire, led by tape to the first shell-hole. I nodded at our squad.

'On me,' I whispered.

Climbing above the sandbagged parapet, I squashed the negative thoughts, knowing my squad was behind me. But there was still a presence, something strange I could not quite work out. Reaching the small cut-out, trying not to get snagged, I crawled through. Following the tape till the crater's edge, I slithered down. My eyes lifted to the dark sky. Apart from some earth that fell, the other three had joined me like ghosts. Roberts and Goodinson were not so quiet due to the tied bundle of one and a half-metre length metal pipe. Looking scornfully at them, I whispered to Blister and Titan to blacken them, then to go over the mission I had already given. Then something I had forgotten to do sprung to mind.

'We need a mission name,' I whispered, breath slightly showing.

Bruce leant to my ear and said, 'How about Mission Push and Go? After the Hippodrome show by...'

'Shut up. Let me think,' I whispered, looking up to the edge of the ridge. 'Operation Edge.' I had to carry on Ant's mission name and the memory of this larger-than-life brother.

Titan forcibly but quietly started taking off Roberts and Goodinson's compromising clothing and kit. He ordered the new recruits to mix dirt with water from their bottles, then smear it over their skin. Blister threatened them with his dagger not to object.

Whilst Roberts and Goodinson got the low down of the basic hand signals and the extra training expected, I hand signalled for Bruce to follow me to the top of the large shell-hole. Gradually, I peered above. Bruce searched through his binos, then he slowly handed them to me. The magnification was fairly good, but nothing jumped out of the ordinary. With all of us now on the edge, I ordered that only Roberts and Goodinson mark the way for the following troops, knowing where the explosive charges were to be set.

At this distance, I told the squad to watch for muzzle flashes, then I silently squat run to the next crater. This one was not so deep, just enough for me to kneel in, but was very wide. An object caught my knee as I gestured for one person to follow. Stupidly, they all got up and ran. I could have exploded with rage. Once Titan, the last man, had made it, I cursed them as quietly as possible, going over what the hand signal had really meant. I knew I was mad as fuck, but to see them quickly clear away, looking distressed, was a little confusing. Bruce, encourage by the others, was pushed down to me. Cautiously, he came over and pointed at the object next to my inner right knee. I frowned.

CHAPTER TWENTY-EIGHT

'Vinnie, please do not touch that unexploded shell,' he hushed.
Fuck.

'It could be gas,' he said. 'You told us not to bring our...'

I stopped listening, slowly taking my leg away. Moving back, I made sure no other unexploded shells were behind me. Seeing the other white teeth light up made me grin as well. Roberts was the first to snigger.

'Had an incident in your trousers?' Roberts whispered.

'Better pants next time,' Goodinson hushed.

'He only wears lacy knickers from *Le Bon Marche*. Didn't you know?' Blister murmured.

Blister and Bruce held back their laughter; instead, tears welling. I chuckled quietly along with them, only for the relief my bollocks were not floating in outer space. As stupid as it sounds, that small bit of camaraderie brought us closer, or that's how I had perceived it. Perhaps it just lightened the mood of what was ahead.

At what I had guessed the halfway point, one by one we slid into a ditch. The soggy bottom had an earthy smell mixed with manure. A lone smashed tree trunk stood tall; bits of tree were littered. This time everyone had eyes on what lay ahead, except Bruce, as I still had his binos. Directly in front was an untouched section of a ploughed field with little chutes pushing up, the only thing living. Panning further, clearly the destruction of our artillery was evident, including the wire fences. However, some of the wire and posts were still standing. Blister whispered he had taken quite a few shots at the German soldiers erecting the new fences. A low chuckle went down the line as Titan had quietly replied that Blister must have been a shit sniper then. I told them to switch on.

With the ground flatter, it was hard to gauge how many Germans trenches there were or where they started. Slightly silhouetted, to the point I wasn't sure if my eyes were deceiving me, were three large mounds, separated about fifty metres apart. I signalled them all in closer.

'This tree is the RV,' I muttered.

Blister whispered to the new recruits what "RV" had meant.

'If it goes noisy,' I continued, 'this is where we head for. Set up an all-round defence. Keep an eye on your ammo stock. If there's no way back to our trench due to the amount of firepower from both sides, follow this ditch leading back to the wooded area, about one klick away. That's the ERV. I've got a hunch there's a farmhouse around there.'

'Emergency Rendezvous I know, but what is a "klick"?' Blister faintly asked.

'Kilometre,' I almost mouthed.

'I really do not think it is a good idea to go to the farmhouse,' Bruce said, concerned. 'It is probably housed with Germans.'

'Is there a property connected to this field we're in?' I probed.

'Well… erm…' he said, flustered.

'Adrian, how fucking far is the farmhouse from the woodland?' I said.

'Nearly a mile, heading back towards France.'

I squinted. 'We'll talk later about this, Adrian. Roberts, Goodinson, you head out on your own to the centre defence and lay the charges. Mark the way. Do not get us compromised. We'll have eyes on you for the first hundred metres, and then we'll head far left. Any questions?'

'Do we disobey Sergeant Rowe's orders to return, or wait here at the RV?' Roberts whispered.

'Like *I've* ordered. We'll meet back here with our German prisoners. Let's Synchronise.'

They looked at each other, dumbfounded.

'Jesus,' I mumbled. 'OK, on my count, set your watches dead on 03.45 hours.'

Watching these brave two disappear whilst the rest of our squad kept watch for the Germans, filled me with pride but also trepidation. Before they even had got to a hundred metres, we had lost sight of them. Now, it was our turn.

Keeping my voice as quiet as possible, I said, 'Lads, to coin Rowe's phrase: this fuckery stops now. This is it: Operation Edge.'

CHAPTER TWENTY-NINE

Crawling over stones and rocks in the ploughed field brought back memories of my E&E in Afghanistan. How vulnerable I was in that terrible situation, and like before, my bollocks were now also taking a hammering. I knew this mission was audacious, border-line lunacy, but a big part of me craved it. I had not felt this desire for ages, probably since Operation Poppy Pride.

My kit bag kept sliding off my back onto the soft soil. It was starting to grate on me. Again, I left my Enfield in front and pulled up the kit. Something tickled the inside of my nose. Face scrunched, I pulled back to reveal chutes. Shit, I was going to sneeze. With minimal movement I faced my arm, disguising a sneeze into it.

'Hey, Tommy. *Wir essen britische Wurst und französischen Wein trinken.*'

I froze, my heart racing. Worrying about a flare, I stealthily crawled into the first crater. On the rim I eased over my rifle, making a groove in the cold soil. Eyes searching, someone tapped me on the leg before coming to the side of me. Titan crawled to my opposite side. Blister, who was next to Bruce, sighted his weapon into the pitch-black.

'What is troubling you, Vinnie?' Bruce said in my ear.

'I think I've just compromised us by stupidly sneezing. We must be close to the enemy. And can you lie still and stop bloody fidgeting.'

'I did not hear you sneeze. Anyway, the Fritz always shout every hour at night. It is all mind games and to keep us from sleeping, but they do not realise we cannot hear them way back there.' He sniggered.

'How do you know they do this every hour then?' I asked.

Bruce's eyes stayed locked onto mine, hiding something.

'What did he shout?' I asked.

'Hey, Tommy. We eat British sausages and drink French wine.'

'Bastards,' Blister hissed.

'Shall I shout back in German?' Bruce whispered, and then took a deep breath.

My heart sunk, until he winked at me. I told him to switch on.

Scanning in the direction of the enemy, continuing in a circle, on the peripheral of my sight I spotted our RV, some eighty metres back. I estimated that we only had the same distance before we reached the strange enemy mounds. It was time to make our move.

Moving the stones and rocks was becoming a pain. Lifting, as if doing a press up, the lay of the land was as mashed up as our side. Cautiously, I had sunk down onto my elbows and gestured for Titan to keep eyes on; a thumb went up. Slowly getting into a crouching position, I silently squat-ran the next ten metres into a large dip. Once the squad had joined me, in a low voice I told them there would be no more crawling until we got to the wire, pleasing them.

The next sixty metres gradually got worse with shell-holes. The area was decimated with remnants of trees, barbed wire protruding from the churned soil, large stones, and occasionally a half-buried unexploded shell; most probably ours. I wondered how many I had trod on that were hidden under the earth. How ironic it would be to disturb one of our own.

Gripping my rifle, I painstakingly kept low, stealthily moving in and out of the shell-holes, all the time keeping alert to any threat. Suddenly, I heard something. I froze, fist up to warn the others. Caressing the ground as I laid down, I then scanned the inky-black. This time I recognised the same sound: a moan; a cry for help. Turning my ear, I pin-pointed it was coming from my left. Blister silently crawled alongside and leant across to my ear.

'That could be Jerries just trapped under the soil from our bombardment,' he said quietly.

'Too clear, Vinnie,' Titan hummed, on my other side. 'You know that sound.'

'Let the bastards die,' Blister said.

Titan was right, I had spent many hours that afternoon listening to the injured and dying. I knew it was burning inside Titan to help the man, but we had to push on with the objective.

'We can't stop now,' I hushed.

He glared at my soul. 'It could be one of ours.'

'Fuck it,' I said. 'We'll at least check him out.'

Taking a slight detour, we kept low, with urgency. Nearing the huge crater, I fixed my bayonet. A smaller hollow opposite gave us good cover to peer over the edge. Was it a trap? Would I get shot or lanced in the face? I signalled for the others to spread out and look over. I held my breath. Gesturing, we simultaneously peeked over. Face down and tangled in wire and posts was a German soldier. He had no weapon close to him. I quietly breathed a sigh. Titan cautiously climbed down first, being careful not to bring down dirt on the injured. Furtively sliding down, I signalled the other two to keep eyes on the enemy lines, possibly being a trap. Titan touched the stained area on the casualty's right shoulder-blade and then examined it, doing the same for the other blooded patches. The German loudly groaned; we flinched. Wincing, he started to thrash about and hoarsely spout off in German. Bruce looked fit to burst. Blister pulled out his dagger. I found myself aiming the bayonet at him.

Jason, unruffled, turned the soldier's head to the side and wiped away the shit from his eyes. Staring at each other, in what I could only explain as shock and awe of being so close to the enemy, Titan smiled and held his thick finger to his lips.

'I believe this is the escaping German trench raider,' Bruce murmured.

'We are wasting our time,' Blister harshly whispered.

Titan gently pulled out a pair of standard issue wire-cutters and showed the victim. The German barely nodded. Frightened at first, as the causality had seen me and Bruce come close, he then became pacified as we all began to cut him free. The loud snipping was heart-stopping.

'You are making too much of a racket,' Blister said. 'Just kill the Jerry.'

Carefully, we pulled him up the bank, laying him on his back. He wailed in pain. Titan rapidly placed a field dressing on the casualty's mouth. I glared at Blister who had told Titan to push harder. Making the injured person more comfortable, Titan assessed him. The obvious were all his cuts from the barbed wire, but he also had blood-soaked jacket and trousers, most probably from gunshot wounds. Titan came close to me.

'The fella has three bullet wounds: left shoulder, left forearm, and right buttock. He also has swollen ankle, multiple bayonet lacerations, and cuts covered in dirt. I am amazed he has gotten this far. Poor beggar.'

Blister huffed.

'We either patch him up...'

'Have you got any more dressings?' Titan interrupted me.

Shit. I could hardly have a go at our medic as I had not brought any. I looked at the other two, they both shook their heads.

'He could be our prisoner,' Bruce whispered excitedly.

'He won't make the arduous journey back,' Titan said.

'Leave the Jerry to bleed.'

I vigorously shook my head at Mark's comment and pulled him close. 'How would you...'

Titan punched my arm and shook his head at me.

The German started to groan loudly and writher around.

'What do we do, Jason?' I asked.

Titan undid his side satchel and showed me the syringe.

I nodded.

'Can I say a poem?' Bruce reticently asked.

'Now?' Titan mouthed incredulously.

Titan and the injured soldier gripped hands; the German knew. Titan injected the soldier. Bruce silently sniffed and wiped his eyes, then cleared his throat,

'If I should die, think only this of me:
That there's some corner of a foreign field
That is for ever England. There shall be
In that rich earth a richer dust concealed;
A dust whom England bore, shaped, made aware,
Gave, once, her flowers to love, her ways to roam,
A body of England's, breathing English air,
Washed by the rivers, blest by suns of home.'

Even though barely audible, Bruce's words struck a chord as the German fell silent.Soundless, we began to get our shit together. Making the way to the rim, Bruce still had his hands together and head bowed. He hadn't noticed we had left as he continued.

'And think, this heart, all evil shed away,
A pulse in the eternal mind, no less...'

Skulking closer to the main wire, I thought about why Blister loathed the dying German so much, too much. Blister had a different look in his eye since we had left. Was he on a different mission? Was he going to go berserk and kill any enemy in his range, blowing the stealth out the window?

Lying in a shallow scrape, I followed the wire down to the right, hopefully to see Roberts and Goodinson with their thumbs up. Sadly, I could not see anything but the carnage us Brits had left. Perhaps their pipes had been screwed together and their explosives were now set. Titan and Blister laid beside me. Eventually, Bruce quietly joined, and he was not happy.

'Bruce, I hope you are not going to recite Shakespeare every time we come across a dying Jerry,' Blister whispered, and nudged Titan.

'It was Rupert Brooke. You are so uneducated,' Bruce said.

'I thought the soldier was a Jerry,' Blister added.

'No, not the dead bugger, the poet.'

'Oh, darling,' Titan said, 'what was the poem called?'

I wasn't sure if Titan's was in an actor's voice or an officer, but it was irritating Bruce.

'It was called *The Soldier*,' he said, above a whisper—both sniggered.

I immediately hand-signalled an end to it. Idiots.

Beyond the wire, approximately five metres, was the chalky ramparts. I remembered Rowe telling us not to put the chalk up because of the dirt mounds and undulating earth would show our trench system. One of the three large mounds were set back about twenty metres. On top, big chunks of soil had been freshly laid over old. Blister was already sizing it up. He gulped as he faced me. What had he seen? Focusing hard with the binos in the little light we had, it became evident: a very wide, twelve-inch-high concrete slot with four heavy-machineguns poking out.

With little movement, I focused in on the other two defensives. Further sandbagged machinegunned areas littered the trench's length in both directions, as far as I could see. The far back trees that had not been destroyed had ladders at the rear, but no snipers were on the plank platforms. Metal plates were lined along the backside of the main trench, but no weapons poked through the slits. Fuck. This was hardcore, but something was rattling me, far worse than I had seen.

I sunk back into our scrape and gestured them to follow me. On my stomach again, I crawled back to the next available shell-hole. Lying next to some dismembered body parts, I signalled the lads in close for sitrep. Faces inches from each other in a circle, I went to whisper, but Bruce spoke first.

'Is this the 'your country needs you' speech?' he said jokingly.

I placed my finger over my lips. 'Lads,' I said as quietly as possible.

'My sixth sense is being whacked. From experience you know when something is wrong or going to kick off. Like when a bustling village market is empty, or the farmers have left their fields, or the towns folk have gone inside.'

'What village?'

Again, I motioned Bruce to stay quiet. 'In Afghanistan, or... look, it doesn't matter. What I'm trying to say is: where is the German infantry? The sentries? Not even one rifle poking out at us.'

'Not even a shout on the hour, five minutes ago,' Bruce said.

'What time is sunrise?' I asked.

'Starts about five forty-five, so a decent light around six-thirty,' Titan answered.

I thought of the approximate three hundred and eighty metres back to our side. Fuck.

'I am scared stiff,' Bruce mumbled nervously.

'You're brave to have come this far, and braver for admitting it,' I said. 'And your breath stinks of garlic.'

It lifted his mood.

'I am frightened as well,' Titan whispered. 'I do not think it is fair Mark continues.'

As Blister never replied, I mouthed, 'Why?'

'Mark lost three brothers to the Kaiser. Two were returning injured from the frontline. The third...'

'The third has never been found,' Mark intervened. 'I missed all the funerals.'

'None of you should be on this mission with the lack of skills, let alone with your baggage, Mark,' I said. 'With darkness fading, we need to abort.'

'Rowe will have us shot at dawn for deserting, and if not him, Taylor will see to it,' Titan said.

We were on a double-edged sword, and they knew it. Our breathing patterns weren't the only thing clouding. I had to decide.

'Right, you lot head to the RV and set a defensive position. If you don't see me by six AM, covertly head back to our trench. If all hell breaks loose from both sides, head to the ERV. Hopefully, Roberts and Goodinson will be waiting back in the main trench, backing up any story to Rowe.'

'What about you?' Bruce hushed, holding his hand across his garlic breath.

'Look, lads, I wasn't supposed to be here, but now that I am, I guess this what was intended. I don't even know if I can die; well, properly.'

I wasn't sure if they were in disbelief or wanted more, but time was ticking on. Knowing I had a lot of ammo on me, I handed over the reserves in my haversack.

'Now fuck off. Silently,' I mouthed.

I didn't wait for their objections; instead, I crawled back to the last scrape.

Taking a silent breath, I mentally prepared myself. Even though the lads were heading to the RV, I had a presence that they or someone else was watching my back. I wasn't going to die today. I would overcome any force with a deadlier reaction.

At the wire, hands slightly trembling, I snipped the lower wire. It cringingly pinged back to the post. Mentally cursing, I cut the second wire, and, with the other hand, I carefully let the tension go. Listening with radar ears, I waited—nothing. Leaving the third wire, I surreptitiously slid my rifle around, painstakingly pushing it under the gap, silently slithering after it. Instinct told me to get the hell out of there, but I crushed it. Inch by inch I pulled myself up onto the parapet. My eyes were flickering all over the place for the slightest movement. The worst part was eying up the four heavy-machineguns, adding to my already racing heart.

Shit. The depth of the trench was far deeper than ours, by at least a metre. Up and down the trench were higher unmanned fire-steps, even the dugouts were empty. No beverage, food, nicotine, or BO could be smelt. I turned backwards and, lowering myself off the edge, dropped. Debris follow me down onto the wooden slats. Six metres behind me was a small ladder propped up against the wall. Bayonet in front, I took in a breath to settle myself. I mentally told myself I could do this, and any enemy that wants to make a fuss would end up dead. I had trained for many years, and executed such killer aggression; although, I was a little rusty. I knew this was a trap, but how they knew we were coming was another matter. I had to become the thinking soldier. Normally, our squad would head for the main defence position or an obvious target, but perhaps the enemy were expecting this.

Sneaking to the nearest trench at right angle to this one, the moon casting a shadow in the deep trench, I made sure I kept covert. Like the war zones I had fought in, each step I carefully placed. I let no negative feelings enter, knowing how to react when the time came. As soon as I smelt it, I crouched, listening hard. A low murmur continued, more than one. Could I take on two? Fucking right I could. Tucked in, I stealthy crept along until I met an intersection. A glow from a dugout lit up a face of a young German, who then passed the cigarette to his comrade. They were armed, and two trench clubs were propped against a timber frame. One club had nasty spikes protruding from the end. Why were these two guards on their own? Where were the rest of the German forces? What were they guarding inside the room? I was only twenty metres from the main trench ladder to escape. What was the best way to tackle these two without causing panic? I smirked at the thought: by strength and guile.

Casually, I stood up. With my head slightly bowed, I started to walk towards them, as if I were just going to pass. The first soldier looked over his mate's shoulder, and then back. I knew on his double-take that he had worked it out. With fast-paced momentum, I placed the pistol to his friend's head, then held the bayonet under the throat of the other. As the first soldier started to turn, I cocked the hammer and pressed hard; he gulped. However, I didn't like the cocky smile of the other German, my neck hairs bristled.

'*Tommy Schwein schmutzig,*' he said.

I shook my head as he reached down for his spiked club, but he kept going, the bayonet tip digging into his neck. My eyes narrowly blazed at him.

'*Nein,*' I whispered.

The other soldier started to tremble against the end of the barrel. I widened my eyes, with a little shake of the head, to tell the other German not to go for the spiked club. Suddenly, he grabbed it. I had no option but to thrust and turn. I pulled the bayonet out.

'I warned you,' I hushed.

The remaining soldier breathed heavy as his comrade gargled to the floor, blood pouring between the dying guard's fingers. Quickly, I shouldered the sling and gripped my prisoner's shoulder. I harshly reminded him of the pistol in his neck. Rapidly, I turned him around to face me and made the 'shhh' noise. His stare watched the blood drip from the blade onto my shoulder. As I dragged him backwards the way I had come, the German on the floor let out a last curdling breath. '*Threat neutralised.*' I'm not sure how long I had been standing and thinking about gaming voice of old, but then something caught my eye—too long was the answer.

Walking strongly towards me from the far end of the trench was a cumbersome figure. I was still ushering backwards in the shadow. The end of the pistol was pushing harder in the shaking German's neck. Fuck, I had recognised the following anomaly. Leaning my captive prisoner into the side wooden slatted wall, I grabbed a grenade. Backing up at speed, making sure my detainee kept between me and the flamethrower, I gripped the pin in my teeth, yanked it out, and then tossed the grenade low. It wasn't like I had to drag the German lad, he fled at the same speed as me.

BOOOM!

A fireball spewed into the air, along with high-pitched screams from more than one person. *'Threats neutralised.'* The illuminating fire lit up the way we were going, heat lapping at our heals. It was so bright and warm that I had visions of the ignited fuel rolling down the trench.

Bang!

'Threat neutralised.' My lightning reactions had made me shoot the German soldier in the face at almost point-blank range, who had just turned the T-junction's corner. The soldier had only managed to get his hand up to shield the light, me being silhouetted.

Checking the corner, I was horrified to see dozens of forms charging down the trench from the direction he had come. Breaking free from me, the young German lad ran towards them. I sprinted towards the main trench, faster than my heart was beating. Fuck the prisoner, I thought. A huge roar of yelling echoed from every angle, then a shotgun fired, followed by a scream. The shouting behind continued. I wondered if the charging enemy had even realised that they had shot one of their own.

Holstering the pistol at speed and swinging the rifle around became natural, even whilst running at full pace. I managed to lob another grenade to the floor. Approximately four seconds later, a large explosion rocked. Debris blew down the trench, but the shouting did not relent. Fuck me, how many were there? At each dugout, I slightly hesitated, ready to use the bayonet on anyone waiting, but I was in luck, and so were they.

A lone soldier jumped into the trench about three metres in front of me. He swivelled around to face me, rifle with bayonet raised.

Bang—lunge!

Keeping the pace, I twisted the Enfield and then whipped it out. Jumping the body, I noticed his headshot wound. *'Threat neutralised.'* Even though the stupid gaming voice had returned, it boosted my drive to escape and evade, especially knowing the Germans were now on top ground. It was now I needed my squad to take them out.

Something swung around from the left. Being too late to react, as I was just about to head right, it slammed into my forehead. I tried to get up, but the world went weird. With another thud, the ringing and blackness filled my mind, taking over the immense pain.

CHAPTER THIRTY

The numbness dispersed as soon as I had managed to open one eye. The other was against something cold. My hands were tightly bound behind my back, adding to the pain that now rifled through me. I guessed whilst I had been knocked out that I had taking a revenge beating. As I pulled back my tongue from my swollen lips, a weird oily taste entered my mouth. Remembering what I had smeared on my face, I contemplated if it was cooking fat mixed with rat juice, perhaps pigeon. Gritting my teeth, I turned my head to allow the other eye to open, the skin pulling at the dried blood on the floor. My head now throbbed even more.

'Fuck,' I muttered.

A strong smell of chlorine hurt my eyes. I remembered smelling it as I had blacked out. Against what was blurry-dark in front, a warm light glowed.

Grunting and groaning, I shuffled myself up into the sitting position against a cool wall, the wrist ties digging in. I let the blood flow from my head. At least in the not so puffy eye I could see my ankles were tied with a heavy strap. A film of grit layered the floor. Above, cracks had formed in the concrete ceiling. Would I be here on the next British bombardment? Blinking further, I faced the whole-hearted light, the sun lighting up my imprisoned mood. However, the spirit went bleak once I had focused on the four mounted heavy-machineguns. Each one had a jacket over the barrel with a pipe leading down to bellows on the floor. Nothing had been used, which was emphasized by no littered spent shells. Why had they not been used? The answer came: they were waiting for the final push on the first of July.

Amongst the crates of ammunition, grenades, and mortars stashed around the edges were hundreds of rat droppings. All I could see from this angle on the rudimentary timber table were some tin mugs and a few pots. Hanging on a crude hook driven into the concrete wall were four respirators. A heavy riveted steel door led into this heavily fortified stronghold. Next to the steel door frame were neatly stacked unlit lanterns. In the other corner were two high-calibre scoped rifles. On the wall, there were five sets of four gouged lines with one scribed through them. Did these tally amounts mean weeks, days, or the number killed by a sniper? I started to picture the British infantryman who had his head taken off on my first morning. Jesus. Had it only been twenty-four hours since I started this Somme hell? My mind turned to the rest of the squad. Had they made it back to 'stand to' without going to the ERV? Was Rowe now planning my rescue?

Footsteps growing closer brought me back to my senses. Inaudible voices came from the other side, then a set of clunking echoed. Even though it had been a long time ago, I started to remember my RTI training, the part of the job I found the most difficult in training and for real. Perhaps they would treat me with some dignity. Then I had a flashback of the Germans I had killed in the trench. The door creaked open; the draft ran across my fingers behind my back. In walked a German officer of similar stature to Rowe. This didn't bode well. He slammed the door, the boom bouncing off the walls and through into my chest, and my throbbing skull. Keep placid, Johnny, I thought.

Keeping his long, dusky-blue back of the jacket facing me, this broad German purposely strode over in his polished brown leather knee-high boots to the heavy-machineguns. He stared down the barrel, the bright light outside causing a long shadow. Then, clattering his embroidered sword against the wooden stacked boxes, he walked over to the slot, peering out, all exaggerated. At one point, I was tempted to make a joke of a 'lovely view', but I had fought hard to stay tight lipped.

Eventually he faced me. Immediately I was drawn to his Dick Strawbridge-like large moustache, especially on such a baby-face. Taking off his gloves and coat, he then placed them on the table. Looking deadpan at me, he began to undo his grey jacket's side-pocket.

'Smoke?' Dick asked.

'Filthy habit, Dick. Could kill you one day.'

He laughed. 'Like we slaughter the *Poilu* and Tommy at Verdun.'

I stayed quiet as he lit his cigarette. Dick blew the smoke my way, then adjusted the German cross that hung below his tight embroidered collars.

'Just you?' he asked.

I thought of my squad back at camp, all feasting on a fried bully beef and egg sandwiches. 'Fortune follows the not so brave.'

Dick brushed the ash of his shoulder board insignia. 'Hmm,' he said. 'Ze other *drei* got away, but it won't be long.'

'What won't be long, Dick?'

'Ah, famous Tom, Dick, and Harry saying.'

'No. Dick Strawbridge,' I corrected.

I shook my legs to get the burning fag off them that he had flicked. Dick drew his sword, the sun reflected of the blade. He rubbed his thumb across the edge, pulling a face as if it had cut him, but all for effect.

'Are you not curious to how we knew you were coming?' he asked.

'Not really,' I lied.

Looking cocky, Dick pulled out a scrap piece of paper. Coming in close, he held it in front of my eyes. It read: Four soldiers plan trench raid. 03:00 hours. Dick screwed it up and, throwing it at my face, smiled at my dumbfounded expression.

'Who the fuck delivered this?' I asked.

'I zink you Tommy call it… mis… mos… mas… ya, mascot.'

'Mascot? What the fuck are you on?'

'But ze poor little monkey filled our German bellies.'

Dick tipped his head back laughing. Rubbing his stomach, he licked his fat moustache at the same time. I remembered a conversation with Adrian about the Australian Army using monkeys as mascots, but who would do such a traitorous thing and compromise us? "I hope the Germans aren't ready for you, dear boy" boomed in my searching mind. I took my stare from my feet, only to face the close-up sword tip.

'Taylor,' I grumbled.

'I hope you Tommy are ready.'

'I hope you get that fucking hideous rat sorted on your top lip, Dick.'

His smile disappeared; his moustache twitched. The blade lowered to my throat; the tip pushed the skin.

'*Nein. Gut für Angst Tommy.*'

'I told the last German nob-head officer in World War Two that I don't speak German.'

I tried to hide my sigh of relief as he pulled the sword away and stood back, replacing it in its sheath. Slowly, he marched up and down, grooming his unkept moustache. Then he looked at his watch. In fact, it was remarkably like my watch. I touched my wrist. Wanker. I had lost enough watches over my escapades.

'Are you not worried about ze *Großen Tommy Angriff*?'

I pulled a face to show I didn't understand him.

'Err… ze Tommy plan?' he asked.

'You mean the over the top push to annihilate your defence? No, Dick, I'm not worried, but you should be.'

'The Empire will crush you and your allies with our *drei bunkern*.'

Evocatively, he started to take off his sword. He tapped the concrete wall before placing the sword on the table, and he then started undoing his sidearm belt.

'Only you know about ze *Maschinengewehr Festung*. I need to make sure you don't talk.'

'There's no need for violence, I will not tell a soul.'

Dick slammed the pistol down and turned to me with a look of hate. I pulled my feet in, ready to defend. Instead of attacking me, he unlocked the steel door and put his head behind it.

'*Gefreiter*,' he yelled.

'*Ja, mein Herr*,' another soldier said.

'*Geben Sie mir Ihren Trenchcoat-club*,' Dick said.

Dick strolled back in, putting his hand through a leather strap that was attached to a wooden ribbed handle, like a policeman's old-type truncheon. However, instead of a wooden baton, the handle which he now gripped was connected to a black, thick coiled spring. As he waved it to get the feel of it, the cuboid iron head on the end sprung back and forth. I swallowed what little spit I had. The original owner poked his head around the door, his eyes excited. I defensively lifted my feet.

'Fuck you,' I said.

Dick swung the club at my boots, the pain shooting up my legs. I shouted more obscenities at him and pulled my sore feet back in front. He made a sudden swing. I reacted to kick it away, but he stopped. Again, he toyed with me as I shuffled around to keep him in front. My legs began to tire, thigh muscles burning. Seeing me grit my teeth, Dick grinned and came in closer, club raised.

A thud outside distracted him for a second, but he looked back at me. It wasn't long enough for me to get to my feet out of the loosening strap. Another soldier, head down and carrying a club, came into the room. As much I tried, I knew I couldn't fend off two for long; acid came into my throat. Dick half-turned to the new comrade.

'*Jäger Angern. Wo bist du gewesen?*' Dick said, shocked.

'*Lassen Sie mein Freund allein.*'

The new soldier swiftly jabbed the metal end of his club in Dick's face. The officer wailed in pain whilst holding onto his nose. Dick then got a harder whack over the head. Once Dick was on the ground, disorientated, he received his last smash.

Shocked, confused, but pleased Dick was out cold on the floor, I stared up at the partly silhouetted soldier. He lifted his shocked face from what he had done, trembling. Instantly, I recognised him, and the blooded club.

'Adrian? What the… what the fuck?' I rambled, overjoyed.

'Are you angry with me?' he said, eyes flitting.

'No… no… how on earth did…'

'Why then did you not call me Bruce?'

I had to laugh. 'Bruce, untie me,' I said, exhausted.

Bruce, shaking all over, sliced through the strap with his German dagger. He then did the same to my wrist restraints, taking a step back after. He stared down at his victim's body whilst I groaned getting achingly to my feet. I twisted Bruce's shoulder away from the battered officer and embraced Bruce. He went ridged, slightly tearful. Bruce was giving off a lot of heat and a lovely clean scent of soap.

'You fucking nut-job,' I said.

'Is that good?'

'No.' I grinned, but he didn't understand. At arm's length, looking at his clean-shaven and sweaty face, I shook my head at him. 'Where and how did you get this uniform? I can't believe what you just did. Boom.' I did the dab gesture, the excitement overcoming my pain.

'What was that?' Bruce asked.

'It's called dabbing. I think it means triumph, but anyway, I really appreciate what you've done, Adrian.'

Bruce lost eye contact, going red in the face.

'Oh, by the way, who is "*Jäger Angern*" that the officer called you?'

Rubbing his collars, Bruce became worried.

'Well?' I asked.

'*Jäger* means Hunter. *Angern* is my friend…' He stopped. 'Vinnie, we need to get back to our side.'

Still in disbelief at how Bruce had managed to get the complete uniform and trick the other German soldiers, I went to the table and picked up the sword. Spotting my trusty pistol, I snatched it, marvelling it for a short period.

'Vinnie, I suggest you leave your arms. Just play along with my wonderful acting skills.'

For a moment, I waited for Bruce to tell me more of his plans, but he just stared, so I placed the sword back on the table. After checking the Webley's cylinder, I stuffed it in the back of my trouser band. Whilst Bruce fidgeted with his uniform, I retrieved my watch, cleaning the blood from it. Time check: 08.32 hrs. Bruce dragged the other unconscious, blooded soldier in. Picking up that man's rifle, Bruce pointed it towards the exit. He ordered me out in German, in a similar tone to Rowe's. Behind me, Bruce shut the door.

Hesitating slightly as I reached the top of the concrete stairs, because of the unknown and the bright contrast, a sharp jab in the lower back made me judder.

'*Bewegen. Es sei denn, Sie meinen Knüppel fühlen wollen,*' he huskily bawled.

'Go easy with the bayonet,' I retorted. 'At least try to give me some orders in English so I understand.'

Bruce whacked me on the shoulder with the club—I grimaced. '*Bewegen. Schnell,*' he sharply ordered. 'Move. Quick.'

If he carried on like this, he wasn't going to last long, I thought.

Once I had become used to the daylight, new cooking smells wafted around the deep trenches. Bruce continued prodding and barking German. Head held high like a British prisoner of war, I proudly walked past the Germans in their dugout. All of them were like us Brit soldiers in the morning: clean face and hands, but filthy clothes and hair. A few looked with awe, some inquisitively, but most with hatred. Even the Alsatians showed their teeth. I supposed I had killed a few of their masters.

I wasn't sure what rank Bruce's uniform was, but nobody questioned him as he bully-marched me through; it was getting on my tits. In an area about the same size where Bruce had been giving gifts to our German prisoners, were huge mortars, like upended cannons. Slightly turning my head, many large shells lined the walls and a pulley-crane system on rails was being maintained.

Bruce pushed the side of my sore face with the club and said, '*Augen vorne,* laddie.'

My fists tightened.

We turned right into the main trench. Even though it was daylight, I had recognised it. However, the growing warm feeling that we might make it was dampened when many armed soldiers lined the walls and funk-holes on the route that we were heading. This time there were many crates propped against the leading wall. Behind masses of piled sandbags were soldiers cleaning the machineguns, clearly standing up and moving about. Why weren't they being taken out by our snipers? A cold chill ran through me, wondering if Blister had not made it back. Every man I came close to stopped what they were doing and stared, some trying to hide their trench art from me. It felt good I had one of my mates behind me, that was until he thumped me between the shoulder-blades. Winded, I sucked in air.

'Do that again, Adrian, and I'll…'

'Halt,' someone interrupted my quiet protest.

A rugged, mean-faced soldier had his pistol at my chest. Bruce came along side and grabbed me by the scruff.

'*Wo denken Sie, dass du gehst?*' he abruptly asked Bruce.

Bruce let go of me and, with his club, pushed the soldier's pistol aside and squared up to his objector. Then, like Rowe had done to me, Bruce slowly started to circle his opponent. At the side of him, Bruce tapped the soldier with his club and moved up close.

'*Ich habe Aufträge zur Rücknahme dieser Tommy und tauscht es gegen unsere Kameraden,*' Bruce said, spit landing on the German soldier.

Bruce leant back and grabbed me by the scruff. The slightly intimidated soldier looked at the way we had come. Two other comrades now stood behind him, pensive.

'*Wer gab dir Aufträge? Ich hätte…*'

Incredibly, Bruce had placed the metal end on the German's lips to shut him up, snarling. '*Diese Fuckery stoppt jetzt,*' Bruce said.

Being dragged through the three stunned Germans, I wasn't sure if I could keep my snigger in, realizing that Bruce had copied Rowe's favorite saying, and in the exact tone. Bruce never looked back as he man-handled me to the front. Yet, I had this over-whelming feeling of uncertainty as I checked behind. The three demeaned soldiers stomped off the other way.

Bruce stopped at the ladder, close to where I had entered. He must have ordered the others around to watch me, as I now had weapons raised at me whilst he climbed the ladder onto no man's land. Bruce yelled in German at me; I didn't know what. After a few bravado pushes onto the ladder, I started to climb. Even though Bruce was harshly yanking me up, adding to the pain of my recent beating, I had visions of our side taking shots.

It was still a shock to see the decimated landscape that confronted me;

also, not having seen the amount of macabre gore last night. I looked back at the German frontline, but this time it was full of eager men sitting behind the steel plates, gun emplacements, and even camouflaged in the trees. Way back sat behind a large berm, artillery cannon ends were only just visible, the entire length of the trench.

Bruce continued to shout in German, even hurling abuse when I stumbled in and out of the craters. A fox scurried out of a crater, along with half a dozen crows, startling us. I spotted the dead German at the bottom of the shell-hole, the British white field dressing seeming so stark. The animals had got to him. Bruce held his hand across his mouth, retching.

'Where did you get the uniform, Bruce?'

He didn't reply.

The shattered tree stump was insight, approximately a hundred and fifty metres. I slightly relaxed, but rushing back to our trench presented another problem, and I wondered if Bruce had thought of it.

'What's the plan with the German uniform? You won't make it by wearing it,' I suggested.

Bruce let go, at last. Undoing the first few jacket buttons, he covertly showed me the British shirt underneath. That's why he was so hot, sweaty, and padded, I thought.

'At the RV, you need to change,' I ordered.

'*Ich nehme keine verdammte Bestellungen von Ihnen; Denken Sie daran, wer du bist.*'

'What?'

'I don't take fucking orders from you, remember who you are,' he hoarsely said.

Jesus. I remembered Rowe saying the exact thing. 'OK, Bruce, you can stop the acting now.'

'*Nein, nein, Sie beobachten uns wird nicht, und es lange vor…*'

'Adrian, speak English, you fool.'

Adrian swivelled around and put the club at my throat, but I pushed it away. It was surreal, knowing we were having a spat and could be shot from either side.

'I am no Fool. It will not be long before they find the beaten officer.'

'How did you get hold of Rowe's club?' I asked.

'You need to get back and save…'

I heard the enemy shouting as well.

'*Laufen. Laufen,*' Bruce yelled.

'What?'

Seeing Bruce run for his life, I had quickly translated it.

Shots zipped close by as I sprinted after Bruce. Among the single shot rifles, sonic thuds waved across no man's land. There was no way I was going to catch him as the whines and whistle came in, so I dived into the nearest crater.

BOOOM... BOOOM... BOOOM!

Debris and the shock crushed me onto the putrid gunge at the bottom. 'Fuck,' I fumed.

I quickly scrambled onto my side, shaking the shit from me. Like horizonal rain, a fierce stream of lead buzzed just about ground level, like nothing I had been through before. Occasionally, the rim's dirt sprayed onto me. I clawed a hollow out of the other side's lower rim and dared to peer through. Smoke bellowed from the earth where I had last spotted Adrian. My first yell for Bruce seemed to stop at my nose.

'Bruce?' I screamed louder.

CHAPTER THIRTY-ONE

Further high explosives rained. All I could do was lay back at the bottom with the dirt. Then there was a lull in the earth shattering, air sonic booms, and the constant stream of rounds whizzing over the top. Had they given up on me? Shaking the shit from me, I scurried up as far as I dared and started to search for Bruce amongst the smoke. I called aloud—nothing. A few thumps made me look behind, but then a whistling made me look up: our mortars; I gave a silent cheer. The cordite smoke that covered the entire German lines was dispersed after the first mortar hit. Seizing the chance, I jumped out of the shell-hole and, keeping low, I started searching and shouting for Bruce. The soft churned soil stuck at my boots.

Suddenly, I saw a club partly covered by dirt. On the move, I grabbed it, then frantically started looking in the near vicinity for Bruce. My heart stopped when I saw what looked like a head, but on inspection, it was a boulder sticking out of the ground.

Zip! Crack!

Crawling fast on my belly, I sunk behind a mound of fresh soil, catching the sight of a German rifle's obliterated stock. It was out of reach; I dared not retrieve it. The mound I was behind vibrated, the soil covering me as the object whizzed over.

'Fuck. Sniper,' I said.

With the loose mound only a few inches above, I had to move.

Without warning, the rifles and heavy machineguns opened fire. Death tore across no man's land, but it was from the Brits. The Germans retaliated by adding all they had. I was caught in the crossfire with nowhere to go, and I could still hear one very close round. Fuck. If I'd had a shovel, I would have dug my way back to Britain. Smaller explosions, unlike our Mills Bomb, sounded further back. I envisaged the iconic stick grenade. I began to shake and breathe hard in the frenzied cacophony of battle.

A new weapon entered the orchestra, it was remarkably close. Lifting my head up quickly, then sharply returning it, I eventually spotted where it was coming from: a crater slightly left, fifteen metres away. The gunner's tin hat ducked, obviously not wanting to get taken out in the enraging battle. A new tin hat came level, then an arm went up, waving at me to run over.

'Are you fucking kidding me?' I muttered.

This time the whole face came up, large beard and all. Titan, like a man possessed, waved me over. The rounds around him and me came in close, we both ducked. The Italian twin-machinegun spewed; that was my que. Like a greyhound at the tracks, I was up out of my cage, chasing the hare. Fortunately, the smoke was doing me a favour from not being seen, but it didn't help my side not having a blue on blue. The number of rounds flying all over the place was frightening. The distance seemed a lot longer than I had estimated, but I still reckoned I was running quicker than Usain Bolt could of; although, I doubted he would have sworn once, compared to the whole way like I had.

Switching from the running event, I dived in like Tom Daley, feeling as if the flak had followed me. Face down, coughing for air, I held my ribs.

'I thought only the new boys laid flat in the dirt,' Blister shouted.

'It is his first time in battle, bless him,' Titan said. 'His shit must have strained through the lace.'

'Worse than the dirty froggies,' Blister added.

Both laughed whilst Blister changed mags.

'You two wankers been brushing up on your banter whilst I did all the work,' I said. Slowing it all down, I then started to laugh with them.

On all fours, sticking my head above the rim to the intense battle, the RV ditch was only about a hundred metres away. Except for the odd recent crater, it was nothing but a ploughed field. Concerned at no concealment, I turned back to them; they knew.

'Where's the Lewis?' I asked.

'We took it back with us?' Titan answered.

'You need some more training, you idiot. Right, we need to make that ditch.'

'Wow, he is getting smarter,' Titan said. 'Perhaps he had a blow to the head.'

'Lucky we have these new steel hats given out this morning,' Blister said.

'Titan, where's your rifle?' I asked. 'I need to take out a few snipers in those trees. The others are behind steel plates, so we have little chance.'

'Erm… "steel plates"? You mean loopholes,' Titan said, bringing around his shotgun, grinning.

'Don't be a twat,' I said. 'Your dad's weapon won't achieve anything.'

'We will see.'

Titan whistled using his dirty fingers and then hand gestured to someone parallel with us. I quickly raised to look, just as the mortars started to rain in from both sides. Roberts smiled at me and did the 'OK' sign. Then he and Goodinson started alternatively taking shots and ducking. Blister let off a short burst, hardly lifting his head. Titan brazenly stood up, reminding me of the fearless Shrek, and leaned into his stance. The recoil shook his body, the vibration filtering through the ground. Again, he fired, the noise as incredible as before. He calmly lowered onto his knees, opening the barrel.

'What the fuck is that?' I asked, and then held my hand out to have a go.

Titan shook his head; instead, placing two huge warm brass shells in my hand. They were about seventy millimetres in length and twelve in diameter.

'Bigger than your teeny todger… little knob…'

'Miniscule winky… bitsy bone,' Blister interrupted him.

Titan took aim like before, whilst everyone started to suppress. This time I watched the direction he aimed. Incredibly, the sniper behind the plate exploded into his red mist. On the second shot, the tree trunk shattered.

'And micro penis,' Titan said.

'What the fuck is that thing?' I asked.

'Point 500 Nitro Express hunting rifle.'

This time his rounds went straight through the sandbags, taking out the gunner.

'Can I have a go?' I pleaded.

'No. You stick to your revolver.' Titan nodded at my Webley laying on the floor.

I frowned, then smiled at Blister, nodding at his Italian sub-machinegun.

'Bollocks,' Blister retorted. 'You would only loose it, like your rifle.'

'And your Mills Bombs,' Titan added.

'Wankers,' I said.

Slowly, the battle fizzled out, except the odd single shot that fired. A wave of smoke rolled over us, along with the familiar smells of cordite and dung. My head was pounding, ears ringing, and I had a throat like a wadi. Blister and Titan were clean out of ammo, claiming they had taken care of the snipers and main gunners, or at least scared them shitless. I still gave them a grilling for running out of ammo. With only a pistol, four Mills Bombs, one knife, and a club between us, there wasn't going to be suppressive cover when I went back to look for Bruce.

'Any of you seen Bruce?' I asked.

'Yes,' Titan said. 'After waiting twenty minutes at the RV, instead of going to the farmhouse, apologies, the ERV, he said it was best to go back to the trenches. He disappeared once he found out...'

Blister shook his head at Titan.

Jason scratched his untidy, large, dirty beard.

'What?' I asked.

'Sergeant Rowe, he must have overheard us when...'

'For God's sake, Jason, shortest version,' I snapped. 'We're not here having fucking a picnic.'

'Sergeant Rowe shot dead Second Lieutenant Bridge, and then beat Lieutenant Taylor nearly to death. Taylor was only saved by the London Dogs, taking all of them to restrain Rowe.'

'Shit,' I said.

'Sergeant has been marched off by the MPs,' Blister added.

'Firing squad in the morning, pal,' Jason finished, and hung his head.

I remembered Rowe had heard Bruce telling us about the abuse. 'Fuck me,' I muttered. 'Bruce came back and rescued me.'

'No jesting? How did that fool...'

'I'll fucking tell you how,' I interrupted. 'That brave soldier somehow got hold of a German uniform, beat a German guard and an officer, and then brazenly marched me out.'

Both looked at me, waiting to see if it was a joke.

'Where is he?' Titan asked.

Throat clamming, I bowed my head, not giving an answer.

'Bastard Jerries,' Blister scowled.

'Where did Bruce get the uniform?' Titan asked.

'I didn't get to find out.'

A whistle from across the way broke the sombre mood. Hunkered down, we all turned at the same time. Titan wiped his eyes. Goodinson looked petrified and, shaking his head, he held up his blooded hand. Titan gave a thumbs down. Goodinson held up a tin hat, clearly with a bullet hole in, then lowered his head. I guessed he was crying.

'Bugger,' Titan said. 'That's Roberts gone. They should not have been ordered to return after bravely laying those Torpedoes.'

'I thought you said Taylor, Bridge, and Rowe were out of it. Who gave the orders?' I asked.

'Some new darling came in, just after Rowe and Taylor were taken. Me, Titan, Roberts, and Goodinson told him about Operation Edge, and he flipped his lid. He then ordered us to find you and bring you back.'

'Who was he?' I said.

'Field Marshall... D... Dominic,' Blister said.

'No it was not, you knuckle head. It was Field Marshall Demblon,' Titan said.

Eyes wider than the crater we were in, I said, 'Are you sure? Huge bloke? Has a South African accent?'

'Oh, I thought Demblon had one of those darky accents,' Blister replied.

'He didn't have a turban though,' Titan added. 'And he was not as big as me.'

The duff sound of mortars firing stopped my questions. Goodinson shouted a warning.

BOOOM...

The first one landed close to us, covering us in shit...

BOOOM...

The second hit close to Goodinson...

BOOOM...

Horrifyingly, we watched the direct hit, body parts fragmented with the soil...

BOOOM...

This one landed to our left flank, shaking us out of the shock. The next one screeched high; they had us bracketed.

'Go,' I yelled.

Blister was ahead as we raced across the rutted field. The explosion never happened; or was it that I was transfixed on getting us to that ditch? However, I heard Titan yell "Gas". It spurred us past Blister. How long would it be before the increasing single rounds that zipped close by would hit one of us? Annoyed that we were running in a line, I shouted to increase our spacing and zig-zag, making us a hard target for the snipers.

Leaving the field, the old craters gave us concealment, but it also made it near impossible to keep our balance. Although his huge size,

Titan charged through like a mad buffalo. For a split-second I wondered why I had my half-empty pistol in hand, maybe for comfort. Blister was falling back, even though he had left his Villar Perosa. I was concerned that he was out of breath and almost out of steam. Surely, he was the fittest out of us.

In the next shell-hole, I turned and yelled at Blister to get a move on. Titan screamed behind me. Switching views, I couldn't see Titan. Fuck. Leaving the red-faced Blister to his own slog, I sprinted to where I had last seen Titan. Just as I reached the RV, Titan stood from the ditch and carried on charging, holding his left ear. I shouted him to stop, then I dived into the channel. Had he forgotten the plan to follow the ditch up to the farmhouse?

The tree splintered over me. Everything racing at speed, I ducked, gradually bringing my eyeline just above the ridge, slightly behind the tree stump roots. Giving encouragement to Blister had spurred him on. He was soaked under his arms. Abruptly, he spun around, screaming, and fell on top of me. Trying to get air, as if being strangled, he dug his fingers into my chest. Jerking to get him off, I managed to twist him to my side. Sharply, he found his breath. Holding his back, he wailed.

Keeping my head as low as possible, rounds zipping close, I pulled off his kit and ripped up his jacket and shirt—stunned.

Laughing, I said, 'And I thought you were slow because you were a fat bastard.'

'Has it gone through?' he gasped.

I slid my hand under the ammo-vest.

He flinched.

'Nope. Only a blister. Or is that where you wear the wrongly fitted *Le Bon Marche* lacy bra?'

'Touché' he said, exhausted, and dropped his face into the ditch, calmly breathing in and out between nervously laughing.

Titan was on the verge of finding the waterhole as he continued to charge. I wondered if his new nickname should be buffalo. Whilst Blister took off his clothes and heavy ammo-vest to try to examinine his right side, I contemplated our next move.

Eventually, as we laid side by side looking up at the pure-blue sky, a large flock of crows flew high. The only noises were the squawking and a slight breeze whipping around us. I was mentally drained and physically battered. My thoughts turned to Bruce. Even though I had not seen him get hit, the gory images of Goodinson were replaced with

Bruce; it hurt. Why had Bruce run off instead of taking cover? He had heard the mortars.

Blister was balancing his new tin hat on branch that he had found.

'What are you doing?' I asked.

'Well, fella, as you missed the handout of the new steel hats, I have to… what is the saying you use… "adapt, improvise, and overcome".'

Blister held up the branch with the hat on—no shot. Then, as high as he could go, started jigging it about. With no shots from the German snipers, he got into a position behind the trunk and hung the vest on the remaining half-branch, then scurried back. By now, I was kneeling with as much interest.

'Maybe the Jerries are going to let us walk back, like they did our sergeant,' Blister said.

'I doubt it, not after the amount I've killed.'

'You have kill…'

'One of us has to test the Germans by heading back first,' I interrupted, 'and we know who that is.'

'Thank you, Vinnie.'

'Cheeky bastard,' I blurted.

For a moment he looked worried, until I winked.

Gingerly, I half-stood, keeping the tree and jacket close by. I then started to squat towards our base, my hairs on end. At the next crater, I called Blister to follow.

The further we ventured back, the more we had the feeling that they were letting us go. Why? Was it because they knew we would be dead when we went over the top? Was this a sporting chance, or a sick game? Like two lost soldiers from battle, we plodded on through the maze of wire and uneven ground, heads slightly down. Blister even took off his hat, tipping the sweat out, making a remark about it being a beautiful summer's day; how surreal.

Lifting my head and sweeping back my scruffy hair, I only then noticed the rifles from our main trench aiming at us. A young lad threw a pair of wire cutters out. Blister groaned, holding his back as he picked them up. I continued to follow a path that had already been taped. Once at our trench, the astonished men helped us down.

'The Fifteenth Sikh's have made it back,' a Sikh said—a few around laughed. 'Where is your turban?'

I was confused at first, but then realised I was still stained from the soil and fat mixture. With no stuffiness about him, I shook the Sikh officer's hand that he held out; medals rattling. He held on and congratulated me, then did the same to Blister.

Most of the original frontline trench soldiers patted us on the back. We even received some cheers, but I didn't want to celebrate. You could tell the reserves that had been brought in, clean and pale-faced, eyes wide, quietly nervous. Our feet kicked the used shells into the duckboard joints. The breakfast odours made my belly gurgle. I did not batter an eye walking straight past a dying lad cursing at the padre to go away and to get his mum instead. Even the medics that helped the injured seemed the norm. Not even the stretchers covered by the thick, grey blankets that were continuously heading down the lengthened dug mass grave bothered me. The main things I did take stock of was the number of ladders leaning against the main wall, and odd wooden contraptions that held a grenade launching rifle. I needed a stiff drink.

39 dead. 49 injured. 1 MIA—Bruce.

Perking up when I embraced the big man, even though he did not man hug back again, Titan's left ear had been cut by a chunk missing from his steel hat rim. I moved aside for Blister who was keen to have a look. Titan shook Blister's hand.

'Titan, you know why the hunters missed their buffalo don't you?' I said.

'Buffalo?'

'Because the hunters had the same shit weapon as you,' I said—Blister and I laughed. 'And you two can embrace, you know.'

'Oh here we go, more homosexual stuff,' Blister said.

'It is not quite the British stiff upper lip thing to do,' Titan added, mimicking an officer.

'What, man hug a mate?' I asked.

'No, wear lady's underwear,' Blister said.

'Say's the lady who has to go into battle wearing a fucking Victorian corset,' I bantered.

As we trudged past the other bemused and shocked soldiers listening to our continued stupid chat, Titan told me where Field Marshal Demblon would be, Rowe's quarters. I asked them both to accompany me to meet him, but both said we all should make ourselves respectable first. Slightly taken aback by my swearing objections, they then decided to follow me.

Some of the men in their fire-bays pitied us after seeing the void behind us. The trench life did not seem the same without his charismatic ways. The other empty feeling was missing the sound of that hard bastard Rowe. It was only now I realised how much I respected him. Rowe had survived the Boer War and had been here from day one. The other long-timer soldiers must be in a tougher place than how I felt. The only positive thing to keep me motivated was Rowe had stopped any further sick shit from Taylor and Bridge. However, I had the negative that he would be facing the firing squad in the morning.

Bringing me out of the undesirable, at the far end of the trench was a horse tied to a post outside Rowe's quarters.

'Oi, cocker,' one of the London Dogs yelled.

I swivelled around, showing I was not in the mood, but he made his way over, his and the camp's smell more unbearable than I remembered. The flies were buzzing around a fresh part of the dugout, with a small wooden cross stuck in the disturbed soil. He grinned, showing the breakfast in its teeth.

'Where's L'Estrange?' he asked. 'I could do wiv some eggs.'

You could do with a toothbrush, I thought. 'Adrian's dead,' I said, choked up.

The other three stopped making Mills Bombs, which I thought was idiotic being on the frontline, and walked towards us. The Dogs demeanour had changed. One took my hand, shaking it.

'I'm sorry, cocker,' he said. 'He was a ruddy good lad.'

The others came and patted me on the shoulder. I was gritting my teeth to keep my emotions in.

'You wanna exchange that nice cudgel there for some meat?' one of them said.

'I'd rather go fucking vegan.'

Nobody understood.

'Where's the boss-man?' I asked.

The new leader pointed at the cross—I grimaced.

The Dogs didn't give Titan and Blister any sympathy or recognition for taking part in a heroic mission to rescue me, let alone Operation Edge, so we made our way to Rowe's quarters. The horse was a beauty. I imagined Adrian having a sneezing fit. As I stroked the horse, Titan and Blister started to make themselves decent. I laughed at them, but inside, I began to get nervous of seeing Georges in such a surreal place. I remembered waking up in the Cambridge Military Hospital in 1944: a mind-fuck. How was he coping with it? How many questions did he have? Would he just ramble them out? I would have to go softly softly.

Without the remaining squad seeing, I let out a sharp breath, then made my way down the timber stairs to catch the monkey.

CHAPTER THIRTY-TWO

Opening the door, the familiar smells hit me. I envisaged Rowe, saddening me. Georges put his ape-like arms around me, the row of medals clanked.

'My *Bru*,' he bellowed. 'Is this a dream?'

As soon as he let go, I jabbed him on the chin. Georges, shocked, rubbed his jaw.

'Firstly, that proves this isn't a dream,' I said seething. 'Secondly, why the fuck did you send four soldiers, of which two are now dead, across no man's land in broad daylight? This isn't some fucking game.'

I smacked the club end on the timber floor. Georges went to speak, but his eyes flicked to behind me. I had forgotten they were there. Facing Titan and Blister, the bewilderment was written on their faces, not knowing how to react.

'Lads, this is Georges Demblon, my old South African barb in my bollocks from the future.'

'Field Marshall,' Georges boasted.

Titan and Blister stood to attention and saluted, and then shouted their ranks and names. Georges was loving this, too much.

'Right, grab your kit and meet us in the trench where the supplies are brought in,' I ordered.

'Why?' Blister and Titan answered.

'You'll find out. Now do it.'

'I cannot just leave my post. I must save the injured,' Titan demanded.

'We do not have the permission to leave,' Blister added.

I nodded at Georges.

'I will see to it. Now do as your boss orders,' Georges said. 'And leave me that fine African hunting rifle.'

Even though Titan and Blister had been given permission by a Field Marshal, although a phoney, they found it difficult to comprehend

300

leaving. However, Titan had been adamant he would not handover his weapon. "Stubborn", like me, according to Georges.

With the door shut, I picked up Rowe's almost empty rum jar and took a gulp. Georges took off his undersized peek cap. I took another gulp.

'Should you be drinking?' he asked. '*Doff* in your condition.'

'Why have you come back, Georges? I was relying on you to wake me up and get me out of this hell-hole.'

'And how would I have known that?'

'Now I'm stuck with you, which makes it even more unbearable.'

'*Eish.*' Georges undone the stretched buttons on his jacket and sat in the chair.

I began to feel exhausted.

'I have some *lekker* news for you, Johnny.'

'You've got us a first-class plane ticket out of here. And stop with the lingo.'

He gave up trying to cross his tight, brown leather knee-high boot over his knee, due to his close-fitting trousers over his muscular legs. Instead, he leant forward and snatched the rum from me. After shaking it, he frowned—empty. I removed the awkward pistol from my trouser band and sat on Rowe's bunk.

'Go on then,' I said.

'Once I had heard your name being bandied about on some crazy mission, realising you were not in the Afghan desert, it makes clear sense to why I had ended up here.'

'Who mentioned the mission to you?'

'Do you first not want to know how I got here?'

'Only if it's the very, very, short version.'

'After they found us in the jungle, I was taken to their mysterious…'

'Speed it up,' I said, looking at my watch.

'Anyone else would get a *snotklap.*'

'Whatever. Just hurry up.'

Georges cleared his throat. 'I told the tribe's chief about me saving the women that was left out for tiger bait. I think they understood.'

'And your better than mine charades forgot to mention that I had helped save the woman.'

'Nico had told me you hated rhetorical questions.' He grinned.

I ignored him and placed my thumping and weary head on the hard-feathered pillow.

'I was taken to the depths of the temple ruins. A drug was injected into my vein by a crude hollow stick.'

'You didn't have to drink some vile stuff?' I said.

'No.'

'For fuck's sake,' I muttered. 'Skip to how you got here. You're boring me to sleep.'

'*Eish.* I awoke not knowing where I was. It was like the meteor shower had hit the African Plains: the end of the Earth. I placed the cartridge in my pocket that the old man had given me and started to wonder aimlessly. I came across a lone horse standing next to a rider face down in a sodden ditch. I was confused about his military uniform, so I turned him over, only to find his face was missing. Of course, it didn't bother me.'

'Sure, yeah,' I mumbled, and turned on my side. 'Get to the point how you ended up here.'

'I searched the side bags on his horse and found some documents relating to finding a Sergeant Sean Rowe, to relieve him from the frontline for a mission in Egypt. The Sinai Desert.'

Immediately, I opened my eyes and sat up excited, goosebumps down my arms. I swung my legs over the bed. 'That's it,' I exclaimed. 'The desert connection.'

'I worked out I was in World War One from the date on the classified letter,' Georges continued. 'Do you not want to hear the long difficult journey of how I ended up here in these quarters?'

'My guess is the officer was a lot slimmer than you, like most. And after shamefully stealing his uniform and medals, you followed the details here, then started asking questions about Rowe.'

Georges realigned his medals, then pulled down his tight, bloodstained uniform. 'I have heard Rowe is going to be shot, why?'

'The same officer scum who most likely asked Rowe to be transferred to another mission, are the same he… taught a lesson. I'll tell you all about it on the way.'

'What do you mean, "On the way"?'

'We're going to save Rowe.' I stood up with his club.

Georges stood tall, placing the small hat on his head. 'How?'

'With your bling and stripes. You help me and the lads save Rowe from the firing squad, and we'll come with you to Egypt.'

'You mean those two *doos.*'

I wasn't happy with his choice of words about my lads, but I had to play him. 'Best sniper and medic I've ever met, Georges. Just think of your command over these guys in Egypt.'

'Why not stay here?'

'And the chance of more medals,' I quickly added.

'Deal.'

I was glad that he had agreed, as I was going to mention about saving his life, as back up blackmail. 'One quick favour whilst you're writing some notes for us to leave.'

'*Eish*. You never change, Johnny.'

'You write a letter to those headed on your document about a Private Adrian L'Estrange receiving the posthumous medal for bravery.'

'Who?'

I gave him a glare.

'I will see to it.'

'Perhaps a real medal, unlike one of yours that you've earned,' I said flippantly.

'Will you treat and respect me as your commanding officer?'

'Of course.'

'Thanks for my pistol back,' he said as I went to leave.

I glanced at the bed, realising I had left it.

Leaving Georges to write his letters to HQ, I came alongside the Dogs. One axed off a head of a rat. The new boss-man was making Mills Bombs.

'You guys know everything that goes down,' I said. 'Where would Rowe have been taken to?'

'Deaf, mate.'

'Huh?'

'Deaf, as in brown bread, mate.'

I sighed. 'You mean death.'

'It's what I say.'

'OK, but where are they taking him to be shot at dawn?'

'Goin' to cost ya,' the boss-man said.

So much for the nice compassion I had received, I thought. 'How about a leg each?'

It confused him.

I thumbed at Georges' horse.

He spat on his hand and held it out.

Deplorably, I shook it.

'Behind the church in Rouen,' he said.

I told them all about the three defensive concrete bunkers and what else was waiting for our troops, instructing them to tell all the higher-ups, realising that I had begun to speak Bruce's lingo.

Georges had pushed his authority to the max by commandeering an unroadworthy and uncomfortable army vehicle. Blister and Titan were over-joyed with it, as if they had never been in a truck. Annoyingly, Georges had designated a driver, rather than any of us drive, ordering us to sit in the rear. The tarpaulin sides were stained and musty. Between the only bench we sat on were rat droppings, perhaps the only luxury for anyone travelling in the back.

Even though it had large suspension springs at the rear, the thin twin solid tyres did nothing for the spine, going down every rut and pothole imaginable. Blister still complained about his back injury. Further away from hell, we passed many laden mules and horses pulling carts, and soldiers whistling and singing *Rule Britannia* and *It's a Long Way to Tipperary*. Some soldiers stared back at us, but not jealous, as I would have thought. Even though I knew what was coming on the over the top plan, was it OK to feel relief leaving your fellow men behind? More guilt engulfed me. Would four men make such a difference? I thought back on seeing the number of ladders being assembled along our main wall. Everyone had seemed excited that extra divisions were being brought in, such as the Sherwood Foresters, as well as a boost in weapons and ammunition.

Looking at Titan and Blister, I guessed they had the same feelings mulching through their mind. To take our minds off this, also above the noisy engine and gear crunching, I told Blister and Titan that our plan was to rescue Rowe and to get him back to England, to repair his mind before going to Egypt. After telling them that we were also going on this new middle eastern mission, the questions flooded in. With some blunt answers from me, I changed the subject and started to come clean about where I had come from: the future. I found myself bragging about how good I had been in every unit, training, and mission. I had never done this before, it felt amazing. There was not only a disbelief from the Titan and Blister about my admittance to the future, but Georges could not believe I was exposing the truth. Incredulously, Titan and Blister had believed Bruce's version of the "future" was a town in Cornwall where I was from.

To try to prove them wrong, I asked both to ask me anything they wanted about the era that I came from. After giving them a lot of encouragement to go beyond if they had got married, had children, and the like, I snapped at them to go even further forward with historical events. After being rocked around for some tense minutes, out of the exhaust fumes came the first question.

'Who wins the FA Cup Final next season?' Blister asked.

They had no vision—I gave up.

With Titan between me and Blister like a huge bean-bag, I placed my head on his shoulder. Listening to them both breathing heavier was hypnotic. With my eyes shut, I started to answer Georges questions about what Rowe had done to face the firing squad, explaining his actions to sort Taylor and Bridge were due to Rowe's sensory overload. Georges was as angry as us about Rowe being punished. I don't remember finishing the question how I ended up on the frontline, my sleepy thoughts had turned to Bruce.

The clunking of the rear half-tailgate awoke me from my nightmare, something I was hoping to never return to. Except the keen Georges, the others appeared exhausted and stunned. Had the black dogs started to chase them? Time check: 12.57 hrs. After a nearly three-hour drive, the driver helped down our stiff bodies. The town was a world far different from what we had been used to, and I had only had the non-pleasure Somme life for less than forty-eight hours. Buildings still stood amongst cobbled roads. Blister knelt and touched the cobbles. Colourful trees lined the orange and red bricked walls. Well-dressed locals were carrying baskets of food and walking their children. The new smells were tantalising. I bet I wasn't the only one vastly thirsty and hungry. In the plume of smoke as the truck left, I did a three-hundred-and-sixty rotation of the freedom; so, this was Rouen.

Noticing some of the unpleasant nose turning looks from the ladies, I guessed we looked like a group of gypsies turning up to a private school. A familiar steam engine chugged in the far distance, letting off a few whistles. Older kids clutching bread and other items wrapped in cloth started to run past. Georges stared at the strikingly dressed pretty women, some coyly looking back. I told him to roll his tongue in, whilst Blister coarsely told him he would have to share them with every other lower-ranked soldier that had. Titan was watching the neatly turned-out nurses heading down the other side street. Bashfully, he half-waved as they turned to him.

'Missing a bit of matron are we, Titan?' I said, hoarse, and then nudged him.

Titan cleared his dry throat. 'There is a hospital based here. I worked there. Yes, fine nurses they all are.'

He hadn't got my smuttiness.

A bell's chime echoed through the streets. We all turned to its direction to see an imposing cathedral tower. Instead of crows, seagulls and other pleasant birds flocked high.

'That's got to be the church the Dogs were on about,' I said lamely. 'Behind there is the firing squad.'

'I know,' Titan said.

'Look at the *aunties* on her,' Georges remarked.

'Excuse me?' Blister said.

'Tits, mate.'

'Oh.'

'You lot could do with some coffee,' Georges said. 'There must be a café in this *dorpie*.'

'*Dorpie?*' Titan said, half-asleep.

'Town. You need to wake up, or you will be no good. I'll think of a plan why you refresh.'

I hated to admit, but Georges was right: I was on my chin-strap.

Titan plodded the way to a café that he said he used to visit to get away from his memories. He had even learnt a little French from the ladies. Most of the staff remembered him, all gesturing how much weight he had lost, but nothing about the frontline grime and smell. Titan became bashful when a stunning lady, looking like Marilyn Monroe, put her arms around him from behind whilst he ate a fresh French stick, nearly choking it into his soup. It was charming to see this giant become such a kitten. Of course, we all took the piss, but I wanted his luck as much as the next man. As we all tucked into the amazingly flavoured food and hot drinks, Titan left the table with this beautiful lady without saying a word, without finishing his food. Blister jumped in and nicked it, whilst me and Georges drooled at Titan's fortune.

Feet up on another chair, glass of red wine in hand, I watched the blue sky above this beautiful town. I had almost forgotten where we were, and why, that was until I spotted a line of injured soldiers marching by. Guilty, I quickly put down my wine and sat up. Every conceivable injury went by, many walking or hobbling on crutches, some on horse driven carts, and a lot on stretchers. They longingly looked at us, even those with one remaining eye. Blister dropped his bread into his soup, pushing it away.

'Blister, go and find Titan. Tell him to get here now,' I ordered.

'But he is probably having crumpet, Vinnie.'

CHAPTER THIRTY-TWO

'I don't care if he's only got his boots on, drag him back.'

'Drag *him*.'

I glared at Blister.

'Yes, Vinnie,' he said.

'Do you reckon I can blag Rowe out of the prison?' Georges asked.

'If not, we'll all have to persuade them.'

Georges grinned. 'Let's hope I can't then. Kick some English arse, like the Springbok.'

'I do recall Ocker talking the same kind of bollocks, but with the Aussie cricket team.'

Five minutes later, just as me and Georges were getting a bit heated over rugby stats, Blister turned up with a very unhappy Titan. The jokes about Titan not getting his dessert didn't fare any better, but it made us feel good.

The procession of soldiers went back as far as the street corner. According to Titan, there were other routes and transport taking the injured off the trains to many hospitals in this area, and the outskirts. The scale of it was unprecedented. Even Georges found it difficult to keep up the pretence to those brave soldiers of all different battalions and nationalities who saluted him, those that could.

As we filtered through them to the other side, the stench was abysmal. Just as I started to walk towards the cathedral area, Blister shouted at me to hold up. I turned to see his shocked expression.

'What's up?' I said.

'I have just clapped eyes on Taylor.'

We all looked at the line.

'Are you sure?'

'Yes, Vinnie, I will never forget that evil bastard. There.'

'Georges and Titan,' I said, 'grab Taylor's stretcher and make your way around to the back of the cathedral. Anyone who stops you, use your medical knowledge and medals as a distraction.'

'What? Why?' Georges asked.

'Just do it,' I said. 'Blister, follow me.'

Blister waved smugly at them, then said, 'Where are we going, Vinnie?'

'On a recce.'

'A what?'

'Jesus. Just shadow me.'

It wasn't hard to find the cathedral, but tougher was the daunting injured we had passed. Making sure the coast was clear, I gave Blister a bunk-up to a high wall. He moaned at how full to the brim he was.

'OK, let me down,' he whispered.

'Sitrep?' I asked—incomprehension. 'What have you seen?'

'A large courtyard with six posts at one end is scattered with straw, and small squares of cloth at the bases. Two benches are at the far end under this wall. There is a key-locked iron gate with a lantern hanging above it, leading to stairs that go down. The only other entrance is a metal gate just on the corner of this wall, where that tree overhangs. No guards or anybody are around.'

'Good work, Blister.'

'Thank you. It is strange that Bellchamber was killed here. What is your plan to get Rowe out?'

'You don't have to do…'

'I want to,' he butted in.

Titan and Georges had both used their skills to get the stretcher-bearers to agree that Taylor had to be taken to another hospital, away from the lower ranked soldiers. It did not go down well with anyone, even with the acting Georges. Once I had discussed the quick plan, Georges went off to bluff his way in. Five minutes later, people were starting to stare. Titan pretended to work on Taylor. Whilst getting what little kit he had out of his side satchel, Blister charmed the crowd to move on as it was disrespectful. Taylor came to and, once he had recognised us, he started to get more vocal. A bullet to the head would have been fitting, but as I had no pistol. Titan gave him a little dose of the magic medicine.

The gate clunked and creaked open. A guard, along with Georges, came out. Field Marshall Demblon, as we had to address him, showed the guard where the absconded high-ranking prisoner was. Carrying Taylor on the stretcher, the guard led the way. Blister stayed on the inside of the now locked gate. At the bottom of the dungeon-like seller were a row of squalid prison cells.

'Put him in here,' the guard said in a French accent.

'Private Bernard, or can I call you Louis?' Georges said.

'*Qui*, sir.'

'Please, call me Georges. Now leave the keys. We will take it from here, and we will lock up after padre Bentley gives the man the last rights.'

'Err,' Bernard said.

'Listen, my little French friend, go and take the weekend off. See some of the lovely ladies, drink wine. I will sort it with your superiors,' Georges said, and nudged and winked at the little Frenchman.

We waited for the guard's decision, ready to use a much unkinder tactic to make him agree.

Bernard, overjoyed, handed the keys to Georges. '*Merci beaucoup, monsieur. Donnez les clés au vicaire une fois que vous avez enfermé,*' he said, still nodding at us all with pleasure.

Once he had gone, we all stopped our stupid grins and nodding.

'What did he say?' I asked.

'I haven't a fucking clue,' Georges said.

We laughed.

Georges handed me the keys. I finally opened the prison door, letting the stench out first. The humour evaporated once we had seen the degrading conditions that such a British patriot and hard-bastard soldier had laid his life on the line since the beginning of the Boer War. He had been left to rot before the final shots. His military stripes had been torn off. Rowe did not even lift his head as we entered.

With him under mine and Titan's safe grip, we laid Rowe on the stretcher, sadness in Titan's eyes. Georges threw Taylor off his shoulder and huffed out. I asked Titan to give him enough dosage to make sure he slept sound until the early hours. It must have been hard for Titan not to administer the whole syringe. Once done, Titan cut off Taylor's rank symbols and stuffed them in the demoted officer's pocket.

Blister closed the gate behind Georges and took the other end of the stretcher, also looking distressed at the dishevelment of this once huge sergeant. Georges handed the keys back in, and then met us around the rear. Now all we needed was a quick escape plan to England.

CHAPTER THIRTY-THREE

Sticking to the back streets, we found an unoccupied store cabin a hundred yards from the train station. We only knew it was empty once we had broken in. Between flour and rat droppings on the floor, we laid down Rowe. The reek from us was unbearable. I thought back to when Titan had told me that they used to let large groups of soldiers coming off the frontline bathe in six metre wooden vats. I really needed that R&R bath.

A quick plan was thrashed out among the four of us: we decided to blend in with the injured, and then head towards the train station to see if there was a way of getting a transport to Le Havre. From there, we could sit with those being ferried back to Southampton. Titan was sent off to see is he could 'borrow' as many bandages as possible from his old hospital. Blister was sent back to town to see if he could charm some food and water, but no alcohol, much to everyone's disappointment. I knew the damage alcohol would have when the black dogs barked.

Looking out the grimy window, another train had stationed. The soldiers began to be unloaded. Another ambulance was quickly being filled to the max, and it soon left. The rest were carried, walked, or helped by cart. I cleaned a small peephole to get a decent look at what they were doing at one end of the platform. Long lines of bodies were laid out, grey blankets thrown over them once any ID was made a note of. Near, but so far, I thought.

I came out of the view of the window as the long and wounded parade came closer. Rowe began to stir, flinching, and waving.

'I did not come to war to shield Belgium,' he muttered, 'but to halt the invasion to my homeland.'

'Sean,' I said.

'We defend this fourteen-mile frontline sector,' he said.

'Rowe,' I hissed.

'It's my hundred-metre frontline,' he growled.

'Sergeant Rowe,' I said.

'Get ready, laddies, to push forward.'

'Sarge,' I shouted.

His eyes flickered open, sweat dripped down his cheeks. 'Private?'

'We're going home. And by the way, that's Corporal.'

Strange patterns formed on the back wall from the marching outside. Rowe closed his glazed eyes. Perhaps he thought he was dreaming. Shit, I thought, and started to check the room. I had left Rowe's club in the café. Its times like this I wish they had mobile phones in this age, so I could text Blister to bring it back with him. I didn't want to rush out into the crowd. They could have guards or officers returning and could start to quiz me what I was doing. Georges' papers only had orders for Rowe to return to England. The last thing I wanted was for us to be held with Taylor for desertion.

The line went on for what seemed an eternity, but eventually it faded out. A whistle blew. Had they crammed the carriages full of courageous new recruits already?

'Georges, wait here whilst I go back to the café,' I said.

'What are you up to?'

'I've forgotten something of Rowe's. I'll be five minutes.'

Georges checked the ammo on his pistol. 'You have not used it then.'

Snatching the pistol from him, I tucked it away and slyly opened the door. Blister startled me as he had pushed it fully open. Titan came running over. They were both exasperated that the line of soldiers had taken so long to clear before coming out of hiding. I was pleased to see Titan, not only carrying loads of different types of dressings, but also a brown blanket and a wooden under the arm crutch. Blister had also come up trumps with some bread, soft-cheese, cakes, and water.

'I had to have sexual intercourse with a beautiful blonde lady to get it,' Blister said, winding up Titan.

Titan sighed. 'If that were true, she would not have felt a thing. Even if I did believe such trickery, I would make sure you wore these bandages for a real reason.'

'Lance Corporal Bentley, when are you going to shave that fucking monstrosity?' Rowe blurted.

'When I get paid a shilling, I will buy a razor. Honest.'

Liar I thought.

'You have a fever, Sergeant,' Titan said, changing the subject.

'Perhaps he fell in a latrine,' Blister mocked.

'Or, he has been eating the cordite to get a Blighty fever,' Titan joked.

'What the devil? You fucking riff-raff,' Rowe growled.

Leaving them to tend Rowe, I casually walked along the streets, saying *bonjour* to the locals. Heading towards the café, two wounded soldiers standing at the counter caught my attention. The reflection off the sun made it difficult to see why they were in there. Getting closer, it looked like they were not getting served; voices had become raised. They were given some food and abruptly pointed to the door.

In the shadows, my heart fell out of my chest. I quickly changed direction. Was I imagining things? Was I that tired? I slid my hand down over my eyes and face, and then slapped my cheeks. I peered back around the courtyard tree: it was him. I swallowed hard, the situation was getting to me: anger, happy, overwhelmed, confusion. How the fuck had Adrian survived? Who was that with him? Both were walking, but heavily bandaged. Why weren't they going towards the hospital with the others?

Playing detective, I followed them, making a mental note of as many landmarks possible so I could find my way back. I shoved the provocative questions to the back of my mind. It was without doubt Adrian's shuffle come walk. Was he suffering from amnesia? But then, why was Adrian doing all the talking? Was it because the other soldier had a bandage around his throat?

As we neared a river, they both started trying doors to properties. Silently happy, they found one and crept inside like promiscuous teenagers. Right, you fuckers, I thought, and sneaked up to the door. Placing my hand on the handle to burst in, I stopped when I heard more than one German voice. Thinking of armed Germans, I slowly took my hand off, then slid to the little side window, but it was not what I had imagined: Adrian was engrossed in a kiss with the other wounded soldier. As they parted, gazing lovingly at each other, they continued to talk German. Incensed, I kicked in the door and charged in under the low door frame. Eyes ablaze, I stood still, staring at Adrian. His mouth dropped open. A putrid stench came from somewhere close. I looked down; he held his bandaged stump. Glaring back at his face, he lost eye contact with me.

'What the fuck is going on, Adrian?' I said.

'How did you get here?'

'Answer the fucking question.'

'Germans marching through Belgium with babies on their bayonets was not true,' he blurted. 'The poster was a lie.'

His friend went to grab my shoulder, so I spun it over and went to hit him. The soldier turned away and held up a hand.

'*Nein. Nein,*' he cried. '*Es ist nicht Adrians Schuld.*'

I ripped down his neck bandage to see no injury. Thrusting him into the wall, my arm against his throat, I started searching him. He had no weapon, so I threw him to the ground. Adrian looked at his lover on the floor, then stared angrily at me. I welcomed to bring it on.

'For someone who has fucking gangrene, you're bearing up well,' I said, and yanked open his large overcoat. Someone else's rotten arm dropped to the floor. 'Fucking bingo.'

The German started to get to his feet.

'I would fucking stay down if you want to walk again,' I said.

Adrian's angry demeanour changed. He puffed out and bowed his head—their game was up. '*Bleiben Sie auf dem Fußboden,*' Adrian said, tears streaming.

I kicked the rotting arm out of the way and grabbed Adrian by the coat, then swung him to the floor next to his mate. Slamming shut the door, I drew my pistol and pointed at them.

'You fucking left me for dead,' I said, seething. 'I wanna know everything, or I'll slot you both.'

Adrian could not keep in the sobbing, but then he began to slow his breathing, as I had taught him. 'We are in love,' he said, and held his partner's hand. 'This is Angern…Wilhelm Angern. He was Rowe's prisoner. I did not want Rowe to shoot him like his mute comrade, so I helped him escape one night.'

'To the fucking farmhouse. That's why you didn't want us to go there, isn't it.'

'Yes.'

I pointed the pistol at Angern.

Adrian shielded him.

'Is that where you have been getting all your goodies to con friends?' I ranted. 'And all along, having sex with him.'

'God no. We are in love, not like Taylor,' he retorted.

'It was his uniform you used to help me escape, wasn't it.'

'Yes, and I did save you.'

'You never even knew I wasn't blown to fucking bits, let alone severely injured when you had left me on the battlefield for your own greed.' I cocked the weapon. 'You helped a German Prisoner escape and didn't ask him about the enemy fortification. Your plan was for us to get killed.'

Adrian stopped sobbing, then snarled. 'I would never let any harm come to you and our men.'

'You disappeared without a trace.'

'We are in love,' he pleaded.

'Not anymore.' I grabbed a heavy feathered pillow from the chaise longue and placed it over the barrel's end.

Back at the store, I barged the door open, ignoring all the questions of where I had been and why so late. Even though the ladies back at the café had wanted to give me more delicious food, I wasn't hungry then, and now. Titan tried to hand me a cake, but I thrust Rowe's club at him. Taking the pistol from my waistband, I threw it at Georges. He smelt it before opening the cylinder.

'Seems to be two missing. Run into some trouble?' he jested.

I gave him an icy stare.

Rowe opened his eyes and said, 'Don't you go getting any funny ideas that you are in charge, laddie.'

I sighed, then stared at the squashed rat droppings.

'Field Marshal Demblon tells me there is a mission for us in Egypt,' Rowe continued.

My pressure was building.

'Big mouth little fucker,' Titan muttered, and gave Georges a dirty look, presumably for telling Rowe of the new mission.

'I like that saying about officer Demblon, Bentley,' Rowe said. 'But Demblon needs a nickname. According to you alone, I am called Sikes.'

I placed my face in my hands and closed my eyes. Wiping the tears away, then taking a big sniff, it stopped the chat. Titan came over and placed a hand at arm's length on my shoulder.

'Please, share your grief, Vinnie,' he said softly.

He was right, this is what I have not done all my life. I deeply inhaled and exhaled. 'If you found out that Adrian had helped a German prisoner escape, only to visit him at night for love and affection, and he had used the German's uniform to help me escape before disappearing off into the sunset with him, what would you do?'

A stunned silence followed, all churning the words over. Rowe shut his eyes, grinding his teeth.

'Would Adrian have come back if you had not been captured?' Blister mumbled.

'Do you mean that same prisoner that escaped from our prison?' Titan said. 'The same Kaiser that L'Estrange was guarding?'

'You are fucking joking,' Blister said.

'Fucking traitor,' Titan ranted.

'Is that where he has been disappearing every night?' Blister said.

'The farmhouse?' Titan launched a kick at the timber planked wall, then pulled his foot back through.

Blister started pacing. 'Love and affection with a man, and a fucking Jerry. Dirty buggers. And he left you to fight alone in no man's land.'

'He is as bad as Taylor and Bridge,' Titan growled.

'I hope you shot them dead,' Rowe said. 'Dirty traitorous swines.'

Georges had stayed quiet, staring at the pistol in his hand. It dawned on them all where I had been and what I had done.

'No one is to ever breath a word of this, not even your last dying breath,' I ordered. 'Agreed?'

They all did.

'Let's get back to Blighty,' I said.

At the train station, Georges spun a few lies saying he wanted to personally get his remaining men back to England, by the order of the King. Sadly, we were informed that no transport was available from here, but to catch a canal barge to Le Havre. Disgruntled at the amount of disrespect to himself, Georges managed to get us a field ambulance to the mooring. We achieved to catch the first boat, perhaps because we had been already medically seen to, although falsely. Playing the casualties, we shared the crammed boat with many real injured soldiers. At least there was no guilt from Rowe on his stretcher taking at least five spaces, but no one complained.

As the River Seine flowed calmly under the bridge ahead, I was the only one of our squad looking forward, the rest pondering what they had left. Standing over the iron construction were two men dressed in civi clothes. One of them dabbed at me, the other waved. I nodded back, waving at chest height as we sailed under it. If the others had found out that I had let Adrian and Wilhelm go to live a better life, they would have hunted them down and killed them. Adrian had not only saved my life, but he had shown me the way of trench life. I had grown to respect the lad. Had he not had a difficult life so far?

Trying not to get emotional of everything that had happened, bearing in mind I was not supposed to be here but with my formidable squad in Afghanistan, I fought hard to shut the door on that horrid episode;

however, now was the time to discuss the next stage of the plan. I secretly asked them to huddle closer. As Georges pulled out a crusty piece of bread from his pocket, many soldiers looking on with envy, something had dropped on the floor at my feet. I picked it up: unused 5.56 ammunition shell. I sharply turned to Georges. He lowered the bread from his mouth.

'What's this?' I asked, trying to gauge his reaction.

'I told you about that,' he said defensively.

'When? Why have…'

'In Rowe's quarters,' he interrupted.

I slightly remembered him saying something about placing a cartridge in his pocket, but I was so exhausted at the time. Georges snatched it back.

'Why have you got it?' I asked.

'The old tribesman had placed it in my hand, curled my fingers, and then held my fist to my heart.'

'Why?'

'I have no idea, my *Bru*, but it reminds me of my roots.' He shoved it back in his pocket.

'Will you two shut up,' Rowe grumbled, and pulled the itchy blanket over his face.

Why would the old man give him one of Ocker's rounds? I thought.

Leaving Rowe asleep, I asked everyone to listen in. I whispered out a plan to how we were going to fool the British authorities that we were injured. I vowed not to let Rowe end up in some asylum, but to take him under our wing until he had his mind back; well, if you could call him normal. Not knowing Rowe had been listening, he said he would sort the clearance for us to be on the new mission with his uncle, a "high ranking darling". Rowe stipulated he was not going to a hospital or an asylum. Becoming angrier, he said he did not need help, it was everyone else that was a failure. I had been in those PTSD shoes. At some point, I would have to tell Rowe that Demblon was not an officer, that I was not from the Cornwall Light Infantry, and we had no documents of who we were. Now was not the time, though.

EPILOGUE

The trip back to Le Havre was excruciating. Not only were we cramped, but nearly everyone smoked. A bombardment onslaught, larger than I had heard before, pummelled the German defensives, ready for the British push. How naive our officers thought that this would weaken the enemy, to become a 'walk-over'.

Eventually, I had the time to think about why I was sent back to this year. Was it to save Rowe? Had it been to find the secret German fortification? Perhaps it was to help Adrian escape with love, something he had missed since his parents disowned him. Maybe I was yet to find out why, perhaps in the Sinai Desert. I had also thought about why I took this leap of faith to return to Afghanistan 2013: to save my squad, my marriage, my dad. Would I ever return? Was someone else coming to rescue me from the weird temple?

One thing was for sure, I had done many years of training and fighting to get to the SAS selection. Passing it was by far the hardest thing I have done from my time. Even after passing, I had been on numerous extreme training and tours, witnessing some terrible stuff. However, just spending a couple of days on the frontline, more skilled than all the soldiers here, my service does not come close to what these courageous men and women went through.

Any sort of hotel in this new town for a decent shit, shower, and shave in the early hours of the morning was off limits. Time check: 07.30 hrs. I knew the first mine and then the sixteen that followed had been detonated. Zero hour was here for the unlucky. Brave faces tried to hide the tears. Rowe pulled up his blanket over his head again, trying to get a better grip of his club that laid next to him.

At the port, we were ferried onto what I could only explain as a cattle boat. Crammed in again after queuing for a numbing hour, we were sent out into the choppy French channel. On the floor was hay mixed with horse shit, including the smell of piss. It was miserable, the mood was the same. With only two small Furness-stoves, the cold was numbing, the journey was hell. Never again would I moan about being on a long flight in the back of a Hercules or sat in armoured vehicle in any desert conflict. I had survived, unlike those who had arrived in July 1916 and fought till November 1916, resulting in 1.2 million and upwards of British, French, German, and other allies. On the first day of the big push, an estimated 70,000 men went missing at the Somme, with more than 57,000 British casualties, and that is not forgetting the mass from other countries: horrific.

Lest we forget.

Lightning Source UK Ltd.
Milton Keynes UK
UKHW020628070122
396749UK00009B/428/J